# FEAR THE WOLF

## ALEX STEWARD: BOOK 1

STEFANIE GILMOUR

Library of Congress Control Number: 2023915872

Printed in the United States of America
First edition 2023

Hardcover ISBN 979-8-9883745-1-0
Paperback ISBN 979-8-9883745-2-7
E-book ISBN 979-8-9883745-3-4

*To my first reader.*

# 1

"YOU WHAT?" EMMA waited, blue eyes wide, at the edge of her seat.

"I smashed the pizza into his face." My blood still simmered from the guy's obnoxious comments. I'd snapped at rude customers before, but most of the time I managed to keep the creature inside me under wraps. I was going to lose my job. Again.

"Into the customer's—"

"His face." I nodded. "Into the customer's face."

"Alex!" My best friend resembled a petite and curvy porcelain doll with blonde and pink braids wound atop her head. She looked stunning in a short white dress, accented with reflective banding. Even more so next to my hastily assembled outfit of dark thrift store clothes. There was always a part of Emma that sparkled. Tonight, it was the large bangles adorning her wrists and a dusting of powder over her cheekbones.

Seated between us at the round table, our friend Anne replied on my behalf. "Really, this surprises you? Alex should be nationally recognized for her low tolerance of frat-boy bullshit." Anne reclined, one long leg crossed over the other, wearing jeans and a logo t-shirt from her favorite local brewery. Her ever-analytical gaze switched to me. "What made you choose pizza delivery? You're practically inviting enemy fire."

"Flexible hours? Discounted food?" I said. "The hope I could get through a workday without a stranger making a remark about my ass?"

"I feel this job prospect wasn't carefully considered before you applied. Let's hope the guy doesn't report you for more than poor customer service," Anne said. "Maybe it's time you get an office job. Trade overt harassment by customers for lower pay than your male colleagues."

"I've tried office temp jobs before. I can't stand being cooped up for eight hours straight." I glanced at Emma, who watched me with crossed arms.

She'd invited us out to The Sound Refuge, a single-story bar with an intimate concert venue tucked in the back. A night with music and the company of these ladies, my only friends, was what I'd needed to soothe the anger from the earlier botched pizza delivery. The low lighting, the din of pinball machines, and the countless conversations were like a cozy blanket.

"You have to ignore jerks like that guy," Emma said. "They pop up everywhere. You can't attack everyone who stares at you or calls you names. Eventually, you'll run out of job options. Choose your battles."

"I chose to believe the guy was being a creep. I'm sure I wasn't the first person he's treated that way." I shrugged. "Maybe he'll think twice next time."

Emma sat back and sighed. Since we met almost three years ago, she'd coached me on acceptable reactions to what she referred to as "challenging social situations." I'd always heard it called "sexism" or "harassment." Her polite refusal to acknowledge it as such could grate on my nerves, but it was also the reason I'd been able to remain in Hopewell for so long.

Unlike Anne, Emma knew a loss of my temper could lead to me growling and sprouting hair in unwanted places. To most people, I appeared as a thirty-something female of average height and average build living in an average Midwestern city. I was ordinary and over-looked. But for a werewolf like me—attempting to stay hidden and carve out some semblance of a life—being overlooked was exactly what I wanted.

And Emma understood the complications such a lifestyle could entail given that she was a bit different herself. Where I tried to manage life as a werewolf, she struggled with accepting her ability to cast magic. My best friend and closest confidant was a wizard.

A corner of Emma's mouth turned upward. "Did you take the pizza out of the box first?"

I recalled the man's shocked expression, complete with pepperoni stuck to his forehead. My fear of getting caught aside, it *had* been kinda funny. "Of course. It was spectacular."

Anne and Emma burst into laughter. I clinked my pint glass with Anne's as she offered me a toast. Smiling, I stood. "Next round is on me. More of the same?" Both nodded, and I stepped away from our table.

I crossed the front lounge, between the high-top tables and the impressive collection of pinball machines, toward the long bar. The floor was covered in an aqua and burnt orange zigzag pattern, and the walls flaunted the blonde brick common in the neighborhood's older buildings.

A bustling bartender took my order. The bar carried the regular liquor, but Anne and I liked the beer, the majority of which was brewed locally.

The bartender served up the drinks. "On your tab?"

I gave a nod and collected the two pint glasses and the tumbler. "Yeah. Last name is Steward. Thanks."

A werewolf's keen sense of smell wasn't needed to detect the bad cologne before I reached our table. Some college-aged guys were attempting to insert themselves into our evening. Anne caught my gaze and rolled her eyes, but Emma was all smiles and fluttering eyelashes as she chatted with the strangers.

Both men wore ball caps, university polo shirts, and an abundance of confidence. They even had matching enamel pins, a black flag with a yellow cross and red crown, in the collar of their shirts. Some sort of club?

I placed the drinks on the tabletop with an unceremonious thud, giving the guy in my seat a chance to vacate.

He glanced back at the noise, saw me, and raised a finger. "Hey darling, can I get a beer?" He looked at his friend. "Do you want anything?"

Emma's eyes flew open wide. Anne frowned.

Anger lit in my gut, causing the beast inside me to stir. *Couldn't I get through one night with my girlfriends without this shit? Just one. Please.*

"You're in my chair." I resisted the urge to haul him out of it.

"Oh, I'm sorry." He chuckled and stood, his height a solid half foot over mine. "I thought you worked here." The guy gave me the blatant once-over most of them felt entitled to.

Was I a slab of meat?

I reclaimed my seat, reining in my frustration, and managed to keep my tone flat. "No worries." Their type was a dime a dozen. Usually, these guys didn't wander far from the sports bars, but once in a while, they turned up at The Sound Refuge.

Emma hurried to take charge of introductions. "This is Alex. She's not very friendly."

I raised an eyebrow and pushed the tumbler toward her. She smiled and winked at me. Anne snorted into her beer.

Pairing me off used to entertain Emma, but she'd given up. Sex was an itch I liked to scratch, but it could turn dangerous fast. My apartment was a no-go since I kept it stranger-free, and going to someone else's place required an exit strategy. Anger wasn't the only primal emotion that, if left unchecked, led to sharp teeth and long nails. Not everyone was into biting and scratching.

Always the diplomat, Emma continued, "Alex, this is Kevin and Brad. A flier was posted at their campus for tonight's EDM show."

"Was it the music or the fact it's an all-ages show that brought you here?" I asked.

Anne choked on her beer.

I smiled at them.

"Sorry." Eyes watering, Anne tapped on her chest. "My drink went down wrong."

The guys exchanged awkward glances. I continued to smile.

*Begone, assholes.*

The one called Kevin (or was it Brad?) finally spoke, "No need to get aggressive, Alex. We noticed a few lovely ladies and thought we'd say hello." He smiled. "We're nice guys."

My face flushed. I clenched my teeth to contain the instant snarl in my throat.

Anne muttered, "For Christ's sake."

Emma exploded into forced laughter. "It was so nice meeting you two, but we'd like some privacy now." She flitted her fingers to shoo Kevin and Brad away. "You know, for *girl talk*."

Kevin smiled at her. "Maybe we'll see you on the dance floor?"

"Doubt it," I said.

"Maybe. Enjoy the show." Emma's smile was genuine. It was a challenge for her to immediately dislike people. I didn't struggle as much. Kevin and Brad left, and Emma jabbed her finger at each of us in turn "You two are terrible!"

"C'mon, Em." I glared after the two men. "If we kept talking to them, they would've followed us around all night."

"We just met them," Emma said. "Quit making assumptions, Alex. Try holding a conversation. They could've been nice people."

"Don't you mean 'nice guys'?" Anne smirked. "Emma, I'm not sure there was any room for Alex in the conversation those two were having with your legs."

"Awful . . . Both of you." Emma smiled, despite her supposed disappointment in us. "Are you two dancing tonight, or will I be relying on Kevin, Brad, and their cologne for company?"

"Sure," I said. "Anything to get my mind off those two." And the fact I'd be job searching again in the morning.

She looked hopefully at Anne, who hesitated. "Maybe."

"You hardly ever get a day off," Emma said. "Seize the opportunity to have some fun!"

"It's challenging enough being a woman at the precinct. I have a pristine and professional image to maintain," Anne said. "I can't be caught flouncing around with you delinquents."

I grinned. "How *is* work?"

"It's busy. We're dealing with an abrupt increase in assaults, which is odd during winter. People usually wait for warmer weather to get rowdy." She frowned. "Last week, there was a reported kidnapping. That doesn't happen often in Hopewell."

"Are there any patterns to the attacks?" Emma's fingers tightened around her glass.

I smiled at her. "Are you gunning for the rank of detective, too?"

"What? No." She blushed and shifted in her chair. "Of course not. Don't be silly."

"There were enough similarities between the attacks for the captain to assign Detective Grey to the case," Anne said. "Hopefully, he'll put me on the detail. I've dropped enough hints."

"How're you handling the stress?" I asked.

"It is what it is. I'm doing okay."

"I have a great solution to stress." Emma raised her hands, and her bracelets jangled. "Dancing!" She hopped down from the chair. "You two are going to love this guy. He's local to Hopewell."

We followed her past the bar to the venue door. Emma, Anne, and I loved attending shows here. There wasn't a bad seat in the house, and the price point often agreed with my perpetually slim wallet. I popped in my ear plugs before the dark room and thumping music swallowed us.

My vision immediately adjusted, allowing me to navigate without issue. Bodies pressed against us as we moved deeper into the venue. The air was thick and moist with the scents of sweat and alcohol. Music vibrated from the speakers to saturate the space. It reached up through the floor, pulsed through my body, and seeped out my fingertips.

Emma linked her arms with ours and wove onto the crowded floor. Emma dancing was a study in sheer bliss. The stage sat at the front of the room where the EDM artist's silhouette bobbed behind a spread of soundboards. Tangled cables spilled over the edge of the table.

Music transformed my state of mind. The right beat, lyric, or guitar riff made a terrible day tolerable. Pair that with a packed, darkened room, and I could temporarily check out . . . forget what I was. I'd been attempting to do that when Emma and I first met.

A guy had been invading my space despite my repeated requests that he step into traffic. Before I could give him a black eye, a small sprite of a woman had appeared, distracted him, and whisked me out of harm's way to another area of the dance floor. Emma had used her body to shield me from any intruders for the rest of the evening.

I haven't left her side since.

Anne, Emma, and I danced into the early morning. When the lights came up and the crowd thinned, we were flushed, sweaty, and couldn't stop grinning.

"You were right, Em. He's really good." I glanced at the stage. And not that bad to look at, either. "There was a lot of old industrial mixed in there."

Emma laughed, her eyes bright. "Isn't he, though?" She took us by the hands. "Come meet him." She led us over to where the EDM artist stood coiling cables. He glanced up, and a look of recognition crossed his features. With a small smile, he set aside the cable and hopped down over the edge of the stage.

He was thin, to the point of skinny, and taller than me. His dark, messy hair contrasted with his pale complexion, and his light eyes were framed by dark lashes.

"Ben!" Emma gave him a hug. She was a hugger. "These are my friends, Anne and Alex."

Ben smiled at each of us and raised a hand in greeting. He was a handsome guy, and looked vaguely familiar, but his intricate tattoos were what held my interest. The symbols were geometric and interlocked, like a poem written in shapes. They began at his Adam's apple, coiled down the side of his neck, and seemed to continue under his shirt and down his arm to his wrist.

I loved tattoo art, but because I was a werewolf, the artwork disappeared in a matter of days. My body expelled the ink as my skin rapidly healed itself. That had been an expensive life lesson.

Emma continued, "The show was so, so good. I couldn't stop dancing!"

Ben placed the fingertips of his right hand to his lips before lowering his flattened hand toward Emma. His smile had widened into a large grin.

Assuming the gesture to be sign language, I looked between the two. I hadn't known Emma was familiar with the language, and hadn't expected someone with hearing loss to be an EDM artist. But why wasn't she signing to speak to him?

"No, thank you for inviting me!" she said. "Please let us know when you're playing again. Alex said she recognized some industry music or something you played."

Ben didn't watch Emma's mouth. Didn't someone with hearing loss do that? When his gaze turned on me, I was caught off guard and my face warmed. Hopefully, I was still flushed from dancing. Words tumbled out. "Industrial music. I liked the nod to Kraftwerk."

He blinked and regarded me with raised eyebrows. Ben looked at Emma, his expressions dramatically emphasizing his signed reply. When finished, he gave me a friendly grin.

Emma giggled. "He says if you promise to be at the next show, he'll play a new song he's working on. He thinks you'll like it."

"Uh." My cheeks burned. "Yeah, okay. Sure. Whenever is fine." *What? Ugh.* Why couldn't my heightened reflexes extend to casual conversation?

Anne saved me from further embarrassment. "I'm sorry, but Emma has worn me out, and I have to be at work in a few hours. It was nice meeting you, Ben. Great show."

Ben signed his thanks to Anne before he waved farewell to us. He climbed back onto the stage to continue packing away equipment. We walked toward the door to the front lounge.

"How long have you known him?" Anne asked Emma. "I feel like you know everyone."

"And you know sign language?" I asked.

"I don't know him *that* well. Ben and I met at Another Chance when I volunteered during college," Emma said. "I'd do my ASL homework there, and he'd help. We bonded over music. Well, EDM anyway. He also listens to some other stuff." She waved her hand, dismissing other genres with a single gesture. "We've been in touch on and off since then."

"Interesting hobby for someone with hearing loss," Anne said.

"Oh, his hearing is fine," Emma said. "I think he suffered an injury to his throat when he was younger. I can't quite remember."

We closed our tabs and exited the building through a crowd of huddled smokers. Anne zipped up her jacket against the icy cold. "Would you ladies like me to walk you back to your cars?"

"We'll be fine. Em is giving me a ride home," I said.

"Okay. Thanks for a great night out," she said.

Emma hugged her. "Thanks for joining us even though you're so busy."

"You're welcome. Good night." Anne jogged across the street toward the parking garage at the end of the block.

We watched her disappear into the structure. Emma linked her arm through mine, tickling my sense of smell with vanilla. We started down the snowy sidewalk in the opposite direction. "I'm sorry. I didn't mean to embarrass you in front of Ben," she said.

"It's all right." I smiled. "No harm done. I don't mind if he knows I enjoyed the music."

"What will you do about the pizza delivery job?" Emma asked.

"I'm pretty sure that's a lost cause." I shrugged. "I still have the rideshare gig. I don't have many expenses, so I'll manage to stay afloat for a few weeks while I job search."

"You didn't wolf out on the guy, did you?"

I hesitated. "Not exactly, though I did want to break him."

She looked up at me, her eyebrows drawn together. "Not exactly?"

"Only my eyes." I've always struggled to hide my eyes. "He reeked of alcohol and fried food. He'll write off the fact the pizza delivery woman had glowing eyes by saying he was drunk." That's what I told myself anyway.

Emma frowned and hugged my arm closer. "Alex, you have to be careful. This is happening more often."

As supernatural beings, we were expected to keep our gifts hidden from the common populace, or *Commoners*, as they were called. People like Anne. Since the vast majority of Commoners had no clue we existed, we could live among them.

"Is everything okay? Are *you* okay?" Emma asked.

"This being inside me . . . She's been agitated. The pizza thing was a small screw-up, but my body didn't listen to me." I frowned. "I'm worried one of these times she'll put a fist through someone's chest."

"Don't say that."

I shook my head. "It wasn't even the most offensive thing anyone has said to me, but it all adds up after a while, you know?"

Emma rested her head against my arm. "Yeah, I know."

We walked in silence a bit and enjoyed the swirling and dancing snowfall. Maybe I'd stuck around Hopewell too long. Whenever a place grinded on my nerves or I screwed up, I'd leave and go somewhere else. But I liked my life here. It felt almost . . . normal, especially with Emma. I might only have two friends, but I didn't want to leave them.

"How're you feeling, Em? You've been as busy as Anne. Is it your job or your parents keeping you away?"

Since Emma accepted a leadership role at Another Chance Ministries, a shelter servicing Hopewell's homeless, her parents were more vocal about their daughter's friend group. As a wealthy and prominent family, they were all about keeping up appearances. Another Chance was operated through Patterson Street Church, where her family attended.

She snorted. "My parents drive me crazy. According to Susan and Charles Arztin, people are only deserving of assistance if they fit narrowly defined 'good guy' guidelines." Emma shook her head. "It's the same 'bootstraps' bullshit we've dealt with for years from donors. It completely disregards what people need to do to survive."

"And your parents don't want their daughter spending time with people who aren't 'good guys?'" I asked.

"Well, not you." Emma laughed when I screwed my face up in mock offense.

"How does Anne escape Susan's judgment?"

"She's a police officer and can't do wrong in their eyes. You, though," Emma ticked off my misdeeds on her fingers, "you have no career path to a six-figure income, aren't engaged to a prominent man, don't spend buckets of money on the latest fashion, and you drive a used car." She pointed a finger at me. "You lazy harlot!"

We dissolved into laughter. Since my life plans had been torpedoed by the whole werewolf thing, I didn't have the drive expected of a ball-busting career woman. Maybe my laissez-faire mindset was collateral damage from living in an area where people set life on autopilot and rode it out until retirement. Or maybe living here provided perspective on how messed up the rest of the country was, equating packed schedules and burnout with success.

Emma wiped away tears. "But I still love them anyway! They're my parents. At least they approve of my friend at Another Chance."

"Does your friend have a name?" I wasn't sure if her pink cheeks were from the cold or my question. Emma didn't withhold details about anything, including the lines of guys she ruthlessly sorted through. I was often happy to see them go. Her taste in fashion was impeccable . . . not so much her taste in men.

"His name is Mitch. I met him at church, and he joined Another Chance's staff part-time. We're working together to develop a mental health program for our clients."

"So *you* like working with him? Because it's not your parents who have to spend time with him." By the way Emma's complexion reddened even more, I suspected she and Mitch were well beyond "friends." Why was I only hearing about him now?

"Yes." Emma smiled to herself.

"Is he a Commoner?" Friendships with them were tricky enough. Romantic entanglements brought a whole new level of hassle.

She nodded. "He and I are going to accomplish great things for our community."

I heard the crunching footsteps behind us before a low whistle and shout. "Hey, Emma!" We stopped and turned to see Kevin and Brad from the front lounge walking toward us. The bad cologne was now fighting with the odor of alcohol. Brad quipped, "You ladies are hard to find."

I narrowed my eyes as Emma clasped her hands together, beaming. "Wasn't the show great?"

Brad nodded absently and glanced at me. "Where's the tall redhead?"

"Her name is Anne." I wanted these guys to leave. I wasn't comfortable with how they were tallying our numbers.

"She's on her way home," Emma said.

Kevin eyed Emma. "We're going to another bar. Want to come along?"

"I'm sorry, but I'm exhausted. I have to—"

"One last nightcap?" He wasn't interested in any answer other than the one he wanted.

"No, really, I—"

"C'mon." Kevin talked to Emma's legs again. "You dressed up like that to spend the night with your *friends*?"

My pulse skipped, and Emma's smile faded. Even *she* sensed we weren't being given a choice. She gave me a worried glance.

Brad waited off to the side, at the edge of my field of vision. A quick look up and down the sidewalk confirmed there weren't any other people nearby. We'd turned down a sparsely lit side street. My sight hadn't been affected, and I'd been lost in conversation. I mentally rebuked myself for not paying attention to our surroundings. That was a foundational rule of *Being a Woman 101*.

Emma shook her head, and her voice wavered. "I'm sorry, but we're going home."

The acidic scent of her fear surrounded us. We were being cornered, and she knew I wouldn't do well if cornered.

When Kevin reached for her wrist, the creature within me struggled to push forward. I stepped toward him and placed myself between him and my friend. The alcohol on his breath overpowered everything else. Every muscle tense, I attempted to keep from shaking. I spoke each word slowly and clearly: "She said no."

His brows knitted together. I imagined the grinding gears of the sluggish organ between his ears. Kevin must not be used to being told no. He looked down at me and pulled his lip back in a sneer.

Anger, mixed with the adrenaline, surged through my body. It would be so easy to snap his arms. Their bones were as frail as their egos. But again, there were understood rules among supernatural beings. For me, that meant no wolfing out in front of Commoners.

"It could've been a good time." Kevin stepped back and shrugged. "Your loss, bitch." His gaze twitched past my shoulder to Brad.

There was an abrupt movement at the edge of my vision, and Brad seized me from behind. His arms tightened around me to pin my arms to my sides. The last shreds of control slipped through my fingers, and my inner wolf forced her way to the surface.

A burning heat exploded from my core and rushed through my limbs. Guttural snarls slipped through my clenched teeth. Cartilage popped and skin stretched as my body bent and broke itself. Knuckles swelled and fingers elongated. In place of my chewed nails were talon-like claws.

"No, please, stop!" Emma lunged to help. It would've been the perfect time for her to fry the jackasses with a magic missile or something, but she wasn't that type of wizard.

Kevin grabbed her arm, pulled her back against him, and covered her mouth. "Shh, no shouting."

Suddenly, the rules didn't seem important. I slammed my head back against Brad's face. His nose crunched. Brad released me and let loose a string of muffled curses. The scent of his blood flooded the air. Despite the frigid night, sweat beaded on my brow from the effort of stopping my body from shifting further.

I spun to face Brad and swiped at his midsection. Fabric ripped as my claws shredded the front of his jacket. He cried out and stumbled back, swinging wildly. His heel slipped off the edge of the sidewalk, and he fell into the street. The guy was doing my job for me.

Panting, I shook my head and refocused on Kevin. I gifted him another smile. Unlike before, this one included a mouth full of sharp teeth. I'm sure my inner wolf's desire shone through my eyes.

*Please, continue to harass us. Give me the reason I need to take you apart.*

Kevin's eyes were wide and he paled. "What the hell?" He shouted at Brad, "She's a shifter!"

I froze. My heartbeat stuttered at his words.

"Take the witch." Kevin shoved Emma toward me and raised his palms, shaking. "Stay the hell away from me, you freak." He nearly fell over his own feet when he tried to turn and run at the same time. Kevin stumbled, slipped on the icy sidewalk, recovered his balance, and fled. After some unflattering thrashing around to regain his footing, Brad followed.

More snarls escaped my body as I suppressed the instinct to run them down. My claws bit into my sweaty palms and my pulse thudded in my ears. I took a long, unsteady inhale. *It's okay.* I slowly blew an exhale out my mouth. *You're safe.*

Withholding tears, Emma looked around to see if anyone else had witnessed the attack. Only the two of us stood on the empty street. Small snowflakes fell quietly around us. The previously jovial mood was gone.

Trembling, she searched me for injuries. "Did he hurt you?"

"I'm okay." I reached with a shaking hand to the back of my head and touched it tenderly. My scalp stung where it'd met Brad's front teeth. "Did you hear him, Em? He recognized what I am." I winced and removed my fingers. They were wet with blood.

Since the immediate danger had passed, the creature inside me gradually receded. My knuckles ached and my gumline burned as my hands and teeth slid back into human form.

Emma wiped at her eyes with the back of her hand. "But they weren't expecting it. And they *knew* I was different. How?" She shook her head. "Is that why they followed us?"

"I'm sorry. I was all right until he grabbed me." My inner wolf was never interested in scaring away threats. She strove to eliminate them.

And she'd almost succeeded once before.

Now that I'd regained composure, my confidence in bending the rules was inconveniently absent. "Do you think they'll tell someone? Would anyone believe them?"

"I don't know."

"They attacked us. What were we expected to do?" That *had* to give us a pass on the rules, right?

Emma chewed at her lip. "I'll ask another wizard. Someone who won't report us."

My anxiety spiked. "Please don't mention me." Kevin and Brad knew what I was, and that was two more people than I felt comfortable with knowing my secret.

"Don't worry, I'll find out what we need to do. You'll—we'll—be okay." Emma rubbed the back of my jacket. "Right now, let me patch you up back at your apartment. My car is only a block away."

We started walking again, our pace faster. There was no more conversation or laughter, only frequent glances into the shadows. My stomach was a mess of acid and unease.

After being forced from my home and family, I moved around the country for close to five years. I never stayed in a location long enough to make friends or build a life, until I found this place. If I lost every-thing here and was forced to run again because of Kevin and Brad, I was going to be pissed.

# 2

EVEN THOUGH I was exhausted, I tried to fight off sleep. If I could put more space between the fight and the moment when my mind slipped into unconsciousness, maybe I wouldn't have the nightmare. It was a regular occurrence, having followed me through life since the day my inner wolf awoke. But the time between episodes had lengthened since I moved to Hopewell. I began to believe I was getting better.

I shivered and turned over in bed, pulling the heavy covers tighter around me. The winters in Hopewell were so gray and cold. My apartment was in an old house, and it was drafty in the cooler seasons. I couldn't afford the bill to keep it comfortably heated 24/7. It made me pine for spring, for more daylight and warmer weather. My heavy eyelids lowered.

*THE CHILLED SPRING air is laced with a floral fragrance. I love running outside this time of year. The smell of the ground thawing and the signs of green shoots appearing are amazing. I avoid the small puddles of rain pooled along the edge of the paved path as I run onto the dirt trailway. My shoes continue their rhythmic pounding on the soil and damp leaves, and new scents hit me. The past semester, my last before graduating from college, had been riddled with stress and anxiety. But here, at this moment, I feel at ease. This is my sanctuary. I am at peace.*

*I hear a second set of footfalls behind me. My steady, confident stride breaks as I look back over my shoulder. A man dressed in runner's clothing has turned onto the path behind me. He raises a hand in greeting as his gait closes the distance between us. I nod, turn my attention forward, and continue down the path. Instead of passing by, the guy paces beside me.*

*"Good morning!" An NYU logo is embroidered on the sleeve of his shirt. It's the same state college that awarded me a running scholarship, much to the relief of my cash-strapped parents. I recognize him as a star athlete from our track team. "It's nice to get outside again, isn't it?" he asks.*

*I politely smile, wishing he'd move on. Instead, he continues talking, consulting some sort of watch he's wearing. "You're keeping a good pace. Are you on the university team? I don't remember seeing you around campus."*

*"No." I'd been on the team with him for four years. I try to sound courteous, but not enough to make him think I'm interested in his company. Usually, the old sweatpants and t-shirt I wear while out running does the trick. Shorts are more practical and comfortable, but I've been taught the more skin I cover, the better the chance I have of being left alone. Why won't he leave?*

*He continues the mostly one-sided conversation. "You should consider trying out for the team. We could use someone like you."*

*Instead of responding, this time I lengthen my stride. I'll be through the woods, off the trail, and back into my parents' neighborhood in a few minutes. I can outpace him until then. I frown to myself as the guy is able to keep up with me. Anxiety tightens my chest.*

*"Are you trying to ditch me?" he asks, humored. The man reaches over and grabs my upper arm to slow me down. "Hold on. I want to talk to you." It causes me to stumble. I wrench my elbow away and turn to escape, but he lunges forward and encircles my waist with his arm. He picks me up, and the toes of my shoes can't gain traction on the ground. I fill my lungs to scream, but he covers my mouth, trapping the cry for help inside me.*

*The man is atop me, red-faced and cursing. He's pissed that it's a struggle to keep me restrained beneath him. He'd prefer I lie still and remain quiet. My screams of anger and fear are muffled behind his hand. He uses his other to tug at the waistband of my sweatpants. I twist and kick, devoting all my strength to breaking free from him. His body weight alone pins me to the ground. He resorts to encircling my throat with his hands and pressing his thumbs into my windpipe. I gasp and choke. The attack robs me of both air and strength to fight back.*

*Spots appear in my field of sight. They obstruct my view of the newly emerged leaves forming a beautiful canopy above me. I smell the rain-soaked soil under the decomposed leaves disturbed by our thrashing. I'm receding within my body. I hold tight to the thin wisps of air allowed me. I see the man above me from a distance, as if from the bottom of a deep well.*

*Something is down here with me. Its eyes burn bright in the dark. It snarls, foam dripping from its maw. Serrated teeth snap at me. The shadowy form struggles against a network of bindings holding it here below. The straps restraining it look worn with age. Some are frayed as if they were hacked at over and over again with a blunt blade. How long has it been trapped, hidden away and forgotten?*

*I reach for one of the bindings. Something inside of me snaps.*

*My near-empty lungs gulp a sudden gust of air. I see the angry eyes of the man again. His breath stinks of his breakfast. He's making another attempt at my clothing. His cold, filth-covered fingers grope uninvited at the warm, clean skin of my stomach.*

*He doesn't know about what has followed me back.*

*I stand above the twitching body of the man. He lies in an unnatural heap in the mess of leaves and mud. His leg is bent the wrong way beneath him. Jagged edges of bone protrude through the fabric of his track pants. He's weeping and calling for help. I'm unsure anyone will hear him. His voice is garbled. Saliva, fragments of teeth, and blood drip from his chin. There's so much blood. It smells bright and tastes like warmed copper.*

*There's a faint repetitive beeping noise. I crouch down beside the man, and he screams. Brushing aside red-speckled leaves, I find my watch. The band is broken, but the watch face is intact. The beeping is a reminder to turn back. Otherwise, when I go out for a run, I lose track of time.*

*I feel detached from my body as my bare feet carry me from the woodline toward my home. I could walk this route with my eyes closed, having traversed it so many times before. The fragrant spring breeze chills my wet face, arms, and hands. There are faint sounds of a woman wailing.*

*When I turn up the walkway, my mother rushes out of the house. The front door is left hanging open, and my grandmother is on her heels. My mom is shrieking something at me and crying. It's difficult to understand what she's saying. She's frantically examining me. Her pretty floral robe is becoming marred with something sticky and bright. My little grandmother is pushing at me, hurrying me inside the shelter of the house.*

*The three of us are in our small, narrow bathroom. I can hear the faucet running in the bathtub. The mirrors are fogging from the steam. My mother is sobbing, attempting to help me out of my torn and dirty running clothes. I'm not able to do so because I can't seem to control my limbs. Instead, I feel my body tremble. I don't notice it at first, but then I'm shaking so hard my teeth are chattering.*

*My grandmother speaks to my mom. Gathering my soiled clothes, my mom rushes from the room. My grandmother turns me toward her and begins to rub down my arms with a damp towel. There's something wrong with my hands. They don't appear to be mine. They are distorted, taloned, and covered in blood.*

*I see myself, or someone like me, in the full-length mirror behind my grandmother. The naked stranger, a young woman, stares blankly back at me. Her eyes are glowing a golden hue, a stark contrast to the smears of blood marring her face and throat.*

I SAT UPRIGHT, letting loose a strangled cry into the dimly lit bedroom. Panting, I was covered in sweat and momentarily disoriented. A mixture of familiar scents seeped into my consciousness, bringing me back to the current time and location. I was alone in my apartment in Hopewell.

I threw the covers aside and swung my legs out of bed. My feet touched the wood floor. The cold surface helped me to feel more grounded. I sat at the edge of the bed for several minutes, focusing on slowing my rapid breathing. "It's okay," I whispered. "You're safe."

A shower always helped to wash away the last lingering images of the nightmare from my mind. I stood and padded quietly across the floor to the bathroom. After showering and getting dressed, I felt almost human again. I checked my voicemail while eating a bowl of cereal and waiting for my hair to dry.

As expected, there was a message from the manager at the pizza parlor. A customer had called to report my inappropriate behavior during a delivery. It went on to explain how unprofessional I had acted. I was told I should consider myself lucky the customer did not decide to press charges. Since laying a hand on a customer is strictly against company policy, my employment with the pizzeria was terminated.

The newspaper I'd found the pizza delivery job in lay on the kitchen table. I pulled it toward me and scanned the other prospects I'd circled. The paper was only a few days old, so maybe some were still available. Rent was due soon, and my bank account was lower than I'd let on when I'd talked to Emma. I could hunt for another job while I was waiting between running rides today.

I brought up the rideshare app on my phone. It didn't take long to decide a cup of coffee was needed before dealing with any customers today. I locked up the single-bedroom apartment, descended the narrow flight of stairs, and exited the large two-story home. The historic 1920s building had been sold in the 1970s, and then sliced and diced into four apartments. Two of us lived on the second floor, while one lucky tenant got the majority of the first floor. The last apartment was a small studio tucked in the back of the first floor.

I made my way to the street where my car was parked. The winter day was even more frigid than yesterday, with a dull gray sky. More snow on the way. I smelled the copious amounts of salt on the street as I brushed last night's snowfall from the car. It was early afternoon, so the usual sounds of the city were already in progress, albeit subdued due to it being a weekend.

My apartment sat up on a gradual hill, at the bottom of which was the downtown district. Over the past few years, Hopewell had experienced a surge in growth. New money was arriving, and the have-nots were steadily being pushed out from the city center. I was one of the lucky renters who'd grabbed an apartment with a great location before the sharp incline in rental rates. If I held onto the apartment, I could continue to afford living near downtown.

The Beacon, my favorite coffee house, sat conveniently between my apartment and the highway on-ramp where I started my work days when I was driving. The trip there was under five minutes, and I was graced with the luck of finding an unmetered parking space. The wonderful aroma of freshly ground coffee greeted me as I entered. The coffee shop was modest in its decor, taking advantage of the exposed brick of the old building. As I waited at the counter, the natural light from the many windows warmed my back and made it feel all the more welcoming. The majority of the seating was available at the bottom of the stairs to the right of the counter. I'd never simply stopped in to sit and have a coffee, and thought yet again, as I did every other time I stopped at the coffee shop, that I should make a point to do so.

By the time I was done running rides, it was late in the evening. Despite the cold, I decided on a walk down to Stanley's for a beer and some video games to mellow me out before bed. Thankfully it was late enough to enjoy myself without being bothered. I could only receive so many unsolicited explanations of a video game before I started to get growly. Where The Sound Refuge shined in pinball machines, Stanley's was a bar and restaurant that boasted an impressive collection of old arcade games. I also adored their jukebox, and a good number of my quarters ended up in that machine as well.

After spending my last roll of quarters, I exited the bar out into the wide alley serving as a second entrance. I was immediately struck by a sharp, metallic scent on the bitterly cold air. Blood. The hair rose on the nape of my neck.

A man was being held against the alley wall by another, much larger, man. A third, shorter figure leaned in close with his finger jammed into the captive's chest. My sensitive ears picked up the attacker's voice, low and gravelly. He demanded something from his victim, but I couldn't understand the language he was speaking. The pinned guy spat in the assailant's face, earning him a solid crack to the jaw from the short man.

I had a fleeting thought of heading back into the bar and reporting the fight, but I didn't want my name in any police paperwork if the situation ended that way. It was a wide alley, so maybe I could slip past them. Then I would dial 911 and drop a tip.

I began to make my exit when I recognized another scent. I took a more careful look at the guy being held against the wall. It was Ben, the friend Emma had introduced to Anne and me. That complicated the situation. Walking away was no longer an option.

I raised my voice as I approached the small group. "What's going on?" Hopefully the possibility of having a witness would drive the two strangers away.

The shorter guy spun toward me, his eyes momentarily widened. I had a habit of sneaking up on people, another feature acquired from the creature inside of me. The man was broadly built with closely cropped hair. He wore a wool-lined canvas jacket, boots, and a flat cap. There were tattoos over his face, neckline, and hands. His beady eyes narrowed. "Get lost, lady."

Between the scent of blood and tone of his words, my inner wolf took notice. Heat and adrenaline surged through my body. I focused on keeping my voice steady. "Let him go."

The short man began to laugh. He looked at his larger partner and back at me. His eyebrows rose, as if someone were pulling a prank. "I'm sorry?"

When I didn't retreat, the man shook his head and wiped his bloodied hands on the front hem of his dark shirt. He walked toward me, and the overpowering stink of cologne burned my nostrils. What was it with self-assured jerks and bad cologne?

He sized me up. "Listen, I'm feeling generous tonight. Turn around, walk away, and forget you've seen anything." The next step placed him in front of me. His face was strewn with scars and speckled in blood. He smiled, exposing almost perfectly square teeth. "No harm done."

I was rapidly losing patience. Bullying was not something I, nor my wolf, responded well to. Anger stirred deep down in my chest. A snarl clawed its way up my throat. "I'm not leaving. Let him go. It's the last time I'm going to ask."

The larger, ox-like man began to chuckle, a deep rumbling sound. The short guy smirked, looking back at his partner before spinning toward me to throw a punch. I sidestepped and caught him by the collar. Propelling his upper body downward, I brought my knee up underneath his ribcage. There was an audible gasp driven out of his body as a burst of steamy air. I released him, and he fell to his knees into the mix of melting snow, salt, and grime on the alley floor. He wheezed as his lungs struggled to refill.

I whirled to face the much larger man. The guy appeared strongly built, so I wanted the advantage of surprise. I crouched low and reached out to the wolf inside for her strength. Warmth surged through the muscles in my legs, and I leapt upward to launch myself at the huge man. My punch connected squarely between the guy's widened eyes before he realized what happened. The cartilage in his upper nose gave way with an audible crunch. I smelled a fresh wave of blood. His head was thrown back and struck the brick wall with a dull thud. The man's large mass toppled to the ground. Without someone holding him in place, Ben slipped down the wall to sit in the slush.

I turned back to the smaller man while keeping his fallen partner in sight. Shortie was standing again with his hand pressed against his gut. He hesitated. It must have been the eyes that spooked him, because I'd somehow kept the claws hidden. My inner wolf thrashed against its prison of my body. She wanted to attack again . . . to put an end to this threat. I thought I'd done well keeping her in check until a low, inhuman growl rumbled out of my body.

Shortie licked his lips and his gaze twitched toward the alley entrance, but he didn't react with the surprise or fright I'd expected. Holding up a hand in a warding gesture, he backed away as he watched me. "No need to let this escalate further, sweetheart. I'll be on my way." At the mouth of the alleyway, he turned and was gone, his partner left behind.

After the man retreated, I crouched beside Ben to assess the damage. His bottom lip was split wide and already swollen. His breathing was short and shallow puffs of steam, and he gripped the left side of his ribcage. He seemed barely conscious, so hopefully he hadn't noticed the whole accidental growling thing.

"You're not looking that good. Do you want me to take you to the hospital?" I asked. "Make sure nothing is broken?"

His eyes took a moment to focus on me. He shook his head, fumbled in his pocket with his free hand, and retrieved his wallet. He showed me his license and tapped on the address area. It was nearby.

The large stranger beside us gave a gurgled moan. I frowned, surprised the man could recover so fast. Not only did the guy have the solid frame of an ox, he was as strong as one too. It was time for Ben and me to move.

"Think you can stand?"

Ben nodded. I leaned forward and he placed his arm around my shoulders. There was a sharp exhalation of breath from him as I pulled him to his feet. I recognized the curse he mouthed.

I asked again, "Are you sure about the ER?"

He nodded, wiping a bit of blood from his mouth and nose with the collar of his wrecked shirt. With him so close, the sight and smell of blood was intense. The beast within me grew agitated and attempted to, yet again, slip from my hold. I clenched my jaw and tried to divide my attention between getting Ben home and not turning into a monster in the process.

I spotted the small surveillance camera mounted near the bar's entrance, and my stomach dropped. How did I miss a camera? My mind quickly went down the *keep-these-things-hidden* checklist. I'd kept the claws in check but messed up on the whole glowing eyes bit. Did the camera record audio? Did I say anything I shouldn't have? How loud had that growl been?

Ben's weight started to sag against me. The cameras would have to be dealt with later. His arm still around my shoulders, and me trying to steady him, Ben and I proceeded awkwardly out of the alley. We only had a few blocks to cover. To the casual passerby, we probably appeared to be good friends stumbling home after a long night out.

The address landed us in front of Rear Window Records, my favorite shop in the city. That's when it clicked . . . where I'd seen him before. "Ben, do you work here?"

He nodded.

"You live here, too?"

Ben let go of my shoulder. He signed something before gripping his ribcage and wincing. I had no idea what he was trying to say.

At my questioning look, he pointed down the sidewalk toward the intersection. He placed his hand against the building's wall to steady himself, then continued to move slowly past the shop's door toward the corner. I followed a few paces before I realized he was walking around the building.

We turned into a long parking lot. A series of stairs and doors ran along the backside of the building to apartments. He stopped at the bottom of some stairs and looked back at me. I recognized his next sign from when he used it with Emma. He thanked me.

"You're welcome."

With strained effort, he started up the stairs.

I didn't let him get too far before catching up. "I'm not trying to creep on you, but please let me get you inside. I'll feel better about leaving then."

He hesitated a beat before retrieving a key on a chain from around his neck and handing it to me. We climbed two flights of stairs, and Ben leaned against me as we paused on the landing. Like the building, the door was old with many layers of paint. It was stuck and didn't open without a fight. I placed my shoulder under Ben's arm again and hauled him through the doorway before closing it behind us. It wasn't graceful. I scanned the walls inside and found the light switch. A dull light above us illuminated the entryway of a tiny studio apartment.

I helped him across the small living area to an old sofa. He looked even more battered in the light of the apartment. I worried I should have taken him to the hospital anyway. "Do you have someone you want me to call? A friend or family member?"

Ben leaned back and gingerly lifted the front edge of his shirt to look at his side. I took the opportunity to do the same, though for undoubtedly different reasons than him. His skin was already bruised beneath the left side of his ribcage. Frowning, he shifted his weight to retrieve his phone from his pocket. He typed something and held the phone out to me, his features twisted by pain.

*Call Emma.*

"Why Emma?" It had sounded like the two knew each other but were hardly close friends. Did Ben know what she was capable of? She was usually so careful. We had to be.

He frowned and fumbled with the phone again.

*Please.*

When Emma answered the phone, her voice was lowered to a near whisper. "Alex? Are you okay?"

"I'm sorry, Em. I'm at Ben's place."

"Really? Well, thank goodness. You really needed to get—"

"No, not . . ." My face grew warm and I turned away from Ben. "I ran into him outside Stanley's. Some guys roughed him up pretty bad, and he's asking for you."

"Oh no. Does he still live above the record store?"

"Yeah."

"I'll be right over."

It got a bit awkward as we waited for Emma. For me, anyway. I'd never been a master at the art of casual conversation. I sat in the single chair at a small table near a kitchenette. The room was a sparsely furnished studio with the standard-issue off-white walls and barely any decor. There was a short hall to the left of the entryway, more than likely leading to the bathroom.

"So, this is your place. How's rent around here?" I asked.

Ben didn't answer. Instead, he remained still, the back of his head settled against the couch and his eyes closed. His breathing was labored. The blood was drying where it was smeared across his chin, jawbone, and side of his neck.

Across from us was a section of floor-to-ceiling shelves filled with records. It was difficult for me not to walk over and nose around the albums. That would be weird to do when the owner was nearly unconscious a few paces away, right? A record player and small television were the only other items located along that wall. At the other end of the room, a full-size mattress rested on the floor. Around the unmade, quilt-covered bed were several towers of books. Some were open, haphazardly placed on the floor around the sleeping area. From the spines I could read, the majority of the titles fell into the subjects of physics and religion.

"Seems like you've been studying." I looked at Ben. "Are you taking some college courses?"

He cracked an eyelid and gave a slight frown.

"No?" Yup. Awkward.

A car door closed outside, and I looked toward the front door. Footsteps sounded on the stairs up to the apartment. The vanilla fragrance of Emma's perfume reached my nose before a soft knock sounded on the front door.

"Alex, it's Emma."

Ben's eyelids raised when I stood and let Emma into the apartment. Upon entering, she gave me a tight hug. Another scent, unfamiliar to me, mixed with her own. Who had she been with so late in the evening?

"Thank you for staying." She released me and hurried over to Ben as I closed the door. Emma slipped off her coat and sat on the couch beside him. Her frown grew as Ben signed to her. I stood out of the way at the corner of the couch.

Nodding, she carefully lifted the front edge of his shirt. She examined the ugly bruises that had already bloomed there, and lightly placed her fingertips beneath his ribcage.

I realized what she intended to do. "Em?" She was going to use magic to heal Ben's injuries. She wouldn't be so casual about flaunting her powers in front of a Commoner, so he must know.

She glanced at me. "It's okay, Alex. Trust me."

I'd seen Emma practice her magic once before, when we found a young, homeless woman suffering from extreme hypothermia on our way back to my car from a show. Emma had saved the woman from dying alone in the cold before taking her to a shelter for the night.

Emma's attention focused on Ben as she pressed her fingertips firmly into his skin. He inhaled sharply, his jawline tense. Her eyelids lowered just shy of completely, and she whispered words I didn't understand. Something clicked into place for me. The short guy in the alley. It was the same language he spoke to Ben.

A gentle gathering of energy from the air around us brushed over my skin. It was similar to the feeling I got before a thunderstorm. The hair on my arms stood up. Emma's brow wrinkled in concentration as she continued to whisper. A dull, red glow gradually rose beneath Ben's skin where her fingertips rested. It reminded me of shining a flashlight through my hand as a kid. She rotated her wrist and he gasped, his eyes squeezing shut. Emma slowly splayed her fingers wider until her palm rested against his bruised skin. The glow faded, and the energy rushed back through the room, as if the space around Emma exhaled.

The tension in Ben's face eased. He inhaled deeply through his nose, and his ribcage rose as he filled his lungs. He exhaled through his mouth as she removed her hand. His eyelids opened, and he carefully shifted his weight to sit up straighter on the couch. He gave Emma a weak smile and signed, "Thank you."

"You're welcome. You'll probably be quite sore for a while."

He glanced over at me before he continued his signing to Emma. She smiled and looked up at me. "He says I have a pretty badass friend."

I would have been flattered if I wasn't feeling so clueless. I was like a child with the grown-ups talking over my head. It was incredibly frustrating. Not only did I not know sign language, I didn't understand all the ins and outs of Emma's world as a wizard. Why was it okay for her to so blatantly display her gift? And if Ben did know she wielded magic, how?

Ben continued communicating with Emma, and her smile faded. She shifted in her seat and gave me an anxious glance. She responded back to Ben in sign. He nodded and gave me a more critical look. Before I could ask what they were speaking about, Emma placed her hand on his arm. "Do you know the people who attacked you?"

He didn't answer, but instead slowly stood from the couch. His breathing sounded more even, not as urgent and strained. He shook his head and limped toward the kitchenette's sink.

"You do, don't you?" Emma frowned after him. "Who were they? What did they want?"

Ben grabbed a dish towel, ran it under the water of the faucet, and started to wipe away the blood marring his face. No answer.

I replied instead, "Those guys didn't seem like average thugs. It's probably best not to get involved with whatever is going on here." I crossed my arms and leveled an annoyed look at Ben. "Any more than we already have." Emma and I had our own problems to manage.

Ben lowered the towel and gave me an incredulous look. He shook his head and turned back to Emma. His signing was more abrupt and fast as he communicated with her.

"You're not being fair." Emma stood. "Alex has a good instinct for situations like this. She's worried."

Ben tossed the towel on the counter and crossed the short distance to the front door. Opening it wide, he stood beside the door with a hand on the doorknob. The cold winter air rushed into the warmer space. He looked over at us expectantly. When we didn't move, he motioned to the open door with a sweep of his hand.

I narrowed my eyes. "You ungrateful bas—"

Emma grabbed the edge of my elbow as she passed, jacket in hand. She led us out of the apartment. I resisted the urge to give Ben the finger as we left. The door shut behind us, and the deadbolt flipped. Emma paused long enough on the frigid landing to put on her coat. She began down the stairs. "Alex," she sounded tired as she spoke, "I'll give you a ride home."

It was a quiet ride until her car was idling in front of my apartment. Emma stared down at her hands resting on the steering wheel. I could make out her worried expression by the lights from the car's dash.

"Emma, can you please explain to me what happened back there? Does Ben know you're a wizard?"

"Ben isn't a Commoner, Alex. He's a wizard, too. I don't have to hide my," she grimaced, "*abilities* from him." She looked guiltily over at the passenger seat. "I didn't tell you after you two met because I didn't think it was important."

"Are those guys who attacked him magic users as well? One of them spoke in the same language you used tonight."

"He did?" She frowned. "Ben didn't mention that. Our language is only allowed to be taught from one wizard to the next."

"If Ben and those guys are all wizards, why would they attack him?" Out of curiosity, I'd once asked Emma to explain the rules she had to follow as a wizard. However, she'd grown uncomfortable and changed the subject. The things that made Emma uncomfortable I could count on one hand, so I never brought it up again.

Emma's eyebrows drew together, and her frown deepened. "I'm not sure. Ben wouldn't tell me much. He believes they were hired by someone from Hopewell, but he also kept saying he didn't know them or what they wanted."

"So, more than likely, he lied to you." I growled. "If he's a wizard, why did he drag you into this? Couldn't he magic himself better?"

She shook her head. "Remember when you asked me if I could throw fireballs and were disappointed when I told you I couldn't because the focus of my magic was healing?"

My face warmed. "Maybe." It had been a valid question.

"Wizards specialize in different areas of magic," Emma said. "When he was still able to practice magic, healing wasn't Ben's focus."

Right, different wizards used different types of magic. "When he was still able? He isn't a wizard, then? But you said—"

"He's a wizard, but he can't cast spells because he's not able to speak. His voice has been suppressed because he's tethered. For supernatural beings it's like being a convict, so he's—"

"Convict? Emma!" My voice spiked in volume and she jumped. I took a deep breath, reining in my outburst. "I'm sorry, but that doesn't worry you at all?"

"No. Ben is a really nice person," she said.

It was an Emma type of logic. "What crime did he commit?"

"I never asked." She noted my exasperated expression and added, "It's rude to ask about that, Alex. It can be really personal. Why would I need to know anyway?"

"To stay safe?" I shook my head. "Listen, Em, my instincts are saying *no* to this situation. I'm seeing red flags."

She frowned. "Yes, I know. I am as well."

"So we're out, right?" I wanted a verbal agreement.

She vocalized her train of thought instead of answering my question. "Something isn't right about this. I don't think it's a coincidental attack. Why would Ben lie? Maybe we should try to find out more about those two men."

"Are you kidding? That's a terrible idea." The last thing I wanted was to give the two guys from the alley a reason to come after Emma and me. "Have you forgotten we already have two problems named Kevin and Brad? Why would we want two more?"

Emma chewed at her bottom lip. "You know how Anne was talking about the assaults they're logging over at the station, and now a kidnapping? Alex, all of those people being attacked are like us."

My mouth went dry. I didn't seek out or associate with those like me. It kept things simple. Manageable.

Emma continued, "As much as you try to hide from them, it doesn't change the fact there are other werewolves in Hopewell."

Of course there were. In an area concentrated with people, like a city, there would be more wizards and wolves. It was simple mathematics. I'd only met a few werewolves when I moved around the country. I hadn't found out my grandfather was a werewolf until the gene that had been dormant in my father's body was triggered in mine. By then, my grandfather had died.

"How do you know wizards and werewolves have been targeted?" I asked.

"It's a small city and people talk. It's been the main subject of discussion in our community for a while now. We're not sure if any other supernatural beings have been affected because they tend to keep to themselves. The Chicago Delegation is threatening a visit if it isn't cleared up soon."

"Chicago what?" It sounded like something I'd place in the *leave-me-out-of-it* file.

"It's the regional governing body for people like us."

I shook my head. "Em, you know I don't do politics. I think we should avoid this."

"What if Kevin, Brad, and those two men are all behind the assaults? We could help by turning them in to the Committee."

*Committee?* What the *hell* was the Committee? My jaw clenched.

Emma's brow softened. She reached over to place a hand on my wrist as I tried to process everything. Part of me found that more annoying than comforting. I wanted to be upset that she hadn't shared any of this sooner, but I realized it was my own fault. I'd told her I didn't want to be involved in the supernatural community. Keeping to myself with only a couple of close friends let me remain hidden. Remaining hidden meant I was safe. And being safe equated to less anxiety about my inner wolf severely injuring someone or worse. Now I was asking Emma questions about the community I'd avoided. That irritated me even more.

"Maybe I could introduce you to a few people," she said. "I think looking out for each other is even more important than usual right now. If you met more—"

I shook my head again. "I'm doing okay with who I already know. I'd rather not keep track of more people who know what I am."

"You have Anne and me. That's it." She added, "Anne doesn't know about us, and I'm a magic user. I don't have all the answers or support you may need."

I sensed her studying me, a feeling I'd never enjoyed from anyone. "I'm doing fine, Em," I repeated. I wasn't going to argue the point further. Keeping myself out of sight from other supernatural beings had served me well so far. I reached for the door handle, signaling the conversation was at a close.

"Alex, wait," Emma said. "There's something else you should know about Ben."

I glanced back at her with a sinking sensation in my stomach. "What?"

Emma hesitated. "He, um . . . he noticed your eyes. Earlier, in the alleyway."

*Shit.* I buried my face in my hands. "No. Dammit. No, no, no."

"I wanted to tell you so it didn't take you by surprise."

"So now I have to convince this guy, who I don't even know, to not mention me to anyone. It's another person to monitor. I should have walked away and left him there."

"No, you did the right thing. Ben had some bad internal injuries," she said. "Tell him it's important he doesn't discuss you with others. He's a wizard. He'll understand that."

I leaned my head back against the seat and groaned. "Because that doesn't sound arrogant at all. 'Hey, we just met, but don't talk to all your friends about me.'"

Emma giggled, which caused me to smile despite the mess I had to sort.

"You're going straight home, right?" I asked. With Kevin and Brad on the loose, and now more details about the assaults, I was worried about her.

She nodded. "Yes, I am. Thank you for calling me tonight so I could help."

"You're welcome." I exited the car. "Send me a quick message so I know you made it back, okay?"

She smiled. "Yes, mother."

I watched her car's taillights disappear into the flurries of falling snow before I walked inside to my apartment. Like me, Emma had never shown interest in the supernatural governing structure of Hopewell. Even though wizards were treated as first-class citizens, she'd always been embarrassed by how she was different. It didn't help that Emma's Commoner mother, despite knowing her daughter had a gift for healing, was strongly opposed to the use of magic. That was, of course, unless it was her husband who practiced. In the case of her daughter, Susan referred to it as "witchcraft" and said it was unnatural. Not having the support of your family while parsing out who you truly are would be hell. I couldn't imagine having done so without my parents and grandmother.

Only in the past couple months had Emma started commenting on the sociopolitical landscape of the supernatural community. The attacks both she and Anne mentioned must have been a trigger. I hadn't questioned Emma about her new interest because, selfishly, I didn't want to get pulled into any drama. She also never seemed to be in danger before now. Because of the comments Emma made tonight, I worried she would try tracking down the strangers who attacked Ben. If I couldn't dissuade her from doing so, I definitely wouldn't let her make the attempt alone.

# 3

DESPITE MY HEAVY eyelids, I kept myself awake with busy work while I waited for Emma's message. I shrugged out of my green canvas cargo jacket. The shoulder and sleeve were stained with Ben's blood. The jacket was a favorite possession of mine, having belonged to my grandfather. I immediately tended to it, gently washing the blemishes from the worn fabric.

The heirloom turned my thoughts toward my family. I loved my parents and grandmother, and missed them, but I'd acclimated to rarely seeing them. We thought it was safer that way. I hadn't left home to avoid the lawsuit or nosy neighbors. It was because of the ominous, rule-enforcing organizations I now had names for. *Delegation. Committee.* My family believed I'd be punished for what I'd done to the man who attacked me. I believed if I remained with them, my family would be in danger as well—if not from the Committee, then from me.

I clearly remembered the day we sat down together to discuss exactly what fate had dealt me. The tone of the gathering was somber, as if we were grieving a loss in the family.

*I SIT AT our small dining room table, flanked by my grandmother and mom. My dad is across from me. I can smell his aftershave. The ticking of the old cuckoo clock on the wall is irritatingly loud and distracting, causing me to clench my teeth.*

*My dad speaks first, "We—your grandmother, mother, and I," he motions to each of them in turn, "—need to share something with you about our family history. You may have noticed that your body . . ." he pauses, ". . . it's changing in unexpected ways."*

*Really? For the last forty-eight hours my mind and body had not felt like my own. I was a stranger in my own skin. I begin to giggle. My dad frowns and looks to my mom for help. She covers her eyes and shakes her head. I'm laughing now. At this moment, I choose to laugh instead of cry. I'd been doing a lot of crying.*

*"Alex, dear, can you please share with us what's on your mind?" my grandmother asks.*

*My manic laughter ceases abruptly. "Changing in unexpected ways?" I shout at my dad. "I'm not having my goddamn period!"*

*"Alexandria Steward!" My mom scowls. "Do not talk to your father in that tone of voice!"*

*I look from one family member to the next. Now that I was talking, the words were coming out in a jumbled rush. "My body has turned into an episode of* The Twilight Zone! *Why is it that I could smell each of you before you even walked into this room? How was I able to get up last night, come all the way downstairs, get a drink, and go back to bed before realizing I hadn't turned on a single light?" My voice is starting to crack. I could feel the tears threatening. "How could I possibly hear the mailman coming up the walk this morning—" I point toward the front door, "—from two rooms away?"*

*I notice my raised hand and immediately fall silent. My fingers are distorted, now longer with enlarged joints. Talon-like nails curve from the end of each fingertip. My stomach threatens to give up its breakfast. Lowering my hand, I look to my family for help. "Tell me what's happening to me."*

*My mom is crying. My dad sits stone-faced and pale. Only my grandmother speaks. She stands from where she is seated at my right side. Her voice is like a balm on a blistering wound. "Alex, dear, let's go into the living room together so we can talk."*

*She places her hand gently on the small of my back and guides me from the dining room. My sense of smell is flooded with the fragrance of lavender. She shoos our family dog, Gromit, off the couch so we can sit down together. I collapse back while she sits upright, facing me.*

*"You carry within your blood a wonderful gift," she says. "It's the same gift your grandfather received from his grandmother, and she from hers."*

*"This," I motion to myself, disdain in my voice, "happened to Grandpa, too?" I stop and hold up my hand, marveling as I turn it back and forth. Was I losing my mind? It was my hand again, not the monstrosity it was a minute ago.*

*"Yes. When you were young, your grandfather insisted the wolf would choose you. But you grew past your early teens without the gene presenting itself. Your parents and I thought it would lie dormant, as it did in your father. But we believe the man who attacked you while you were out running woke it. You were being protected." She gives me an empathetic smile. "Don't be disheartened, though. It's possible to live your life alongside it. I'll tell you everything your grandfather shared with me. We prepared for this when I was carrying your father, and again when your mother and father were expecting you."*

*I shake my head. "Grandma, do you know how crazy you sound right now?"*

*"Of course I do, dear. I sound as batty as your grandfather did when he told me." She places her small hand on my knee. "Imagine having fallen desperately in love with the man of your dreams, and right before he proposes marriage, he tells you he's a werewolf."*

I FINISHED WITH the jacket, hung it up to dry, and checked my phone. No message from Emma yet. I dialed her number and waited as the phone rang, chewing my thumbnail. Her phone directed me to her voicemail. Where was she? Had Kevin and Brad been waiting outside her house? Growling, I ended the call and dialed her again. This time she answered on the third ring.

"Hello?" Her voice was groggy.

"Emma? I've been waiting for your message."

"Oh, shit." Fabric rustled. "Alex, I forgot. I'm so sorry."

"What the hell? You *forgot*? I was getting worried."

"I know. I'm . . ." There was a deeper voice, barely audible, on her end of the line.

My chest tightened. "Em, are you safe? Is everything okay?"

"Yes, I'm okay. I'm at home in bed."

She had someone staying with her, then. Was he this Mitch guy she'd mentioned? Whoever he was, he must have been the scent I noticed on her at Ben's apartment. My concern was replaced by a surge of irritation. I didn't hide it from my voice. "Good night."

Emma didn't notice. "Good night."

As I got ready for bed, I found Ben's key in the back pocket of my jeans. "You've got to be kidding me." I tossed the key on the nightstand and texted Emma to ask what I should do with it. She replied with a phone number, a "*good night*," and a snoozing emoji.

I glanced at the key again before texting the number she sent.

*It's Alex. I still have your key. When and where can I meet you to give it back?*

I grabbed a quick shower and climbed into bed. Turning over, I pulled the covers up around my chin. I couldn't get to sleep. My conversation with Emma kept replaying in my mind. She'd suggested I meet other werewolves so I could figure out how things were run here for those like me. Even though she felt like a sister, we were different.

I knew the basic rules of hiding my gifts and not letting my wolf make a meal out of Commoners. So far an unremarkable lifestyle, dull gig jobs, and a tiny social circle had kept me hidden, out of trouble, and safe. But my patience with everything, and my hold on the beast living in my body, was rapidly fraying. Maybe it was time to get a few pointers from the local werewolves, because if my inner wolf severely injured someone, it'd be the end of us.

I'D JUST DRIFTED to sleep when my buzzing phone fell off the bedside table. I woke with a start, looking about as it continued to vibrate on the hardwood floor. Leaning across the bed on my stomach, I reached down and retrieved the phone in time to miss a call from Emma. I called her back, wondering if she felt guilty for making me worry.

Her voice was bright. "Good morning! I thought you might want to join me at a community meeting tomorrow."

Nope. She was already well past my irritation with her. "What? Why?" I curled up on my side back under the covers and stifled a yawn.

"It's a small group made up of our people. We can let them know what happened to Ben and the two of us. This could help us get some answers." There were sounds of traffic on her end of the line, as well as the tapping of her shoe's heels on the sidewalk.

Uneasiness brewed in my stomach. "Community meeting" sounded like a one-way ticket to *everyone-wants-to-know-my-business* town. "I don't know, Em. Do we need to tell a whole group about Kevin and Brad? Tell them what happened to Ben and let them handle it. Plus, you know I'm terrible at groups of people."

"That's why you have me as a friend! Please? Come along, and if it all creeps you out too much, we can leave." Bells began to toll in the background. She must have been downtown. There were a dozen or so churches down there. Patterson Street Church, where her family attended, was one of the larger, more established congregations. "I'm heading into service, so I'll text you the details and we can talk more about it later."

"Did you even sleep?" I asked, wishing I were still sleeping.

"Bye!"

The woman was a machine. I wasn't sure where Emma managed to store all her energy. My phone chimed with the info she'd promised. I noticed another new message. It was a reply from Ben.

*I'll be working at Rear Window this afternoon. Stop in at any time you'd like.*

I made an attempt at more sleep, but shortly after noon, my growling stomach urged me out of bed. As usual, my refrigerator was empty. I'd have to hunt down some lunch. It wasn't far to Rear Window Records, so I decided to walk. The frigid winter air would wake me up.

After I grabbed something from a small sandwich shop, my route passed by the alleyway entrance to Stanley's. Police tape and a few parked patrol cars blocked the alley, and an officer turned away curious pedestrians. I remembered the camera and the same anxiety-induced dread I felt when I'd first noticed it returned. Had the camera picked up any footage of me?

Hanging around a crime scene I'd been involved in wasn't the brightest idea, so I continued to Rear Window Records. I filed the alleyway camera in my *to-deal-with-later* mental folder. Soon I stood outside the front door of the record store. Emma and I didn't leave Ben's place on the best of terms. Elegantly handling confrontations had never been my strong suit. I took a deep breath and entered the shop.

Rear Window contained rows and rows of bins, each housing albums for sale. Posted along the brick walls were old concert posters, photographs, and t-shirts. The Struts played on the overhead speakers while customers browsed the wares.

I approached the U-shaped counter and its archaic-looking cash register. Behind the counter, a young employee stood directing a customer to his desired genre section. Her short platinum blonde and blue hair was pulled back into pigtails, a fringe of bangs above her brown eyes. I didn't recognize the band logo on her strategically tattered shirt. The name tag she wore read "Sara." She greeted me with a smile. "Can I help you find something?"

"I'm here to drop something off for Ben," I answered.

Her smile flickered, and she hesitated before responding. "Sure thing. I'll call him up here." She looked me over. "Who should I say is asking for him?"

"Alex."

"I'll go grab him." Sara crossed the store to a curtained doorway, pushing aside the fabric. She shouted into the back room. "Ben, someone by the name of Alex is here for you." She returned to the counter. "He should be up in a few."

I stepped aside so she could help two teenagers waiting in line behind me. There was a new release display near the curtain. I hummed the song playing on the shop's speakers to myself as I browsed the latest album titles. There was a reason I didn't come here often. I'd spend what little money I had on music.

There was a light tap on my shoulder. I turned quickly, surprised I hadn't heard anyone approach. Ben stood behind me, his hands lifted in mock defense. A small smile played on his lips as he watched me with raised eyebrows.

My face flushed. "Sorry, you startled me."

He lowered his hands and reached into the back pocket of his jeans to retrieve a small notepad. Taking a pencil from where it was tucked behind his ear, he scribbled a quick note. He flipped the paper around toward me. *Sorry for being an ass. Situation would have been worse without you.*

Ben began writing again. He looked much better with the blood cleaned from his face, hair, and clothing. His bottom lip was still split and swollen but no longer bled. The beginnings of an ugly bruise ran along the bottom edge of his left eye socket, and his eye was bloodshot. Maybe that's why he wore glasses. He looked good in the dark, thick frames. The notepad flipped toward me again. *Can I thank you with a coffee?*

I looked from the notepad to him. The friendliness I'd noticed at The Sound Refuge had returned. But I was here to return his key and ask him to never mention me, not to set up a coffee date with him. "Um, I'm not sure. Can I give it some thought?" I'd refuse the invitation via text.

He shrugged and nodded.

"I passed by Stanley's on my way over. The police are there looking around." I frowned. "There was a security camera in the alley I hadn't noticed until we left for your apartment. I wanted to let you know in case the police ID you and show up to ask questions."

Surprisingly, the news didn't seem to bother him. He wrote in the notepad again. *Don't think they'll find anything, but thank you.*

How could he be sure of that? What else did he know? "On second thought, the coffee is starting to sound good. Is there somewhere you have in mind? Maybe when your shift ends?"

He smiled and nodded again. He flipped the page and scribbled something down on the notepad. *The Beacon? 8:00?*

I could get in a day's worth of driving before meeting him. "That works." The Beacon would allow for more privacy, and I could talk to him about the cameras and keeping my name to himself. "See you then?"

Ben nodded. He tucked away the notepad and pencil as I pulled his apartment key from my pocket. He accepted the key in one hand and signed his thanks with his other.

"You're welcome." I raised a hand in farewell. He mimicked the gesture. I exited the shop, thankful the whole encounter was over without incident.

I GOT TO The Beacon early to pick out a table. The coffeehouse wasn't very busy. At this time of day, most people had traded coffee mugs for pint glasses. I selected a table for two on the lower level near the back of the shop. It was quieter, more private, and allowed me to place my back to the wall while watching the staircase down from the main level.

Ben arrived on time and caught sight of me halfway down the stairs. He gave me a questioning look as he pointed at me and then tipped his hand like drinking from a mug.

"Regular coffee, please. No cream," I requested.

He gave me the universal "one moment" sign and turned to ascend back up the stairs. A few minutes later he made his way to the table I'd selected for us. He placed the steaming mugs on the tabletop, one in front of me. The coffee smelled wonderful.

"Thanks."

He retrieved his notepad and pencil from his jacket and tossed them on the table. The legs of the chair screeched on the cement floor as he pulled the chair out. I gritted my teeth at the shrill sound. I tried to get my thoughts in order as he got settled and scooted up to the table.

"Ben, I have a favor to ask of you."

His eyebrows rose.

I dropped my gaze to the coffee mugs. "Em told me you'd noticed I'm a bit . . . different. Not many people around here know that about me." I glanced up. "It's important to me to keep it that way. I'd prefer you not mention me . . . ever . . . to anyone."

Ben's head tilted to the side as he studied me. He more than likely thought I was either a diva or crazy. Maybe a bit of both.

"Please," I added as an afterthought.

He smiled and nodded before he took a sip of coffee.

That had gone smoother than expected. "Thank you," I said. Hopefully he was a person who was good for his word. "I couldn't help but notice earlier that you weren't concerned when I mentioned the security camera at Stanley's."

The friendly smile faded. He shrugged.

"Why not? Because I sure as hell am."

He drummed his fingers beside his mug a few times before he picked up his pencil and flipped open the notepad. I leaned forward to watch him write. *He fried the camera. No camera means nothing to see.*

I looked up and sat back in my seat. "You saw him wreck the camera?" Ben nodded.

I wasn't sure whether or not to believe him. The lack of certainty was uncomfortable. "Ben, I'm bad at mincing words, so I'm going to tell you what bothers me about this whole situation," I said. "Emma is a close friend of mine, like a sibling. I care for her a lot."

He nodded again.

"You, on the other hand, I don't know."

Ben shifted in his seat, leaning back in his chair. His arms crossed over his chest.

"I feel you're withholding some information about those two thugs. If you're not willing to tell me who those guys are or what they wanted from you, my imagination will fill in the blanks. I'm going to assume it's nothing good." I frowned. "As of right now, I see you endangering Emma. You chose to involve her in your situation, and then you refused to tell her the full story. I don't like it."

He sat up, scribbled something on the notepad, and spun it on the table to face me. I read the single word on the page. *Understood.*

I looked up at him. He stared at me calmly from across the table. Feeling a surge of irritation, I leaned forward. My elbows rested on the table, and I struggled to keep my tone civil. "So tell me what is going on."

He scanned my face and wrote in the notepad. *Your eyes.*

Widened, glowing eyes reflected in his glasses. My stomach lurched. I dropped my gaze before sparing several sideways glances around the rest of the room. Had anyone else noticed? The only other people there were involved in conversation or reading. I closed my eyes and exhaled slowly, trying to regain composure.

Ben's pencil scratched on the paper before he pushed the notepad across the tabletop. I opened my eyes. *Asked Emma about you. Be extra careful around Hopewell.*

Before I could ask what he meant, Ben flipped the page, and the pencil moved across the paper again. *Those types of guys are hired by someone. Paid in promises. Person holding their leash is probably well connected. Told Emma they aren't our problem, so she shouldn't be in danger.*

I shook my head. "Em believes she can protect people by puzzling out these strange assaults happening around the city. She thinks the two guys who attacked you could be part of it. I'm worried she'll get hurt." I frowned. "I've tried talking her out of it, but she isn't letting it go." I was beginning to think the only way to keep her safe and not risk my cover was to get the info she wanted for her.

"There are still rules of conduct for wizards, right? Why would those two men disregard the laws and go after you?"

Ben paused, turning the pencil over the tops of his fingers. He lowered it to the page. *I'm not protected under those laws.*

When I looked up from reading, he lifted a finger to touch his throat.

"Because you don't talk?" What had Emma said about his voice? Something about it being blocked because of a crime.

He flipped to a blank page and drew two perpendicular lines on the paper. It was a cross. I looked up at him again, and he pointed to his throat a second time. Camouflaged among the linework of the tattoo, right over his Adam's apple, was a cross. The color of the symbol was slightly different from the ink used in the tattoos. It was like a brand that would be burned into the hide of livestock. If you weren't looking for it, you wouldn't even know it was there. Ben wrote beneath the cross on the bottom of the page. *I'm tethered.*

I opened my mouth to ask why, paused, and then closed it again. I took a sip of coffee instead. Though my curiosity demanded to know how he'd ended up with a tether, Emma had also said it was impolite to ask. Maybe her attempts to train me in the nuances of social etiquette weren't as fruitless as we'd thought.

There were footsteps at the top of the stairs. A barista walked down to our level to retrieve a tray of used mugs and dishes. The young man cleared the empty tables, checking on patrons as he passed. Upon hearing the sound of clattering mugs, Ben glanced back over his shoulder. He tore the last few pages from the notepad, crumpling them.

The barista approached the table. "Need anything, Ben?"

Ben grinned at him, tapping his middle and index finger on his thumb.

It must have been the sign for "no" because the young man turned his attention to me. "Miss?"

"No thanks." I smiled.

He left our table to head back to the stairs and the front counter.

"Ben? Did those guys say anything that might tell me what they were hired to do?"

He shook his head.

"Or where they're from? Or who hired them?" I asked.

He shook his head again.

"Why you? Were they going specifically after you?"

He frowned this time. Ben fidgeted with the pencil before writing. *Don't know anything else about them, and don't want to.*

Conversation over. He wasn't going to give me anything else. Right now, at least. "Yeah, okay." I drummed my fingertips on the table. "I need to learn more about them before Em finds herself in a bad situation." She knew more about navigating politics than I did, but that wasn't going to help her in a dark alley with those two goons.

Ben's phone buzzed on the table beside his mug. He checked it, and I finished my coffee as he replied to the message. When we stood to leave, he waited for me to proceed up the stairs before following.

The barista gave a wave as we left. "Have a nice night."

Ben returned the gesture and exited the coffee shop after me. We stood there awkwardly in the cold a moment before Ben smiled and jabbed his thumb back over his shoulder. I assumed he wanted to go back home.

Nodding, I smiled as well. "Thanks for agreeing to respect my privacy. And for the coffee, of course."

He lifted a hand in farewell before turning and starting down the sidewalk. I watched him depart, unsure if he was being completely forthcoming with me. Emma liked and trusted him, but people she didn't like were few and far between. I'd hoped to get more information about what the two men wanted. Instead, every small detail I'd extracted from him had felt like a struggle. Why was that? Was he scared those two men would find him again? Or was he protecting someone?

I returned home and was curled up on the sofa when my phone buzzed on the table. I expected it to be Emma. I'd agreed to go to the community meeting and had messaged her to ask if we could meet at my place beforehand. My plan was to have a heart-to-heart, *this-is-the-worst-idea* chat with her about poking at the two guys who attacked Ben.

Instead of a reply from Emma on my phone, it was a message from Ben. *Thanks for agreeing to coffee. Enjoyed the interrogation. Up for trying a film at my place?*

I blinked at the words on the screen. I asked my empty apartment, "What?"

Another message appeared in the thread. *Sunday evening? 9?*

I chewed at my thumbnail. Emma said Ben was harmless, and my gut told me I still hadn't heard the whole story from him. If Emma agreed to back off looking into the assaults after I talked to her, I could cancel on Ben. If she didn't, hopefully Ben would spill more details on what his attackers were up to. I could pass on the info to Emma, and she could report it, eliminating the need for her to pursue the men herself. I typed in my reply and sent it. *See you then.*

# 4

WHEN THE NEXT day dawned and Emma still hadn't gotten in touch, my concern grew. She'd never leave a message unanswered this long. After a quick breakfast, I grabbed my jacket and left for her workplace. I could catch her there before I started my day running rides.

Another Chance Ministries was a block or two from the city center. The central location was unusual. As new development in the form of restaurants and retail shops had sprung up, Hopewell had tried its best to push the shelters further south down the street. By keeping the homeless population out of sight, it could better ensure the comfort of tourists, and therefore revenue. Also, residents could conveniently forget about the city's homeless. They'd rather enjoy their happy hour sushi without someone panhandling in front of the restaurant.

I waved to a few familiar faces as I entered the old building. I'd helped out before when Emma came up short on volunteers. Mixed scents of breakfast food, damp clothing, and cleaning supplies met me inside. Many people were ducking into the building to get a hot meal and catch a break from the freezing temperatures.

An older woman waved her hand to catch my attention and motioned me over to her table. She sat in front of a steaming Styrofoam cup of coffee and two store-bought sugar cookies on a napkin. Her gray hair was pulled back into a messy bun beneath a knit stocking cap. Standing, she wasn't much taller than Emma.

"Good morning, Barbara," I said.

I'd spent time with Barbara at a social event for Another Chance. She had tried, unsuccessfully, to teach me to knit a hat. She was clear in her instruction, but I didn't have the patience for the skill. As a consolation prize, Barbara had given me the hat I'd worn the past two winters. With my abundance of curly hair, it didn't exactly exude chic, but it kept me warm.

"Good morning, sweetie. Are you here to see Emma?" Her short stature and warm smile reminded me of my grandmother.

"Yeah. Have you seen her?"

A few more wrinkles appeared in Barbara's brow. "She and I usually chat while I have my coffee, but I haven't seen her for a few days. Is she sick?"

I frowned. "Not that I know of." Emma never missed work.

Barbara leaned toward me and beckoned me closer. I crouched down beside her seat. She glanced around and then lowered her voice. "I thought she might be spending time away with that handsome blond fellow, but he's in their office."

I glanced across the dining area to the small cluster of doors. A light was on in Emma's office. "Is he still here?"

"Yes. I believe so."

"Thanks." I stood.

Barbara smiled, pleased to have helped. "You're welcome."

When I reached Emma's office, I found the door cracked open and heard movement from inside. I rapped lightly on the door with my knuckles.

A man's voice answered, "Come in."

Opening the door, I got a noseful of the unfamiliar scent I'd detected on Emma. It nearly overpowered the traces of her vanilla perfume lingering in the office. I studied the man seated at her desk. This must be Mitch.

He looked up from something he was writing. "Can I help you?" He had blue eyes and meticulously cropped blond hair. His clothing looked well-fitted, complete with jacket and tie. Custom tailored, maybe? I could almost smell the money on him.

"Is Emma here?" I asked.

"No, I'm sorry. She won't be in the office today." He folded his hands together. "Is there something I can help you with?"

"I'm Alex, a friend of hers. Do you—"

"Alex?" He stood, and his smile was damn near perfect. "So, you're Alex. She's spoken a lot about you."

"Oh?" *Well, she hasn't said much about you.*

He stepped around the desk and extended his hand. He was my height, but built broader. "I'm Mitch White. Emma and I are colleagues." His last name, though common, stood out to me.

I gave him my polite smile and accepted the handshake. "Nice to meet you." *Finally.* "I really do need to contact Emma, but she's not answering my calls or messages. Have you seen her?"

"Yes, briefly, this morning."

The tension in my chest eased a bit. "Do you know where I can find her?"

"She's extremely busy with meetings today," Mitch said. "I'm sure if it's important, she'll return your call. I could pass along a message to her if you'd like."

I wasn't sure what was more irritating: his assumption that whatever I needed was unimportant, or the fact he was playing gatekeeper to my closest friend. "Or you could tell me where she is."

His eyebrows rose, and he crossed his arms over his chest. There was that perfect smile again. "I'm sorry. I don't feel comfortable handing over her schedule."

"She's my best friend, Mitch. She won't care."

He shook his head. "I can't give her schedule to anyone who asks. It's company policy."

Was it? Frustration burned in my stomach. "Ask her to call me as soon as she can about our plans tonight. It's important." Now that I knew she was safe, I could wait until before the community meeting to talk to Emma. If Mitch was the only way to make that happen, I'd have to deal with it. I frowned, then added, "Please."

He nodded. "I'll be sure to pass along your message. It was nice to finally meet you, Alex."

I gave him a glance up and down. My tone was civil, but I couldn't conjure the smile again. "Likewise."

I exited Another Chance wondering if Emma would get my message. My gut was telling me there was a chance she wouldn't. Was he the reason she couldn't be bothered to get back to me? I checked my watch. There was no time to search for Emma before the meeting tonight. If I was going to make rent this month, I needed to spend the time bringing in some more money.

LATER THAT NIGHT, I arrived at the address for the meeting as a tweaked bundle of nerves. Not only was I going to walk into an organized group of complete strangers, I still hadn't heard from Emma. So much for my plan of talking with her before the meeting. It would have to be afterward now.

I messaged and then called her to see if she was already inside the restaurant or would arrive soon. No answer. Maybe it was noisy inside and she didn't hear her phone, or she was already caught up in conversation with someone.

The Village Pub was a squat restaurant tucked a door back from one of the main city streets. The street-facing wall contained several small windows and was covered in a harvest-themed mural. It took me three different passes by the front door before I seized the cleaver-shaped door handle and went inside.

The pub was invitingly warm compared to the frigid winter evening. A wave of mixed aromas and sounds greeted me. I could smell the traditional, deep-fried pub food, along with cooking beef. There were traces of different colognes and perfumes from the patrons. Laughter punctuated the hum of conversations. The smokey smell of burning wood drifted toward me from the crackling fireplace on the back wall.

The cozy, low lighting helped to ease my anxiety. Bright fluorescents in unfamiliar public places gave me the feeling of being exposed or put on display. I wandered down the narrow walkway between a line of booths and the bar. Scanning faces, I looked for Emma.

"Excuse me, hon." A waitress passed by with a tray full of beverages.

The back of the room included more booths and tables, the bathrooms, and the order window, where I caught a glimpse of the kitchen staff bustling about. Clanks and crashes could be heard as the chefs called up orders for the waitstaff. I didn't see Emma anywhere. Did I have the right place?

I retraced my steps past the bar and found a room off the entryway I'd overlooked. A couple dozen people talked between the tables. It seemed to be a mix of ages, from early twenties to mid-sixties. I looked for Emma and was again shuffled aside as a waiter bustled through. I stepped over the threshold of the room, and the noise level of the room drastically increased. It was if a glass door kept the noise contained within the room.

"Hello! Are you looking for the meeting?" a cheery voice asked. It belonged to a young woman with bright, alert eyes and long, softly curled hair. She clasped a clipboard tight to her chest.

"Ah . . . yes?" I glanced behind me at the room entrance before turning back to her.

Before I could ask, she gave a dismissive wave. "This room is partially veiled. We don't have to worry about Commoners at the pub, but we can get loud. This keeps the noise down." She extended her hand. "I'm Amy, the organizer behind these get-togethers."

I accepted the handshake with a smile. "Nice to meet you."

Amy's handshake was dainty. "And you are?"

*Dammit.* "Alex."

"Thank you so much for joining us, Alex. The more people we can have looking out for each other, the better. How did you hear about us?"

"My friend Emma invited me." I gave a longing glance at the door. "She should be here any minute." Where was she?

"Emma Arztin! Really?"

I nodded.

"That's great. She's been a wonderful addition to our group," Amy said. "Pull up a chair and have a seat. I'm sure she'll wander in. People usually do. In the meantime, I'm going to get us started."

I thanked her and sat at a two-top table near the back in view of the front door. I flagged down the waiter as he passed. I'd need a drink to make it through the gap from now until Emma arrived. He left with my order.

Amy walked to the center of the room. She placed her fingers to her lips and gave a sharp whistle. It rang painfully in my ears, and I noticed several others cringe at the noise. Were they werewolves as well? I shifted in my seat and considered leaving.

"Was that really necessary, Amy?" a voice yelled from the other side of the room.

She hugged her clipboard and blushed. "Oh my gosh. I'm so sorry. I wasn't thinking." There was chuckling throughout the room. "Good evening, everyone! Thank you to those who are returning, and welcome to those joining us for the first time. I thought we'd begin by updating each other on what we've been noticing in our neighborhoods."

My gut clenched, and I broke out into a sweat. Was this going to be a sharing circle kind of thing? Was I expected to introduce myself and talk in front of all these strangers? If so, I was out. I eyed the front door.

"Andrew will be taking notes for us. Whoever wants to go first can begin." Amy sat down next to a young man with a small laptop.

A middle-aged woman stood. "Hello, everyone. I'd been hearing stories of these harassments and assaults. They seemed to be only that—stories—until this past week when our family was affected. My daughter walked home from school with her friends and was followed to within a block of our home by a stranger. While the girls waited at a crosswalk, he started to question my daughter."

This sounded like another day in the life of any girl. I remembered my own walks to school—the men who'd watch me from behind their steaming work thermoses, or male peers who'd critique my body aloud with their friends while we waited at crosswalks. A flare of heat fired in the pit of my stomach. I looked back over my shoulder. Where the *hell* was my beer?

The woman's face reddened as her voice wavered. "He asked her if she knew what her mother was, and if she was a defect too. He told her she isn't wanted here, and if her family doesn't leave, he'd kill us. She's ten years old! She was terrified and came home in tears."

Amy asked, "Was your daughter able to describe him?"

"Everyone was bundled in winter clothing. She said he looked as old as my eldest son, who is in his late teens. I called the police and filed a report. They asked me to bring my daughter to the station to work with a sketch artist. She was too upset to do so at the time, so we have an appointment this week." The woman took her seat.

A man closer to my age, his wrist in a cast, stood. "Evening."

Greetings were returned from around the room.

"My wife and I took a bus home a few nights ago from downtown. It was late and too cold to walk. Two men who looked to be in their early to mid-fifties got off at our stop. After they followed us for a bit, they turned onto a different street. When we reached our street, they were standing on the sidewalk waiting for us. They must have circled the block. The men started to threaten us. It got heated, and then they attacked me. My wife called the police, and they ran."

I wondered if this guy was a wizard or a wolf. The only way I could sense wizards was when they were casting magic. As for werewolves, it was scent. Maybe he was neither, but something else instead? Other supernatural beings lived in Hopewell with us, but I wasn't aware of what they were. Like Emma said, they kept to themselves anyway.

"They told my wife and me that we're monstrosities that don't belong in their city," the young man said. He gestured at the woman who spoke before him. "It's the same kind of behavior her daughter dealt with." Murmuring spread through the group as he took his seat.

As I listened to the reports, I wished the information could be shared with Anne. Did any of the police know about us? If not, how many assaults on wizards or wolves were not being reported? Keeping their supernatural gifts a secret could be a challenge for the victims if the police poked around in their personal lives.

"Your beer." The waiter appeared with my pint. I debated hugging him for it.

Another person stood to speak, but I was distracted by the faint sound of the front door. A cool breeze swept in around the chair legs. I looked back over my shoulder to see if it was Emma, but the stink of cigarette smoke and a distinct musky scent preceded a man and woman who entered together.

The woman's raven-colored hair was cut into a blunt bob, and she wore a sleek and contemporary jacket over fitted, dark clothing. She caught the waiter's arm on his return trip to the bar. She held up two fingers as she spoke to him.

The man who walked in with her looked down at me from where he'd stopped at my chair. His nostrils twitched. "You're new." It wasn't a greeting, but more a statement of fact. He was similar in age to the woman. His brown hair was shaved and razored into a soft mohawk, and he wore plaid pants and a black hoodie. "Mind if we join you?" He pulled out a chair, spun it to face my own, and sat down.

His scent, the primal earthy aroma I'd only encountered a few other times in my life, swirled around us. The beast inside me recognized it and shifted in my chest. I held tight to my pint glass and focused on my breathing.

The dark-haired woman entered the room and stood beside his chair. She placed a hand on his shoulder, but her focus rested on the front of the room and the person speaking. The man, however, continued to stare at me as he sat with his elbows on his knees. His eyes narrowed as he studied me.

I finally looked directly at him and raised my eyebrows. "Is there something you need?"

He leaned toward me, and his eyelids closed as he took a deep inhale of air through his nose. His face and ears had multiple piercings. The man grinned, and when his eyes opened again their color had shifted from brown to a deep copper hue. "Why haven't we met before? I thought Trish and I knew everyone around here."

Instantly, the hair rose on the back of my neck, and my pulse accelerated. I'd never looked so closely into the eyes of someone like me. Another werewolf. It was disconcerting.

The waiter brought the woman, presumably Trish, two tumblers of amber liquor over ice. She took both, tapping one against the seated man's shoulder. He leaned back in his chair and looked up at her as he accepted the glass. "Thanks, love."

She glanced down at him. "Nate, please leave her alone and pay attention." She tipped her glass back and returned her attention to the front of the room. He rotated in his chair to face the speaker too, resting an ankle up on his knee. Trish rubbed her hand over the back of his shoulders.

I tried to refocus. An older man spoke. "The two young men waited until only a few people were in the shop with me. Then they dumped the tea bins onto the floor. They demanded we stop taking business from other proprietors and said we're not welcome here." The man raised both a hand and his voice. "We've been a part of this city longer than they've been alive! My partner and I've always been good citizens and neighbors. We pay taxes. We follow the laws. Why are they harassing me at my place of business?" He directed his next statement at Amy. "I don't think we should wait. We should demand this be addressed by the Committee."

There was that word again. *Committee*. Emma had mentioned it in the car when she told me the assaults were targeting people like us.

Nate called up to him, "Frank, you've been around long enough to know it doesn't matter if you've followed their rules or not. Money has to exchange hands before anything benefiting us is put on the Committee's schedule."

Amy spoke up in a measured tone as Frank sat down. "Nate, we don't know that. We haven't even sent a request."

Nate chuckled. "A written request is a waste of time. It's the same story as it's always been. The Commoners' representatives are scared of us. Why would they want to make our lives easier? They don't want us here either. Hell, these mystery assailants are doing them a favor."

Trish spoke. "Unfortunately, there is some truth to what Nate says. Our adversaries outweigh our allies on the Committee. I've been relaying your encounters, but we are underrepresented, and it is difficult to convince the majority that this is a serious issue. A letter to the wizards' representative, Reginald Sharpe, would alert him to your concerns. However, I also advise taking more direct action. Consider being at the next Committee meeting to personally share your stories."

The Committee must be the local level of the governing body for the supernatural. Wolves, wizards, and Commoners-in-the-know all sitting down at a table together? I wondered how that worked. Not too well from what Trish said.

There was murmuring within the group before Amy motioned for silence. She spoke to the entirety of the room. "Is there anyone willing to draft our concerns in a letter?" Several people raised their hands. "Great. Can you meet each other after we convene?"

Nate muttered, "Our people are being harassed, and she wants someone to write a letter."

I remembered the encounter with Kevin and Brad. An uneasy type of realization crept into my consciousness. "So if we're attacked, we're not allowed to defend ourselves?"

Nate looked at me for a moment, as if he wasn't sure whether I was being serious or not, before he started laughing. "Did you hear that, Trish? Why hadn't we thought of that? Problem solved."

Smirking, Trish spoke. "Where did you say you were from?"

I returned a flat look. "I didn't."

"Fair." She went on, "If we commit a violation involving a Commoner, and it is reported, the Committee will almost always side with the Commoner. It often doesn't matter if the action was taken in self-defense, so we don't rely on that."

"That's ridiculous," I said. "What are we expected to do?"

"We steer clear of Commoners as best we can." She motioned around the room. "It's why we've created places like this, safe spaces veiled from them."

"I didn't even know they existed before tonight," I said.

"But now there are Commoners who are confronting us at our places of business, outside our gathering places, and near our homes." Trish frowned. "Something has emboldened them. They know who we are and purposely target us."

"How are they identifying and finding us?" Even *I* knew werewolves were supposed to hide our shifting, to blend in with Commoners. Unless wizards were casting magic, I wouldn't be able to identify anyone as such.

Nate answered, "We're not sure yet. I think someone is making a lot of money sharing that information." His gaze jumped from one person to the next, and his voice lowered. "Even one of these self-righteous wizards would roll over for the right amount."

Amy's voice broke into the conversation as she called back to us, "Nate? Trish? Any news in your area?"

Trish spoke up for the room to hear. Everyone immediately fell silent. "We cleared out a group of several men a few nights back. They'd come sniffing after our employee when she came into work." She patted Nate's shoulder. "Everyone kept their composure. The only thing injured when they left was their pride."

A voice from the crowd asked, "Is there any way we can help? Set any wards on your building?"

Nate's reply was abrupt. "We don't need magic to protect us."

I glanced at Nate. They don't? Emma's magic seemed to come in handy. I don't know why other wizards' magic wouldn't be useful.

Trish added, "The offer is appreciated. We'll let you know if it comes to that." She took a small object from her pocket and held it aloft. "While the men were being hauled back outside our building, this pin was knocked loose. I noticed all four of them were wearing it. We all know the power a symbol can hold. It may not be relevant to our shared situation, but I brought it here tonight for everyone to see just in case."

Amy asked, "Can it please be passed around?" Trish nodded and handed the pin to me.

I looked it over and frowned. "I've seen this before." The enamel pin was of a black flag with two yellow, perpendicular stripes dividing the area into quadrants. In the top left was the icon of a red crown.

"Alex, do you have something to add?" Amy asked.

My eyes widened. I was a kid caught talking in class. "Um, Em and I . . ." Knowing now that I could get in trouble for flashing some fang to scare off Kevin and Brad, I wasn't sure how much I should share.

Someone from the other side of the room asked, "Can you speak up, please?"

I despised speaking in front of groups of people. My face warmed, and my mind raced as I began again, "Two guys hassled my friend and me after a show. They were wearing these pins in their shirt collars."

Trish's brows drew together and the muscle at her jaw twitched. Small conversations sprung up across the group as I passed the pin to the person seated at the table in front of me.

"Everyone, please take a close look at the pin," Amy said, "even if you haven't been a victim." She set the time for the next meeting, promising there would be a letter drafted for everyone to review and sign. People began to disperse. Nate and I both stood. He moved his chair out of the way, clearing the narrow aisle back toward the front door.

"Nate." Trish pointed over toward Amy, who still spoke with other attendees. "I'll see you at the bar." She pointed to me next. "Grab her."

Nate grinned at me and jerked his thumb toward the bar. "Join us for a drink?"

I glanced at the front door. Still no Emma. My concern for her from this morning returned in waves. It wasn't like Emma to not show up without at least sending a text. Maybe I was being paranoid. "Give me a minute," I said.

Nate left for the bar, and I got out my phone to call Emma again. There was a message from her sent only ten minutes prior.

*Won't be at the meeting. Talk later.*

My face burned, and my stomach roiled with acid. What the hell was she doing? Why didn't she tell me sooner so I didn't have to suffer through this alone? She knew I hated things like this. And what about an update on Kevin and Brad? Would I be in trouble for scaring them off? Growling, I shoved my phone back in my pocket and beelined to the bar.

Nate saw me coming and slapped the barstool seat next to him. I sat down, and he motioned the bartender over. "Two bourbons and . . ." he glanced at me.

"A stout, please."

"A stout," Nate finished. As the bartender moved away to get the drinks, Nate turned on his seat. His left elbow rested on the edge of the bar, and his chin on the heel of his hand as he asked bluntly, "So, who are you?"

*Ugh.* "Alex. I'm a friend of Emma Arztin's." Or at least I'd thought so.

"Emma . . ." He drummed his fingers against his cheek, looking upward as he tried to recall the person attached to the name "Emma, Emma. Don't think I know her."

A voice spoke from my other side. "She's that little curvy one with the really posh clothes and car. The wizard who started coming to these meetings a few months back." Trish took the barstool to my right, and the bartender served our drinks. "Charles Arztin's daughter."

Nate pushed one of the tumblers past me to Trish. "Yeah, okay. The one who always smells so nice." He grinned and gave me a knowing wink. "So, that's where you've been hiding. You've been slumming with the wizards?"

Trish chuckled and shook her head. "Don't answer that. It only encourages him." She offered her hand. "I'm Patricia Drake, and that's Nathan Osterberg." I exchanged a handshake with her as she asked, "Have you been living here by yourself? I don't remember hearing your name before."

"I'm not much of a people person," I said. I'd hoped not to be anyway.

Trish replied, "You're a wolf. We're stronger together. You need your pack."

The hell I did. "That's what Emma tells me. I'm not convinced yet." I watched the clusters of people leaving the meeting. "What is this Committee everyone was talking about?"

Nate gave a derisive snort. "It's a clusterfu—"

"Nate, please," Trish said.

He grinned but fell silent.

"The Committee is Hopewell's governing body of representatives from the lupine, wizard, and Commoner communities," Trish said. "It was created to maintain harmony between the different groups. There is a mutually agreed upon set of rules, created and enforced by the Committee, that we all follow. If a problem arises between the communities or a rule is broken, the Committee addresses it."

"But right now this Committee is unbalanced, so they won't look into these weird attacks?" I asked.

Trish nodded, her lips pressed into a fine line.

"How many of these representatives are wizards and wolves?" I asked.

"Reginald Sharpe is the representative for the wizards. I serve as the spokesperson for the lupine," she said. "That is all. We only have a few sympathetic ears among the Commoner reps."

I shook my head. "That must be frustrating."

"No shit," Nate said. "People are scared, and the wolves are getting pissed. It will only be a matter of time before everything blows, especially if the Commoners keep violating our sanctuaries."

I looked around the bar. "How many places like this are in Hopewell?"

"Our city is small, so there are only a few," Trish said. "We own one, Hell's Bells, across the river. Most lupine places don't obfuscate the doors with magic, so occasionally we'll get some Commoners."

Nate shrugged. "Usually the younger ones are all right. It's when they get older that they can be a pain in the ass."

Trish set her hand on my wrist. "Come by some time and let us show you our place. Do you listen to music?"

I couldn't help smiling. She'd said the magic word. *Music.* "That's a bit of an understatement."

Nate startled me by slapping my back. "We'll put you on the list."

Trish smiled. "There isn't a list."

I finished my beer, exchanged phone numbers and farewells with Trish and Nate, and left the two of them at the bar. I paused beneath the creaking, wooden sign outside the restaurant's front door to send Emma a message.

*Survived the meeting, no thanks to you. We need to talk. Soon.*

When I reached the street for my apartment, I passed it and kept driving toward Emma's home instead. After an evening of hearing stories of others being harassed and assaulted, I had to check on her despite my irritation. Her car was in the drive, and the lights were off in the house. It seemed early for Emma to be in bed. I chewed at my thumbnail, debating whether or not to knock on the door and possibly wake her up.

As I was trying to decide what to do, another car pulled up beside mine in the driveway. I looked over at the driver. It was Mitch. Emma was seated beside him. The same rush of anger from earlier, when I read Emma's text, ran through me. This time it was answered by my inner wolf. She stirred, and a snarl slipped past my lips. I got out of my car and walked around it toward Mitch's.

He exited the driver's side of the car and smiled like he was pleased to see me. "Hello again, Alex."

"Piss off, Mitch." I continued to the passenger door.

Emma opened her door and got out of the car. She looked happy to see me as well. "Alex, what're you doing here?"

Taking her by the arm, I pulled Emma aside. She resisted, allowing me to move her only a few steps away from the car and Mitch. Her eyebrows furrowed and her breath appeared as a burst of steam in the cold air. "Stop it!" She yanked her arm from my grasp. "You're being rude."

I lowered my voice. "I was really worried about you. You didn't make it to the meeting you invited me to, and you're not returning messages. What am I supposed to think after you've told me what's going on with these assaults? And then what happened to us with Kevin and Brad? I considered having Anne file a missing person's report. Is everything okay?"

She pulled her jacket tighter around herself. "Yes, of course it is. I can't pick up every single call."

"Emma, would you like me to wait inside?" Mitch asked.

Did he have a key? *I* didn't have a key to her house. I glared over at him. "Did you forget to tell her I needed to talk to her tonight?"

"What?" Emma looked from me to him. "You two have met?"

Mitch spoke to Emma, but his cool stare was for me. "Alex visited Another Chance this morning while I was in the office. I told her you were busy and would return her call when you were able to."

The creature inside me responded to his stare as a challenge. I clenched my jaw and looked away from him, taking a deep breath in an attempt to calm it.

"I see." Emma offered me a small, tired smile. "I'm sorry, Alex. I noticed a few messages, but I've been extremely busy and haven't got to them yet. We've been working all day and rushing to meetings every night. I'm starting to drop a lot of balls. I promise I'll get better at this with time." She shivered. "What did you need to talk to me about?"

"Emma, I'm going inside. Will you be long?" Mitch asked.

Another surge of anger burned inside of me. I wished he would leave so Emma and I could talk. Things were going to get hairy if he stuck around much longer.

She glanced between the two of us. "No, I'm coming."

"What? Em—"

"It's late, and I'm getting cold standing out here." Emma gave my arm a pat. "I'm sorry I worried you. I'll call you tomorrow, and we can talk more then."

Jaw clenched, I nodded. I didn't trust a growl wouldn't escape if I opened my mouth.

Emma walked to Mitch and disappeared into the house with him. It caused a dull ache inside my chest. Abandoned, I stood alone in the cold beside Mitch's car. The growl I'd been withholding rumbled through my chest.

I didn't like Mitch, and I didn't trust him either. Maybe I'd been focused on the wrong type of danger to Emma. It's possible the real threat wore a charismatic smile and a well-tailored suit.

# 5

"YOU ATTENDED A community meeting?" The *thank-goodness-our-daughter-is-being-social* was fully present in my mom's relieved smile. "That's wonderful!"

"Why would you do that?" Dad asked. He wasn't the extrovert of the two.

I grinned at his reaction. "Yeah, not my usual scene, but my friend Emma invited me." I propped my phone up on the table and leaned back in my chair. "It was at this pub that doesn't allow Commoners. I didn't know such places existed."

"Were there other werewolves, dear?" Grandma's voice came from off camera.

"Mom, move closer so she can see you." Dad tilted his phone, and my grandmother squeezed into the frame with my parents.

"Um, yeah. It was kind of weird to meet them," I said. "I don't really seek them out, you know?"

"Why not?" Grandma asked. All three of them waited.

"It's easier if fewer people know what I am," I said.

"*Who* you are," Grandma said.

"I know we've all been extremely cautious, but you've lived there for a few years now," Dad said. "If you plan on staying, maybe knowing another werewolf or two would be a good thing. It may even keep you more safe."

"Alex, stop chewing your nails," Mom said.

I lowered my gnawed thumbnail from my mouth and sat on my hand. "I don't know, Dad. Maybe."

"It'll be good for you to make some friends," Mom said.

"I already have friends, Mom," I said.

My mom smiled. "You have two."

"But remember to be careful," Dad added.

I chuckled. "Yes, I know. I'll be careful."

"Is there anything we should know or that you need before we say goodbye?" my mother asked.

I thought of the job loss, which I'd conveniently forgotten to mention, and the upcoming rent bill, which I'm sure I'd figure out. Somehow. I shook my head. "Nope. All good here." This was the part of the monthly call that was the hardest. "Be sure to give Gromit some ear scritches for me. Love you guys."

"We love you too, sweetheart. Stay safe." My mother blew a kiss and Dad and Grandma waved goodbye.

The screen of my phone went black. The wave of homesickness hit me hard, and tears itched the corners of my eyes. Maybe it was all the shit I was worrying about with Emma that made me not only miss my family, but also the life I'd left behind.

I briskly wiped at my eyes and stood to put on my jacket and boots. Anne had sent me a dinner invitation earlier in the day, and I immediately accepted. It would be the perfect opportunity to talk to her about my worries for Emma.

"THE WHOLE THING was odd. Emma wasn't herself." I took another drink of my beer as I sat atop Anne's kitchen counter.

When Anne and I hung out, it usually involved either exercising— we both ran—or food. She loved crafting recipes, and I loved to eat. She had a rare stretch of free time before her evening shift started, and invited me over for dinner. I wasn't going to miss one of her home-cooked meals.

Anne talked over the sizzling frying pan as she stirred its contents. The mix of the sesame oil, ginger, and cooking vegetables smelled so good. "That is strange. Emma is our social butterfly. Even when she's busy, I usually receive a quick note to let me know when she'll be able to get back to me."

I pointed at Anne. "Exactly! She acted like it wasn't a big deal that she'd ignored her messages. That isn't like her. And this Mitch guy? Have you met him?"

She shook her head. "No, I haven't met him. I didn't even know there was a Mitch." She removed the lid of a small pot on the stove. "Can you put the rice on the table, please? I'm almost done here."

I set aside the beer bottle and hopped down from the counter. "He works at Another Chance with her. Apparently, they met at church. Since when does she pick up guys at her parents' church? What does she call the people there again?"

Anne handed me a ceramic bowl. "Stodgy?"

"Yes." I frowned, recalling Mitch. "He was very Übermensch. She'd told me her parents like him a lot, which I totally understand now that I've met him. It also explains why he seems awful, right?" I dumped the rice into the bowl.

"Alex, I'm not sure you've given this guy a fair chance. We don't really know him yet." She switched off the range, grabbed an oven mitt, and transferred the stir-fry into another serving bowl. She swatted away my hand as I tried to snatch a sweet pepper. Anne walked to the table set for two.

"She'd gone MIA, without a check-in or an explanation." I set the bowl of rice on the table and took my seat. "Now I find out this guy has been in the picture. It seems pretty suspicious to me."

Anne nodded. "I understand what you're saying, but she's also been under a lot of stress with this new position at work. It's tied to the main ministry for her family's church. Maybe she's acclimating to the new workload."

"But he's staying over. I'm almost positive. We should've known this already. Emma always shares those details whether we want to know or not." I shook my head. "Then she said she'd call me today. I still haven't heard from her."

Anne motioned me to help myself to the food. "I know you're concerned, but let's pause and take a breath. If Emma is serious about him, maybe we set something up to meet this Mitch guy. The four of us could go out together. It'll be casual, and we can learn more about him."

I handed her the dishes after helping myself to food from each. "I guess so." It sounded like a terrible idea. I didn't want to spend any more time with Mitch than I had to.

Anne noted my lack of enthusiasm. She chuckled. "I'll arrange it and send you an invite."

I pointed to my plate with my fork. "This is amazing, Anne. Thanks for feeding me." It was one fewer meal I'd have to buy and so much tastier than ramen or cold pizza.

She smiled. "Thank you. And it's not a problem. I like cooking for people. Food always tastes better when it's shared."

I devoured a few more forkfuls of the delicious meal. "I walked to Rear Window the other day. Patrol cars and police tape were outside of Stanley's. Did something happen?"

Anne nodded. "I was helping work the scene. It looked like another assault, but more severe than the others. There was blood on the building walls and around the alleyway."

I looked down at my plate to avoid her gaze. "Any leads?" I'd settled into the habit of lying by omission with her. It wasn't *actually* lying, right?

"The detectives were hoping for some security footage, but the cameras had fizzled out. Talk about awful timing. We only have an eyewitness account from the person who called it in. The problem is, he was too inebriated to have a clear recollection of the scene. The recording of the call was cringeworthy. He raved about shadows with glowing eyes. It took the dispatcher several tries to figure out what the call was even about."

A weight lifted from my shoulders. The possibility of being caught on surveillance footage could be crossed off my *shit-to-worry-about* list. "Any progress on the string of attacks?"

She paused in thought before answering, "No, but we had a missing person's report filed that has been bothering me. It was passed along to Detective Grey as an FYI because the person in question was previously a victim of one of the assaults."

"And you think it's linked?"

She shook her head. "It's a single report, so as of right now, I only have a nagging suspicion."

Anne's gut feelings, like my own, had a track record of being pretty accurate. I thought of Kevin and Brad attacking Emma and me, and of Trish bringing that pin to the meeting. "Do you think a group could be responsible for the attacks, like some sort of organization?"

She raised an eyebrow. "You and Emma seem really interested in this case." It was a simple statement that carried a whole lot of suspicion.

I'd strayed too close. Conversations with Anne could be tricky. I focused hard on my food and tried to ignore the sudden pounding of my pulse in my ears. Shrugging, I said, "What you do is interesting."

There was a pause, and I felt her studying me. After what seemed to be hours rather than seconds, she continued. "Yes, we're sure now that the assaults are coordinated by some type of group. We've also noticed a repeated reluctance among the victims to provide much detail in their reports. Detective Grey thought the attacks may be gang-related, but his contacts across the city are saying no."

I'd hesitated to share information with Anne, fearing I'd somehow be pulled into the ongoing investigation. Like the other victims of the attacks, I didn't want the police parsing through my personal life. But this was too important not to pass on to her. "Hey Anne, remember those two guys who tried to pick up Emma at The Sound Refuge?"

She chuckled. "Which night?" When she looked up from her plate, she noticed I wasn't joking. Her mood sobered. "Kevin and Brad?"

"Yeah. After the show, they accosted Emma and me while we were walking back to her car. The reason I'm bringing it up is because I think it's related to your case."

Anne's eyes widened, then her jawline became taught. She set down her fork.

"I didn't give it much thought at the time, but Kevin and Brad wore matching pins. Then I met some people yesterday who'd thrown guys out of their club for harassing an employee. Those guys wore the same pins."

Anne sat a few moments in silence before asking, "Why didn't you tell me you and Emma were assaulted?"

"They ran off after I nailed one of them in the face, so we were okay. I'm sorry."

She stood and grabbed an envelope from a pile of mail on the counter. She flipped it over, placing it and a pencil beside me. "Tell me more about this symbol." Her *I'm-going-to-solve-this* brain had prevailed over her *I'm-pissed-at-my-friend* heart.

"It was a flag with a yellow background." I attempted to sketch out the pin. "Then there was this black cross that divided it, with a red crown in the corner." I pushed the drawing over to her.

"I'll look into this." Anne made some additional notes and put both envelope and pencil aside. "If something like that ever happens to you or Emma again, which I hope it doesn't, please tell me as soon as possible, even if you don't believe it's a big deal."

"Okay."

She picked up her fork and returned to her meal. "So, what do you have planned for the rest of the evening? Work?"

I appreciated her trying to push past her irritation with me. "No, I'm done working for today. I'll be relaxing and watching a movie tonight."

"It's not one of those awful romance films you like, is it?"

I tried not to sound too defensive. "Rom-coms are not romance films. They're comedies that happen to have a relationship as a key plot point." I turned my attention back to my food as well. "I'm not sure of the movie. I have an invite to go to someone else's place to watch it, so he'll be picking it out." I didn't look up when I heard Anne's fork stop moving.

"Huh. Anyone I know?"

"Sorry," I smiled, "the position of managing my social life is taken."

She grinned. "I'm here when you're ready to share the details."

We didn't have much time after dinner before Anne had to get ready for her shift. I helped her clear the table and clean up before pulling on my jacket to leave.

"Thank you for the information on the pin," she said.

"You're welcome."

She surprised me when she embraced me in a tight hug. Anne and I were good friends, but we'd met through Emma and weren't as close as Emma and I were. "And please, if anyone tries to harm you again, let me know."

After leaving Anne's apartment, I was on my way to spend the remainder of the evening at Ben's.

IT FELT WEIRD to be back at the apartment I had recently stormed out of, this time holding a six-pack of beer to share. I raised my hand to knock, but the door opened before I got the chance. Ben stood in the doorway with a welcoming smile and signed, "Hello." He held out a hand in an offer to take the beer.

"Hi there. Thanks." I handed over the six-pack, stomped some snow loose from my shoes, and stepped into the apartment. He closed the door behind me as I took off my shoes. The place was the same as before with a bit more organization to the stacks of books by the bed. "You need an extra bookshelf or four."

Ben's smile grew as he retrieved a bottle opener from a kitchen drawer. I wandered over to the shelves full of records and browsed the titles. I'd never seen a collection as extensive. From what I could see, the music spanned a period from around the mid-fifties to the present and covered multiple genres. He joined me, handing over a beer.

"Thanks. Books and music, then?" I asked.

He nodded and set his bottle aside to retrieve his notepad from his back pocket. He scribbled on the page. *And film. You?*

"Music, definitely. I couldn't function without it. I like movies. I run."

He wrote in the notepad. *For fun?*

I chuckled. "That's something Em would say. Yeah. It helps mellow me out and organize my thoughts." I shrugged as I continued to browse his records. "I spend time with Anne and Em when I can. They both have pretty demanding work schedules, Emma even more so now." I pulled out an album with a screenprint of a banana on a white cover. Smiling, I looked at him. "This is a classic. Do you ever use music from this far back when you play at shows?"

Ben wrote. *Not exactly. Use more current music inspired by it. That's something for here.*

The different styles of music aligned a lot with my own tastes. "I covet your collection. I don't know how you can work in a record shop and not buy everything in there. Or have you?"

Ben was grinning when I looked back at him. He began to sign something but stopped as he remembered the language barrier. He took a step closer so I could see the notepad again. I was surrounded by the pleasant scent of some sort of spice. His dark eyelashes were so thick, I could barely see his eyes as he looked down at the paper. *It's difficult. Have a few jobs and not many expenses. Want to listen to a few?*

Ben looked up from the notepad at me. His eyes were somewhere between a blue and gray color, something I hadn't noticed before. A small smile curved the corners of my mouth. "Yeah, if you don't mind." I walked to the sofa and got comfortable, tucking my legs underneath me. "Go ahead and pick out a few."

He pulled the album I'd asked about and selected several more. Opening a well-loved record player, he set the music up to play. Ben retrieved his beer from the shelf and joined me. He sat down, pulled his knees up, and rested his heels on the front edge of the sofa. Lou Reed crooned to us from the record player.

"Did you grow up here?" I asked.

Ben signed, "Yes." He pointed to me, raising his eyebrows.

I shook my head. "No, I'm a transplant from out of state. I've lived here for close to three years."

He scribbled on the notepad. *Why here?*

"It's quiet. Not much goes on. A lot less chance of any problems for someone like me."

He smiled. *You sure?*

Laughing, I said, "No, not anymore. I'm feeling a bit overwhelmed right now, to be honest." The comment was out before I realized it. I took a quick swig of my beer.

He wrote. *Why's that?*

Because even as I attempted to keep my best friend safe, some jackass was taking her away from me, and she didn't seem to care. I turned the bottle in my hands, debating how much to share with Ben. "Ah . . . I don't know the fine print on how things work here for people like us. I've avoided dealing with it until now. I mean, I'm aware of the obvious rules. I know to keep what I am hidden so I don't make the villagers nervous."

Ben grinned. *Never a shortage of torches and pitchforks here.*

"Emma invited me to go to some meeting to connect with more wolves and learn how our communities operate. Remember the assaults I mentioned at The Beacon? The people at this meeting are trying to get a committee to look into the attacks more closely." I frowned. "Sorry, all of that was to say the meeting was at a place called The Village Pub. I learned it was created as a safe gathering space for people like us so we can be ourselves. I guess there are a few other places like it around the city?"

Ben signed, "Yes."

"I'm not sure how the Commoners are kept out," I said. "Are the buildings invisible?"

He shook his head and wrote in the notepad. *They don't notice the places.*

"Do you have a favorite?" I asked.

*The Beacon.*

I blinked. "What? The Beacon is one of ours?"

Ben nodded and tried to hide a smile by taking another drink from the bottle he held.

"So I panicked for nothing?" I gave him a light punch on the shoulder as he feigned to the side. "You're right: You are an ass. Why didn't you tell me when I nearly had a panic attack?"

*Wanted to let you know how lovely your eyes are. You got anxious, so didn't want to make a big deal of it.*

I blinked again, realizing the miscommunication. My cheeks grew hot, and I diverted the attention away from me. "Do you want to join us at one of those meetings?"

With no hesitation, he signed, "No."

"Misery loves company?" Maybe after he heard the others talk about their experiences, he wouldn't be so reluctant to open up about the men who attacked him.

Ben shook his head.

I fell quiet, casting about for some way to lead up to the questions I was here to ask. "You said you have a few jobs. Where else do you work besides Rear Window?"

Ben wrote in the notepad. *At The Sound Refuge. Do sound part-time.*

"I don't remember ever seeing you. We go there a lot."

He smiled and wrote. *No one goes to see the sound person. We hide in the booth.*

"I thought maybe you worked at Stanley's too," I said.

His smile faded. He signed, "No."

My face warmed again for a different reason. My clumsy attempt at being covert had been spotted. I looked at the bottle I held, scraping at the edge of the label with my thumbnail in the awkward silence.

Standing, he pointed to his empty beer bottle.

"I'm all right for now," I said. "Thanks."

I watched Ben return to the counter to open another bottle. It gave me an opportunity to appreciate how he moved, the build of his lean frame and long limbs, and the contrast between his light eyes and his mess of dark, thick hair. Warmth spread throughout my chest as my inner wolf stirred. I decided I wouldn't mind getting to know him better. Downing the last of my beer, I stood and padded over to the counter to join him.

He placed the bottle opener aside on the counter and turned, completely colliding with me. The full bottle fell and began to empty its contents onto the floor. We both crouched to reach for it, colliding again—this time with our foreheads.

Someone cursed, and for once, it wasn't me.

I blinked, confused. His eyes widened. I narrowed mine. I stood and backed away from him. His complexion paled as he slowly stood, holding the half-empty bottle. It had been barely more than a whisper, but I'd heard him. What else could he do that he wasn't supposed to be able to? Should I be worried? I looked past him to the door. I could make it out of here if I had to.

He swallowed. "Alex, please don't leave. Let me explain." His voice was so faint that someone hard of hearing wouldn't even notice it.

I snorted. "You sure as hell are going to explain. What are you trying to pull?"

"I'm not—I can't—" Ben placed the bottle aside. "Can we sit down?"

My eyes still narrowed, I studied him. His body was tense, and his features were a mix of guilt and anxiety. He was also scared. I smelled it. If he did attack me, I was pretty sure I could snap him in half like a twig. "We can sit. If you get evasive, I walk."

He nodded. Ben took a dish towel from a rod near the sink and dropped it onto the floor. He tapped it a few times with his foot to soak up some of the spilled beer. The next bottle he opened shook slightly in his hand as he turned back to me.

I motioned to the sofa. "After you." Despite his nervousness, I sat at the front edge of my seat in case a quick exit was needed. I watched him closely. "Isn't a tether supposed to silence a wizard?"

"Yes. I found a way to . . ." he searched for the words, "work around that. Not right away, but several years ago."

"You broke your tether?" I couldn't imagine that being smiled upon.

"Not exactly. More like slipped a hand from the cuffs. The barrier blocking my access to the energy we use is less . . ." he paused again to find the best word, "solid." He frowned and shook his head. "It's hard to explain to someone who hasn't practiced magic before."

"I don't understand why tethering is such a big deal if someone can get around it."

Ben's pale complexion turned pink, and he fidgeted with the bottle he held. "It hasn't been done before."

I raised my eyebrows. "Oh."

"Yeah."

"So you can cast spells again?"

Ben's eyebrows drew together as he hesitated. He looked down at the bottle he held. "I don't feel comfortable talking about that."

I gave him a pass on that one. He'd already had multiple opportunities to use magic and set me on fire or something equally unpleasant. "Who else knows you've found a work-around?" I asked.

He took a drink. "No one else from here."

"From here?" I raised an eyebrow. "Ben?"

"Those two guys in the alleyway." He frowned at the beer bottle. "I'm not sure how, but they knew."

A growl rumbled in my chest. "I thought you didn't know anything else about them."

Still frowning, he looked up at me. "How was I supposed to tell you? If anyone finds out I cheated the tether and it gets back to the Committee, they could have me executed."

"Executed? Why would you even chance messing with the tether, then? Wait it out."

Ben shook his head. "I tried, but I thought about it every day. It's this large, intimate part of me that's been," he motioned at his chest near his heart, "locked away. I'm not whole anymore. Even now it's not quite the same." He set aside the beer bottle. "It's the reason I eventually got into EDM. I needed to weave words to create something new."

My first thought was tethering sounded awful. My second thought was now I had leverage to ensure Ben would keep quiet about me.

"Please, don't tell anyone," he said, "including Emma."

"I don't keep secrets from Emma." Even if I suspected she was keeping secrets from me.

"But she's safer by not knowing," he said. "If I get caught and she doesn't know anything, her conscience will be clean. They wouldn't be able to convict her of being an accomplice."

"So, you're saying now that I know about this, we're considered partners in crime?"

"The Committee has a track record of trying to take down as many of us at once as possible."

Fantastic. Being saddled with this isn't what I'd expected when I walked through his door.

"I'm sorry, Alex."

"And how do I know you aren't some hate-filled warlock secretly plotting your revenge?" If I kept it quiet, and he went on a rampage, people could get hurt.

"I've studied the lupine," he said.

"That doesn't answer my question."

He continued, "You wouldn't be here alone if you believed I posed any real threat."

Dammit. He was right. Ever since my inner wolf awoke, I've listened to my gut's ability to identify danger in people and situations. It'd kept me safe for years. The way Ben held his cards close to his chest was more irritating than menacing. "I'll take that beer now."

He got another beer from the counter, opened it, handed me the bottle, and settled back beside me on the couch.

"If those two guys know you're breaking the rules," I said, "aren't you worried they'll turn you in?"

"Like I said before, they're probably here to do someone else's dirty work. I don't think they'll risk drawing attention to themselves by reporting me."

"When I found you in the alleyway, the short guy talked to you in another language. What was he saying?" I asked.

Ben hesitated. "That's when I found out they'd heard I weakened my tether. He wanted me to tell him how."

"Did he say why?"

"No." Ben swallowed, and color appeared in his cheeks. "And it wasn't much of a two-way conversation."

I frowned. "Someone else knows about you, then, otherwise how would those two know?" Maybe being of a criminal persuasion, the short guy wanted to pocket the technique to escape a future sentence. "It seems that type of information would be valuable. They might try tracking you down again for it. Don't you want to find out more about them so you're prepared?" And I could get my answers about the two men, keeping Emma out of any possible danger.

He shook his head. "I'd prefer to avoid them."

It wasn't the answer I'd hoped for, but I understood. Regardless, it would be beneficial to keep Ben close in case the men did attempt to confront him again. Plus, I enjoyed looking at him. And he smelled nice. "Are you busy tomorrow night? I met some people at The Village

Pub who own a venue called Hell's Bells. They invited me to check out some music there. Want to come along?"

Ben glanced at me, suspicious of the invitation. "I'm serious about avoiding those guys. I won't have additional intel for you, and I'm not going to go look for them."

"No worries." I winked. "I plan to take the night off from my detective work."

"That's good. You're pretty bad at it," he said.

I laughed and gave him another mock slug.

He smiled and rubbed at his shoulder. "Yeah, I'll go. I like checking out new music. It sounds like a good time."

We spent the remainder of the evening in conversation and listening to music. Even though Ben's voice was a whisper due to the tether, his whole demeanor seemed mellow as well. He smiled easily and had the same streak of genuine friendliness Emma had.

I was able to relax, and the creature inside me took note. She uncurled and slunk forward, breathing in his scent and observing him through my eyes.

He was the youngest of three kids, while I was an only child. We both lived a distance from our parents. I was close with mine. He didn't communicate often with his. I preferred a few select, close friends, while he was more comfortable with a larger group of casual acquaintances.

Ben asked about my journey prior to settling down in Hopewell. He was eager to hear about the different areas of the country I'd visited. His travel was restricted to the Midwest due to his tether. Even then, he had to request permission from the Committee to leave the state. If they discovered he'd traveled beyond those boundaries, his sentence would be extended.

Our accidental shared secrets eased my hesitation of discussing such details with him. Afterward, I realized I hadn't told Emma much about my life between leaving home and signing my lease here. It wasn't because I wanted to keep it from her. She never inquired, so I never shared.

It was shortly after midnight before I noticed the time. Ben waited by the front door with me as I laced my shoes up. He stood with his long arms wrapped loosely around himself, his forehead creased. We lingered a few uncomfortable moments before I said, "I understand what's riding on me keeping my lips sealed. As long as you promise to do the same for me, I won't tell anyone."

Ben looked like he was going to be sick. I'm not sure he believed me. He nodded, swallowed, and managed, "I understand." He opened the door. "Goodnight, Alex."

# 6

I WAITED OUTSIDE Rear Window Records in my car, anxiously looking between the clock and the shop door. Emma had always been my emotional crutch in social situations involving new people and places. With Hell's Bells being a werewolf hangout and me exchanging names with my first wolves, I was jumping into the deep end of the pool without my swimming buddy.

Ben exited the store, pulling his jacket tighter against the cold. He approached the car, smiling as he opened the passenger door.

"Hi there," I said. "Thanks for coming along."

Ben got into the car, signed a greeting, and slid the seat back to accommodate his long legs. He still wore his glasses, but the bruising on his face had progressed to a shade of purple.

I added a disclaimer. "I've never been to this place, so I'm not sure if the music will be good."

He looked up from buckling his seatbelt, shrugged, and smiled again. Unlike me, Ben didn't seem to be bothered by trying something unknown and new. He settled back in the seat for the ride, tapping his fingertips on the armrest in time with the music on the radio.

Hell's Bells wasn't difficult to find. It was across the river on the west side of Hopewell. The small parking lot was packed. A crowd of people with a hazy cloud of smoke hovering above them stood outside the front doors. The windows were dark, plastered over with show billings and posters. We walked past the patrons outside, and in addition to the cigarette smoke, I picked up on the musky primal scent I'd noticed on Trish and Nate.

Inside the front door, we were stopped by a doorman as tall as Ben and about three times as wide. As he checked our IDs and placed paper bands around our wrists, I looked around. The main room held an arrangement of worn sofas and chairs. The lighting was mainly dependent on tableside and floor lamps. The decor gave it more of a cocktail lounge than a hole-in-the-wall bar feel. The bar itself was deeper into the room, past a wide stairwell and a hall on our right. Music drifted up the stairs from below.

We got drinks before descending the stairs into a noisy, dimly lit room. The odor of stale beer and sweat lingered in the air. People stood in small groups shouting at each other over the volume of the music as they waited for the live performance to begin. The ceiling was low with exposed pipes that dripped with condensation. All the bodies gathered in the tight space generated a lot of heat.

The density of the crowd increased as we walked further into the room toward a low stage. Speakers were stacked precariously in the corners. Unrecognizable symbols were spray-painted across the brick wall behind the stage. The other walls were covered with an assortment of old show posters, band logo stickers, random graffiti, and chewing gum. The floor had that mysterious sticky texture found in all good venues.

Ben and I enjoyed our drinks and people-watched while we waited. The audience here skewed younger and a lot more animated than the venues I usually frequented. I popped some ear plugs in to help mitigate the noise for my sensitive ears. I noticed the majority of the other concert goers had done the same. I didn't see that often, especially at shows with a younger audience. It was a visible reminder most of the other people here were like me, something that carried a sense of comfort I hadn't expected.

A fight broke out beside us, jostling us from our space. The sounds of snarls erupted from two entangled guys, causing the hair to stand up on the back of my neck. As we backed away, there were flashes of golden eyes and sharp teeth. Their friends and other audience members finally pried the two apart. One young man was unceremoniously hauled up the stairs by the back of his shirt. The remaining guy thrust his fists into the air, the gesture punctuated by howls and whoops from those standing around him. I looked over to Ben. He raised his eyebrows at me, grinned, and took off his glasses to tuck them safely away in his shirt pocket.

The pre-show music and lights were cut, replaced by the sound of a single squealing, protesting guitar chord. The sound of it ran up my spine, giving me goosebumps. The whole audience erupted into cheers. The stage lit up, revealing two guitarists and a drummer. A wave of bodies surged toward the platform. Ben held his drink aloft as people pushed past him to get closer to the band. I laughed at how ridiculous he looked—a pale scarecrow posted in the tide of dark-clothed bodies. I made a half-hearted attempt to remain beside him, but soon gave in to the movement toward the stage.

The singer stepped up onto the stage and took the microphone from the stand. The audience erupted into a fresh wave of ear-splitting cheers as she wrapped the mic cord around her wrist a few times. She looked back at her bandmates, gave a signal, and then barreled into a cover of RVIVR's "Wrong Way/One Way."

The bodies around me exploded into thrashing and jumping movement, and my drink was knocked from my grasp and gone. The primal beast deep inside me instantly responded, and in this place, there was no need to keep her hidden. My insecurities were forgotten. I naturally fell into the dancing of the crowd as if I'd always been a part of this group. It was exhilarating.

Several songs later, I found Ben near the edge of the audience, safe from the tidal-like pull of the crowd in front of the stage. I was covered in sweat and possibly beer, and I couldn't stop grinning. I laughed as I approached him. Every cell in my body buzzed. "This is amazing!" I shouted at him.

He was grinning too. He nodded and threw up the sign of the horns.

I lifted my damp hair off the back of my neck, fanned myself, and looked around. "I need some water or I'm going to pass out."

Ben shook his head and tapped on his ear. I stepped closer and leaned in to repeat myself. Instead, I became abruptly aware of the heat coming through the front of his shirt and how insanely good he smelled. The scents of some sort of spice and his sweat triggered the same spine-shivering sensation in me from earlier. The beast inside me was drawn forward.

I wondered what he tasted like.

My pulse sped up, and I stepped back. My heart thudded against my ribcage. Ben gave me a questioning look and tapped on his ear again. Flustered, I pointed to the ceiling before I pushed away through the crowd toward the stairs.

I took the steps two at a time, emerged into the lounge, and found the bathroom down a dimly lit hall. Under the flickering fluorescent lights, I dampened a paper towel with cool water. As I dabbed it along my throat and neck in an attempt to cool down, I caught my reflection in the mirror. A pair of charcoal-rimmed, golden eyes stared back at me from the dingy surface. I ran my tongue over my teeth and felt enlarged canines. It was either the dancing or Ben—probably both—that had enticed my inner wolf to the surface. My mind was still debating if Ben was okay, but the beast living within my breast was sold. I closed my eyes and focused on bringing my pulse back to a normal pace.

When my heartbeat and senses returned to a more neutral state, I pitched the paper towel into the waste bin and left the restroom. Ben waited at the bar with two glasses of water. He offered one to me.

"You read my mind." Although I was glad he hadn't. "Thanks." I downed the water in one go.

"Alex!" a familiar voice called. Nate and Trish strolled across the lounge from where they'd been seated with several other people. Nate leaned on the bar next to me and motioned to the room around him. "Welcome home."

Trish smiled as she slipped up next to him. She spoke around the cigarette she lit. "Better late than never, right?" She exhaled a stream of smoke and pulled an ashtray toward her. "Who's the wizard?" She tapped the end of the smoldering cigarette into the tray as she eyed Ben.

"This is Ben. He's a music junkie like me. We met at a show he played last week," I said. "Ben, this is Trish and Nate. They own the place."

Ben raised a hand to greet the other two. Nate's mouth turned upward in one corner. He slunk from his place beside me and narrowed his eyes as he circled behind us. He stopped, nostrils twitching, on the other side of Ben. Ben's posture stiffened and he remained still, not making eye contact with Nate. Instead, he focused on the glass of water in front of him.

"Your kind doesn't usually come over here to see us, wizard." Nate cocked his head, studying Ben. His brown eyes warmed to the deep copper I'd seen before. "Yet, here you are with Alex. Why is that? Why aren't you across the river with your own?" He lowered his voice to a conspiratorial whisper. "Or is it true your people find the tethered even more offensive than they find us?"

Ben's face paled except for the bruising and some color high in his cheekbones.

"Back off." I glared at Nate. "I invited him."

He looked past Ben to me and grinned. His teeth had shifted to points.

"Nate," Trish warned.

His tone turned more jovial. "Well, you're in luck, wizard. We don't care who you are or what you've done." Nate clasped the back of Ben's neck. "You don't make any trouble for us, and we don't rip your throat out. Got it?"

Ben's brow furrowed, and he nodded. I moved to stand and intervene, but Trish placed a hand on my arm.

"Great!" Nate swiped his hand upward to ruffle Ben's hair. "We should get along fine." He sauntered back to Trish's side. His eyes remained copper as he said, "Ladies, I hear a pit calling my name. If you'll excuse me . . ." He put his arm around Trish's waist, pulled her close, and licked the side of her face from chin to temple.

She laughed and punched him in the arm. "Get out of my sight." Trish affectionately watched him depart as she took another pull on her cigarette. She looked back at me and smiled. "Sorry, he has a habit of pissing all over things every time a new guy walks in." She motioned at Ben with her cigarette. "You can bring him along anytime you want. It's always a motley crew around here. He'll be safe."

"Thank you."

His jawline tense, Ben watched Nate depart as well. He stood and pushed in the bar stool with his knee.

"Ben?"

He looked at me, fanned himself, and pointed toward the front door. I nodded in understanding, and he walked away to step outside.

After he left, Trish tapped the ash from her cigarette. "Has he told you what he did?" At my puzzled look, she added, "To get himself tethered. Those are usually only doled out among the wizards for high crimes."

I shook my head. "No. We're still getting to know each other."

"What sort of feeling are you getting from him?" she asked.

"From what I can tell so far, he seems like a good person."

She smiled. "Then he probably is. We wolves survive by relying on our senses. You can trust your ability to find genuine people among the insincere."

"I didn't know tethering existed before Em told me about it recently. It's a type of punishment for wolves and wizards?" I asked.

"It's the way we're all kept in line. When wizards are sentenced, they get a type of hex put on them." Trish made the sign of a cross in front of her throat. "They're branded and no longer possess their true voice. The tether keeps them from casting spells by silencing them."

I frowned. "For how long?"

"It depends on the crime. If the Committee is politically weighted one way or another, the numbers are skewed. Around here, we have always been the minority voice on the Committee. Sentences are longer than elsewhere." She snubbed out the remains of the cigarette in the ashtray. "Wolves and wizards who are tethered walk around with the brand on their throat as a warning to the rest of us. 'Follow the rules and don't speak out or you'll be silenced too.'"

"I don't see how that would work with us," I said.

"The effects of tethering are different for lupine. It blocks our ability to shift. All the power you feel roiling inside you is instead funneled straight into your mind."

I thought of the extreme intensity of the emotions that caused my body to shift. Then I imagined those emotions continuously saturating my mind instead while I was denied the ability to act upon them. The blood drained from my face.

Trish nodded. "It's horrific. Most lupine don't survive a tethering sentence. It's trying for the wizards as well. Their relationship with magic is part of who they are, like our inner beast is part of us." She motioned toward Ben's empty seat. "One of the largest differences between our community and his is that we don't shun our tethered. Everyone messes up now and then, right?"

Looking down at my hands, I nodded. I thought of my own past. If I hadn't fled my home, I wondered if I would have been tethered for my actions by some local Committee. My family feared for my safety, so I left. Had they known about tethering? A sudden feeling of home-sickness tightened my chest.

"Alex, most of us aren't as polished as your wizard friends appear to be, but this community is here whenever you need it. Around this city, people forget empathy isn't constrained to stone walls, lines of pews, and a list of rules. It can be found in dark basements, elbow to elbow with sweaty bodies, listening to kickass music."

Trish's words caused a lump to form in my throat and my vision to blur. I quickly wiped at my eyes with the heel of my hand. Swallowing, I nodded again. "Thanks."

She smiled. "Have a good time tonight. I hope we see you two again." Trish reached behind the bar and retrieved a business card. "And pass this on to Ben. Have him message me." She handed over the card. "We're always looking for new talent to promote here."

"Thank you," I said. She left me and rejoined the group of people seated across the lounge. I looked at the card. It read *Hell's Bells—Music and Mayhem; Patricia Drake, Owner,* and listed her contact details. I tucked it into my pocket. Ben hadn't returned, so I headed for the parking lot to find him.

Past the group conversing and smoking outside the entrance, Ben was posted up by himself against the side of my car. The glow from his phone reflected in his glasses. He looked up from it when I drew closer.

"Do you want to stay for the band's second set?" I asked.

He shrugged. I could tell he was done. He looked awkward and out of place for the first time since we'd arrived that evening. I offered a smile. "Let's leave. We can always drop in again some other time, right?"

Ben nodded.

We got into the car, and I offered him the business card. "Trish said to contact her. She wants to know more about your music."

He accepted the card and read it over. He raised an eyebrow, looked up at me, and jabbed a thumb back at the building.

"Yeah, to play here."

He shook his head as he put away the card. Ben sat back and turned his attention out the passenger window. The glass squeaked as he wiped the gathering condensation from it. His mind was focused elsewhere while we drove in silence back to his apartment.

The packed snow crunched under the tires in the lot behind Rear Window Records. I put the car in park and turned down the radio. It didn't take keen senses to know something weighed on Ben's mind.

"Thanks for coming along with me tonight. It felt great to have someone share in my excitement about the music. Em would have gotten bored and gone upstairs to socialize."

Ben glanced around the empty parking lot. Instead of reaching for his notepad, he replied in his whispered voice. "You're welcome." He unbuckled his seatbelt. "The music was really good."

"Hey, is everything all right?"

He avoided my gaze. "Yeah. Thanks for inviting me." Ben leaned forward and reached for the door handle. I hit the automatic locks, stopping him. He looked over at me, his eyebrows drawn together.

I didn't believe him. We'd enjoyed time together, and I didn't want the night to end on a sour note. "Ben, please talk to me. Was it Nate? I didn't know he'd be such a dick to you. I met them at that meeting, so I don't know them well yet. From what Trish said, I wouldn't take it personally."

"No, it wasn't him." He leaned back in his seat. "Not exactly." A faint odor of fear grew as he spoke, "People see the tether and make assumptions about me. It bothered me at first, but I stopped caring. And then when I met those two with you . . ." He paused, struggled to find words, then restarted. "Whatever this might be," he motioned between the two of us, "it feels good. I liked burning time with you tonight. So I care about what you think, and that makes me nervous."

"Did I somehow make you uncomfortable?" I asked.

Ben gave a weak smile and a shake of his head. "No. Not at all. I'm worried that eventually you'll start asking more questions, and then I'll have to decide whether or not to answer." The smell of fear pressed in around us. I bit my tongue, allowing him to process his thoughts at his own pace. He fidgeted with the paper band around his wrist. "I was tethered because I made a mistake. I reacted without thinking, and someone was killed."

I swallowed. "That would've been awful. How old were you?"

"Sixteen."

By the look of him, that had to be around fifteen years ago. I wasn't sure what to say. The thought made me sick to my stomach. The worst punishment I'd received at that age was being grounded for a month after sneaking out to go to a concert. At sixteen, I'd also not had to deal with what lay dormant in my body or the harm it could inflict.

He glanced over at me. "Are we good for now?"

I felt he asked more for his own peace of mind than mine. I was okay with that. I nodded. "Yeah, we're good."

He unlocked his door and got out of the car. "Goodnight." He pushed the door shut and walked toward the stairs up to his apartment. I waited until he was inside before leaving.

Ben's admission of guilt was on my mind as I left the parking lot. After speaking with Trish tonight, and now hearing of Ben's experience, I doubted this tethering thing was a good solution. On the surface it seemed like a way to ensure law and order among the supernatural communities. However, people don't fall into neat categories of "good" and "bad," and the current disciplinary solution of tethering didn't take that into consideration.

There had to be a better way.

# 7

THE ROUTE BACK to my apartment took me past Patterson Street Church. I slowed when I spotted Emma's car in the parking lot. Last time we spoke, she mentioned having a lot of meetings to attend. Despite Anne's efforts to calm my nerves, the situation with Emma didn't feel right and took up a lot of mental and emotional bandwidth.

I turned my car around, pulled over to the side of the street, and turned off the headlights. Within the hour, a small group of people exited through the front doors of the church. Their muffled voices and laughter carried through the crisp evening as they crossed the street to the parking lot.

Emma and Mitch parted from the group and walked to her car. I reached for the door handle and paused. If I got out of the car and confronted her here in the parking lot, it might appear overbearing. She hadn't called like she promised today, but maybe she'd still do so tonight. Was Anne right and I wasn't giving Mitch a chance? All I had to go on was a weird gut-level suspicion of the guy.

While I struggled with the decision, the universe made it for me. The headlights of Emma's car switched on, and exhaust floated up into the cold air. Her car left the parking lot and started down the street. When they had a block head start, I pulled away from the curb to follow. Anne's voice reprimanded me in the back of my mind, but I ignored it and listened to my gut. Instead of driving home, she took a ramp onto the expressway. Were they going to Mitch's place?

We drove ten minutes before exiting to a sprawling retail area. Her car turned into a strip mall parking lot lined with some chain restaurants, a salon, and a few random retail businesses. I used the next driveway to enter the lot and parked at a deli a few doors down.

Emma's car idled in front of what looked like some sort of healthcare business. Security lights lit the building's interior enough for me to see a lobby similar to a doctor or dentist's office. Contemporary furniture in a palette of grays and whites with red accents was arranged throughout the space. A long white counter served as a receptionist's area.

Mitch left the car, unlocked the front door of the lobby, and entered the building. He paused at the wall beside the front door before he walked farther into the office and past the counter. It must have been his office when he wasn't at Another Chance. I lost sight of him from my vantage point. A glance over to Emma's car found her talking on the phone. So she had time to make phone calls, but not to return mine.

I took out my own phone and found a map of the area. The business Mitch entered was called The Mind Center. Its website listed it as a biofeedback therapy center. The center focused on therapy services for different mental health ailments, offering bio readings and discussion of lifestyle choices as a way to improve quality of life. It all felt sci-fi and odd to me.

Several minutes later, Mitch reappeared in the lobby. He again paused at the front wall and then left the building and relocked the door. He approached the driver's side door of Emma's car, and the window lowered. I caught glimpses of her as the two conversed. He handed something to her, leaned down closer to kiss her, and then walked away as the car window closed. He got into the driver's seat of another car several parking spaces away.

I chewed at my thumbnail, looking between the two cars. Up to this point, I'd been trying to keep track of Emma. Perhaps it was time to look a bit more into Mitch. When Emma and Mitch's cars turned in opposite directions out of the parking lot, I followed the latter.

Emma's home was in a small wealthy suburb on the eastern edge of Hopewell. I assumed Mitch lived in the same general area, but I followed him back downtown. His car pulled into a gated parking lot for a clump of modern condos. The condos were built above some boutique shops, a restaurant, and a market. I couldn't imagine the price tag for living in one of those places.

I parked my car along the edge of the street. Not many other people were around since the shops and market were all closed. The only other signs of life were the people dining at the restaurant.

Mitch left his car and walked toward the building. A short and stocky figure wearing a flat cap, jacket, and boots emerged from the shadows and tailed him across the parking lot. I recognized Shortie from the alley fight, but Mitch didn't even seem to notice him.

"Oh no," I muttered. Even if I was suspicious of Mitch's influence on Emma, he was still, for some reason, important to her. I probably shouldn't sit by and watch while he got mugged.

I left my car and hurried around to the sidewalk, my focus on the two men. My single-mindedness was what Anne would have called "a rookie mistake."

I rushed toward the parking lot to intervene. Something large flashed in my peripheral. A rough jerk on the back of my jacket caused my feet to leave the ground, and I was airborne. I landed on my back on the hood of my car with a hollow, clattering thud. The force of the fall knocked the wind from my lungs.

As I lay gasping, the Ox lurched toward me. The bridge of his nose sat at an unnatural angle, and the amount of purple bruising near his eyes and nose made him appear almost raccoon-like. He glowered down at me as he drew back his arm like a battering ram. I rolled to the side before his fist connected with the windshield in an awful-sounding crunch. A huge spider web of cracks spread across the glass.

I continued my barrel roll away until I fell off the edge of the car's hood. It wasn't a second too soon. Another crunch, this one metallic and in the area recently occupied by my body, was echoed by the car's protesting shocks. How strong was this guy?

And would my auto insurance cover the damage?

My inner wolf responded to the threat, and a low growl seeped up from inside me before I could stop it. I gathered my feet beneath me and kept my body lowered in a crouch. Trying to control both my shifting and the situation with the Ox was a bit of a struggle. Emma said Mitch was a Commoner, and the rules said no wolfing out in front of Commoners.

I loosened my hold on the creature inside me enough to further brighten my field of vision. It made the cross-like brand on the Ox's throat all the more visible.

He was tethered? Was Shortie as well? It must be why they'd been after Ben. But then why would they be working a job that put them at risk of further punishment? From across the hood I asked, "Why're you here? Who hired you?"

The Ox responded with a scowl and lumbered around the car toward me. This time I easily ducked away when he lunged at me. I rounded the back corner of the car and darted toward the gated lot, Mitch, and Shortie. I leapt over the low metal fence and pulled off a half-decent landing on the slippery pavement. There may have been a moment of flailing arms, but at least I remained upright.

Both Shortie and Mitch had taken notice of my encounter with the Ox. Mitch's attention jerked from me to Shortie, and his eyes widened. He spun and dashed to the door of the building.

Shortie squared himself up to face me. "Is this a joke? What're *you* doing here?"

"What do you want from him?" I only had to delay long enough for Mitch to get safely inside. There had to be some sort of security guard or other residents in there that would deter these goons from pursuing us. I crept toward Shortie, trying at the same time to keep tabs on Mitch's progress. He was busy dropping his keys at the doorway.

"Sweetheart, that's really none of your business."

His words caused the creature inside me to twist and writhe. I allowed her more freedom, and my hands shifted, but so did my teeth. "It is if you two keep accosting people I know." Now that I knew what to look for, the cross-like mark on his throat was obvious.

Shortie began murmuring a string of syllables. I gasped as a tug of magical energy rushed past me. It felt different, more abrupt and reckless, than when Emma prepared her healing spells.

*What the hell?* Everyone had told me a tether prevented a wizard from casting. Shortie smiled cruelly as he tightened his hand into a fist. Blue flames licked around his fingers.

*Nope.* This was above my paygrade. I broke to the side and sprinted toward Mitch and the building. The air crackled, and a white-hot column of flames hurtled past the side of my body. Pain sliced across my shoulder, and the stench of burnt hair filled my nostrils. The blast made contact with the brick wall of the building ahead of me. It left a long smear of charred, smoking stone in its wake.

Mitch had finally made it inside. He attempted to pull the door shut after him, but I jammed the toe of my boot between the door and the frame. Mitch yelled in surprise and stumbled backward. I slipped through the doorway.

"Wait!" I held up a clawed hand to Mitch. He continued to back away from me, pale and shaking. "I'm not going to hurt you," I said. I spun to look out of the building. The parking lot was empty. Neither Shortie nor the Ox was in sight. With a sinking feeling, I turned to Mitch. He stood panting near the opposite wall of the small lobby. He eyed both the elevator and me.

"Please, don't run," I said. My shoulder throbbed, and I began to realize the full weight of what I'd done. How much trouble was *this* going to cause? "I know everything seems crazy right now and you probably want some explanations. But first, those two guys, have you seen them before? Do you know them?"

Mitch recovered remarkably fast for a guy who was rescued from a flame-wielding stranger by a clawed and glowing-eyed woman. Had Emma already told him about herself and other supernatural beings? Was she *that* sure she could trust him?

He watched me warily, but his voice barely trembled. "I've never met those men."

"You should report them as soon as possible." I glanced around the lobby for any other entrance doors. "Tell both the police department and this place's security staff. I can help you with descriptions. This may not have been a chance encounter. They've attacked someone else I know." Mitch didn't have to worry about remaining hidden, and maybe a bit of extra pressure on Shortie and the Ox by the police would help.

I checked my shoulder and noticed my fingernails appeared normal again. That meant my teeth would be, too. I could only hope the same went for my eyes. My body was able to take a beating and rebound much faster since I'd become a werewolf. This injury felt different. Fabric was missing from both my jacket and shirt where Shortie's attack grazed me. Blisters had already formed, and my skin burned as if it were on fire.

"Do *you* know who they are?"

I blinked and looked back at Mitch. "What?"

"I won't have you endangering Emma with the company you keep," he said.

I laughed. "What are you talking about? Why would I try to hurt Emma? I'm trying to keep her safe."

"You're jealous, aren't you?" He looked me up and down. "She's on a selfless path for the benefit of her community while you continue to flounder. You have no focus. What have you ever done for anyone other than yourself?"

I swallowed back a snarl. He didn't even know me!

"You don't want her to succeed because then you'll be alone."

Was he serious? "There's no time for *Life Goals with Mitch*," I said. "We need to report these guys before they attack someone else."

His features darkened. "I suggest you leave before I call security and have you escorted out."

Frustration and anger boiled up within me in quick succession. I clenched my teeth to keep from saying anything stupid. I'd messed up already by flashing my claws in front of Mitch, and I didn't look forward to explaining it to Emma. I didn't want to make the situation worse. Turning, I shoved open the door and exited back into the frigid evening.

I hopped back over the fence onto the sidewalk. Flashing lights caught my attention from the restaurant next door. A police cruiser was parked nearby. A young couple conversed with a patrol officer who studiously took notes. Someone had called about the ruckus.

My car sat by the curb, looking as if I'd hit some type of large animal. The windshield was completely wrecked, the hood was crumpled inward, and I was down to a sole headlight. How was I supposed to make rent if my only way to make a buck was in the shop for repairs? And how much would those repairs cost?

I glanced back over my shoulder toward the police car. The couple had left, and the officer sat in his car talking on a radio. I got into my car and tried to start it. The motor whined and then stalled. My stomach proceeded to tie itself in knots. I tried to start the car again, but this time I didn't get any response from the engine. Frustration fueled the growling noises that escaped my body. I closed my eyes and rested my forehead on the cold steering wheel. A tow truck it would be, then.

I dialed Emma's number. Hopefully she would give me a ride back to my place, and I could tell her everything that happened with Mitch. Shortie and the Ox had targeted him, but were they actually looking for Emma? She'd been spending so much time around Mitch. And what was with Shortie being a human flamethrower even though he was tethered? Just when I thought I was getting a handle on how things worked, everything shifted sideways.

Emma's phone continued to ring several more times before I was kicked to voicemail. The prompt for me to leave a message, recorded in her voice, caused an unexpected ache in my chest. I bit at my lip and dialed her number again. "Pick up the phone, Em." My call went into voicemail a second time. "It's Alex. I need to talk to you. This is important. I ran into the two guys tonight who attacked Ben. They were after Mitch. Please, call me back as soon as possible. Be careful."

After calling a tow truck to have my car hauled to the nearest repair shop, I took a cab to Hell's Bells. Trish and Nate had been at the community meeting to discuss the odd attacks. I wanted to share details about the two thugs I'd run into again and get their thoughts on the tethers that may not really be tethers. The bouncer greeted me, and I asked for Trish and Nate. He spoke into a small microphone on his shirt collar, and moments later they appeared from the back hall.

"Alex, we didn't expect you back so soon . . ." Trish's nostrils quivered. She'd caught the scent of the burns. "Where's Ben? What happened?"

"He's at home. After I dropped him off, I took a detour on the way back to my place and ran into a bit of trouble."

Nate retrieved a bottle and glass from behind the bar. He took a seat beside me on one of the lounge's sofas and poured a glass of whiskey. "Who did this to you?"

I winced as Trish helped me out of my jacket. The pain from the burn had spread across my shoulder. I accepted the drink Nate offered. "Two guys I'd run into before. I'd interrupted them when they were attacking Ben several nights ago. Tonight they were after a Commoner with ties to Emma. At least one of them is a wizard. He clipped me with these crazy blue flames."

Trish frowned and glanced at Nate.

"And both men were tethered," I added.

Nate's eyes widened and Trish shook her head. "That's not possible. He wouldn't have been able to use magic if he was tethered."

"Trish, I felt it. I know it was a spell." I began to doubt that I'd seen the mark on their throats. "Maybe he wasn't tethered. He did have a lot of tattooing around his neck."

"From what I know, a tether has never been broken. It's a complex spell," she said. "Even attempting to remove a tether before a sentence is served is punishable by death."

Ben came to mind, and his attempt to rid himself of the tether. It hadn't mattered to him that he could lose his life over it.

"We're going to have a problem if there's a wizard trying to toast Commoners," Nate growled.

Trish nodded. "I'll take this to the Committee right away."

His eyes flashed. "Come on, Trish! How much longer are we going to wait? We'll suffer the fallout right along with the magic users. We should find these two who attacked Alex."

I remained silent, feigning interest in the whiskey and not wanting to interfere with the tense exchange. The Committee wasn't my first choice either, but probably for different reasons from Nate's. After talking to Ben and Trish, I thought of it as an ominous organization that specialized in punishing, not helping, people like us.

Trish sounded tired. "Nate, please . . ."

He immediately checked his tone but didn't stop talking. "I'm sick of sitting here with my tail between my legs, shackled to this Committee, while our people are being attacked. We need to stop talking and act."

Yes. I wanted Shortie and the Ox dealt with so Emma and I could focus on our original problem: Kevin and Brad. Since I was a wolf and Nate seemed so anxious to take action, maybe Trish and Nate would help me.

Trish closed her eyes and rubbed at her temples.

Nate leaned forward. "You've tried, love. You've been more patient with those Commoners than anyone else here could have managed. But in the end, we're stronger than them. We don't need the Committee's permission to protect ourselves."

"Ben believes the two guys who attacked him are hired thugs," I offered. "Is it possible someone brought them in for a job?"

Trish lowered her hands and nodded. "More than likely, that is the case. The wizard and wolf communities are small in Hopewell. Any wizard runs the risk of being recognized." She looked at Nate. "Even if we move on this independently, we should ask Reginald for help. He could have insight on the wizard who attacked Alex. Yes, we're strong, but our numbers are fewer."

His jaw clenched, Nate leaned back. He looked away from us without responding.

Trish turned her gaze on me. "We have to be careful around magic users. Their attacks can be deadly to us. Though not as quick to cripple us as silver, injuries caused by magic take longer for our bodies to heal."

"They hurt more, too." Hopefully, I'd never get a chance to compare a magic-induced wound to an injury caused by silver. I glanced at Nate. "Whiskey seems to help."

Nate didn't acknowledge my comment, but Trish smiled. "Alex, if I bring you to a Committee meeting, would you be willing to report what you saw tonight?"

My gut reaction was to decline. "Do you think they'll actually help us? You said at The Village Pub that you've already tried and they didn't seem to think it was a big deal."

"I hope since one of the attackers was a wizard, and the possible intended victim a Commoner, the Committee will view the assaults in a new light—as a shared problem," she said. "Would you be able to describe the two men?"

"Yeah, okay." The thought of working so close to the Committee made me uneasy. But if it was willing to help, it might have more resources to track down Shortie and the Ox, and the means to get rid of them. My progress working solo was disappointingly slow.

"Thank you. Stay as long as you need to rest and heal. Drinks are on us." Trish looked to Nate. "Can we speak in the office, please?"

Nate stood without a word. He strode past the bar and back down the hall. Trish followed.

Finishing my whiskey, I poured another ample serving and settled back onto the sofa. I sent Ben a message, asking him if we could talk soon. If I was going to have any future unfriendly relations with a wizard, maybe Ben would know something about protection from magical attacks. Ideally, I could ask Emma, but if she knew what I was up to, she'd insist on being part of it. There was also the more obvious issue of her not returning any of my messages or calls.

I looked up information on The Mind Center next. Beyond the company's website, I found multiple articles discussing The Mind Center's approach to therapy as controversial. Not many of the techniques were backed by research. The center was built and run by the White family. I realized why Mitch's last name, though common, had stood out to me when he introduced himself. In past fundraising efforts, Emma had mentioned the wealthy family as key donors.

Several hours later, as the club closed at morning's approach, the pain from the burn began to subside. Usually by now, the first thin layer of new skin would have knit itself over the injury.

After getting my address, Trish walked me to the front door. She gave me a light hug farewell. "Get some rest. I'll pick you up later today for the meeting."

I spent the last bit of money I had on me for the cab ride home. The emotional rollercoaster of the evening, along with the multiple doses of whiskey, made me sleepy. My phone buzzed in my pocket, and I paused on the stairs to check it. The message was from Emma.

*Mitch told me what happened tonight. I'm so disappointed. Why were you following him? I don't know why you're acting like this. Please, you need to back off and stop threatening him.*

Standing on the stairs, I gaped at the message. "Threatening" him? That asshole. He lied to her. But I'd left a voice message telling her what happened. Didn't she receive it? Was he monitoring her phone? The thought raised my hackles and a growl rumbled in my chest. If that was the case, this Mitch guy absolutely had to go.

# 8

TRISH FINISHED A cigarette while she waited outside my apartment. The clothing she wore was business casual, and her makeup minimized. It made her appear more like an accountant attending a finance meeting than a club owner. She nodded in approval at my outfit, an understated pair of dress pants and sweater. It wasn't my usual choice in clothing, but she'd asked for something more than denim, but not too stylish. "The less intimidating you appear, the better." She gave me a wink. "This group struggles with the concept of strong women, and we have shit to get done."

As we got into the car, I asked, "How's Nate today?"

"Still sleeping when I left." She smiled. "Nate has a deep love for our community and is very protective of it. He is also an impatient person. It's challenging for him to sit still while something as bureaucratic as this Committee churns." She glanced at me. "How are you feeling? Were you able to rest?"

"I got a little sleep." The pain in my shoulder had settled into a dull throb. I was feeling the pain in my wallet more this morning after I'd received a call from the auto shop. My rent was due, but the money I'd set aside for it was now going toward car repairs. It would take awhile to earn that much back by running rides.

Being on my way to speak in front of strangers only made the anxiety worse. "You know, I'm not sure this is a good idea after all. What if I say something wrong or offensive? I've told you everything." I chewed at my thumbnail. "Maybe you can do the majority of the speaking, and I could fill in the details in case you forget anything."

Trish gave me a sympathetic smile. "I already reported our concerns in the last meeting. It will carry more weight if it comes from someone other than me. You also have a first-hand account of those two men. I'll be right there to support you." She sighed. "We have to dance this dance first in hopes of gaining some assistance. Then, if the Committee still doesn't move on it, we'll decide on how to take action on our own. I'm hoping that isn't necessary."

"How many people will I be talking to?"

"A little over a dozen," she said. "The majority of the group are leaders from older, established houses of worship. Despite separation of church and state, religious leaders wield enormous influence in this area."

Things were beginning to add up with this Committee. Unfortunately, that did nothing for my confidence. "When I think of church, I don't think of people who are okay with 'witchcraft and monsters.'"

"I suspect some members would prefer supernatural beings to live elsewhere. I'm sure they will make themselves known to you today. But there are also several who see the value in diversity and welcome the collaboration." She gave me a glance, smiling. "Serenity and Martin are two younger Committee members who give me hope."

I nodded. "And the people who aren't religious leaders?"

"There are a few officials from the city's board of commissioners and a detective from the police department. As I mentioned at The Village Pub, there is only one representative each for the wizards and the wolves," she said.

Detective? I wondered if they knew Anne. "Is it a good idea to involve so many Commoners?" I asked. "Isn't one of the things that keeps us safe the fact that the majority of people are blissfully ignorant of our existence?"

"It seems counterintuitive, but it's a model established by the wizards and used for centuries. The Commoners have always held their tongues."

We didn't have far to drive before we arrived at a Romanesque stone building. The sign at the entrance read *Union Street Church – 1920*. An older man dressed in a fitted suit and bowler also approached the building. He tipped his hat to Trish, holding open the door for us. "Good morning, Ms. Drake. Is this the young woman who will be speaking today?" He was tall and slender with a neatly trimmed white beard and mustache. His bright eyes were cornered in deep lines.

"Good morning, Reggie." Trish nodded. "Yes. This is Alex Steward. She has some important findings we believe are linked to the assaults. I hope it provides the Committee information it needs to take action." Trish turned to me. "Alex, this is Reginald Sharpe. He sits on the Committee as the representative for Hopewell's magic-using community."

Reginald tipped his hat to me with his free hand, smiling. "Welcome, Miss Steward. Thank you for agreeing to help us."

Something about his friendly smile and the way it reached his blue-gray eyes was familiar. I found myself more at ease with him than I usually did upon first meeting a person. I gave him a nod. "Nice to meet you, Reginald."

All three of us entered the main hallway, and then one of several doorways lining the left wall. The doorway opened into an immense sanctuary. Our steps echoed down the main aisle as we walked past row after row of pews. The stone walls and stained-glass windows rose up around us, past the wings of a balcony, and met far above in a vaulted ceiling. Up at the front of the sanctuary, on a raised platform, was a circular table. Seated around the table were close to a dozen figures. There were multiple conversations taking place as the three of us took our seats.

As we waited for the meeting to begin, I looked around the table. The age of most members seemed older than Trish, with both men and women present. However, the majority of the people at the table were older white males. They must have been the religious leaders Trish had mentioned. The city officials and the detective were easily identifiable by their suits.

When the meeting was called to order, Trish spoke of the increasing number of assaults the community had noticed on wizards and wolves alike. She mentioned the attack on Ben, the harassment of her employee, and the stories shared at The Village Pub. I watched the others around the table as she presented the information. Despite her giving multiple examples, many of the people looked skeptical.

A balding man with a doughy complexion and bulbous nose interrupted, "The majority of these attacks happen after nightfall?"

"Yes, William, the majority do," Trish answered.

"Crime rates increase during the evening. It's a consequence of living in an urban area. People who remain within the safety of their homes instead of staying out until dawn are less likely to be mugged." The man spoke to all but gave a man in a rumpled suit a smug smile. "You don't have to be a detective to realize that, do you, Sam?"

The detective gave a pained smile of acknowledgement. Was this the Detective Grey Anne wanted to work with on the case of these assaults? Did she know more than she'd let on?

Another man, hawk-nosed with dark hair and gray beginning to show at his temples, spoke, "This wizard who was attacked in the alleyway was involved in a case the Committee addressed over a dozen years ago."

William chimed in, "Are you saying he's tethered, Aiden? He's a convicted criminal?"

Reginald stated, "He is currently serving a sentence."

William gave an exasperated look across the table at Trish. "With everything we manage in the city, you believe it's also our responsibility to protect convicts? You're well aware the tethered are not granted the same protection as those who follow our laws."

Hearing the specific consequence of a tether from Ben had felt different from hearing it spoken aloud by William. Did we all get one chance to get it right? Otherwise, we weren't treated as people anymore?

Folding his hands in front of him, William continued. "Ms. Drake, we all understand you take it upon yourself to be a protector of your people. However, is it possible your emotions may be getting the best of you in this situation? It is a stress-filled responsibility to serve on this Committee." Several others nodded in agreement.

Trish gave William a slow smile. Her jawline twitched. I could only imagine what she was thinking. The man was irritating the hell out of me, and I was suffering through my first encounter with him. I wasn't sure how Trish dealt with him on a regular basis.

Reginald took note as well. "Yes, Ms. Drake desires the best for her people. It is something we should all aspire to as leaders. I have received a letter from a group of uneasy wizards. It outlines similar concerns. I feel if we are not quick to reprimand this awful behavior, the aggressors will be emboldened. Attacks could increase and grow more severe."

A middle-aged woman with shoulder-length hair, a priest's collar, and glasses spoke. "I agree with Reginald. No matter who it affects, this type of behavior is inexcusable."

"Serenity is right," stated a young man across the table. "By being a part of the Committee, we've pledged to equally support each other and the people we represent."

Father Aiden waved away the man's comment. "Yes, Martin. We all know what is expected of us."

"Do we?" Martin asked, arching a brow.

I lowered my gaze and tried to withhold my smile. There was a quiet moment as Father Aiden studied the younger man. William snorted and muttered to himself.

Trish broke the tension by holding up the flag pin she'd brought to the meeting at The Village Pub. "This was being worn by the men we recently threw out of Hell's Bells. I wasn't sure it held any importance until Alex," she motioned to me, "told us it was worn by two young men who attacked her and Emma. Emma Arztin is a wizard with a public service record outshining most of our own." Trish handed the pin to Reginald to pass around the table. She addressed William. "You would, of course, be familiar with Emma's work. She attends your church."

"This is all speculation!" William turned pink and pointed a finger across the table at me. "Who is this, Aiden? Are we allowing anyone to sit at this table?"

*What the hell?* My face heated up. How did this become about me being here? The guy was acting pretty defensive about Trish's observations about the pins.

Aiden frowned at William. "Alex Steward is an approved guest of Ms. Drake's."

The outburst had landed awkwardly with the other members as well. There was a lot of fussing around the table as people shuffled notes, cleared their throats, or exchanged confused glances.

William shook his head, spluttered, then scowled at Trish. "Since you feel so strongly about this, Ms. Drake, how do you suggest we proceed? Ask everyone we meet to turn their pockets out so we can look for a ridiculous little pin?"

Trish narrowed her eyes. "I don't pretend to know the answers." She held her hand out to me. "Alex witnessed three attacks firsthand. She agreed to join us today to share her experiences. My hope is the information will guide the Committee toward a swift and effective solution."

Trish took a seat and all eyes turned on me. I broke out in a cold sweat. Taking an unsteady deep breath, I began. Everyone listened as I recounted Kevin and Brad, and how they seemed to know Emma was a wizard. Conveniently, I left out the part where I wolfed out and scared them off.

I also shared my two encounters with Shortie and the Ox. I recalled as many details as I could about the men, hoping a thorough description would spark some recognition. "The smaller guy attacked me with some sort of flame spell."

William startled me by slapping his hand on the tabletop and interrupting. "There we have it! Reginald, it seems you have some wizards who have gone rogue."

It was Reginald's turn to be flustered. "Are you sure he cast a spell?"

"Yes," I said. "I felt it. It happened while I tried to protect the Commoner." Should I mention the maybe-tether?

"One of my parishioners!" William exclaimed.

I frowned and looked at William. "You know Mitch?"

"Of course I know him, girl," he said. "This is Hopewell. Everyone knows the White family."

Serenity asked, "None of the previously reported attacks have involved magic, have they?"

"No," Trish said. "None that have been shared with us." She looked at the man in the rumpled suit. "Detective Grey?"

He shook his head. "Not that I know of. It's been slow-going on my end. Like usual, no one wants to talk." It aligned with what Anne had told me.

"And what is this of a wizard targeting a human?" William asked.

Reginald scowled at the man. "Come off it, William. We're not other-worldly aliens."

"I think something odd is going on with those two men," I said. "The larger guy was tethered, I'm positive. But I think the wizard may have been as well."

A deafening silence filled the room. Everyone was staring at me. Reginald's complexion turned gray as he regarded me, wide-eyed.

"The wizard? Who cast the spell?" Aiden asked me in a measured tone. "You believe he was tethered?"

Heat rushed up from my collar through my face for what seemed like the umpteenth time. "I'm not sure. I think so?"

The room exploded into cross arguments, the voices echoing in the large sanctuary. My heart sank. I might have to turn in Shortie and the Ox without the Committee's help after all. I'd try to contact Ben again for any info on dealing with less-than-friendly wizards. And, finally, I should confront Emma about the multiple threats swarming around her.

Trish stood, the movement catching the attention of the other members. She waited as the arguing petered out. Her eyes were a radiant gold color, but her tone was civil. "It's disappointing to witness how dysfunctional this group has become. I've attempted to bring the wolves' concerns to this shared table multiple times. They are frightened, and rightfully so. Each time, we've been disregarded. The lupine will no longer wait for this Committee to take action while those in our community are being harmed." She looked to each committee member as she announced, "Please take note, I will be granting full permission to the lupine to defend themselves. If this is in any way held against them, there will be a much larger issue for this Committee to resolve."

William pounded his fist on the tabletop and stood. He shouted across the table, "Are you threatening us, Ms. Drake?"

Father Aiden spoke, a hint of distaste in his tone. "Please compose yourself, William. There's no need to raise your voice." He turned his gaze on Trish. "Patricia, please be seated. We can discuss what actions to take next to put Reginald's and your minds at ease. I'm sorry to hear you feel we haven't acknowledged the lupine's concerns."

Trish tilted her chin slightly upward and fixed Aiden with her golden stare as she weighed his words. She finally shook her head. "No. The lupine are done giving this Committee our time and energy. Until a solution is presented to us, we will no longer participate in these meetings." Trish placed a hand on my shoulder. I stood as well, and we left the table. A burst of renewed arguments began in our wake.

Back in the car, Trish spent a few moments in silence, collecting her thoughts. She finally looked over at me with a disheartened smile. "Thank you for speaking to them."

"You're welcome." I waited until we were on our way to my apartment before asking, "Did you really mean what you said about granting wolves the permission to protect themselves?"

"I meant every word of it." She glanced over at me. "I've spoken to Reggie about adding wards to your apartment for protection. He'll join us after the meeting concludes."

"Protection? I've rented this place for two years and have been perfectly safe without any spells cast on it," I said. Plus, I didn't know Reginald, so I didn't want him at my apartment. I wasn't sure if I even wanted Trish there. "Those two guys don't know where I live."

"But Emma does, so that means Mitch does. We don't know how those two men are connected to Emma and Mitch. What if they follow them here? Wards will shield your apartment against malicious magic."

I PACED MY apartment as we waited for Reginald to arrive. I'd already burned time messaging both Emma and Ben to check in on them. Neither had answered. Every several passes by the window, I stopped to push aside the curtain and peer down to the street.

Trish sat at my small table in the kitchen texting with Nate. Her thumbs moved over the keys. "Alex, I'm sensing you're uncomfortable with this. Why is that?"

"It's weird." I let the curtain fall back into place and resumed my pacing. "Do you trust him? Reginald?"

She didn't look up from her phone. "Yes."

The doorbell rang. I left Trish in the apartment and descended the sharply inclined staircase to answer the door. Reginald waited on the covered porch. He tipped his hat to me when I opened the door for him.

"Greetings, Miss Steward."

"Please, call me Alex."

He took off his hat and followed me up the stairs. "These old homes are wonderful. It's a shame so many were hacked to bits for apartments."

We entered my apartment, and Reginald nodded to Trish. "Ms. Drake."

Trish didn't return the formality. She set her phone aside and gave him her full attention. "Reggie, please tell me you have good news for us. Did something get accomplished after we left? What was decided?"

He turned his hat in his hands by the brim and cleared his throat. "I have news of progress, albeit more gradual than you may prefer."

Trish rolled her eyes and cursed. Gradual wasn't what I'd prefer either.

Reginald continued, "The majority of the Committee are not convinced there is an actual emergency to address. A few members are even of the opinion the situation has been dramatized. They believe details are being embellished to further advance our . . ." He hesitated, turning his hat in his hands again.

Trish growled, "Our what, Reggie?"

He cleared his throat again and tugged at his shirt collar as if it had become uncomfortably tight. "Advance our agenda."

Trish's eyes flashed. It caused the hair to stand up on the nape of my neck, and I took a step back from the two. Trish rose slowly, not taking her eyes from the wizard. "We've bent over backward for years to keep them comfortable. We've hidden ourselves away so they feel safe. We've followed their never-ending list of demoralizing and pointless rules. And now when we ask for their help, we have an 'agenda?'"

Reginald raised a hand, his palm facing Trish. The air began to buzz with energy. My eyes widened and my pulse skipped. Trish felt it too. She gave a low, rumbling growl. Her whole body quivered like a coiled spring, but she remained by the table, watching the wizard closely.

He spoke to her in a soothing tone. "Be still, my friend. I understand your anger. Your words did not fall on deaf ears today. There was a majority of Committee members who agreed the situation required further investigation. Every member is charged with combing through their ranks to look for the symbol you presented and persons who may be inclined to instigate these hateful crimes."

"What about the guys who attacked Mitch?" I asked.

"Since at least one of them appeared to wield magic, I was assigned the task of identifying them." Reginald spoke to me but kept his gaze locked with Trish's. "I require your help with that, Miss Alex. I need a more detailed visual profile of the two men."

"I already gave a description of them during the meeting." I frowned, not sure what else I could do for him.

Trish's nails sunk into the cheap surface of the table. Her eyes an intense gold, she asked, "Why should one of my people further endanger herself to help that incompetent collection of fools?"

One of her people? We'd only met a short time ago.

"I don't believe the two are working under orders from either of our communities. I find it extremely alarming the wizard may have cast a spell while tethered. The sooner I can identify them, the sooner I can possibly find who is controlling them." Reginald spared me a glance. "If Miss Alex agrees to help, the lupine will have full access to any of my findings, despite their departure from the Committee." He asked Trish, "May I approach her?"

I looked between the two. And since when had I needed a pack leader making decisions for me?

"That is Alex's choice to make," Trish answered, "not mine."

"What exactly do I need to do?" I asked.

"Could you please step over to me, Miss Alex?" Reginald didn't lower his hand until I stood next to him. "I will need you to envision the two men you encountered. When you have a firm picture of them in your mind, I will briefly glimpse what you remember. It will not be painful or leave any lingering sensations."

Frowning, I asked, "So you'll be looking through my memories?" That would not be okay.

"I will only see what you wish to show me. You have my word. I will respect your privacy."

Shifting my weight from one foot to another, I glanced over at Trish. Not seeing any signal from her that I shouldn't do so, I closed my eyes and recalled what Shortie and the Ox looked like. I remembered the features of the two, the build of their bodies, and the clothes they wore the first night I ran into them.

Reginald's voice sounded beside me. "Are you ready to begin?"

I nodded. He whispered unfamiliar words in a low tone. His speech had a cadence similar to a person reciting poetry. Once again, a type of tingling ran across my skin as the air in the room seemed to shift toward us.

"I'm going to place my hand on your forehead," he said.

The pad of his thumb pressed against my skin an inch above the bridge of my nose. A soothing coolness spread outward from the point where his skin met mine. I pictured the men in the alleyway with Ben. Shortie's scarred face when he first noticed me. The Ox's expression of surprise before I struck him. Reginald abruptly lifted his thumb, causing me to gasp as all the energy focused on that point rushed away from us. I opened my eyes, blinking. My vision was momentarily blinded by brightness before the room came into focus again.

He looked at me with a troubled expression. "I apologize. I was surprised by what I saw."

"What is it?" Trish asked, "Do you know who they are?"

"No, I do not." He looked at Trish, his brow furrowed. "But Miss Alex is correct. Both of the men are tethered."

Trish frowned at Reginald. "How is that possible?"

"The tethers have been altered with additional glyphs. It's highly disturbing news. I have some research ahead of me this evening." He added almost absently, "Ms. Drake, Miss Alex, I can arrange the wards now if you both don't mind stepping outside."

Trish stood. She and I walked toward the front door of the apartment. Reginald lifted a finger. "Miss Alex, do you mind waiting a moment so we can speak in private?"

I looked again at Trish, and she nodded—not permission, but an assurance I would be safe to do so. "Sure."

When I heard the front door at the bottom of the stairs close, Reginald straightened himself. His tone was business-like. "I couldn't help but notice the injured man in your memory. Do you know if he received medical care?"

"Ben? Yes. Emma healed his more serious injuries." When Reginald responded with a pained smile, I asked, "Why?"

"Benjamin is my grandson. We haven't spoken in a long time. It was startling to see him in such a state." Reginald added in a disapproving murmur, "And in such dire need of a haircut." He cleared his throat. "Do you know if he is doing well?"

"Uh . . ." I was still trying to absorb the new bit of information. Grandson? "Ah . . . yes, I think so? He seems to be." Despite his injuries, he definitely *looked* quite well.

Reginald gave a curt nod. "Good to hear. Thank you for intervening and ensuring his safety."

A twinge of guilt reminded me how intervening hadn't been my first choice. "You're welcome."

He motioned around the apartment. "If you'll excuse me, I will prepare your home now."

"Okay. Sure." I moved to leave, but then paused to turn back to Reginald. "Am I going to need some magical password to get into my own place now?"

He smiled, amused. "No, Miss Alex, you will not. You may come and go and allow guests as you please."

"Okay, good." I said. "Trish said these wards will protect my apartment from magic?"

"Yes, that is correct," Reginald said. "In your case, if the wizard you reported attempts to enter your apartment or spy on you, he will not be able to rely on his magic to do so."

Spy on me? At my home? I thought of the Ox and the ruined state of my car. "Couldn't they kick down the door if they wanted?"

"Yes, I'm afraid so. The wards do not protect against physical attacks. For that, you will have to rely on your gifts as a werewolf."

"Okay. Thanks." I frowned to myself as I descended the stairs. The whole situation with Shortie, the Ox, and now the Committee was getting extremely uncomfortable. And why hadn't Ben mentioned his grandfather was on the Committee when I'd talked about it? He was *still* withholding information from me.

I joined Trish outside. She remained agitated as she stood by her car, smoking a cigarette. She offered me the open carton.

"No thanks." I looked up at my apartment windows and caught brief glances of Reginald moving past them. "Apparently he's Ben's grandfather."

Trish raised her eyebrows. "I knew Reggie had grandkids, but I assumed they lived out of town like his daughter and her husband."

"How long have you known him?" I asked.

"Over a dozen years?" She exhaled a stream of smoke. "He and his wife took me in for a short time. We became friends. He's always been supportive of my efforts to give the wolves a voice on the Committee."

"If the wizards have access to magic, can't Reginald use it to run the Committee?" I asked. "He could tell the others what the rules are going to be around here. No more headaches for us."

She laughed and shook her head. "Wouldn't that be nice? As I understand it, not many wizards wield magic powerful enough to accomplish something on that scale. They also follow an additional framework of rules among themselves when practicing magic."

"So there aren't any great and powerful wizards to fix this for us?" I'd prefer there to be. I could get this problem cleared off my plate, Emma would be safe, and we could go back to our carefree evenings with Anne at The Sound Refuge.

"An all-powerful wizard doesn't exist. They can't. Reggie explained to me that magic simply doesn't work that way because of the focus wizards choose." Trish smiled. "I know he's up there in the ranks, but I don't think he'd lord his magic over others even if it were possible."

"Seems like a nice-enough guy, I guess."

Trish arched her brow. "Like his grandson?"

I smiled and shrugged.

She exhaled a stream of smoke and motioned to the apartment windows with her cigarette. "He's lucky you saw what you did. Let's hope it will speed up the process of finding those two and who's pulling their strings."

I wasn't willing to wait for that to happen. I'd thought the Committee would be able to help me protect Emma, but now I had my doubts. It was past time for Emma and me to sit down together and talk. I wanted to clear the air of everything: what to do about Kevin and Brad, what not to do about Ben's attackers, and finally, addressing the issue that was Mitch.

# 9

AFTER REGINALD FINISHED setting the wards, I asked Trish to stick around a few minutes at my apartment. If I could find Emma, I might need a ride. Trish waited in her car while I dialed Another Chance, hoping to dodge Emma's voicemail and catch her at work.

"Good morning. Another Chance Ministries. This is Emma Arztin speaking."

I couldn't believe my luck. "Hey, it's Alex. You're a hard woman to get a hold of."

There was a pause on the line, but thankfully she didn't hang up on me. "Hello."

"Can we go somewhere and sit down together, just the two of us?"

"You mean without Mitch?" There was a tone of accusation in her voice. She was still pissed about me following him home.

I slowly exhaled, trying to keep the frustration from coloring my tone. "Yes."

"He said you'd try something like this."

"There's so much we need to talk about. It's really important to me. I'm free for the next few hours if you have time." There was another gap of silence on her end of the line. I could hear my heartbeat in my ears. "Em. Please."

"We can't be too long. Do you want to meet at the diner?"

Emma and I had a favorite diner we frequented enough to be known between the two of us simply as "the diner." It sounded great, but my wallet was currently sitting on empty. "Only if you're buying. I'm low on cash right now."

"I can be there in about twenty minutes. Will that work?"

"Sure."

Trish dropped me off at the diner, and I grabbed a booth near the back corner for some semi-privacy. When Emma arrived, I didn't wait for her to take off her fluffy coat and hat before I hugged her. My heart swelled as my nose filled with the scent of vanilla. "I've been so worried about you."

Her hug was tentative, but she giggled. "You're being ridiculous."

"I already ordered us drinks," I said, releasing her. "Thank you for meeting me."

Emma gave a small smile as we sat down. "You're right. We are overdue for a talk."

The waitress delivered our coffee and tea. I placed my order and handed over my menu. While Emma consulted the menu, I was alarmed by the differences in her appearance. Her round cheeks seemed gaunt, and shadows lurked beneath her eyes. The usually vibrant strands of pink in her hair had faded. My friend looked like a diluted version of herself.

She gave her order and surrendered her menu. "How's the job hunt going?" she asked.

"Well, it hasn't been going as much as it should. When I read the job listings, there wasn't much available that would pay enough. I've been driving instead, but my car is in the shop right now."

"Oh no. What happened?"

I didn't want to derail the conversation. "Um, it needed some work done."

"I'm sorry. Car troubles are the worst."

"Yeah." I thought of the price of the repairs. "I'll be scouring the papers with a bit more purpose after we're done here. I need to make a hefty chunk of change fast."

Emma bit at her bottom lip. "I know someone who's hiring," she said. "But she's a good friend of my mother's. The job lead came into

Another Chance. It's a delivery job that requires some sort of driving certification many of my clients don't have." She took some paper and a bejeweled purple pen from her purse. The ink smelled like grape bubblegum as she wrote.

I had mixed feelings about the offer. Keeping my distance from Susan Arztin was always a good idea, but I needed the money. I accepted the slip of paper with the business's information. "Thanks, Em."

"Be sure to pass along my name as a reference," she said. "I can talk to her about getting you some sort of advance."

I smiled and nodded as I pocketed the slip of paper. My mind spun as I tried to decide where to start the conversation about Mitch. "About last night . . . I don't know what Mitch told you, but I didn't threaten him."

"He said you followed him home and chased him into the building from the parking lot. When he tried to shut the door, you forced your way in after him."

*Shit.* My face warmed. "Well, I . . ."

Emma frowned. "Really, Alex?"

"There's much more to it than that. Didn't you get the voicemail I left?"

"I didn't have any messages or calls from you last night. I swear, half of these calls I'm accused of not returning don't seem to exist."

She wasn't getting my messages? "Did you see Mitch last night after I supposedly chased him down?" The anger already burned in the pit of my stomach.

She hesitated. "I don't see what that has to do with anything, but yes, he came over afterward. You're acting strange, Alex, and it makes him nervous. It has me worried as well."

I closed my eyes, desperately trying to keep my temper in check. Mitch messing with Emma's phone was a real possibility. The guy was a piece of work.

Emma placed her hand over my own. "Please, quit being so aggressive toward him. Give Mitch a chance."

"Shortie and the Ox were there waiting for him, Em," I said from between clenched teeth. "I was trying to *protect* Mitch."

"Who?"

I opened my eyes. She was frowning at me again. I shook my head. "The two guys who'd attacked Ben were waiting for Mitch in the parking lot of his building."

Her eyes widened.

"They seem like really bad news, and I'm worried they were actually there for you. What if they're the heavies who are sent when idiots like Kevin and Brad screw up?"

Emma paled.

"I tried to distract the two so Mitch could get safely inside. When Shortie tried to roast me with a flame spell, I fled too. That's why I ran into the building after Mitch."

She swallowed and looked down at her teacup. "Mitch didn't say anything about strange men in the parking lot."

Of course he didn't. "When I asked Mitch to report the guys to the police, he threw me out."

Her gaze twitched back up to me. "He wouldn't do that."

I gave a short laugh. "Em, why in the world would I make that up?"

"I don't know." She frowned, and pink appeared in her cheeks. "I don't understand why you're acting the way you are. Mitch says you're jealous of he and I spending so much time together."

Anger flared in my stomach again. I clenched my jaw so tightly I thought I'd crack a tooth. What was Mitch doing to Emma? She'd never leaned into a guy this hard, and she seemed oblivious that she was doing so now.

"I know my relationship with Mitch has been hard for you, Alex. With that and my new position, I don't have as much free time right now. I'm sorry. Once I become more comfortable at work, we can see each other more . . ."

I interrupted. "Ask him about the two men."

"Okay, okay." She held up her hand. "I will. In exchange, you have to promise to stop following him."

My heart sank. "I have a bad feeling about this guy, Em."

"You haven't been able to spend time with him like I have. He's a sweet and thoughtful person." Emma smiled. "Mitch and you are both extremely important to me. So please, promise me you'll be kind to him and not follow him around."

She wasn't seeing what a manipulative jerk Mitch was being. Why wasn't she seeing it? It seemed so obvious to me. I didn't know how to show her without getting pushback.

"Okay, I promise." I tried a different angle. "Did you find out what we should do with Kevin and Brad?"

Emma's cheeks turned a deeper pink.

"You haven't asked anyone yet?" It'd been priority number one to her after they'd attacked us.

"No, I haven't." She shrugged. "We're okay, don't you think? No one has contacted you about wolfing out in front of Kevin and Brad, right?"

Her flippant attitude contradicted the anxiety we'd shared that night. Something was definitely off.

"I've found out a few things since it happened. Can I use your pen?" I reached for a napkin.

She handed me the purple pen.

I sketched the flag symbol from the pins and pushed the napkin over to her. "This symbol is turning up in the assaults targeting our people."

Recognition dawned on Emma's face. "That's the symbol for the Noble Sons. They're an all-male Bible study group Pastor William created shortly after he was installed as head pastor."

Was that why William reacted so strongly to Trish presenting the symbol at the Committee meeting? "What else do you know about them?"

"It's grown pretty fast. I heard there are people joining from outside our church." Emma lifted her gaze from the napkin to me. "What do the Noble Sons have to do with Kevin, Brad, and the assaults?"

"Kevin and Brad wore pins of that group's symbol on their shirt collars."

Emma sat back in her seat. "Are you sure? I don't remember seeing that."

I nodded. "I noticed the pins when they were at our table at The Sound Refuge. At first, I thought it was a fraternity symbol. But then the symbol showed up again. Remember the community meeting you invited me to?"

Emma busied herself with refolding her napkin in her lap. "Yes. That's the evening you were waiting at my house, and then were so rude to Mitch and me."

If I didn't let the comment go, I was certain to end up in another *Mitch-is-great-and-you're-being-awful* spiral. "I went to the meeting, and you were right. People are frightened by the assaults targeting our kind. A club owner threw some guys out of her business because they were harassing her employee." I tapped the pen on the napkin. "Those guys were also wearing pins with this symbol on it."

Emma bit at her bottom lip. "Maybe it's a coincidence?"

I blinked. "What? How?"

She took a tentative sip of her tea. "I worry I was being caught up in some type of group paranoia by going to those meetings."

"I don't think you were." Begrudgingly, I added, "And you were also right about making an effort to meet other people like us. I'm getting to know new people and learning a lot."

"I've been struggling with some guilt about that. I hope I haven't steered you wrong. You've had no problem living here without engaging people like that."

I frowned. This didn't sound like Emma. "What do you mean? People like what?"

"You know," she motioned vaguely at the air, "people who fabricate issues to be upset about, and then upend everyone's way of life until they get what they want. If you think about it, we already have the opportunity to lead a great life here. We should be thankful we're able to coexist with normal people and not be hunted like monsters."

*Normal* people? Leaning forward, I lowered my voice. "Have you considered we're not hunted because we're always hiding? We can never be ourselves in public because the Commoners would lose their collective shit."

"But do we really need to act differently? Normal people make it through every day without being like us," she said.

There it was again. The word "normal." She'd been self-conscious of being different from Commoners, but she'd never spoken like this before.

Emma's elbows rested on the top of the table as she rubbed at her temples, frowning down at her tea. "Plus, some of our people can be dangerous. Look at the two men who attacked Ben. It's understandable there is some mistrust from—" She abruptly cut off her words and sat up. She smiled at the waitress as we were served our food. "Thank you." Emma started her meal.

"Is Mitch a part of this Righteous Lads group?" I asked.

She gave me an exasperated look. "Noble Sons. No, he isn't a member of the group." Emma raised her brows and smiled, pleased with my befuddled expression. "He isn't comfortable with the group's shared beliefs. He thinks they're too literal in their interpretation of scripture."

"Em, have you told Mitch about yourself?"

"Yes."

My stomach twisted. Had she told Mitch about me as well? Is that why he'd recovered so fast when I slipped up and revealed my werewolf features?

She moved food around on her plate with her fork. "He's helping me work through it. I can't control what I was born into, but I can choose who I become. It was selfish of me to embrace something so unnatural."

Upon hearing Emma's words, my mouth went dry and my stomach began to burn again. Was this what Mitch was telling her? She was selfish for embracing who she was? I tried to maintain control of my temper and keep my tone conversational. "You have an amazing gift. It helps people. It's not something to be ashamed of or something to 'work through.' I've witnessed you save someone's life. Look at what you did for Ben."

Emma's hand started to tremble, causing her fork to tap on her plate. Her smile flickered and then was gone. She set the fork carefully down and covered her face. Her small body began to shake.

I left my seat and sat down beside her in the booth. Placing my arm around her shoulders, I said, "Hey, tell me what's going on. Let me help."

She sniffled, using her napkin to dab at her eyes. "I'm sorry." Frowning, she shook her head. "I don't know what's happening. My mind has been so noisy these past few weeks. My thoughts are all over the place. Words come out of my mouth that don't sound like mine. I think I'm overtired from work."

Emma hid a lot of her stress. It was a skill she'd been taught by her parents. If cracks ever did appear in her near-perfect facade, like now, I was startled by it. But this time it was something I could help her with. If I could find out what Mitch was up to and expose him to Emma, she could get better, and I would get my friend back. The only problem was that to do that, I'd have to break my promise to her.

# 10

EMMA GAVE ME a ride back to my apartment. "Remember to call about that job," she said. "When you go in for the interview, send me a message so I know to expect a call from them."

I nodded. "Thanks again, Em."

She smiled and waved before leaving. It was hard to say goodbye to her. My meal and conversation with her instilled a renewed sense of urgency in me. Whatever Mitch was doing to her had to stop asap. I sent off a text message to Anne and Trish. *Group with flag symbol called Noble Sons. Emma ID'd. Meets at Patterson St. Church.*

Trish's reply was immediate. *That's William Jensen's congregation.*

*Yeah. It's a Bible study group he organized. People joining from outside the church too.*

Her next reply was a simple "Thank you." Hopefully she'd pass the info along to Reginald. With multiple people looking into the group, we'd get to the bottom of everything sooner.

I called the number Emma had given me and, after dropping her name, was fast-laned into scheduling an interview. The earliest I could get was an eight o'clock morning appointment two days from now. At least my car might be done by then and I wouldn't have to take the bus. The weather this time of year caused the bus schedule to become unreliable. I couldn't miss the interview since Emma put her name on the line for me.

Investigating Mitch further required resources I didn't have, a big one being a working vehicle. Between asking Trish or Nate for help, I

felt Nate was the safer option. The impatience and frustration he'd displayed the last time I was at Hell's Bells might work in my favor. When
I called to ask him for help looking into Mitch, he agreed.

Nate messaged me when he got to my apartment. His car, a rusty
sedan the size of a small boat, waited at the edge of the sidewalk. I got
into his car and my senses were immediately assaulted by a blast of talk
radio and the overwhelming stink of cigarettes.

"Thanks for giving me a ride," I said, "and not thinking I'm a stalker."

He chuckled and turned down the radio. "Tell me more about this
guy we're looking into."

"There's something bothering me about how Mitch reacted after I
ran those other two off. Instead of being freaked out that he was almost
mugged by a guy wielding blue fire, Mitch started lecturing me on how
I was endangering Emma."

"Are you sure he's a Commoner?" Nate pulled away from the curb
and started driving.

"Emma said he was. When I met her for lunch, I learned she'd told
Mitch she's a wizard."

Nate raised his eyebrows and gave a low whistle. "That's a commitment. She must be serious about this guy. So, he's a Commoner
in-the-know."

"Maybe? He didn't have any questions when he caught me with
my claws out." I shook my head. "The more time Emma spends with
Mitch, the more oddly she's behaving. She said her mind was 'noisy.'"

"And you think Mitch is the cause?"

"Yes."

Nate nodded. "She's okay with you spying on her guy?"

My face flushed. "Em isn't thinking clearly right now."

"Got it." He grinned. "Discretion is advised."

"The place we're going, The Mind Center, is some sort of pseu-
do-therapy business owned by Mitch's family. The practice sounds kind
of shady. I want to look into it further, but I'm not quite sure how."

"I can help with that. Getting into places I'm not wanted is a staple in my skill set."

We arrived at The Mind Center near the end of their business hours. Fortunately for us, the interior designer thought it best for the business to have large windows to let in natural light. At this dark time of year, the office became a fishbowl. The interior lighting gave us a clear view of clients and staff moving around inside the lobby and front office. Nate drummed his fingers on his knee, the heel of his boot bouncing as he watched the people.

"That's him." I pointed. Mitch conversed with a young man, a receptionist, at the front desk.

"You said there might be an alarm?" asked Nate.

Mitch took something from the front desk and walked to the back of the office. He disappeared from view.

"Yeah, I'd followed Em and him here after hours. He went into the building, and before he left, I think he armed one. He messed with something near the front door."

Nate nodded. "Right. Be back in a few." He got out of the car, closed the door, and started toward the building.

I panicked, rolled down the window, and tried to catch his attention. "Nate! What are you doing?!" He ignored me. My pulse thundered in my ears, and I broke out into a cold sweat. I rolled up the window and sank down into my seat, watching him enter the building. This was a much more direct approach than what I'd had in mind.

He walked up and leaned casually on the main counter. The receptionist greeted Nate. At first, the young man's body language communicated discomfort, maybe even fear, as he stood rigid behind the counter. Nate smiled and gestured as he conversed with the guy. I held my breath and waited for security to be called.

Instead, the receptionist began to relax. His head tilted back as he laughed. Nate grinned and tapped on the counter with his fingertip. The receptionist returned the grin, nodded, and looked at a monitor behind the counter. A few more minutes passed before the young man wrote on a small card and handed it across the counter. Smiling, Nate exchanged a few more words before he turned away from the counter. His smile disappeared as he pocketed the card and exited the building.

He opened the car door, took a seat, and yanked the door closed behind him. "You were right. They have an alarm system armed from a panel at the front. Seems pretty basic, though. I could probably get us in there tomorrow night if you're ready."

My pulse lurched. Nate spoke about breaking into the building as if it were a normal, everyday task. "What? How?"

"The office gets cleaned every other evening by a contracted company. I know the guy who owns it." He looked toward the lobby. "We'll be able to search the place when we schedule a time to have it to ourselves."

"What was the business card for?" I asked.

"The receptionist gave me one in case my cleaning company wants to make a bid for their business. He gave me his phone number, too." Nate looked back at me, grinned, and held up the card. "You interested?"

"A date with the receptionist or some light breaking and entering?" I wondered what Anne would think if she knew I was considering this. Extreme disapproval was my guess.

"Either."

Getting into The Mind Center was a nonconfrontational way for me to find out more about Mitch and what he was up to. I wasn't agitating him by following him around and asking direct questions. I was secretly breaking into his office and sorting through his stuff.

Technically, I wasn't going back on my promise to Emma. And if we didn't get caught, Anne would never know. I had to find out what Mitch was doing to Emma. "I can't believe I'm saying this, but I'll take the latter."

BY THE NEXT evening, I'd picked up my car, handed over my rent money to the repair shop, and driven out to a large cinema complex across the street from the strip mall. I crossed the street and slipped behind the line of squat buildings. After pausing to message Nate, I crept along the back of the businesses toward The Mind Center. A van belonging to a cleaning service idled outside the employee entrance.

Nate hopped out of the passenger side and walked around the vehicle. The man seated behind the steering wheel was too busy watching his phone to notice me.

"Who's this?" I asked.

"A friend of a friend." Nate handed me a pair of latex cleaning gloves. "Put these on. We get fifteen minutes once we're in there."

"They don't have cameras?"

"Yes, but not any that haven't been on the fritz since yesterday." Nate clucked his tongue and gave a shake of his head. "Tech is always so unreliable."

"So they won't be on when we're in the building?"

"Nope." He withdrew a key card from his pocket, referenced his watch, and then held the key to the lock at the back door. It beeped, and the door unlocked. He pulled it open, and I followed him into a hallway. A cleaning cart stood in the hall, and the sound of a vacuum came from the front of the office.

Nate led me down the hallway to a door where Mitch's name was engraved on a metal plate posted on the wall. He used the same key card to unlock the office door.

"Do we have to worry about the person up front? Or are they also a friend of a friend?" I asked.

"You're a quick study." He opened the door. "They'll let us do our thing as long as we're out of here in the time promised."

I followed Nate into the room and a lingering cloud of Mitch's cologne. "You got all of this from one chat with the receptionist?"

"C'mon Alex." He grinned, flashing a set of pointed canines. "Who could resist this pretty smile?"

I snorted. Show-off. The display of effortless command of his shifting made me wonder how long Nate had been a werewolf. It also made me wonder if I'd *ever* reach that level of control.

Mitch's office was extremely tidy with the same modern furniture as the front lobby. A desk faced the door, and the wall behind it was covered in framed certificates.

Nate gestured at the wall. "In case you were wondering, this man is accomplished."

I chuckled as I sifted through the sparse stacked contents atop the desk. Several framed photos sat on its surface as well. A couple were Mitch receiving handshakes from old guys in suits. One pictured Mitch and William. Another smaller frame held a recent photo of Mitch and Emma. Seeing it, I gritted my teeth and sat down in the office chair to check the desk drawers.

Nate asked, "Is there a key in there for this cabinet?"

The drawers to the desk were unlocked. I opened up the middle one and lifted a tray filled with office supplies. A small key lay underneath. "Of course there is." Office administrative assistant happened to be part of my temp-job history, and never would I have imagined it would benefit me in this way. I tossed the key to Nate. He opened the cabinet and started thumbing through the hanging files.

I closed the middle drawer and opened the bottom left to find more hanging files. I pulled out a group of folders from the files and set them atop the desk. While flipping through them, I noticed one was dated last week. "Nate, what is that tea shop owner's name? The one who spoke at The Village Pub?"

"Frank?" He closed the drawer, walked over to stand beside me, and looked at the *patient name* field I pointed to. Nate nodded. "Yeah, that's him." He flipped through the next couple of folders. "I know these people."

I frowned. "They're all patients here?"

I searched through the stack of folders with a sinking sense of dread in my stomach. Sure enough, "Emma Arztin" was printed in stark black and white on one of the labels. Browsing through the pages, I read aloud bits and pieces of notes, "Hallucinations? Periodic delusions of grandeur? Patient believes she can heal people through magical means. Symptoms possibly exacerbated by peer group." I felt sick. "Are they 'treating' Emma here? There's nothing wrong with her." I looked at Nate.

Genuine concern was on his face. "She's not the only one. He has files on some of ours as well." He held up another folder. "How often does your friend have appointments?"

I flipped through the pages. "Twice a week, but not here. The facility location is noted as 'off-site.'"

He looked through the folders I'd set aside. "A lot of these are listed as off-site too. The appointments start at this office and then move to an off-site location after several visits."

I took out my phone. "Help me grab photos of these names." We logged the names of the file folders before we returned them back to their drawers. Further digging for any information about a second location didn't turn up anything.

A rushed exploration of the building revealed several rooms, most likely used by the counselors and clients. We didn't find any other useful information. Nate and I were retracing our steps toward the back door when I smelled the fresh wave of cologne.

"Alex?"

I froze. Nate cursed, and I turned to look back. Mitch stood in the hall staring at us, open-mouthed, with a keycard in his hand. The loud whir of the vacuum must have drowned out the sound of his footsteps.

He looked from Nate to the gloves on our hands, and back to me. His widened eyes narrowed. "What do you think you're doing here?"

There was no answer to smooth over the fact we'd broken into his place of business. I frowned at him. "What are you doing to Emma,

Mitch? Messing with her mind? Trying to convince her you're something other than a complete asshole?"

His face turned red. He shook his head and chuckled. "Unbelievable. I'm calling the police." He retrieved his phone and dialed.

Okay, so maybe the "asshole" thing was a step too far. I glanced at Nate.

"Are we leaving?" he asked me in a lowered voice. "If so, now would be the time."

"It's me," Mitch spoke into his phone. "I'm sorry, darling. You may want to come inside. We're going to be stuck here for a bit."

The blood drained from my face and my knees weakened. Emma was with him. "Mitch, please, ask her to wait in the car. She'll get really upset if she comes in here. You can prevent that from happening."

Mitch smirked. "Would you two like to get comfortable before I make my next call?" He ushered the two of us to the lobby. Nate and I sat down in the extremely fashionable and completely uncomfortable chairs. Mitch dismissed the woman cleaning the room.

Emma entered and stopped dead in her tracks upon seeing us. "Alex?" She looked between Nate and me. Her eyes widened and her hand flew up to cover her mouth. It wasn't too challenging to figure out what we'd been up to. Mitch explained anyway.

"I have to report these two for breaking and entering." He added, "I'm so sorry you have to witness this." Mitch stepped back behind the counter to make another call, presumably to the police department.

The sudden tears that sprang into Emma's eyes hurt more than any words she said next. Her face turned a bright red as she scowled. "You promised, Alex! Yesterday! You promised you'd stopped doing this."

"Em, why can't you see what he's doing to you?" Tears threatened the corners of my eyes as well. "You're not yourself. He's hurting you, and you're . . ."

"No! Stop it." She squeezed her eyes shut and shook her head. "Stop trying to make him a villain. He's helping me. *You're* the one hurting me. You're forcing me to choose between him and you." She opened her eyes, and the tears ran down her cheeks. "I need you to leave us alone. *Both* of us."

I felt as if I'd been sucker-punched in the heart. "Em, no, I'm sorry. I'm so worried about you. This time I'll—"

"No. You can't seem to accept Mitch or the person I want to become." She wiped at her damp cheeks with her gloved hands. "I don't want to be around you anymore, Alex."

"Darling, are you okay?" Having made his phone call, Mitch moved to Emma's side to place a hand on her shoulder. He glared over at me. "What did you say to upset her?"

My core flushed with heat as my wolf leapt forward. A snarl erupted from my body. I sprang out of my seat at Mitch, but Nate caught me by the arm. Mitch encircled Emma's waist and pulled her away, as if I would attack my friend instead of him. The gesture infuriated me even more.

I struggled against Nate's hold until he twisted my arm and yanked me back down onto the seat beside him. A canine-like yelp escaped me. His hand remained like a vise clamped to my arm. His tone was low and controlled. "Not now."

Emma started to cry in earnest and pushed free from Mitch's hold. "I'm sorry. I can't wait here," she said to him. She left the building and went back out into the cold evening to the car.

I deflated beside Nate. He released my arm and gave my shoulder a pat. "So, we're waiting this out?"

What was the point of running now? It'd be prolonging the inevitable. Mitch could easily direct the police to where to find me. I bit at my lip, continuing to keep the tears at bay, and nodded.

"All right then." Nate settled back into his chair and closed his eyes. "Wake me when our ride is here."

I didn't understand why Nate hadn't cut and run earlier when he had the chance. Why was he staying here? And why had he taken the chance of getting caught in the first place? He barely knew me.

The police cruiser arrived what seemed like a lifetime later. Nate and I were escorted to the car while an officer spoke to Mitch. I tried to get Emma's attention as we passed Mitch's car. She was looking away from us and speaking on the phone. The realization of what I'd done hit me, accompanied by a hefty dose of adrenaline. I started to shake, and my thoughts raced.

What the hell had I been thinking? Had I really been caught breaking and entering because I couldn't stand my best friend's boyfriend? Now I would be hauled to jail, and my name would appear on some police record. Worse, I'd broken the trust of the person who'd accepted me for who I am and meant nearly everything to me.

On the ride to the police station, I thought of the file I'd read on Emma. The notes taken about her, as if her gift were a mental illness, made my blood boil. The creature curled in my chest responded. My breath came in quick bursts as I fought to maintain my control. No, this was larger than disagreeing with my friend's choice in guys. Whatever harm Mitch was inflicting upon Emma, I now knew it reached beyond her. If Mitch thought this was the last he'd see of me, he was sorely mistaken.

I wasn't sure who to spend my sole phone call on. Nate had told me he would contact Trish, and she would have us out by the next morning. Knowing Anne would find out about my epic screw-up sooner or later, I chose to call her. The message I left was a combination of nervous chatter and a plea to see me if she could.

The cell I spent the night in was cold and smelled awful. I sat awake in the corner with my back to the wall and the collar of my shirt pinched over my nose. Only two other women were with me, and one seemed to be continuously vomiting from a bender. It did nothing to help my own feelings of nausea brought on by one part anxiety, one part the rank stink of the room.

Anne didn't appear until the following morning when she escorted me from the cell. I tried to talk to her, but she only replied with a slight shake of her head and a clenched jaw. Either she was as pissed with me as Emma, or she wasn't allowed to converse with me. I silently slunk beside her out to the area where Trish and Nate waited.

"There she is!" Nate grinned from where he stood beside Trish at a counter. "How were your accommodations?"

I frowned and shrugged.

Anne gave my arm a slight squeeze. "I'll call later." She frowned at both Trish and Nate, turned away, and left.

Trish signed a few more papers before she turned to us. I expected her to be upset, but she acted like this was another task on today's to-do list. She waved for us to follow her out of the station.

"Please think twice before you visit a White's place of business again." She looked between Nate and me. "Avoiding those charges cost a large favor that I would have preferred to save for something else. Mitch White was asking for the full ten years for you both."

Did Trish and Nate have a regular habit of paying off the police? Is that why Nate wasn't worried when we were arrested?

"Sorry, love," Nate said. "Next time we won't get caught."

"I'll take you to your cars, but then I have a meeting to go to," Trish said.

Meeting. The interview. My pulse lurched. "What time is it?"

Trish glanced at her watch. "A short bit after ten."

"No." I shook my head and covered my face. "No, no, no." The tears I'd been holding back since last night hovered in my eyes again.

"What is it?" Trish asked.

"I had an interview this morning, and I missed it. I needed that job." I was going to lose my apartment.

Nate snickered. "Why am I late to this interview? Well . . ."

Trish's tone was terse. "Nathan."

He smiled and gave me a slap on the back. "Reschedule. Your goldfish died or something. No harm done."

Sniffling, I nodded. "Yeah, you're right. It'll be okay. I'll call them after I get the car."

Trish dropped us off at the cinema to retrieve our cars. I drove back, parked my car outside my apartment, and called the business. After a few transfers and a brief wait on hold, the first person I'd spoken to, the receptionist, answered the phone again.

"Alexandria?"

"Yes, I'm here. Hello."

"Good morning. I'm sorry to keep you waiting. I've checked with HR, and we will not be able to reschedule the interview. There are two candidates who will be extended offers today."

"Oh."

"Thank you for your interest. We wish you the best of luck. Goodbye." There was a click as she hung up.

I lowered my phone and released a shaky exhale. I'd failed Emma not once, but twice, within twenty-four hours. And how would I find the money for rent now? Exhaustion and hunger were not helping the increasingly difficult struggle to keep my shit together. I forced myself to move from my car and up to my apartment. I made it as far as the couch. I collapsed onto it and cried myself to sleep.

# 11

I AWOKE SEVERAL hours later, smelling awful and feeling ravenous. I showered, dressed, and ate a bowl of ramen while I checked my phone messages. Trish had called to check in on me. A message from Anne, which I delayed responding to, had a liberal use of capital letters and cursing. The general gist was *what in the hell were you thinking*. None of the messages were from Emma.

I'd messaged and called Ben to set up a time to meet and talk. After I'd been attacked at Mitch's condo building, I hoped Ben would have some insight on the magic Shortie used. Since Ben hadn't replied yet, I worried that Shortie and the Ox somehow found him. I put on my jacket and boots and headed out again for Rear Window to see if he was at work.

Entering the shop, I smiled at the sound of The Smiths drifting from the speakers. I spotted Sara, the young female employee, and Ben behind the counter. She rang up a purchase for a customer at the register. Ben's back was to me as he referenced an ancient computer and crossed items off a clipboard. A few piles of records were stacked next to him on the counter.

He was safe. The tension in my body released. It was replaced by a pleasing warmth in my chest as my inner wolf responded to the sight of him.

The customer passed by as I approached the counter. Sara spotted me. She turned and gave Ben a nudge in the side of the arm. "Someone's here for you." He glanced at her and then looked over his shoulder at me. Ben's coworker took the clipboard and motioned him away from the computer. He smiled at Sara, moved aside, and walked the few steps to stand opposite me across the counter. He signed a type of salute.

"Hey there." I scanned him over and didn't see any additional harm. "You weren't replying to my messages. I thought I'd make sure everything was okay."

Ben pulled the small notepad from his back pocket. He opened it to a blank page and set it on the counter. He scribbled, *I'm all right. Thanks.*

We stood looking at each other awkwardly across the counter. When we parted last, he hadn't been in the best of moods. Something still felt off. I glanced at his coworker and back at him. "Do you have a break soon so we can step outside and talk?"

Sara spoke without turning from her work at the computer. "You can go take your break, Ben. We're not busy right now, and if I have to listen to one more Smiths song I'm going to throw myself off the roof of this building."

He grabbed the notebook and made his way from behind the counter. I followed him along the rows of album bins and past a motorcycle parked beside the rear exit. The back door led to an empty, enclosed stairwell utilized by the entire building. He took a seat on the stairs and slid over so I could sit beside him.

"There isn't anything else I can do for you," he said.

I was taken off guard by the blunt statement. "Are you still upset about Nate?"

"No. You want more information about those two guys, and I don't have anything to give you." He shrugged. "I guess I'm not sure why you're here."

His words stung, so I snapped back, "I'm here because you weren't answering your phone. I was worried you were dead in an alley somewhere." My tone lost a bit of its bite. "And yes, I'm asking for your help. I ran into Shortie and the Ox again."

"Who?"

"The two guys who jumped you in the alleyway."

"What? You hadn't told me that in your messages." His eyebrows drew together. "How did they find you?"

"They didn't exactly 'find' me," I said. "I followed Mitch, a guy Emma is spending time with. When we arrived at his condo, the two were there waiting for him."

"Why were you following a guy Emma knows?"

"I don't trust him. She went missing for a while, and now she's acting odd. She looks really unhealthy and is saying very un-Emma-like things." I frowned. "I think he's messing around in her head at this weird therapy center he runs."

"Is Mitch a wizard, too?" he asked.

I internally cringed. "No, he's a Commoner she met through her church."

"Did he see you shift?" Ben waited, and I externally cringed. He said, "You should let Emma know before he does."

"She already knows." I ran my hands through my hair. "She's really angry at me right now for looking into Mitch."

We sat in disgruntled silence and stared at our shoes. I scuffed at the concrete with the sole of my boot. "I met your grandfather."

Ben flinched as if he'd been struck. "What?"

"I witnessed your attack and can describe the two men, so Trish asked me to join her at a Committee meeting. She's trying to get the Committee to take action on the assaults. I was introduced to Reginald there. He asked how you were doing." I glanced at Ben. "Thanks for the heads-up."

Ben shook his head and glowered at the floor. "You're rushing into the middle of this and dredging up all this shit without understanding what you're getting into. None of this is your problem. I wish you'd stop poking at it before it blows up on us."

"Hey," I growled, "I agreed not to tell anyone about you. I plan on keeping that promise. You have nothing to worry about."

"I'm not worried about you keeping your promises, Alex," he said.

I jabbed my thumb back at myself. "I, on the other hand, have to keep Shortie and the Ox from possibly hurting my best friend while she's determined to date a puritanical jackass who's attempting to scramble her brains if I don't stop him. She's currently furious with me, but I don't know what I'd do if I allowed something to happen to her. She's the sister I never had . . . my family. There's no life for me here without Emma."

Ben looked over at me. "I understand you want to help Emma, but you have to be careful with anything involving the Committee. It's full of bigots. Its whole purpose is to oppress us. It could get dangerous really fast. If anything goes wrong while they check into those guys, they'll fabricate some reason to lay the blame at your feet so they don't look at fault."

I threw my hands up. "But I want to keep Em safe, and I can't do it on my own! If I hadn't met Reginald, I wouldn't know the two guys have altered tethers. I was so wrapped up in chasing them off, I didn't notice that important detail. Reginald thinks it's why Shortie was able to attack me with a spell."

"Altered? What kind of spell did the guy use?"

"The *Hurling Blue Flames at Alex* spell? I have no idea, but it definitely was magic. I could feel it. If you know any way I could defend myself against magical attacks, I'd appreciate you sharing it."

"Instead, would you consider dropping this?" he asked.

"But the guy ruined my favorite jacket!" I stuck my fingers through the hole in the shoulder and wiggled them at Ben.

He looked at my fingers, then me, and began to smile. "It *is* a nice jacket."

"I know you don't want to get into this too deep. I understand the risk. I only need a tip or two if you have them. My current tactic when dealing with those two guys is to run away. That's not sustainable. I don't know many magic users, and Emma isn't talking to me." I paused, then suggested, "I guess I could ask Reginald."

"No, wait. I know someone who specializes in shields." Ben pushed up his shirt sleeve and turned his wrist to expose the underside of his forearm. He tapped his index finger on a pentagram within the artwork tattooed there. "A shield is like a ward you wear. It will deflect most magic-based attacks."

I shook my head. "That's not going to work for me. I can't get tattoos. They fade away within days."

"Sandra has inked lupine before. Her area of magic is protection. She weaves it into the shield."

I chewed at my thumbnail. Yet another person I didn't know who would then know about me. "You trust her?"

He nodded. "With my life."

At this point I didn't have many other options. "Yeah, okay, I'll give it a try. What do I need to do?"

Ben pushed his shirt sleeve back down. "I'll message her to set up the appointment. Part of the power of a shield is its meaning to the wearer. You select a symbol that embodies protection to you."

I nodded. "Okay." I reached over and took a hold of his hand. I knew how it felt to be pulled into a situation you'd rather avoid. "Thanks. I really do appreciate your help with this."

He looked down at our hands and spread his fingers to slip them between my own. The simple act had an immediate effect on me. My pulse jumped. The primal being nesting inside me stirred and stretched. She recognized his scent and was drawn closer by his touch.

When Ben looked at me, golden eyes reflected back in the lenses of his glasses. I leaned forward the few inches needed and kissed him. We parted, and his eyelids were still half-lowered. He was smiling. No further encouragement needed, I kissed him again. My inner wolf pushed forward. She wanted more than a taste of him. It was suddenly hot in the otherwise chilly stairwell. He caught my hand before it slipped beneath his shirt in search of bare skin. The action abruptly reined in my senses. Ashamed by my obvious lack of control, I blurted, "I'm sorry."

Ben smiled, shook his head, and pulled my clawed hand up to place it against his chest. He covered my hands with his. His quickened heartbeat thudded against my palm, and his face was flushed. I smiled despite my embarrassment. "You too?"

"Yeah."

His place was upstairs. I eyed him. "How long is your break?"

He chuckled. "Not long enough."

"Another time, then?" I grinned and stood. A deep inhale and slow exhale helped my hands to slide back into their human form. "I won't keep you any longer."

We walked back through the shop together. Sara had swapped the Smiths album for some Distillers. Ben picked a neon piece of paper up off the counter from among an assortment of fliers. He handed it to me, his eyebrows raised. I took the offered paper. It was an advertisement for an upcoming concert at The Sound Refuge. Derezzed, one of Emma's favorite EDM artists from the West Coast, would be headlining.

Ben wrote on the notepad, *A way to begin amends with Emma?*

I smiled, imagining her excitement. "She is going to lose her mind when she sees this. Maybe I'll send it to Anne, and she can let Emma know about it." I read the name of the opening act. "Wait, Ben, is this you playing beforehand?" I looked up, and he grinned.

Sara leaned on the counter and teased, "You'd think they could book some decent, local talent to open for such a well-known act."

Ben replied to her comment with a smirk and threw in a middle finger for good measure. The younger woman winked and returned the gesture as I laughed.

I folded over the piece of paper, shoved it into my back pocket, and raised my hand awkwardly. "See you soon, then?"

He nodded, raising a hand. Sara waved goodbye. "Later, Alex."

When I exited Rear Window, I snapped a photo of the same flier posted in the front window. I sent it off to Anne with a request to forward it to Emma. If Anne sent an invitation, Emma may actually go and enjoy herself. By the time I returned to my apartment, Anne had sent back a reply.

*I'm not going to be a mediator. We can talk tonight after I'm off work.*

BEN MESSAGED ME later that day. *Meet me at Thread the Needle tonight at 10:00.*

Anne called as I left for the tattoo parlor that evening. After an unhelpful synopsis of her earlier text messages, including how utterly irrational I was acting, she fell silent. I wasn't sure if she'd spoken her peace or run out of breath.

"I'm afraid something really terrible is happening and we're going to lose her," I said.

"That isn't a reason to break the law," Anne said. "Why didn't you come to me?"

"I did."

"Okay, I admit I dropped the ball. I told you I'd set something up for the four of us and I didn't," Anne said. "I'll send Emma the concert information for Derezzed and let her know we'd like her to bring Mitch. I want to meet him. You, for the sake of your friendship with her, want to give him a second chance."

"I'm not sure Em will want to give *me* a second chance." Saying the words caused a pang in my chest. "She's never been this angry with me."

"I know."

We ended our call, and I drove to Thread the Needle to meet Ben. The tattoo parlor was located above a bar. When I reached the door, I read the shop hours and noticed the closing time had been a couple of hours prior. I got my phone out to message Ben but stopped. His tall silhouette approached from down the sidewalk.

"Hi there." I pointed to the hours posted on the door. "They're closed. Think we could try again tomorrow?"

He stepped up into the doorway, pressed a button by the door, and waved at the security camera mounted above the doorway. The door lock buzzed. Ben opened the door and motioned for me to follow. We climbed a narrow, creaking staircase to a second-floor landing. The name of the parlor was etched on the glass of a door left ajar at the top of the stairs. Ben lightly knocked a few times before he pushed the door open.

A middle-aged woman with waves of salt and pepper hair falling past her round face walked across the small lobby to greet us with a large warm smile. "Hello, Ben. Good to see you again. It's been too long. Come in, come in." She waved us into the shop and closed the door. Her flowing dress and lace shawl allowed us a glimpse of the colorful tattoos covering her arms and legs. The majority of the artwork portrayed plants and insects. Like Ben's, the designs wove seamlessly together into a tapestry. A fragrance of vanilla and lavender lingered around her. She turned to me. "You must be Alex? I'm Sandra."

I offered a hand. "Nice to meet you. Thank you for working so fast and fitting me in on such short notice."

"You're welcome." She shook my hand. "Ben told me what symbol you've chosen. I have a few designs for you to review." Sandra walked behind a display case showcasing body jewelry for sale. She retrieved a folder from beneath the case and set it atop the glass surface. Within the folder were three different sheets of paper.

Each page displayed a different, beautifully rendered interpretation of the moon. My eye was immediately drawn to the design in the center, created in rich black ink with white ink accents. The composition contained a full moon flanked by a waxing crescent moon on the left and a waning crescent moon on the right. The detailing was skillfully nuanced, causing the moon to stand out against a charcoal-like swatch of dark sky. I placed my finger on the page and looked up at Sandra. "This one."

Sandra waved Ben toward the row of chairs across the small lobby. "Ben, you know where to find a drink if you want one. We'll call if we need anything." She picked up the design. "Come along with me, Alex. I'll get the stencil made and we'll be ready to start." She pushed aside a long, heavy curtain, and I followed her along a hallway deeper into the shop.

We walked past a couple rooms before turning into one. I asked, "Ben said you've done this before for people like me?"

She clarified, "Lupine?"

My face warmed, the word still feeling odd when said aloud in reference to me. "Yes."

Sandra gave me a kind smile. "Yes, among others. If Patricia Drake doesn't bring them in, most lupine eventually find their way to my parlor. The Committee doesn't always uphold its promise of protection equally. I offer my gift to fill the gap." She motioned for me to take a seat in a reclined chair.

"Have more people been looking for your help because of the recent attacks?" I settled into the chair.

"Yes. More wizards than usual." She rolled a stool over beside my chair and sat down. "Can you show me exactly where you would like to wear your shield?"

"Would it work here?" I placed my fingers near the top of my breastbone. She nodded, and I unbuttoned the front of my shirt. Sandra prepped the area of skin as I asked, "How long have you been creating shields for people?"

"It's been many years. Ever since I moved here from the West Coast as a younger woman. The focus of my magic is protection, so it's a natural fit." She turned the stool to begin preparing her equipment. "When did you arrive in Hopewell?"

"I've been here for almost three years. I mostly keep to myself."

Sandra glanced at me. "Ben says he met you through a mutual acquaintance. Another wizard?"

"Yes." An ache pinged in my chest. "Emma is like a sister."

"It's rare for lupine to say that about wizards. It's nice to hear."

Sandra turned back toward me. She handed me a mirror and placed the stencil. I nodded my approval, and she transferred the design to my skin. "Would you mind sharing with me why you chose this symbol? It will allow me to fortify the shield even more."

I hesitated. A sudden wave of homesickness hit me. "I know it seems pretty cliché since the moon amplifies a werewolf's gift. But the symbol reminds me of my grandmother."

"Was she the family member to pass her gift on to you?" Sandra asked.

"Actually, no. That was my grandfather. My grandmother and I are really close, though. She pretty much raised me since my parents worked a lot and my grandfather passed when I was still a kid," I said. "Her name is Lunella."

"Thank you, Alex." Sandra's voice and smile lulled me into relaxing back into the chair. "Is there anything you need before we begin?"

I shook my head. She applied ointment over the prepared skin. As she turned the machine on, I barely felt the gentle shift in the air around us. Sandra's needle was swift and sure as she expertly rendered the artwork in ink. I tried to keep my mind busy listening to her so I didn't focus on the pain. The soft singsong words of her spell were slightly audible above the needle's buzz. As the image took form, an additional sensation beyond the bite of the needle flowed into my body. Tendrils of warmth unfurled beneath my skin from the freshly inked area. They fastened up over each side of my collarbone and around my chest, as if to form an unseen breastplate.

Sandra finished the linework and shading within a couple of hours. She handed me the small mirror again to review the work. I placed my fingers on the halo of reddened skin around the artwork. "This is beautiful. Thank you."

"You're welcome, Alex." She gave me instructions on how to care for the tattoo, the timeline drastically shortened because of my body's accelerated healing. She assured me it would not disappear. After dressing the wound, she walked me back to the parlor's front room. Ben looked up from a small paperback he'd been reading. He closed the book and stood, his eyebrows raised in question.

I grinned. "I love it."

On the way back to my place, I was in better spirits than earlier. The beautiful design etched under my skin provided me some comfort. Maybe because it made me feel even closer to my grandmother. Or maybe I felt more prepared and protected if I ran into Shortie again.

I called Nate from my car. "Are you available for another stakeout tomorrow night?"

He chuckled. "I realize you're new to the criminal lifestyle, but this is where we put our feet up and let things cool off before going out again."

"No illegal stuff. Emma has these evening meetings at her church. I want to hang out and make sure Shortie and the Ox don't show up for her." If those two did turn up, I wouldn't mind having Nate along to help deal with them.

"Yeah, all right," he said. "You driving?"

"Sure. I'll call before I'm on my way to pick you up."

I left my car and climbed the stairs to my apartment. A message from Anne popped up on my phone. *She said you can come only because you agreed to give Mitch another chance. Otherwise, she doesn't want you there.*

It was going to be extremely difficult to be polite to Mitch, especially with what I knew he'd written in Emma's patient file. I sent off my reply. *I'll see you at the show.*

When I opened the door and walked in, my boot landed on an envelope. I crouched to pick it up and frowned. The name and address of my landlord was in the upper-left hand corner. I already knew the contents of the envelope before I opened it. It was a warning letter stating my rent was overdue, therefore violating the terms of my lease. I had seven days to supply the payment, or my lease would be terminated.

# 12

THE NEXT EVENING, Nate and I sat in my dark car and watched the glowing entryway of Patterson Street Church. Mitch's car, Emma's car, and several others were in the lot across the street.

Nate looked up at the steeple, lit with floodlights, as if it were the main attraction at a carnival. "Take a guess at how many churches are down here."

I shrugged. "I don't know. Judging by the Committee size, a dozen? I've never given it much thought."

"Nearly twenty. Not all of them have representatives on the Committee. Some refuse to be a part of it." He looked over at me. "Hopewell's entire lupine population barely fills one of those churches, yet those bastards are constantly grasping for more control over us. You should hear some of the things Trish says the Commoner reps ask for." He shook his head and looked out the car window to the entryway of the building again. "She doesn't tell me everything because she knows how pissed I'll get. I wish I could support her more with the Committee, but I can't stomach it. She's so much stronger than me."

"At least she has Reginald to stand with her," I said. "The two seem to get along well."

Nate looked back at me and smirked. "That pompous ass? He only cares about his own. I've suggested to Trish we permanently cut ties with the Committee. We wouldn't be the only supernatural group flying solo around here."

"I've never met any of the others," I said. In fact, I wasn't sure how many supernatural creatures shared the city with us. "Have you?"

He nodded and scratched behind his ear. "A few. Trish has a vampire she'll tap for information now and then. The fae are scattered around. The place is lousy with gremlins and other sprites."

"I had no idea there were so many different . . . types. Like us." And another layer hidden deeper than my life as a werewolf.

"They keep a low profile," Nate said. "If those groups are able to pull off going alone, I know the wolves could."

"Why doesn't Trish want the wolves to separate from the Committee for good?" I asked.

"She thinks everyone is safer when we stick close to people who might hurt us. We survive by playing along with their ridiculous rules. It leaves them no ground to stand on when they're still not happy about us living here." Nate looked out the window again and narrowed his eyes. He leaned forward and used his jacket sleeve to wipe steam from the glass. "Are those your guys?"

I spotted two figures lurking outside the patch of light cast on the sidewalk by the glass-walled lobby and entryway. The drastic difference in their heights gave Shortie and the Ox away. "Yes." I reached for the car door handle.

Nate grabbed my forearm. "Sit tight. Let's see what they're up to first."

A small group of people gathered in the lobby. The doors opened, and Emma exited with four others, leaving Mitch inside talking on his phone. My pulse skyrocketed, and my attention darted to Shortie and the Ox.

From our viewpoint, their breath escaping as occasional wisps of steam was the only indication that they weren't statues. Neither of them made a move toward Emma. Were they hesitant because she was with other people?

Not noticing or not caring about the two strangers, the small group crossed the street together. I recognized one of the men. "That older guy is William, the pastor here. He was at the Committee meeting." All of the cars except for Mitch's left the parking lot.

Shortie and the Ox approached the doors of the church. I frowned, my hand tightening on the door handle, and glanced at Nate. He focused on the two men. I noticed a similar coiled tension in his body that I'd witnessed in Trish's when she was at my apartment. Unlike her, he trembled as he held himself in check. His breath came in short bursts through his nose. Shortie and the Ox walked into the lobby. Mitch looked at the two and started to talk with them.

I released the door handle. "What the hell?" Maybe my stunt in the parking lot of Mitch's condo building wasn't a rescue. Instead of being a hero and saving Mitch, I'd unknowingly made a pest of myself and interrupted a meeting.

Mitch's gestures grew increasingly animated as he yelled at the two men. Shortie's reply appeared more collected. Mitch nodded and ran his free hand through his hair. He reached into his jacket and withdrew an envelope he handed to Shortie. By the time I thought to get out my phone and capture some video evidence, Shortie and the Ox exited the building.

I tracked the two in the rearview mirror. They moved down the sidewalk and toward the center of downtown. "I'm going to follow them and see where they're going next." I glanced at Nate. "Want to come along?" Mitch I could find at any time. Shortie and the Ox were more slippery.

"Of course." Nate flashed his pointy-toothed grin. "I'm not going to let you have all the fun."

The wait for Mitch to get to his car and leave so he wouldn't see us seemed agonizingly long. As soon as the car's taillights disappeared, Nate and I jumped out of my car and pursued Shortie and the Ox on foot. I could barely make them out down the street. We broke into an easy run along the buildings' shadows to close the distance. The stink of Shortie's cologne grew stronger, but we lost sight of them when the street ended at an intersection.

I stopped in the shadow of a large building on the corner and looked up and down the sidewalk of the main street. I felt Nate near me, waiting for my lead. I pointed across the street. "Right up there." The two men traveled along the sidewalk as if they were out for an evening stroll. "They're heading into a busier area. It's going to be well lit down there."

Nate shrugged. "It's your call, Alex."

"If they lead us back to where they're staying, I can keep an eye on them," I said. No more surprises. Plus, I really wanted the envelope. Was Mitch feeding them some type of intel? But the way he'd been yelling at Shortie and the Ox, Mitch must be more than an informant to them.

Nate nodded and pulled up his hood. "Let's go, then."

We turned the corner and continued along the main street at a more casual pace. Shortie and the Ox walked together with only an occasional exchange of words. We followed them through a pedestrian walkway downtown, past some shops, restaurants, and a crowded outdoor ice-skating rink. Nate and I remained a block behind them. Between the strong fumes of Shortie's cologne and the Ox's towering stature, I was able to track them.

The crowd thinned as we approached one of the bridges spanning the river that cleaved Hopewell in half. Since there weren't other pedestrians to blend in with, we waited for the two to cross before we even started over the bridge. On the opposite bank of the river, a large carousel lit up the city's museum's windows. Beyond the museum was a large hotel.

"They must be staying over there." I expected the men to pass the museum to the hotel, but instead, they turned left off the sidewalk before reaching the museum. They descended a set of stairs to a riverfront walkway that ran perpendicular to and underneath the bridge.

Nate muttered a curse as the men vanished from our line of sight again. We lengthened our strides and eventually broke into a jog to finish crossing the bridge.

Nate's voice sounded behind me. "I'll take the opposite stairwell." He broke to the right to cross the street. Another set of stairs, mirroring the one Shortie and the Ox had used, led down from the sidewalk to the same riverfront walkway.

I slowed as I drew close to the staircase the men had taken. Even with my newly minted shield, my confidence that this was a good idea was dwindling. But I'd pulled Nate into this, and he'd already started down the other stairs. It was too late for second-guessing.

At the top of the staircase, a dose of adrenaline caused my body to tremble. My inner wolf sensed the possible danger, and she stirred inside me. Knuckles popped as my hands distorted, unbidden, and grew curved claws. Without my prompting, my vision brightened. The smell of cologne strengthened. I slunk down the staircase one silent footfall at a time, straining to hear anything over the water from the river and ambient noise of the city at night.

An eruption of shouts and snarls reached up to me from the riverfront walkway under the bridge. Shortie and the Ox must have been waiting for us. Hurrying down the remaining steps, I felt a violent wrenching of energy from the air. I spotted Nate and the other two beneath the bridge before a flash of blinding light blew out my night vision. I shook my head and rubbed at the dark spots obscuring my vision. Blinking rapidly, I glimpsed Shortie dash toward me. I dropped into a crouch and readied myself, struggling against my inner wolf's desire to lunge ahead, take him down, and open him up.

Another rushing sensation from the air around me, Shortie's spell preparation, was interrupted by a grotesque ripping sound. His face contorted into a grimace. Shortie stumbled forward to his hands and knees on the paved walkway. The aroma of fresh blood reached me. I clenched my teeth against the immediate urge to leap atop the fallen man. Nate stood behind Shortie, his eyes the color of liquid copper and his distorted hands ending in bloodied claws.

The looming figure of the Ox lurched toward Nate. With my night vision restored, I dashed forward past Shortie and toward the other two. Nate instinctively crouched as the Ox swung wide where my friend previously stood. Turning on his knee, Nate swiped upward into the towering man with his claws. The awful tearing noise of cloth and flesh sounded again. The Ox gave an animal-like bellow of pain and pawed at his injured side.

Glowing eyes tracked me as I passed the Ox. So, not a wizard as I'd originally thought, but more than likely a werewolf. That explained his quick recovery in the alleyway with Ben and his ability to crunch my car like tinfoil. But why hadn't I picked up a scent? I should have noticed it.

I leapt up onto the railing along the pathway and then sprang onto the back of the Ox. Hooking my arm around his throat, I held tight as he spun and reached for me. The odor of all the blood made my entire body buzz. An odd haze crept in around the edges of my mind. I tightened my jaw, as if it would hold back the beast inside me, and doubled my efforts to stay focused on taking down the Ox.

Nate had seized the opportunity to open another gash in the larger man's side. The Ox caught Nate's arm this time, effortlessly pulling Nate off his feet and pitching him against the metal railing edging the walkway. Nate's body collided with and flipped over the top bar. He scrambled and caught the bar with one hand while the rest of his weight fell with a dull clang against the outside of the railing above the rushing water of the river.

I drew up my knees and braced them against the Ox's back. It gave me more leverage to tighten my hold around his neck as I huddled against him. He grasped back at me in an attempt to pull me off. I made myself as small a target as possible. Finally, he stumbled, and his flailing weakened. The Ox slowly sank down to a knee. His large mass teetered. I released my hold and scurried out of the way before he collapsed, unconscious, over onto his side.

With the Ox out of play for now, I turned my attention back to Shortie. His hands hovered above his injured legs as a rippling blanket of blue flames enveloped his limbs. The rank stench of singed skin made me gag. He was trying to cauterize the gashes.

Nate grabbed the railing with his other hand and hoisted himself upward. His boot found the bottom rung of the railing, and he hopped back over onto the walkway. He jogged over to me. Rubbing at and rotating his shoulder, he nodded at Shortie. "Do you want him conscious?"

"I think so." If possible, I wanted him to answer some questions. I had a feeling he wasn't going to be as cooperative as I'd like. We started cautiously toward him, and I suppressed another gag as the stink of the burnt skin strengthened.

Shortie looked up as he heard us approach. He raised a palm toward us. "Don't come any closer!"

Nate and I both halted. "What has Mitch hired you to do?" I asked.

Shortie winced, his raised hand unsteady. "Like I said before, it isn't any of your business."

"Why would a wizard and a wolf take marching orders from a Commoner?" I said. "What could he offer the two of you? Is it money?"

Shortie's chuckle was as gravelly as his voice. "You're determined to be a part of this, aren't you? We can do that. Maybe we'll take you off his hands for free."

Nate snorted beside me. "You're wasting time. Our large friend was pretty vocal. I'm sure someone has called this in by now." As if on signal, police sirens sounded east of us from the main downtown area.

I gave the sirens an irritated glance before I looked back at Shortie. "This is your last chance to talk before the police show up. I'm sure Mitch will be thrilled when he has to pick you two up from the station."

Shortie scowled.

I smiled. "Tell us what you were hired to do, and we'll help you avoid the police."

He shifted his weight and finally lowered his hand. "Get me outta here and away from the cops first. Then I'll talk."

I walked the remaining steps to where he lay prone on the sidewalk. His clumsy attempt to "heal" his legs had slowed the bleeding. I offered my hand, and Shortie eyed my claws before he accepted it. He looked up at me, exposing the cross-like brand marking his throat. As Reginald had noticed in my memories, Shortie's tether had been embellished with additional symbols. My eyes widened in realization. "It's your tether, isn't it? Mitch had it altered so you can cast magic again. Did he promise to free you from it once you're done working for him?"

Shortie's grip tightened. He yanked me forward, almost causing me to fall atop of him. Energy was ripped from the air, and flames licked the palm of his other hand. I jerked my forearm up to protect my face and closed my eyes. He uttered a single word. A roaring sound and an incredible amount of heat enveloped me. A strange tingling sensation spread across my body, and a searing pain burned on my breastbone where my shield lay. The odd sound faded, and I opened my eyes. Shock and confusion were frozen on Shortie's face.

"Holy shit!" Nate rushed to my side. "Are you okay?"

Shortie and I stared at each other in disbelief a moment longer. He released my hand and floundered to turn over and scramble to his feet. With a snarl, I flipped him onto his back again and used my knee to pin his shoulder to the scorched and blood-smeared pavement. I reached inside his jacket and yanked out the envelope.

"Alex, you're cutting this a bit close. Let's not push our luck here." Nate looked up to where flashing lights were approaching from down the street. "I enjoy visiting the boys at the station, but not more than once a week."

I pocketed the envelope. Shortie and the Ox would have to deal with the police on their own. Nate and I quickly retreated down the riverfront walkway, away from the bridge. We put a block behind us before the police cars arrived. A pedestrian bridge got us back across the river, and we reentered the heart of downtown before our gait slowed to a natural walk.

"You all right?" Nate asked.

I nodded, but my body intermittently shook as it crashed from its adrenaline rush.

His bloodied hands were discreetly tucked into the pockets of his hoodie. "I thought your ass was toast back there. I'd already started putting together an apology to Trish in my head. How long have you had your shield?"

My voice trembled. "I got it yesterday."

He gave a low whistle. "Sandra for the save, yet again."

"You know her?"

"Yeah, of course." Nate grinned. "All the lupine do. We refer to her as the Good Witch. Trish takes the new kids to see her."

My next question sounded like an accusation. "Then why in the hell did I have to pry my invitation to meet her out of Ben? I told you guys there was a wizard trying to blast me with blue flame spells!"

He shrugged. "You must have already had an appointment when Trish called. Lucky for us, it was before tonight." He wiped his hands clean on the t-shirt beneath his hoodie. "So, the big guy is a wolf. The wizard must have been cloaking his scent."

"I wondered why I hadn't noticed he was one of us."

"And you think Mitch is promising to remove their tethers as payment?" He shook his head. "I don't know. If I were those two and could already cheat my tether, I'd kill Mitch and get the hell out of town."

I thought of the altered brand I'd seen on Shortie's throat. "I don't think they're cheating their tethers." If it was a permanent fix, why would they have bothered with Ben? "The tether was modified with extra marks in the design. Maybe they're not really free of it yet. What if there are strings attached?"

Nate snorted. "That sounds more likely. Give them a taste of what they're missing to make sure they follow through with the job." He held up a finger. "The more interesting question is, who did Mitch get to alter the tether and then remove it when the job is done? Trish says tethers are a complex spell, so the wizard would sling strong magic."

I shrugged. "Reginald is the only wizard I know like that, but then again, I don't know many wizards beyond Emma."

"Nah. He's the guy who slaps tethers *onto* people around here. It'd be too obvious." Nate fished out a cigarette and a lighter. "And why would a wizard stick his or her neck out for a Commoner?"

"You said it yourself: For the right amount of money, a wizard isn't above being bribed. Mitch White is a walking trust fund."

"Good point." Nate stopped at an entryway of a closed shop to escape the wind. The flicker of the flame lit his features briefly. "What do you think you're going to do next?"

I stopped beside him. "I'm not sure yet. I'm still processing all of this."

"Keep your ear to the ground in case those two goons file a report and pull the police into the whole mess," he said.

"Why would they do that? They'd have to identify themselves."

"If Mitch has invested the right amount into the police department, that may not matter. It's always a toss-up on where the Commoners' law enforcement lands in situations like these. Another option is to permanently remove those two. Otherwise, they'll be getting in the way while you puzzle out what's happening with Emma."

I frowned. "I'm not going to kill them, Nate."

"They're tethered. You get a pass on the rules." He shrugged and exhaled a stream of smoke. "It's up to you, but you're naive if you think they'll be as considerate. That wizard attempted to torch you. I'm sure he won't hesitate if he gets the chance to try again."

"Yeah, I know." Still, I couldn't take a life. My inner wolf, though, she never gave it a second thought. "But it's not who I am."

Nate grinned. "Yet."

I studied him. A nagging suspicion had been forming in the back of my mind ever since we were arrested. "Why are you doing this?"

"Doing what? Smoking?" He shrugged. "There are worse habits to—"

"Why are you and Trish doing so much to help me? I hope you're not expecting money, because I'm broke." I frowned again. "And I don't like owing people favors."

"You're a wolf. We look out for each other. It's what we do."

Was it that simple? Trish had said the same thing. Being among the other werewolves at Hell's Bells had felt so natural, so . . . normal. I shook my head. "There has to be more to it than that."

Nate pointed back across the river with his cigarette. "Why did you take the chance at getting nuked over there for that envelope you're carrying?"

"You know why." I was getting tired of justifying my actions. "I want to know what Mitch is doing to Emma and the rest of our people so I can stop him."

"I'm sorry . . ." Nate cupped his free hand to his ear and leaned forward. "Mitch is doing to Emma and *who*?" He waited with raised eyebrows.

"That's different." I growled even as my face grew warm, knowing it wasn't much different at all. "I thought he was harming Emma, but then found out he's possibly hurting a lot more people like us. We shouldn't be targeted for being different. Now I feel responsible for everyone."

"Why?" He shrugged and leaned back. "Fuck them. You don't know them."

I gritted my teeth.

"Listen, sometimes people are simply there for each other," he said. "Our community is here for you. Trish and I are here for you. If and when you choose to give back is your choice. No one is keeping score or expecting payment." Nate dropped the remains of his cigarette and ground it out with his boot. He stepped back out of the entryway. "Let's get to the car and go home. My shoulder needs a drink."

I DROPPED NATE off at Hell's Bells. He invited me in, but I declined the offer. The only thing on my mind was getting back to my apartment and opening the envelope. I promised to send a message afterward to let him and Trish know what I'd found.

At home, I got myself a beer and settled onto the couch. I tore open the blank envelope and withdrew its contents. My eyebrows raised as I counted through a stack of high-value bills. The sum would cover my rent, food, and gas expenses for at least the next eight months. I wondered if the amount was as valuable to Shortie and the Ox. Would they come looking for it?

Setting the bills aside, I also found a folded map of Hopewell. Locations were highlighted in green, along with several orange marks. Both The Village Pub and The Beacon were circled in green. Trish's club was highlighted in orange. Several other locations I hadn't visited were flagged. I ran a finger over the map to find Ben's apartment. It was thankfully clear of any markings. Then I noticed dozens of blue marks in the residential neighborhoods. My heart stuttered. The house with my apartment was highlighted in blue.

My gaze jumped to the front door. Had I locked it? Holding my breath, I strained to hear any trace of movement. Nothing. The envelope and map forgotten on the table, I slowly stood, shut off the main light, and padded over to the windows. My fingertips caught the edge of the curtain and I cautiously pushed it aside. Only the dark, snow-spackled street and the occasional pool of light from the streetlamp were outside.

I thought of the go bag stashed in my bedroom. It's something I'd had since the day I was forced from my parents' home. Ten minutes, and I could be on the highway with Hopewell in the rearview. A long, rumbling growl sounded inside my chest. No, there wouldn't be any running away this time. I couldn't leave Emma and the others with Mitch.

Returning to the sofa, I snapped a photo of the map. I sent a message with the photo to Nate. *It's a map identifying our homes and community spaces*. I didn't mention the money, but I counted out my rent payment and sealed it in another envelope. If anyone came looking for the missing cash, I could pay it back at that time. Hopefully.

My phone rang. Startled, I almost dropped the second envelope. "Hello?"

"Trish is making calls to arrange a meeting with select stooges from the Committee as soon as possible," Nate said. "She wants you to come over and talk to them about what we learned tonight. When a day is locked in, she'll let you know when to be here."

"Of course. I'll be there." The fact Shortie and the Ox had been carrying around a map with my apartment highlighted made it personal. If Mitch was willing to pay criminals ridiculous amounts of money to work for him, I wouldn't put it past the blond jerk to send Shortie and the Ox after me.

# 13

AFTER BEN GOT out of work at the record store the next day, we bundled up with hats and scarves and walked to The Sound Refuge. It was already quite cold. The wind found its way down between the buildings to blast past us and leave swirling snow in its wake. I bumped playfully into Ben as we walked. "Are you nervous? The performer you're opening for is a pretty big deal."

If he was, he was doing an excellent job of hiding it. He took his hand from his pocket and signed, "No." He glanced over and pointed at me with raised brows.

My anxiety had increased throughout the day. "Yeah, I am." Now that I knew Mitch was working with a pair of hired thugs and somehow "treating" supernatural beings at his clinic, I wasn't sure how I could be civil toward him. "Emma is giving me a second chance, but I'm not feeling confident I can pull it off."

When we arrived at the venue, Ben had to leave to set up his equipment. I reached out for his hand. "Hey, good luck. I'm looking forward to your set."

He smiled, signed, "Thank you," and released my hand to head for the door to the performance space.

I grabbed a drink and settled into a booth near the front windows. It was early enough in the evening that the place was still fairly quiet; only a handful of patrons were scattered among the booths and tables. I looked out the window for some possible people-watching to take my mind off my nerves. The wind had died down, and full, lazy snowflakes were falling. With the booth sitting against the large window, I felt like I was in a snow globe. Anne approached from down the sidewalk and raised a hand in greeting as she passed.

At the booth, she pulled off her scarf and hat. "Hi!" Her cheeks were rosy, and the fragrances of the freshly fallen snow and winter air lingered on her jacket. "Thanks for coming early so I can remind you about playing nice with others. I also have some news to share." She slid into the seat opposite me. There were shadows under her bloodshot eyes.

"Have you been stressing over this as much as I have?"

"I'm not sure that's possible." She gave a tired smile. "Work is not letting up. Our missing persons caseload is increasing. We've also been struggling to catch a break on these assaults. But between your pin, Emma ID'ing that group, and some off-the-clock hours, I think I have a lead."

"Have I told you you're amazing?" I wished I could pull in Anne on Shortie and the Ox, too. She'd probably find out who they were faster than Reginald could.

"Yes, but I don't mind hearing it again. Like Emma confirmed, the symbol you sketched for me is an emblem for a group calling themselves the Noble Sons. It's a national organization."

"Em said the group was formed at Patterson Street Church," I said. "Is that a local chapter?"

Anne nodded. "Exactly. There are several states where this group was cited for hate crimes. Instances included harassment, property damage, and at times, assault. All attacks carried a similar theme of 'You don't belong here.' Sound familiar?"

"Yeah, sounds like the jackasses we're dealing with in Hopewell."

"Considering the majority demographic around here," Anne said, "I'm surprised the group hasn't popped up sooner. Membership is limited to men. Most are Caucasian from age sixteen to their sixties. They tend to have nationalistic, conservative-leaning views, especially in regards to women."

"So, a boys' club of insecure man-children." It was the embodiment of my living nightmare. I'd broken a lot of noses attached to men who'd fit those membership requirements.

Anne chuckled. "Exactly. Their mission statement could be 'Founded to Piss Off Alexandria Steward.'"

"And I suppose you can't round the group up and charge every last one of them?"

"Currently, we are far from anything resembling that," she said. "I completed the background research to pitch to my superiors and Detective Grey. I need to convince them this is something we should invest time and resources into."

"How do you not implode while working on these cases?" I asked. "It's frustratingly slow, and there are so many damn rules. You aren't able to protect people because first you have to get a budget passed?"

Anne lifted her eyebrows. "Yes, it's frustrating, but it's also part of my job. I can't do whatever the hell I want, like breaking into a business to get information I need."

Ouch—no fair. I frowned. "It was a momentary lapse of judgment." That had yielded valuable intel about Mitch and The Mind Center.

"It's crazy you got out of those charges. Your accomplice must have been well-connected." Her eyebrows drew together. "How have you been? Are you doing okay?"

The Anne Scan had been activated. I shrugged. "Going to squeak by on rent this month. I really need to get a second job."

"How was the movie you went to after our dinner?"

Confused, I asked, "Movie?"

She tilted her head and chuckled. "That good, huh?"

"Oh, *that* movie." I realized she was referring to my invitation to Ben's place. It seemed like ages ago. "I'm sorry. My worries about Em are taking up a lot of my headspace right now."

Anne nodded. "I understand. We'll get to know Mitch better tonight. Then we can hand over the verdict to Emma."

I gave Anne a smile. She was trying to make me feel better, to validate my concerns, but dealing with Mitch wasn't going to be so simple.

We'd put a pint behind us by the time Emma and Mitch arrived. When she saw Anne, Emma's face lit up. Mitch followed her, brushing the snow from the shoulders of his expensive-looking wool coat. Anne and I both slid out of the booth and stood. Emma encircled Anne in an energetic hug.

"Mitch, this is my friend Anne," Emma said.

Anne smiled and shook his hand. "Nice to meet you, Mitch."

Mitch raised his eyebrows. "Solid, strong handshake. Good to meet you too, Anne."

Emma glanced at me. Her smile faded. "And you've met Alex."

I forced a polite smile for Mitch. "Hello again."

"Hello, Alex." Mitch's smile was near-perfect. "I want you to know I consider what happened at The Mind Center in the past." He put his arm around Emma and gave her a squeeze. "No damage was done. Let bygones be bygones."

Emma beamed up at him. I clenched my jaw. *No, Mitch, you attempted to have us prosecuted to the fullest extent possible, and you were told it wasn't going to happen.* This was a show for Emma. He could've easily pulled me aside to talk in private instead of flaunting his false forgiveness.

As they shed their coats, hats, and scarves, I was startled by Emma's appearance. Her hair was pulled back into a simple ponytail, and her clothes were less, well, "Emma." Both her makeup and jewelry were extremely understated. I glanced over at Anne. She'd noticed as well.

Anne spoke up as the two settled into the booth. "Emma, how've things been?"

Emma gave a laugh and a knowing glance at Mitch. "We've been so, so busy. It's crazy. There's a lot of work to do in Hopewell. It honestly feels a bit overwhelming. I'm glad Mitch joined the team to provide some guidance."

"What's your background, Mitch?" Anne asked.

"Psychotherapy. Emma and I are working on a program for the downtown homeless population. Many don't have access to mental health treatment. We want to change that."

He actually seemed genuine in his concern, which only pissed me off. It'd be much easier to dislike Mitch if he were a straight-up awful person. Emma had been wanting to provide such a program at Another Chance since I'd met her. Now, because of his connections, she was able to achieve that.

I stood. "Can I get some drinks for us?"

Mitch answered, "We can wait for the waitress."

I gave him a thin smile. "You're drinking with the peasantry tonight. It's serve yourself. Anne, a porter? And Emma, an Old Fashioned?" Both nodded.

"I'll take a beer," Mitch said.

I left the booth for the bar. After I placed the drink order, selecting the least-expensive swill possible for Mitch, I looked back across the room as I waited. Mitch sat with his arm possessively around Emma as she spoke with Anne. It took me two trips to return with the drinks, walking back into the middle of the conversation.

"It's all about making good choices, really," Mitch said to Anne. Emma looked down at her folded hands. Anne had both eyebrows raised, nodding slowly as he spoke.

She turned her gaze on me. "Mitch was explaining to me why people find themselves homeless." Her eyes ever-so-slightly widened, and she raised her glass to take a sip of her beer.

"I feel it's more complicated than that, though," Emma said. "Not everyone has been given the same—"

"We've all been given the ability to make our own decisions," Mitch said. "Some people repeatedly choose to make bad choices."

I snorted. "It all sounds so simple when you put it that way. You'd think we'd have homelessness solved by now." Anne gave me a nudge under the table. I asked, "Em, what were you saying?"

Emma looked up and hesitated. She tried again to voice her opinion. "Making bad decisions isn't everyone's story. There are many complex reasons people find themselves caught within poverty."

"Alcoholism, substance abuse, unemployment . . ." Mitch said.

I narrowed my eyes. "Domestic abuse, rape, abandonment—yeah, all pretty bad choices." This time Anne gave me more of a kick than a nudge. I shot her a glare.

"There's no need to get irritated, Alex," Mitch said. "Everyone is entitled to an opinion."

Anger lit in my gut. I didn't dare open my mouth lest an inhuman response slipped out.

Mitch checked his watch and gave Emma a kiss on the cheek. "I'm going to the restroom before the show starts."

As soon as he was out of earshot, Emma scowled across the table. It was the first time she'd looked directly at me since they'd walked in. "Is this what making a genuine effort to get to know him looks like? Arguing with him?"

I leaned forward. "Em, *you* don't agree with that bullshit."

"Emma, you already know so much more than he does about the community you work with," Anne said. "A lot of your effort is going to be spent giving him a reality check. Do you have the time or energy for that?"

She shook her head. "It's complicated. His family is extremely active in our church. Their company, The Mind Center, is offering a lot of the therapy services pro bono that Another Chance wouldn't be able to afford otherwise. He really is a nice person, too. His intentions are good."

"Are you trying to convince us or yourself?" I asked. The words had spilled out before I could stop them.

Emma's complexion reddened. "You're being a bit dramatic, don't you think? You don't know him like I do."

I received another nudge beneath the table from Anne, but I ignored it. "How much do you *really* know about this guy? Not everyone who acts nice is a good person."

"Quit talking to me like I'm an idiot, Alex. Just because I don't immediately distrust people doesn't mean I'm being naive," Emma said.

"Alex and I want to make sure you're safe," Anne said.

Emma's eyes widened, and she looked from Anne to me and back. "Both of you are going to do this?"

Frustrated, I sat back in my seat and looked toward the restrooms. Mitch entered the building through the side door. He returned his phone to his pocket, walking past the men's restroom and a row of pinball machines on his way back to the booth. What'd he been doing? Was there something so urgent he had to make a call this late?

Anne shook her head. "We aren't teaming up against you or Mitch, Emma. Please don't think that. I—" She glanced at me. "*We* truly wanted to spend some time with you both and give him a fair chance."

I admired Anne's effort to include me, but I knew I'd already fallen short of Emma's expectations tonight. My revised goal was to make it to the end of the evening without losing my temper with Mitch, and to find out what that phone call was about.

Mitch and his perfect smile rejoined us at the booth. "Time for the show?" I gritted my teeth. He looked around at us all before he rubbed Emma's shoulder and asked her, "Is everything okay?"

She slid from the booth. "Yes."

"Everything okay with you, Mitch?" I asked. "Work bothering you during off hours?"

His brows drew together, and his smile wavered. "I'm sorry?"

Emma glanced at me with a frown. She linked her arm with Mitch's and smiled up at him. "Wait until you hear this artist. She's amazing." They walked toward the back venue.

Anne spoke as we followed several paces behind. "As a suggestion, try not saying anything to either of them. I think your safest bet for the rest of the night is to smile and nod."

I smiled and nodded, which made her laugh.

The crowd was already fairly large when we entered the back venue. It wasn't long before the show started. Anne, Emma, and I took to the dance floor and left Mitch to wait at its edge. Emma began to smile and then laugh as she danced. The tightness in my chest loosened. There were still glimmers of Emma in there.

Ben was a tall, lanky silhouette on the stage as the tempo picked up. He wove spoken audio from film throughout the layered music. The pulsing of the music's beat was visually magnified by lighting. Emma, Anne, and I were soon nestled snugly between other dancing figures on the packed floor. The show must have sold out because of the main act.

After the final song and applause, the house music and low lighting of the venue came back up. The three of us wove through the heat of the crowd to the stage. Emma caught Ben's attention with a wave. He returned the gesture and signed something. She nodded and looked at Anne and me. "He has to move his equipment and then he'll join us."

We met Mitch at the back edge of the dance floor. He smiled at Emma. "I didn't know you liked dancing so much."

Fanning herself, Anne grinned. "Nonstop, this woman! Somehow it recharges her."

Emma laughed, her eyes bright. "This music and dancing always make me so happy."

"You don't find the music to be really repetitive? I had a hard time telling one song from the next." Mitch continued to smile, but Emma's dimmed.

"The more familiar you become with the genre, the more you can pick up on the nuances," Anne said. "Since you don't really know anything about this music, it's understandable you couldn't tell the difference."

Mitch's smile cooled. I scratched at my nose to hide my grin. Anne's tolerance for Mitch seemed to be waning. Good.

"If you ever want to learn more about EDM, though," she pointed at Emma, "this lady is an expert."

Emma looked past us and grinned. Her hand shot in the air and she gave an excited wave. I turned. Ben attempted to make his way to us through the crowd. People stopped him every few steps. He repeatedly signed his thanks to what must have been compliments. Finally, he arrived beside me with a friendly grin and a small wave of greeting to the whole group.

Ben's scent, strengthened by the hot room and his sweat, filled my nose. My wolf's defensive stance relaxed and a pleasant warmth flushed through my body. We wondered how salty Ben's skin would taste right now. If there was some dark corner where we could find out. I promptly lowered my eyes, but I couldn't stop her from taking another slow inhale.

Mitch's voice was more effective than a cold shower. "I'm Mitch White, a close friend of Emma's." He offered his hand to Ben. "Nice to meet you."

Ben nodded and accepted the handshake.

"Ben and I met at Another Chance," Emma said. "I happened to be in an ASL class. He helped me through my homework."

Mitch snapped his fingers and pointed at Ben. "Yes, now I remember Emma mentioning you. Would you ever consider returning to teach an introduction to ASL as a community class? We're currently constructing a model for those who receive Another Chance's services to then lend their talents to give back."

I looked at Ben. I'd thought he was a volunteer at Another Chance with Emma, not a client.

Emma gave Ben an apologetic look, signing to him. I recognized the sign for "sorry." Ben signed back his reply before he gave Mitch a grin and a thumbs up. Emma's face reddened. Mitch looked expectantly at her. She gave a small smile. "He says thank you for offering and he'll think about it."

Ben tapped my shoulder with the back of his hand. He curled his other hand into a C shape and lifted it to his mouth, his eyebrows raised in question.

I nodded. "Yes, please."

We left the group to walk up to the second bar situated back in the venue. As we waited in line, I gave Ben a nudge with my elbow. "You were really good again tonight. I liked watching you up there."

Grinning, he signed his thanks. He took out his phone and rapidly punched in a message. *Something I love to do. You all look amazing from up there. Like a massive creature moving around the floor. You're all part of the music for me.*

"It felt great to be dancing with Em and Anne." The ache caused by my arguments with Emma flared in my chest. I must not have been hiding the hurt well because Ben gave my shoulder a gentle squeeze. "What do you think of Mitch?" I asked.

He typed into his phone. *First impression: I don't like him. Don't care if people know I needed Another Chance. But someone else might? Told her he's clueless or an ass.*

Now if only Emma could see that. We ordered our drinks and rejoined the group.

Mitch checked his watch and looked at Emma. "We shouldn't stay too much longer. We have an early morning tomorrow."

I glared at Mitch as Anne asked, "Emma, you don't plan on watching the show? She's one of your favorite artists."

Emma looked at Mitch, uncertain. "We'll stay for a bit. I'd like to hear the first few songs at least."

The lights went down, and the crowd roared a welcome. A steady beat thrummed from the stage. Anne reached out and snatched Emma's hand. She smiled as Anne took her out onto the floor. Ben and I followed, and all four of us joined the dancing mass of people moving like a heartbeat in time to the music. I grinned as Emma became energized by the music she loved so much. It made me miss her more than ever.

We were several songs in before I spotted Mitch signaling to Emma from the edge of the floor. Frustration burned in my stomach as she danced away toward Mitch and playfully twirled up to him. He wasn't smiling. He took one of her wrists from above her head, pulled it down, and drew her nearer to him. Her smile waned, and she lowered her other hand as he continued to speak near her ear.

The snarl sprung up out of me before I could stop it. Thankfully the music's volume overpowered the sound. I glanced at Anne. She had stopped dancing and watched the two with a frown. Not having a fraction of Anne's patience, I pushed my way through the crowd on the dance floor toward Mitch and Emma. My hearing allowed me to parse out his words before I reached the two.

"If she's your favorite artist, don't you have her albums? You could listen to her some other time?" Mitch said. "You're the director of an organization now. These people don't have a presentation first thing tomorrow morning."

"Is everything okay, Em?" I asked.

Mitch looked at me, frowned, and released Emma's wrist. "We're fine."

"She can speak for herself." I glared at him. The creature inside me reacted to my growing anger. I wrestled with keeping her at bay.

"Yes, I can speak for myself." Emma said to me, her brows drawn together. "Go away, Alex."

I flinched and looked from Emma's angry expression to Mitch. *Now* he was smiling. My inner wolf lunged. I pushed forward past Emma and seized Mitch by the front of his finely tailored shirt. "You manipulative jackass."

Both Emma's and Mitch's eyes widened. Emma's voice rose. "What are you doing? Stop!"

"Why don't you tell her the real reason you didn't press charges against Nate and me?" I lifted Mitch to stand him on the front tips of his leather shoes. "It wasn't out of the kindness of your heart, was it? You didn't have a choice."

Emma's rounded eyes turned to Mitch. "What?"

Mitch tried to pry my fingers loose from his shirt. His face had reddened and his tone was sharp. "No, I didn't. Why? Because the criminals you associate with must have bribed the police."

"Whoa!" Anne was at my side, a hand on my arm. "Alex, let go of him. Right now."

I released Mitch. His weight dropped back onto his heels and he took a step away. He straightened the collar of his shirt, his usual charming smile replaced by naked anger. He glanced at Anne. "Are you on their payroll, too? Is that why you set this up? To frame me as some sort of monster in front of Emma?"

Anne gaped at him. "What? No."

Emma looked between us, her face flushed and her eyes shining with tears. "This was an awful idea. I knew we shouldn't have come here tonight." She looked at Mitch. "I'd like you to take me home."

"No, Em, I'm sorry," I said. "I lost my temper."

"Because you throw tantrums whenever you don't get your way, Alex. You have no self-control! I'm constantly having to keep you out of trouble," Emma said. "Do you know how exhausting it is to be your friend?"

It felt like she'd physically struck me. Did she really feel that way about our friendship? That she had to babysit me? That I was a hassle?

"And when I take time for myself, for my career and a possible relationship, you won't let me be happy." Her eyes closed, and she pressed her fingers to the space between her eyebrows as if she had an awful headache. "Why?"

I needed her to stop talking. The ache in my chest was nearing unbearable. My voice wavered. "I'm sorry. Please stay."

She shook her head. "No, I'm going home. This was a waste of time." Emma turned from us. Mitch attempted to place his arm around her as they walked toward the door, but she pushed him away.

I sunk my teeth into my bottom lip, torn between feeling hurt and pissed, and not wanting to cry in a room full of strangers.

Anne rubbed the back of my arm. "Want to go sit down for a few?"

Wiping at my eyes, I nodded. Anne gave a glance back at Ben, who'd been waiting for us. The three of us left the loud room to sit around a small table up front.

Anne covered my hand with her own. "First, I want to say I'm sorry about dismissing your worries. Mitch seems to be a controlling asshole. I have no idea what is going on in Emma's head right now. I wonder if the new job responsibilities are taking a real toll on her confidence, and for some reason this guy is the rock she's clinging to."

My vision blurred, and I blinked back tears. It felt good to hear the affirmation.

Anne continued, "But, there's no 'rescuing' her from him."

"What?" My fingers curled into fists. Ben settled a hand lightly at the small of my back.

"As an officer, I've seen this happen several times, Alex. A friend or family member calls us in to pull a loved one out of a bad relationship. The whole act is messy and can endanger and traumatize the person even more. It's better to wait, be a supportive friend, and let that person be in charge of making the decision to leave."

I withdrew my hand from beneath hers. "I can't do that."

"I understand. I love Emma, too. I'm going to struggle with it as well, but I believe it's the best way we can help her." Anne watched me as I simmered. "She'll come around, Alex. We need to keep the conversation going and just be there. Let's not give up on her."

Doing nothing would be giving up on her. Allowing some guy to slowly destroy her from the inside out would be giving up on her. But I wasn't going to tell Anne because she would stop me. I fabricated a weak smile and nodded instead.

Anne let out a deep breath. "Are you two staying for the whole show?" She looked at Ben when she asked. I wondered if she was worried about what I'd do after she left. Maybe she knew me better than I'd thought.

Ben tapped his fingers where they rested at the small of my back. I looked at him, and he raised his eyebrows. He was leaving the decision to me.

"Yeah, I think so. I need to decompress a bit," I said.

"Okay. I'm going to head home. The spectacular failure of my plan has worn me out." Anne stood, her next questions directed toward me. "Can you give me a call tomorrow? Maybe we can get lunch?"

I stood as well to give her a hug goodbye and then one last smile and nod.

"Great set, Ben. Good night, you two."

He raised his hand in farewell.

Anne left, and another wave of anger and hurt passed through me. My inner wolf paced within my chest. She was waiting to follow one of those emotions to the surface. My eyes squeezed shut, I inhaled slowly and deeply, and exhaled. I needed something to distract me. Something to interrupt my mind's constant reply of Emma's words.

A light touch landed on my elbow. I opened my eyes to see Ben standing beside me, his forehead wrinkled. He was wearing a small frown.

"I'm okay," I said. "Will you stay and dance with me?"

His brow smoothed, and he nodded. We returned to the back venue and the dance floor. I gave Ben a mischievous grin and hooked his front belt loop with my finger. I pulled him into me and kissed him. As we danced, I remained close to him, enjoying his delicious scent and the occasional brushes against his body. With several drinks in my bloodstream and the trance-like quality of the music, my stress and anger fell away.

I PULLED UP the collar of my jacket against the cold as we stepped out onto the sidewalk after the show ended. The wind had picked up again, and the snow fell more heavily. Not even the smokers lingered to brave the chill outside the venue doors. The traffic was nearly nonexistent at this hour, as most people had found their way home by now. Ben yanked the knit hat out of my jacket pocket and pulled it down over my head, partially obscuring my vision. I laughed, and he dodged away as I took a blind swipe at him. As I adjusted my hat, he pulled on his own before offering me his hand. I clasped my fingers with his, and we started strolling the handful of blocks back to his apartment. Since his place was nearby, I'd left my car there for the evening. Our shoes made muffled crunching noises as we walked over the layer of fresh snow. It must have continued to accumulate while we were inside.

A slight itch at the edges of my senses caused me to stop and look back. My sense of hearing was hampered from hours of loud music, despite the ear plugs I'd worn. I let go of Ben's hand, which made him halt as well. He turned, scanning the buildings, sidewalk, and street behind us. I could only make out the distant sound of the freeway and the light sound of our breathing. Ben gave me a questioning look. "I thought I heard something," I murmured.

We continued walking, and every few steps Ben gave me a glance. I heard an extra set of footsteps in the snow. Were we being followed? From the edge of my vision, a shape slipped into the larger shadow of the parking structure across the street. A prickle raced along the back of my neck, which triggered a low rumbling in my chest. I peered across the street and strained to see any more movement through the falling snow.

Ben touched my shoulder and signed "no." His hand ran down the length of my arm to my hand. He tried to gently pull me with him, urging me to continue. Only a short walk across a parking lot remained before we reached his apartment.

I freed my hand again but continued to walk with him. I kept my voice lowered. "I only want to take a look." We'd almost made it across the nearly empty lot before the extra footsteps reached my ears again. My adrenaline spiked. It seemed to be only one person. I struggled to maintain control of my twitching muscles. I spun and saw him this time, his location given away by the bright lights of the parking lot. The figure froze, then turned and dashed back along the edge of the lot. With a snarl, I took off from Ben's side to give chase.

"Stop!" I yelled. The figure shot across the street and into the alley between the parking garage and a neighboring building. I plunged into the narrow alley in pursuit. My eyes adjusted to the low light, while my quarry was hindered by limited vision. His breathing became labored as we wove along the slim pathway. A familiar odor of privilege, in the form of designer cologne, reached me as I closed the distance between us. I got a better look at his back and recognized the jacket.

Growling, I lengthened my strides and gave him a rough shove. His balance was thrown off center, and he was sent sprawling sideways off his feet. The edge of his left shoulder struck the alley wall. He bounced off the wall and crashed on the ground, rolling a few times until coming to a stop in a flurry of snow. It took me a few feet beyond to stop on the slippery pavement. The person was lying on his side, groaning and clutching at his shoulder as I walked back to him. I reached down and hauled him to his feet by the front of his expensive wool coat. "I thought you had an early morning."

Mitch glowered and swept aside my hand with his right arm to free himself. The movement caused him to stagger back against the alley wall. He was out of breath, his tidy hair was mussed, and his face contorted in pain. "We know you stole the money and map. Who sent you to spy on us?"

"We?" I raised my eyebrows. "Is that who you were talking to when you got lost on the way to the bathroom tonight?"

He sneered. "I don't have to answer any of your questions."

"You're completely entitled to that opinion." I pushed him roughly back against the wall by his injured shoulder, causing him to wince. Holding him firmly in place with one hand, I used the other to fish his phone from his pocket. It was locked. "Smile for me," I prompted. I held the screen up to face him, and the phone unlocked.

"You bitch!" He struggled to free himself. "I'll have you arrested for this."

"For being followed home at night?" I flipped to his recent calls. There was a name timestamped from right before the show. "Pastor William Jensen. Is William part of whatever crazy scheme you've concocted?" I returned the phone to his pocket and gave it a pat. "Or are you another 'yes-man' like your two hired lackeys?"

Mitch chuckled darkly. "Emma is wrong about you. What purpose could you possibly serve to anyone? You're too far gone to be saved."

I slammed his shoulder into the wall, eliciting a cry of pain. The sound was extremely gratifying. "Why is it when I have you alone, you sound like a raving lunatic?"

"Lunatic? Me?" He grimaced. "Interesting observation coming from the likes of you."

With each word he spoke, my anger grew and my control over the beast inside waned. "Tell me what you're doing to Emma. Then you'll explain the map."

Even though pain was clear on his face, Mitch chuckled again. "How could a selfish abomination like you understand? Emma wishes to cast aside her sinful nature and become human again. I'll be the one to help her. Stay out of our way or I'll have you permanently removed."

He was trying to take away her spellcasting abilities? Could he do that? "How are you filling her head with your bullshit?"

"Why do you want to know?" The hard edges in his tone softened. "Was Emma right? Do you want help, too?"

*What?* My eyes widened and I swallowed. "She said that?"

"You try to paint me as a villain, but my work helps people change for the better. They can live normal lives without fighting, day after day, to blend in, to be accepted." He paused. "Alex, do you want to be free of the monster possessing you?"

I stood frozen, my mind spinning. *Did I? No more hiding. I could see my family again. Have a career. A home. Maybe eventually a family of my own?*

My inner wolf wrestled loose and charged forward. I clenched his left shoulder, the claws puncturing the coat's fabric and his skin. He cried out again. My teeth grew into points. I shouted inches from his face, "Tell me what you're doing to Emma!"

The sound of footsteps caused me to glance at the corner of the alley and parking garage. Ben cautiously walked toward us, his gaze locking with and holding mine. He brought the bottom edge of his right hand down like an axed onto the open palm of his left hand.

Mitch jerked, and I caught his left wrist in my free hand, stopping it inches from the side of my face. Swinging from a chain clutched in his hand was a crucifix. I gave him a sharp-toothed grin. "I think you have the wrong type of monster, Mitch."

He returned a smile laced with hatred. His weight shifted, and I was struck in my left side. A sudden excruciating pain flared out from the point of contact. I released him to clutch at my side, my fingers closing around the handle of a blade. They were instantly seared as if the blade had been pulled from a fire. The stench of burned skin flooded my nostrils. Cradling his shoulder, Mitch stumbled away from me. He broke into a jog and then a clumsy run down the alleyway.

I moved to follow, but Ben grabbed my elbow and pulled back. My inner wolf immediately turned to the new target. I spun on Ben, snarling, and bared my teeth. "Let go of me!"

He released me and jerked back, his hands held up at chest height between us.

The pain in my side intensified. I grabbed the handle again, and a sharp whine escaped my lips. As soon as I yanked the blade loose, it clattered to the alleyway floor. I pressed my scalded fingers to my side and realized my mistake as blood steadily seeped from between them.

Ben approached again, his steps slow and careful, lowering his hands. Without his gaze breaking from mine, he shrugged out of his jacket, folded it over, and offered it to me.

His wariness flooded me with shame. My gaze lowered, I accepted the bundled jacket. "Thank you." I slipped it between my bloodied fingers and the wound. I'd found a guy who was okay with me being a werewolf, but then I had to go and lose my shit, reminding him I could eat him.

With the knife gone, the pain dulled to a deep throbbing hurt. I tried to regain control of my breathing. Pressing the jacket to the wound with my left hand, I uncurled the tightly clenched fingers of my right. Burns marred my palm and fingers. Fear crept into my consciousness, dousing any residual anger. "It's silver." I looked up at Ben. "He was carrying silver." Mitch had followed us, armed with a weapon meant to cripple me.

Ben retrieved the knife from the ground and helped me back to the street. I was thankful we were so close to his apartment because I felt lightheaded by the time we reached the stairs. My vision spun and spots marred its edges. "I need to stop," I murmured. Ben helped lower me to sit on the bottom stair and crouched beside me. I was dimly aware of him trying to sign something to me. The last thing I remembered was drops of red slipping from my wet fingers to bloom on the snow.

# 14

AN UNUSUAL MIXED smell of coffee, antiseptic, and vanilla drew me up out of sleep. Ben's scent hung heavy around me. My eyes opened to the ceiling of his apartment. I rolled to my right side to prop myself up on an elbow and immediately regretted it. A dull pain flared up my left side from near my waist. Wincing, I laid back down on what I now knew was the mattress he used as a bed.

Footsteps drew my attention across the room. Ben walked toward me, dressed in worn plaid pajama pants and a red hoodie. His dark hair stuck up at odd angles where his glasses were perched atop his head. The mattress jostled when he sat down on its edge, and his brows drew together. "How're you feeling?"

"It still hurts really bad," I said. "Why does it still hurt so bad?" I turned down the edge of the quilt to assess the damage. My jacket, shirt, and jeans were gone. Instead, I wore only a band t-shirt and underwear. Had he changed my clothes? And I wasn't awake to enjoy it? The corners of my mouth turned up. "When I imagined waking up in your bed for the first time, you had fewer clothes and I had fewer problems."

He smiled. "That would have been awkward with Emma here."

"Emma was here?" I gingerly pulled up the edge of the oversized t-shirt. A pink scar, a small echo of the curve of my waist, ran along the tender area on my side. "She came to help?"

"Yes. You passed out, and I didn't know what to do," he said. "Want some coffee?"

"Yeah." The fact Emma answered his call for help sparked a flicker of hope. "She knew you were asking for help for me?"

"Yes." Ben stood and walked away across the apartment to the kitchenette to rummage in the cupboard. A pillow and blankets arranged as a makeshift bed on the old sofa made me smile. He returned with two mugs of coffee.

After a groan or two, I managed to sit up and rest my back against the wall. I wiggled over to make room for him and reached up to accept the coffee. "Thank you."

Ben's eyes were bleary. "I didn't think you'd be okay with the hospital. I got you up here, but the gash wouldn't stop bleeding. I knew silver complicates lupine healing, so I texted Emma for help." He took a sip of his coffee. "She asked that you call when you woke up."

"Did Emma have any opinion on her guy lurking in dark alleys with a silver weapon?" Surely *this* would help my argument against Mitch.

"When she asked what happened, I told her we were mugged," he said. "I thought you'd want the option of what details to tell her."

I looked around for my phone. "What time is it? I need to call her before Mitch fabricates some crazy story about what happened. I should go talk to her in person."

"Do you think that's a good idea?"

I frowned at him. "You can't expect me to relax here while my best friend is being suckered by a sociopath."

"The silver really messed with your system. Emma suggested you rest so your body can heal," Ben said. "Plus, your clothes were soaked with blood, so I threw them in the wash. You can't go anywhere without pants."

Was he sure about that? I scowled and clasped my mug tighter, which caused my palm and fingers to throb. I switched the mug to my other hand and studied the off-color scarring on the underside of my right hand. Silver added a new level of scary complication to the mess I found myself in. "Fine. Can I at least get out of bed?"

He grinned and leaned in to kiss my cheek. Before I could grab the front of his shirt and pull him down on top of me, injury be damned, he drew back and stood. With his support, I was able to get to my feet. Ben helped me put on a pair of sweatpants and a hoodie to ward off the chill of the apartment. There was minimal cursing on my part. I grew lightheaded from the short walk to the small table near the kitchenette. Maybe I wouldn't be able to run around looking for Emma as soon as I'd thought. I lowered myself into the chair at the table, my side burning.

Ben handed me my phone and a blanket. "After Emma left, I messaged Trish to make sure there wasn't anything else I needed to do. She wants you to call too."

I called Emma first and was immediately shuffled to voicemail. She wouldn't have blocked my number, would she? Was her phone off? Frowning, I left my message.

"Em, it's Alex. Ben said you asked that I call you." The words weren't coming easy. I wished she would've stayed. "You're . . . what you can do . . . I'm not sure what would've happened if you hadn't answered Ben's text. Thanks, Em. Please call me back. I'd like to see you and to thank you in person." I ended the call, wondering how long I should wait for her reply. She'd been so angry with me.

When I called Trish, she sounded relieved to hear my voice. "How are you?" she asked.

Wincing, I answered, "I knew silver was bad news for us, but I haven't felt anything sting like that before. How long do I have to wait before it heals?"

"It will take longer than other injuries to completely mend. Give yourself time to rest."

I didn't want to put my feet up and relax. I'd been attacked with silver, and my apartment was on some sort of hit list.

"Mitch carrying a silver blade is worrisome," Trish said. "The Committee had outlawed the use of silver weapons in Hopewell since before my time."

"Where would he have found the knife, then?"

"I don't know."

"Trish, Anne found out more about the Noble Sons," I said. "It's a national hate group."

There was a pause before she spoke. "Is Mitch part of this group?"

"Emma says he isn't." Like whatever shady business he was up to at The Mind Center, Mitch was probably hiding his involvement with the hate group from her. "He'd called William last night while we were at The Sound Refuge, though."

"Thank you for letting me know. I've set the meeting with some select Committee members for tomorrow morning at Hell's Bells. We can discuss everything you've found and how to respond to it. Would you like someone to come get you?"

I frowned, realizing how my injury could hinder me. "I'll call if I need a ride."

"If you need anything at all or if Ben finds any information on the weapon, please call me or Nate."

When I ended the call, I looked over at the sofa where Ben had flipped his glasses back down onto the bridge of his nose and was paging through a book. Several others were stacked on the small table beside him. Resting on the cover of the top book was the knife Mitch used to stab me. I recognized the handle.

"Trish asked you to call if you learn anything about the weapon," I said.

He nodded absently.

"Ben?"

He looked up at me.

I arched an eyebrow. "You volunteered to look up information about the knife?"

Ben stood and brought the knife and the book over to the table. Now that I saw the whole weapon, it looked more like a dagger. Intricate engraving wrapped along the silver handle and blade. "I've seen these symbols before, but I can't remember where. I've been trying to find them," he said. "They're similar to religious symbols, but I don't think that's what they are."

I was surprised he'd agreed to help after resisting for so long. "So you've decided to be a part of this?"

He rubbed at the back of his neck and shrugged. "I have a thing for symbols. They're interesting." He stifled a yawn.

"Sounds riveting." I smiled. "Thanks for looking out for me."

"You're welcome."

"You don't need to stay up with me if you want some sleep."

He checked the time. "I have to go downstairs soon anyway."

I called Anne as Ben got ready for work. She asked me to join her for an early lunch before her shift and agreed to stop by and pick me up. I would struggle to sit still by myself at the apartment, so I was thankful for her invitation. However, with Anne being a cop, I was unsure how she'd react to my confrontation with Mitch.

I retrieved my clothes from the dryer. My shirt was ruined. The long gash from the dagger had ripped open the side and hem. I was able to wear my own jeans and jacket, though the jacket also had a new tear in the side panel. Ben helped me down the stairs, and I waited at the entrance of the record store for Anne.

Apparently I didn't look my best, because her forehead creased and the corners of her mouth dipped down as I walked to the car. I tried to keep the wincing to a minimum as I opened the door and got in.

Anne stated slowly while she watched me, "I feel I missed something after I left last night."

I exhaled, thankful to take the weight off my feet. "A bit."

"Alex, what happened?"

Hesitating, I tried to decide on the fly how many details to share, a mistake when around Anne. "We were on our way back to Ben's place, and I got into a tangle. The person had a knife."

Her concern flipped to alarm. "What? Are you okay?"

"I'll be fine. Ben got me medical care. The knife missed anything important. It'll heal up, but it doesn't feel the best right now."

"Did you report this?"

"Not yet. It's complicated."

Anne frowned. "What about getting stabbed is complicated?"

"It was Mitch," I said.

Her eyes widened. "Do you want me to drive you to the station? We can file a report."

What I wanted was to go after him. "No," I muttered to the dashboard. "It's not worth the hassle." My complaint would more than likely be dismissed because of who he was. Guys like him didn't have to deal with the consequences of their actions. "And I grabbed him first."

"You attacked him?" The volume of her voice in the car made me wince. She lowered it, but the anger was still there. "Alex, what were you thinking? He could report you for assault. We discussed how to deal with him. What if he gets a restraining order? How will you support Emma then?"

I frowned. Okay, so I hadn't considered that when wanting to hammer the jerk. I swallowed. "I don't know. He tried to follow us without being noticed. I guess I was so irritated from earlier, and then he creeped on us. I didn't have a good handle on my temper."

"The three of us left before the show ended," Anne said. "Why would he go back to follow you? What did he want?"

Because I'd intercepted and stolen the envelope containing his evil villain plans and dirty money. But of course I couldn't tell Anne that. I looked away from her and out the windshield. "He didn't make any sense. He talked about these crazy plans for Emma and how I should step out of the way."

"He threatened you, too?" she asked.

I nodded. And possibly tried to take my life. The look in Mitch's eyes right before he stabbed me, that intense hate, made me suspect he was well aware of what the silver would do. I was running out of time to deal with him.

"Please let's go downtown to write up a report," she said.

"No." I frowned at her. "A report isn't going to make a difference. With the family he's from, he'll come out on top." I'd take care of him myself. Somehow. Soon.

As if reading my mind, Anne said, "Stay away from him, Alex."

My frustration escalated to anger. "You might be okay with it, but I'm not going to let Emma be brainwashed." Listening to Anne tell me what to do for the next hour wasn't going to work. I reached for the car door handle. "I'll pass on lunch."

Anne raised her voice as I got out of the car. "I understand you want the best for Emma, but you're fixating on this. It's already dangerous for you. We need to be careful."

I slammed the door shut and was awarded a sharp pain in my side. It didn't improve my mood. Anger burned deep in my chest. If I couldn't remove Emma from the situation she was trapped in, I'd have to find a way to eliminate the situation. The creature inside me stirred at the thought, and my pulse quickened. I'd told Nate I wasn't a killer. Was it only a matter of time before the wolf inside me would get her way?

I focused on my breathing as I walked around the building to the parking lot. My vision had started to spot from the pain in my side, so I waited behind the wheel of my car until it cleared again. I sent Ben a message letting him know I'd be resting at my apartment. By the time I reached my place, my side throbbed. I popped a pain pill, set an alarm on my phone, and crawled into bed. It didn't take long after my head hit the pillow before I fell asleep.

THE ALARM WOKE me several hours later. I was ravenous from having missed lunch. Poking through the refrigerator, I rounded up a plate of leftovers. As I ate, my phone buzzed with a message from Ben.

*I remember where I've seen the symbols. I'm off in thirty. Can you meet me there?*

Chewing on some cold pizza, I clicked on the map link he included. It was the address of St. Anthony's Cathedral downtown. I sent him a reply. *See you there.*

When I arrived, Ben was waiting for me. He offered his arm for support, and we slowly walked together across the snow-covered square. In an area where open space was at a premium, an entire city block was dedicated to the cathedral and its grounds. The yellow limestone building reached up out of the ground toward the sky with its towering spires and pointed, Gothic windows. Since it was a place of worship, the front doors were unlocked during the weekdays. People from the community were welcome to come and go as they pleased.

We entered the building, stomping the snow from our shoes. The sound echoed down the hall. The odors of damp rugs and salt tracked in from outside gave way to those of spent candle wicks, dust, and incense. I wandered into the sanctuary and the mere size of it caused me to lower my voice. It made me feel small and insignificant. I whispered to Ben, "This place is enormous. You've been here before?"

Ben's gaze lifted to the vaulted ceiling. It was colored with pale tints of blue similar to those in his eyes. He withdrew his notepad to answer my question. *Used to go to church here as a kid.*

I leaned back against a pew, spotting a huge pipe organ crouched in the balcony above the entryway. It looked like a large creature ready to pounce. "Must have looked even bigger as a kid. Seems like a fun place to play hide-and-seek."

He wrote on the page again. *It was intimidating.* He turned to exit the sanctuary, waving for me to follow.

We walked back out into the main hallway. It led us past some smaller rooms, offices, and a chapel. He stopped at a set of stone stairs winding downward. A mesh, metal gate was pulled shut across its threshold. He lifted the gate's padlock and frowned before letting it fall back in place.

I watched his notepad as he wrote. *Come back on Sunday? Should be open then. Could look around during church service.*

I glanced up and down the empty hall for any people or security cameras. Not seeing any, I stepped up beside Ben. I wrapped my fingers around the lock. Carefully reaching down inside myself, I called to the creature for her strength. Warmth surged through my arms, and I gave the lock a rough tug downward. It snapped open. I gave him a smile, removed the lock, and carefully folded aside the gate. "Oh look, someone left it open." I replaced the padlock on the open door of the gate, and we descended the staircase.

The smell of damp stone and earth filled my nostrils. The air grew naturally cooler. The lighting was subdued, giving the large, low-ceilinged area a haunted feel. Some type of verse, engraved in large Gothic letters, ran the length of the room. Small, dimly lit alcoves lined the walls and contained different artifacts sealed away behind more metallic mesh gates.

I tried to discern what was written on the wall. It was in a different language. Maybe Latin? "So, what exactly is going on down here? Is it a treasure vault?"

Ben stood near an alcove across the room. He wrote on his notepad as I walked over to his side. *Where they keep lesser relics. Main one upstairs in altar.* He walked to the next alcove, searching for something. Glancing back at me, he pointed into the area.

I joined him as he pulled out his phone and activated the flashlight to better light the area. Behind the metal gate stood an ornate pedestal. Atop the pedestal was a wooden box about the size of a shoebox. It was elegantly carved with metallic clasps. "Are those silver?" I asked.

Ben shrugged and shook his head. He crouched and shone the light into the alcove to illuminate the face of the pedestal. I gingerly lowered myself beside him as he pointed at the carvings in the stone surface. It was the same design as on the dagger Mitch had used. Ben set down his phone so he could write. *Thought I'd remembered symbols. Been here as long as I can remember, but don't think it belongs to church. Symbols aren't right for that.*

I looked back at the pedestal and noticed a figure below the symbols, but hoped I was seeing it incorrectly. Picking up Ben's phone, I shone the flashlight down the rest of the pedestal. Carved in the stone was a man in medieval dress. He stood among a flock of sheep, brandishing a spear in one hand and a key in the other. He drove the weapon down through the skull of a large wolf with pointed teeth and a lolling tongue. Suddenly feeling uneasy, I stood to distance myself from the alcove's contents. "If this doesn't belong to the church, how did it end up here? Do you think it was stolen?"

Ben stood as well and wrote. *Maybe it was hidden here?* He tapped on the small handle of the gate and looked at me with raised brows.

Handing his phone back to him, I took hold of the handle. Footsteps sounded in the hallway above us. I released the handle and pointed up. Ben switched off the light. I scanned the room for another exit out of the room but didn't see one. I turned to Ben. He knew the question before I asked and shook his head.

Footsteps descended the stairs. The aromas of soap and incense reached me. A voice called ahead. "Hello?" The figure of Father Aiden, the priest I'd seen at the Committee meeting, came into view. "I'm sorry, but this area is closed to visitors during . . ." He stopped, looking both surprised and confused. "Miss Steward?" I could tell among his top five guesses of who he'd find down here, I wasn't one of them.

I smiled awkwardly, surprised and not thrilled that he remembered my name. "Ah, hello." I motioned around us. "Nice place you have here. Very . . . old."

He looked past me to Ben and back. "I apologize for the mistake, but this area should not have been left open to the public today. Is there something I can help you with?"

"Actually, yes. What can you tell us about this?" I jerked a thumb at the ornate box.

Aiden walked from the stairs to stop beside us and look into the alcove. "It is a relic that belonged to Saint Hubertus." He studied us. "We can continue our conversation upstairs. Perhaps there are other questions I can answer."

I nodded. "First, can we look inside the box?"

"Absolutely not." His tone was civil and stern like at the Committee meeting. "Please," he motioned to the stairs, "I will join you both in the main hall shortly."

I glanced at Ben. He tucked away his pencil and notepad. We ascended the staircase and waited in the hall while Aiden did whatever it was he had to do. I kept my voice lowered. "I'm struggling to get a read on this guy. Are you all right sticking around and seeing if he says anything to help us puzzle out the dagger and how Mitch got it?"

Ben chewed at his bottom lip and eyed the front door. I wasn't sure if it was Aiden's presence or the fact we got caught down there that made Ben uneasy. He looked back at me and nodded.

Aiden ascended the stairs and tried to resecure the gate, but the lock wouldn't close. He paused and frowned to himself. Turning a cool gaze on us, he asked, "Can you both please accompany me to my office?"

We followed him back to the grouping of administrative offices off the main hall. Beyond an empty receptionist's desk and some cubicles was a book-lined study. Aiden held the door open for us as we filed into the room. He closed the door with a soft click and walked to a handful of chairs. "Please, have a seat." He sat in one of the chairs and waited for us to sit down.

Aiden spoke to Ben first. "Benjamin, I was sorry to hear what happened to you. What a blessing Miss Steward was there to deter the attackers. Even with your tether, I want you to know the Committee is taking the attack seriously."

Ben swallowed and shifted in his seat but didn't look at the priest. His gaze was lowered to the carpet.

"Why does it make a difference if he's tethered or not?" It's something I'd wondered at the Committee meeting. "Shouldn't the Committee be looking out for all of us either way?"

"Yes," Aiden said. "But some Committee members believe if a citizen decides not to follow the rules that are in place to keep everyone safe, that person also does not deserve the benefit of the Committee's protection."

"That's bullshit," I said. "A blanket rule like that ignores how complicated people are."

Aiden's smile was pained, as if suffering a child's outburst. He waited a moment longer than needed to make sure I was done talking and then continued as if I hadn't raised a question. "The Committee is currently attempting to understand the outbreak of violence against supernatural citizens. The attack on Benjamin will be dealt with."

He leaned back and fixed us with a critical stare. "And now, please tell me why your interest in relics caused you to trespass into the area where they are kept."

I thought of attempting a lie, but my face had already betrayed me with a flush of heat. It wasn't worth the effort. "I've seen something up close and personal that had that saint's symbol on it. Is anything missing from that box?"

Aiden studied us over steepled fingers. I had an unnerving sense he was peering inside my head. I didn't care for the feeling. After a silent moment, he replied, "Yes. Where did you last see the weapon?"

Weapon? So, the box had contained the dagger. I shifted in my seat. The mending wound in my side began to throb. "A Commoner used it to attack me."

Aiden's features darkened but his tone remained even. "Who was it?"

This guy must have been used to people automatically providing him with answers whenever he asked. "Keeping silver weapons in a box in your basement doesn't seem like the best idea when you have wolves for neighbors."

There was a twitch in Aiden's cool and collected facade. "It is import-ant I know who stole the daggers from the reliquary and attacked you. Wielding silver against the lupine is strictly forbidden in Hopewell."

"Stole the 'daggers'? So more than one is missing?" That wasn't a comforting thought.

"There are three in total. All have been taken." He repeated, "Who attacked you, Miss Steward?"

Not knowing if Aiden was friend or foe made it difficult to decide how much to share. I shifted in my seat again. "It was Mitch White. He is a member of—"

"—William's congregation." Aiden frowned to himself.

"I've already let Trish know what happened," I said.

Aiden nodded. "She plans to confront William?"

"You'll have to talk to Trish if you want to know that."

"I've sensed Patricia's growing frustration for some time now. I understand it," he said. "However, for the Committee to achieve what it was meant to do, all parties must be honest and forthcoming with each other. She should bring her concern about William's parishioner to us instead of approaching William alone. It would be the more dip-lomatic and effective solution." He paused, watching me before asking, "Do you understand?"

I snorted. "Except the wolves aren't part of the Committee anymore." I wasn't Trish's errand girl, here to carry back messages to her and was irritated he would think so. My patience with Aiden was dwindling. "I told you about Mitch, now tell me why you have silver daggers hidden in your church and how he got them."

Aiden frowned. "Child, this is not a game."

Was he serious? I'd taken one of his missing daggers to the gut. A growl rumbled in my chest. "I'm well aware of that."

Ben reached over for my hand. His eyebrows were drawn together, and he gave me a small frown. He lightly rubbed the pad of his thumb over the back of my hand.

I took a deep inhale through my nose and exhaled, attempting to calm the agitated beast inside me. I repeated, "Why are the daggers kept in this church?"

Aiden studied me with raised eyebrows before answering, "The weapons are guarded here so they are not misused."

"I'm sorry to break it to you, Father, but you're doing an awful job of it. Or did you lend them to Mitch in exchange for a large deposit to the collection plate?"

Aiden's features immediately darkened again. He narrowed his eyes. "I'm sorry for whatever happened to you, Miss Steward, to give you such a jaded opinion of houses of worship. I assure you that is not how this church operates. I do not know how he came into possession of the daggers. I just now found them missing."

"How do you plan on fixing this?" If this place was in charge of keeping the daggers out of the wrong hands, I'd think Aiden would feel responsible if they went missing.

"I will inform Patricia and then the remainder of the Committee. We will speak with William about his parishioner and recover the daggers so no further harm comes to you or any other lupine."

Except Ben and I had one of the daggers in our possession, and I wasn't going to give it back until I knew for sure Aiden would follow through with what he promised.

Ben gave my hand a light squeeze. He glanced at the door and back at me.

I gave a slight nod before replying to Aiden. "Thank you." I stood along with Ben. "Good luck with William."

"Miss Steward, one more thing." Aiden stood as well. "Looking further into the missing daggers is the Committee's responsibility. Despite Patricia's claimed independence on behalf of the lupine, gross violation of the Committee's rules by any individual is still considered grounds for punishment."

My face flushed. I was growing tired of men hurling threats at me.

Aiden watched me with the same unreadable expression as before. "I trust you can find your way out?"

Ben and I left the office. We walked down the hall toward the main entrance of the cathedral. I muttered, "I have no idea if he was telling the truth or not." There hadn't been any scent of fear, and his body language revealed nothing other than mild irritation with me. I stopped and leaned against the wall in the entryway. My injured side ached. "Do you think he's going to alert William?"

Frowning, Ben looked back over his shoulder toward the offices. He offered his arm and pointed toward the front doors.

I pushed away from the wall and took his arm for support. "Was Aiden the priest when you attended here?"

We exited the large building. Ben shook his head as he retrieved the notepad from his back pocket. We stopped in the empty courtyard. I huddled close to him against the winter evening and watched him write. *No, but he was there at my trial and tethering. Don't want to irritate the Committee. Can't do more years with this tether.*

"I'm sorry," I said. He was worried about being punished for being caught snooping. I should've thought of that before I asked him to stay during my conversation with Aiden.

*Could have left. Now know where dagger came from.* He gave me a small smile.

"And to be watching for two more," I said. "Do you want to let Trish know what we found out about the daggers, or should I?"

He shrugged and pointed at himself.

I gave Ben a ride so he wouldn't have to walk back in the cold. My phone buzzed as I watched him climb the stairs. It was a text from Trish. *Tomorrow at Hell's Bells. 8 a.m.*

On the short drive back to my place, I wondered if the meeting Trish was calling would result in anything. How would it be any different from the larger Committee meeting? I called Nate while still in the car in front of my apartment. "It's Alex. I need your help with something."

"Yeah?" he said. "What're you thinking?"

"I want to find the second location of The Mind Center," I said.

"Why?"

"I want to get inside."

# 15

WHEN I PULLED up in front of Hell's Bells the next morning, it looked abandoned. The windows were dark, and the building's peeling paint and rough edges were more apparent in the daylight. The gray sky and dirty snow didn't help its desolate appearance. I passed an immaculately kept silver sedan on my way to the front door where a sun-bleached "closed" sign hung. After a rap of my knuckles on the glass, there was movement within.

Trish answered the door. "Good morning."

As on the outside, the building's interior was oddly quiet. The few times I'd been to Hell's Bells, it thrived with conversation, laughter, and music. Currently, a circle of warm light lit the lounge area where Reginald sat. Trish and I joined him.

"Good morning, Miss Alex." His good-natured demeanor was absent.

I sat down beside Trish on one of the sofas. "Are any other Committee members coming?"

Reginald appeared grim as he waited for Trish to answer me. She shook her head. "No. Everyone else canceled late last night."

"What? Why?" I looked between the two.

"Aiden contacted me last night," Reginald said. "He reminded me of the Committee's obligation to always meet as a whole. We are discouraged to organize or attend meetings exclusive to select members. I assume the others received the same phone call."

My pulse skipped. It must've been after Ben and I visited the cathedral. We'd tipped Aiden off that Trish was taking matters into her own hands. "Trish, when I saw Aiden last night, he said he was going to call you. Has he?"

She shook her head again.

My stomach dropped. "He asked if you were going to confront William. I told him he'd have to talk to you about it." I frowned. "I'm sorry if I messed anything up. I was trying to help."

"I know." Her eyes were steely. "Do you have the map?"

I handed the folded paper to Trish as I spoke to Reginald. "Nate and I got it from Shortie . . . I mean, the two men who attacked Ben. One is a wizard, but we found out the other is a wolf."

Trish looked from the map to Reginald. "Reggie, did you hear back from Chicago?"

He nodded. "The most recent roster of the tethered in the Midwest region is being sent to me from the Chicago Delegation. It should allow us to identify the men and their past infractions."

"Mitch White gave those two guys the map. They seem to be working for him," I said. "He's a member of the Patterson Street Church."

"That's William's congregation," Trish reminded Reginald. She leaned forward to hand the map to him. "Mitch White is also co-owner of a counseling clinic called The Mind Center. Alex and Nate found the client list I shared with you. When I checked in on the wolves from the list, those I was able to contact were evasive about their experiences at the clinic."

Reginald reviewed the map. "Perhaps they are private individuals and didn't want to discuss such personal matters. No wizards from the list you sent have contacted me about strange therapy sessions."

A flicker of annoyance passed over Trish's features. "Two of the wolves were reported missing."

My eyes widened, and Reginald looked up abruptly from the map he held.

Trish continued, "One's name was given to the police by his friend. Another was reported by her concerned coworker. Neither have immediate family in the area for me to question. Both were patients at The Mind Center."

"My friend Anne is on the police force," I said to Reginald. "She mentioned their missing persons reports are increasing. You should check the list again to see if any wizards have disappeared too."

"Isn't the White family the largest financial supporters of William's church?" Trish asked. She motioned to the map. "Do you think they pressured William for this information? Wolves and wizards living in Hopewell are reported to and kept track of by the Committee, so William would have access to it."

They were? Why hadn't Trish told me about that *before* I agreed to attend the Committee meeting?

"Take care, Patricia," Reginald said. "That is a serious accusation against a Committee member, and we do not have evidence linking William to anything Mitch is doing. It's possible William is not aware of it."

"Emma identified the symbol on the pin, the one Trish brought to the Committee meeting. It's from a group called the Noble Sons," I said. "Em said it's a Bible study group William organized at her church. Isn't it kind of odd William wouldn't have said anything about the pin when Trish showed it to everyone?"

Reginald frowned to himself and handed the map back to Trish.

"Mitch also called William the evening he attacked me," I continued. "The call was logged on his phone. It seems like an unlikely coincidence Mitch rang up his pastor before trying to follow me home unnoticed."

"Mitch was wielding a silver dagger," Trish said. "Alex found out last night that similar daggers are missing from St. Anthony's. Those daggers are known Hunters' weapons."

*Hunter?* What in the *holy hell* was a hunter, and why hadn't I heard of it before? The same uneasiness I'd experienced when Ben and I found the box for the daggers passed over me.

Trish continued, "Even if William is unaware of what is happening— and I am not convinced that's true—he is the Committee representative for Patterson Street Church. Mitch is his responsibility, and the attack on Alex should be addressed immediately. The lupine are promised protection by the Committee from Hunters and their weapons."

I licked my lips. "Hunter?"

Trish clasped my hand in hers as she spoke to Reginald. "We have the dagger. The map is evidence that our people are being targeted at their homes and community places—places they believe are safe. We don't have the time to follow Committee protocol. My priority is the safety of the wolves."

Reginald ran a hand over his face and short beard. He nodded. "I understand."

"I'll be visiting William tomorrow after his church service to ask questions and remind him of his responsibilities," Trish said. "Reggie, will you come with me?"

The wizard nodded again. He looked disheartened and tired. "Yes, I will."

"Do you want me there too?" I asked.

"No," Trish said. "Let us handle this."

Trish stood and Reginald followed suit. He gave me a nod. "Thank you for your work, Miss Alex."

"You're welcome." I worried I'd done more harm than good. My visit to the cathedral was more than likely the reason Aiden had robbed Trish of her allies for this meeting. He wouldn't have known about it otherwise. I waited on the couch, chewing at my thumbnail, while Trish walked Reginald to the door.

She returned to stand in front of me, arms crossed. Trish looked down at me, silent. Her mouth was pressed into a thin line, and her eyes glowed a soft gold.

Wilting beneath the weight of her stare, I mumbled, "Trish, I'm really sorry. We weren't expecting Aiden. We didn't know it was his church."

She slowly drew in a breath and exhaled as slowly. "The information you and Ben gathered was valuable. Thank you. Nevertheless, I'm asking you not to engage Mitch, William, or the unknown wizard and wolf until after tomorrow."

Anne would have been happy to hear this. If it were anyone but Trish, I'd disregard the request. I'd follow up on my call with Emma instead.

"Do you feel safe in your apartment?" she asked.

"That depends. What exactly did you mean by Hunters?"

Trish gave a slight shake of her head. "Hunters themselves are extremely rare nowadays. We would have a large body count instead of missing individuals. Hunters' *weapons*, however, were fashioned to inflict harm specifically to supernatural beings."

"Like the daggers."

She nodded. "Now go home and rest. Heal. Reggie and I will put an end to all of this."

It wasn't a request. I stood without another word and slunk from the lobby. Outside, the silver sedan was still parked in the drive. Reginald exited the car.

"Miss Alex, a word with you?" he asked.

I stopped, fully expecting another reprimand. "What is it?" I asked, more sharply than intended.

He didn't notice or didn't care. "When Aiden called last night, he mentioned Benjamin was with you at the cathedral."

"Yes. Ben recognized the symbols on the dagger's hilt and remembered them from some relics in the basement."

Reginald nodded. "He's easily distracted by a good puzzle. However, as I asked Ms. Drake before you arrived this morning, please do not encourage this behavior from him." He frowned, and the lines on his forehead deepened. "In our investigations, we are skirting the edges of what the Committee rules allow. As I'm sure you've noticed by now, my grandson is serving time under a tether. If we are punished for our actions, his would be far more severe because of his previous offense."

"Are you asking me to tell Ben he's not allowed to help us?" I asked.

Reginald nodded again. "Yes. That is my request."

No, I wasn't going to manage their relationship for him. Absolutely not. They would have to talk to each other. "I'll pass along your concerns, but I'm not going to tell him what to do," I said.

Reginald studied me for a moment, frowning. He gave me a curt tip of his hat. "Have a pleasant day, Miss Alex."

I watched him get into his car and depart. Nate had said Reginald was the person on the Committee to cast the tethering spell when someone was convicted. How could he do that to his own grandson? And now he expected me to keep Ben out of trouble? No wonder Ben was still pissed at him.

What a shitty start to the day. I hoped it would get better from here.

I DIDN'T IMMEDIATELY return to my apartment after leaving Hell's Bells. The day dragged on as I attempted to make a few bucks by driving instead. Even if caught in the shifting sands of politics, a lady had to pay her rent. This month's near eviction had narrowly been avoided, but next month's was looming right around the corner. My thoughts turned to the sizable chunk of change I'd recently acquired from Shortie.

I stopped by the bank and deposited the remaining cash from the envelope. I told myself it was for safe-keeping . . . for now, anyway. By midafternoon, my side ached again, and I'd run out of patience waiting for Emma to return my phone call. I wasn't able to focus on my job and decided to end my workday and go home.

My attempt to call Emma landed me in voicemail again. Growling, I hung up and redialed her number.

"Hello, Alex." Her voice sounded distant and groggy. "You can leave a message if it's important instead of repeatedly calling."

Except she never responded to my messages. "Em? You sound funny. Are you okay?"

"I'm not feeling well. I think I've caught a cold." There was a rustle of bedcovers.

"A cold?" I paused, thinking through the question before I asked the obvious. "Aren't you able to heal yourself?"

Her tone sharpened. "What do you want, Alex?"

"Ben said you'd asked me to call after you helped with my injury. I did, but I never heard back from you."

There was a pause. "Yes. I'm sorry. I forgot." There was more rustling. Her voice became clearer. "How's your side?"

"Sore but healing."

"Did you recognize the person who mugged you? Ben didn't know, but I thought of Kevin and Brad."

I hesitated. "When and where can we talk in person?"

"I'm busy tonight. I was hoping to sleep off this funk so I could keep my commitment."

An immediate growl surfaced in my voice. "With Mitch?"

The line was quiet a moment before she answered. "No." More silence. "Em?"

"Alex, my head hurts. I can't deal with this right now. I have service tomorrow morning with my parents. If you want to, you can meet me afterward."

Her parents? That meant her mother, Susan, would be there. "I could come over now. Maybe bring you some soup?" Isn't that what people usually did for sick people?

"Goodbye, Alex." The line clicked and went dead.

Should I go over to her place anyway to check on her? I lowered my phone and stared at the screen, chewing at my thumbnail. If I did and nothing was wrong, she'd be mad and I'd lose my chance to talk to her. At least it sounded like Mitch wasn't with her.

I decided to stay home and slept the rest of the afternoon. I awoke in the evening feeling better than I had since my less-than-pleasant encounter with Mitch. Ben had to work at The Sound Refuge, so I ordered takeout and stayed in. Maybe a night of films and resting on the sofa would keep my mind off Mitch. I soaked in a hot bath, then suited up in flannel pajamas and a pair of ridiculously fuzzy slippers my parents had gifted me. I flipped through my small collection of rom-coms, discreetly tucked away behind other films, and popped one into the player. A quick trip to the kitchen, and I had a beer and the food I'd stuck in the stove to keep warm.

On my way back to the living room, I heard voices in the stairwell. One belonged to my neighbor across the hall. I paused at the apartment door and listened to footfalls descend the stairs. Those also belonged to my neighbor. After a few moments of silence, a heavier set of steps began to advance up the stairwell. The old stairs squeaked and groaned beneath the stranger's weight. The hair rose on the back of my neck and arms at the sound. I quietly set down the open bottle and container of food on the living room table. Straightening, I leaned toward the closed door to listen. The stranger's footsteps stopped in front of my door. I slowly backed away. A rumbling growl brewed in my chest.

A large crash collided against the door. The frame of the room shuddered, and the door buckled inward against its hinges. I cringed as small flakes of plaster fell from the ceiling down around me. A second crash brought a large fist through the door. The hand grabbed at the shards of broken wood to pull them away.

The creature inside me wrestled away some control. My hands shifted with a popping of cartilage. I couldn't suppress the snarling noises coming from my body. I backed farther away from the apartment entrance, not taking my gaze from the shattered door. The heel of my slipper hit the opposing wall's floorboard. I froze, waiting. The odor of gasoline drifted across the room.

The scent flipped the switch in my brain from fight to flight. I dashed to the row of tall, thin windows facing the street. As I did so, the remains of the door were torn from the entryway. My clawed hands scratched at the frame as I struggled with an awkward, older window. It slid halfway open before it jammed. Footsteps crossed the apartment behind me. I spun to face the intruder.

The Ox set the gasoline can he carried aside on the floor. His eyes shifted color as he grinned down at me. When I bolted for the exit, he was quick enough to block it with his huge frame. I'd only given the doorway a fleeting glance, but he'd noticed. The punch that struck my jaw had enough force to send me sliding back across the floor. I rolled quickly to my side and propped myself up on an elbow. My ears rang and my healing wound ached. I briskly shook my head to right my senses.

The stench of gasoline became more pungent. The whooshing sound of it being lit was followed by a wave of heat. I staggered to my feet, my vision still unfocused from the Ox's punch. The middle of the living room and the area in front of the door was enveloped in flames. The Ox lumbered toward me. I backed away and bumped up against the large windows I'd tried to escape through earlier.

A huge flash of light and a booming noise came from behind me. The whole house trembled this time. I ducked away, looking back. Familiar blue flames dispersed across the windows' surfaces. The wards held against the magical attack, preventing the windows from being blown in. Shortie was waiting outside.

The fire alarm screeched, first in the apartment and then in the hallway. The smoke filling the apartment overwhelmed my sense of smell. My eyes teared, and I began to cough. Spinning away from the windows, I collided with the Ox. He seized my upper arm and dragged me back through the apartment toward the door.

I twisted and bucked against his hold, which caused the stab wound to scream. With the claws of my free hand, I sliced at his hand and forearm. He bellowed and drove the side of my body against the wall. I swear my teeth rattled in my head. My gasp of pain filled my lungs with more smoke, and I started coughing again. The Ox's grip tightened, and my arm grew numb from the elbow down. He half-carried and half-pulled me from the apartment into the hallway.

We crashed and stumbled our way down the stairs together, my body beginning to tire. The fresh, icy air hit my lungs hard as we emerged from the building, which caused yet another fit of coughing. Shortie's voice commanded, "C'mon! Hurry it up." A few more steps and all three of us were on the sidewalk together.

Shortie limped into my field of vision. "Wards on the house, too? You've become an immense pain in my ass."

I struggled to focus on him. My head still spun from my collision with both the Ox's fist and the wall. I mumbled, "If you'd answer my questions, I'd stop bothering you."

He shook his head and chuckled. "You think you're in any position to be making demands of us? Let me explain to you what actually will be happening tonight. You're going to tell us where to find our money. Then you'll be coming along with us, nice and calm-like. All those questions you have, you can ask our employer himself. You'll get the VIP *treatment*." He gave the word emphasis before he grinned and looked up at his partner.

A deep bass voice behind me parroted, "VIP treatment." The Ox gave a rumbling chuckle. "You're pretty clever, George."

Shortie scowled. "Dammit, Leo! How many times do I have to tell you not to use my name?" He stopped, blinked, and his scarred and tattooed face turned crimson.

These two didn't seem like the brightest crayons in the box. I gave a bleary smile. "No wonder Mitch got you two to agree to work for him."

Leo the Ox growled and gave me a rough shake. "Want us to take away more than your apartment? Keep talking."

Shortie George barked at his partner, "Hey! She's messing with you. Stay focused." He stepped closer and glared at me. The stink of his awful cologne saturated the frigid air. "Sweetheart, you're the one on your way to get your brain baked. We'll be the ones running free again after this job. Who's got the smarts now?"

I managed a laugh. The movement caused another flair of pain in my side. "You really think Mitch is going to honor his agreement? What Commoner willingly gets a wizard and wolf released from their tethers? Does he even have a wizard lined up to do that?"

Leo's low voice carried notes of concern. "Wait, does he? I can't go back to being tethered, George." Leo's scent as a werewolf may have been disguised, but a pungent odor of fear wafted from the larger man.

"If you finish whatever crazy scheme he's hired you for, Mitch is going to have your tethers reinstated, not removed," I said. "You'll be right where you started."

"I can't go back, George." Leo moaned. "My head was full of fire."

George jabbed a stubby finger into my collarbone. I flinched as he shouted in my face. "We're getting these tethers removed. If that arrogant blond bastard doesn't make it happen, we'll be hunting down your scrawny friend again."

The threat caused my chest to tighten. "Don't touch him," I said. Even these two didn't fully trust Mitch. Ben was their backup plan.

George slowly smiled. "Only this time, you won't be around to stop us from beating the answers out of his punk ass. You'll be useless, no better than some Commoner."

The creature inside of me responded with a low growl. Nate was right. These two were going to be a persistent problem. They wouldn't conveniently go away if we stopped Mitch.

Leo spoke the moment before I heard the fire sirens from down the hill. "The firetrucks are coming, George. What about our money?" He gave me another shake. "Where's our money?"

"You should have asked that *before* you set my place on fire, don't you think?" I asked. "You might be able to salvage it yet." My comment had the opposite of the intended effect. Instead of releasing me, Leo's tightening grip on my arm caused his claws to bite through my skin.

"Be quiet!" George yelled. "Let me think." He limped a few steps away, closed his eyes, and took a deep breath. "All right. We take the girl to the boss, and we don't hand her over until he pays us more."

When he opened his eyes and looked at me again, he withdrew a switchblade from his jacket pocket. "Let's level the playing field before we get into the car." He flipped open the blade. "Tell me where I can find that shield of yours."

I twisted my body and let my weight collapse against Leo's hold. The abrupt motion caused his balance on the icy walk to shift. We crashed to the ground. He released my arm to catch himself, and the blood returned to my fingers in a rush. I scrambled back from the men. When Leo reached for my ankle, I drove the heel of a slippered foot into his face. He grunted in pain, caught the slipper, and yanked it from my foot.

I clumsily stood and staggered away from Leo. George lunged at me. I raised my forearm to protect myself, and he sliced a gash across it. It wasn't a normal switchblade. The cut burned unnaturally hot even after the blade slashed past me. The horrible scent of singed skin filled the air. When he deftly flipped the blade to his other hand and swiped at me again, I dodged out of the way.

The howling of the fire engine sirens grew louder by the moment. It was echoed by the additional sounds of police sirens. George was livid but started to retreat. "Leo!"

Clutching one of my soggy slippers, Leo hurried with his partner to a rusted blue sedan parked along the street. I didn't catch the plate number, but I did notice it was from out of state. The car pulled away even as the fire trucks, an ambulance, and a police car arrived.

I stood panting on the sidewalk in a daze. Flames leapt from the windows of my apartment. Cradling my injured arm, I attempted to focus on the mantra to calm the beast within me. "It's okay. You're safe." My teeth began to chatter from the cold and the adrenaline.

A paramedic rushed up to me. Her lips moved, but I struggled to understand her words. She guided me to the ambulance where she and a teammate wrapped a blanket around me and dressed the laceration on my arm. They were too concerned with the wound to notice my still slightly elongated fingers twisted in the blanket.

"Alex?" Anne was in full uniform, having been the police officer to report to the call. She looked relieved. "I recognized your address when it came up. Thank goodness you're safe." She added, "But you're missing a shoe."

I looked down at my single, soggy slipper and back up at Anne. When she hugged me, I burst into tears.

ANNE LET ME wait in her warm cruiser as the fire department tended to the building. I worked through the descriptions of George, Leo, and their car, and related most everything that occurred—sans the blue magical fire and werewolf claws. She drew the connection between my description and the men the police found beneath the bridge downtown. Leo must have still been passed out and George unable to get away fast enough because of the injuries to his legs.

"What did you say their names were?" Anne asked.

I rubbed at my aching temples. "George and Leo."

"That doesn't sound familiar, but they could have given us false names when we found them. The short guy said they were mugged by a couple of men, and he was attacked by their dog. It didn't look like any dog attack I've seen before. Was he favoring his leg at all?"

"Yes. He was limping a bit."

Her brow furrowed. "I got a weird vibe from those two when we found them. The larger guy is like a human bear. Those muggers would have to be brutes to knock him unconscious." Anne shook her head. "I tried to look into them further, but my boss told me to stop. He said I was wasting department time and money on a hunch when I should be concentrating on the assaults."

Nate had said the police department could swing either way. With Anne's boss diverting her from George and Leo, I wondered if more of Mitch's money was involved.

"But now that they tried to snatch you, I have reason to follow up on the two," she said. "Thanks for that."

I snorted. "I'm always happy to help a friend," I said. "Do you think George and Leo are working with the Virtuous Dickheads?"

Anne chuckled. "The Noble Sons? I don't know. Since our missing persons reports spiked, I'm inclined to link them with that instead. Would you be willing to look at some photos to confirm we're talking about the same two men?"

I hesitated. "Could I do so anonymously?"

Anne studied me, making me shift in my seat and break eye contact. "Sure," she said. "Can you meet me at the station tomorrow?"

"Okay."

When I was allowed access to my apartment, I changed out of my torn and soggy pajamas. My clothes reeked of smoke, the scent turning my stomach. I retrieved a few sets of clothes, my jacket, and my phone. I also grabbed the go-bag—kept on hand in case I needed to leave on short notice—from the top shelf of the closet. Living every day with one foot out the door had taught me not to get too attached to any material items.

My landlord showed up, as well as my neighbor. The majority of my apartment was lost, but thankfully the flames didn't make it across the hall to the second apartment. The landlord didn't know when renovations would begin, but said she'd contact me soon with a timeline. She also didn't have any other apartments open. Since I'd avoided the extra expense of renter's insurance, a hotel bill wouldn't be covered. I didn't want to dip any further into the money I'd taken from George or Leo if I could help it.

Anne tried to convince me to stay at her place, but I refused. "You have a small place. I don't want to crowd you."

The truth was, I didn't want to bring my mess to her doorstep when George and Leo tried to find me again. If she was ever forced to acknowledge the existence of supernatural beings, battling a wizard and werewolf in her tiny living room wasn't how I'd prefer it to happen. Plus, I'd successfully hidden my true self from her so far. I didn't want that to change.

"Trish and Nate will let me stay at Hell's Bells," I said.

"How well do you *really* know them?" she asked. "You haven't talked about them often. Are you sure you don't want to stay with me?"

"They've helped me out a few times already."

"Like breaking and entering? Great people." Anne raised an eyebrow. "Are you sure?"

"I'll be okay."

My drive to Hell's Bells included a lot of anxious glances in my rearview mirror and nervous scans of the intersection at every stop light. I had no idea if George and Leo had lurked around the neighborhood, waiting for me to leave the burned wreck of my apartment, and followed me.

I arrived at Hell's Bells an hour or so before it closed. Trish sat in the front lounge holding court with a small group of people. Our eyes met, and she excused herself from their company. I walked to the bar and waited for her.

She wrinkled her nose when she sat beside me. "Why do you smell like smoke?" Her tone was stern, but her features softened when she brushed back my hair to examine my swollen jawline. "Did they find you? The wizard and the wolf?"

Biting at my bottom lip, I nodded, stubbornly trying to hold back more tears. My eyes were already red and swollen from crying on Anne's shoulder. Trish took my hand and led me down the hall, past the bathrooms, and around the corner. The hall continued to a doorway and a sparsely furnished one-bedroom apartment. She made some tea, and we sat at a small kitchen table while I relayed the details of the evening to her.

"I'll pass along the names of the two men to Reggie. Tell me more about your police officer friend," she said.

"Anne? Her investigative senses are tingling. She suspects there is more to George and Leo than a police report for a random mugging and dog attack. It sounds like she is going to be looking into them further."

"Can you keep me updated on her progress?" Trish said. "She might find some information we would find helpful."

"I could try. It's difficult to sneak anything past Anne, including intent. She asked me to meet her at the police department tomorrow to ID the two guys." I frowned. "I'm nervous she already knows I'm not sharing the whole George and Leo saga with her."

Trish nodded. "It's a tricky balance to have Commoners as friends and keep our secret. Nate and I no longer consider ourselves close to any."

The more I tried to figure out what Mitch was up to, the harder it would be to keep things from Anne. I wished I could tell her everything. "She offered to let me stay at her place tonight, and I made up some excuse as to why I didn't think it was a good idea. I don't like having to do that to her."

"It was necessary," Trish said. "You can sleep here as long as you need. We have several cots, or you could use a sofa out front after the club closes in the evenings."

"Thank you." Her offer eased a bit of the tension I carried. I felt safe with Trish and Nate.

"You're welcome." She smiled. "You smell awful, though. Bring in your clothes, and I'll throw them in the wash. You can shower and borrow some of my clothes until yours are clean."

When Hell's Bells closed for the night, Nate and Trish retired to the apartment. Trish went to bed while Nate rummaged for something to eat in the cramped kitchen. He sat down beside me with some reheated takeout and looked over at my phone. "What're you doing?"

I frowned at the screen. "Trying to find where that second location could be for The Mind Center. It can't be too hidden. No one would go to an appointment in an underground cave or secret hideout, right?" I looked at him. "Have you had any luck?"

He answered around a mouthful of food. "Some leads, but nothing solid yet. We can drive around later today to follow up on a few if you want."

"Yeah, okay." I put away my phone and stifled a yawn.

"Sorry I missed the reunion at your place with our two friends."

"I'm sorry you did, too. George, the short one, was still feeling the injuries you gave him. He had silver on him tonight."

"You seem to be attracting a lot of that shit." Nate glanced at my bandaged forearm and looked at me. He cocked an eyebrow. "Think I should raise my rates for helping you?"

I snorted. "Smartass. Aren't you supposed to be anywhere but here right now?"

He chuckled, stood, and crossed the small apartment to throw out the empty food container. "Holler if you need anything."

I tried to sleep on a cot wedged in the tiny living room, but my side ached, my forearm stung, and my mind wouldn't quiet. I surrendered to the fact I wasn't going to get any rest and sat up at the table drinking more tea instead. The dryer buzzed from the hallway. I changed my clothes and repacked the remainder of my clean laundry.

Now I had to wait to meet Emma at her church. Instead of meeting her after the service, I'd catch her before she went into the building. She couldn't possibly slip away. I'd tell her everything—what had happened with Mitch, George, and Leo, and about the connections between Anne's missing persons reports and The Mind Center's client list. The only possible person to stand between me and that long overdue conversation with my best friend was Emma's mother, Susan Arztin.

# 16

THE SUNLIGHT SEEMED harsh in its brightness as I waited for Emma outside the church. Trish had given me pills to take the edge off the pounding in my head and ache in my joints. My curly hair's frizz hid the bruise forming on the back edge of my jawline.

Most of the parishioners had already filed inside when Emma arrived alone. She crossed the road from the church's parking lot and gave me a small smile. "I wasn't sure if you would brave my mother today, and here you are willing to sit through a church service with her."

"I'd hoped to catch you before you needed to go in," I said.

"Sorry, I always run late on Sunday mornings. No getting out of service for you." Emma sounded more alert than the last time we spoke on the phone.

"Are you feeling better?"

"Yes," she said. We moved up the walkway together, past a security guard and into the church. "I need you to be patient with my parents. I've had so many arguments with them lately, I'd prefer not to throw any fuel on the fire."

A knot formed in my gut. I'd never seen eye to eye with Emma's parents, especially her mother, Susan. Emma and I had been friends ever since we first met at The Sound Refuge. So naturally, her mother, who was concerned with keeping up appearances, directly credited me with her daughter's love of donning "provocative" clothing, consuming "copious amounts" of alcohol, and staying out "dancing around" until morning. Susan was in complete denial that her daughter would be doing all of the above regardless of whether I was her friend or not.

I followed Emma into the large sanctuary. My sense of smell was flooded by the overpowering fragrances of warring designer perfumes. Emma led me past row after row of pews lined up like soldiers. Unlike the stoic, stone sanctuary where I'd attended the Committee meeting, this space was awash with light. Both the vibrant stained-glass windows and the wooden vaulted ceiling gave the sanctuary a feeling of warmth.

Unfortunately, the sense of welcoming warmth didn't extend to the congregation members—or at least to one in particular. As we took a seat beside Emma's parents, Susan smiled thinly at her daughter. Her smile disappeared when she noticed me. "You didn't mention you were bringing along a friend today, dear," she said. "And you're late. Again."

A blast of sound from the large pipe organ drowned out Emma's reply. A small group of people walked to the front of the sanctuary. I recognized William dressed in Sunday vestments and a stole. He didn't seem to notice me, his focus set ahead to the altar.

It was difficult for me to stay focused. My mind repeatedly wandered off, speculating about what would happen when Trish arrived after the service. I depended on Emma for cues on when to stand and when to sit. She shared her hymnal with me so I could pretend to sing.

Unlike her family members, mine weren't regular churchgoers. My parents didn't object to religion, but it was never a household priority. Sunday was another day off from school for me as a kid, and a morning to sleep through as a teenager.

I was grateful when the service finally ended. The perfumes didn't help my headache, and I was gradually losing the struggle to stay awake. We got a cup of coffee in a large communal room with a stage and high ceilings. I hadn't realized how hungry I was until I snagged a cookie from a tray being swarmed by children.

Emma's mother approached us, preceded by a cloud of designer perfume. I shored up my defenses. Every conversation with Susan was a battle. She greeted me with a frosty smile. "Good morning, Alexandria. It's so nice to see you in church."

Or, *It's so nice to see you in church instead of passed out in a gutter, you heathen*. The culture of passive-aggressive remarks disguised as kindness could have been founded in Hopewell. Susan Arztin was a master at it. I pushed aside my knee-jerk, inappropriate-for-church response and managed a neutral, "Thanks."

Even though Susan was petite like her daughter, she somehow still managed to look down her nose at me. She raised her perfectly shaped brows. "How's work?"

I glanced at Emma, telegraphing a plea for help. "Work is okay. It pays the bills." Barely.

"Your name recently came up when I had lunch with a friend. You'd scheduled an interview with her company and then didn't show?" Susan smiled. "You have to be careful, Alexandria. It's a small city. Business leaders know each other, so word travels fast."

Emma frowned and looked at me. "You didn't interview for the job?"

My face warmed. "Um, I—"

"Has Emma told you about the amazing strides she's made in her new position at Another Chance Ministries?" Susan beamed. "Her focus, hard work, and dedication are creating positive change for Hopewell."

"Thank you, Mom." Emma didn't smile.

"Are you unwell, dear?" Susan's voice lowered as she studied her daughter. "You're looking a little sickly. Some makeup this morning wouldn't have hurt." She sighed. "But I suppose you were running late like usual and didn't have time."

I clenched my jaw and exhaled slowly through my nose. My jawbone throbbed. I was too tired and my body ached too much to handle a prolonged interaction with Susan. "Em, should we go?"

A familiar voice greeted us. "Good morning."

My stomach lurched, and I turned to face William. Trish had asked me to stay away from him. In my defense, he'd found me.

His smile was smug. "Emma, I noticed you brought a guest to join us this morning."

"Good morning, Pastor William." Emma smiled. "Yes. This is my friend Alex Steward."

"Alex? I have a nephew named Alex." He asked me, "Is that short for something in your case?"

Already agitated by Susan, I bristled. "I prefer Alex."

"Alexandria," Susan supplied him.

So much for making outsiders feel welcome. Against my better judgment, I lifted my chin and watched William as I told Emma, "Actually, William and I have already met." I smiled at him. "You're fairly new, right? I don't remember you being here the last time I joined Emma at church."

William's smile faltered. "You visit us on a regular basis, then?"

Susan interrupted our exchange. Her expression was a combination of confusion and concern. "I'm sorry, Pastor William, but where have you met Alexandria?"

He smiled warmly as he turned to Susan. "She was a guest at a meeting held by community faith leaders."

Susan scoffed, looking at me. "You have a church?"

Emma's eyes widened. "Mother! Please. You're being rude."

I shrugged to let Emma know I didn't blame her for her mom's WASPish behavior. "I was attending the meeting as a concerned community member."

Susan frowned and looked at her daughter. "Is this something you should be a part of?"

"It's my responsibility as a leader at Patterson Street Church to attend on behalf of the congregation," William said. "Only one representative is required, so there is no need for Emma to give her valuable time."

Susan nodded, backing down. Emma gave her mother a thinly veiled, irritated look. I believed if it was solely up to Susan, her daughter would sacrifice meals as well as sleep to climb the social ladder. I'd never see my friend again.

William's tone turned businesslike. "Susan, if you have a few spare minutes, I'd like to discuss some items with you concerning the upcoming Hopewell mayoral campaign."

Emma jumped at the opportunity to make our exit. "Go ahead, Mom. Alex and I are getting some coffee together. I'll see you later this afternoon for family dinner." Emma took my arm and guided me away.

"I don't know how you can stand her," I muttered as we left the building. I scanned the sidewalks and parking lot to spot Trish but didn't see her or Reginald anywhere.

"She's my mother, and she loves me in her own way," Emma said. "I'm sorry for her behavior. As I mentioned before, her worldview is pretty narrow. She struggles with understanding the concept of her privilege."

"She seems to get along well with your pastor, and he's a guy I'd rather not spend time with. Birds of a feather?"

Emma raised an eyebrow. "You noticed? When I looked over during the sermon, you were falling asleep." I tried not to appear guilty as she continued, "Yes, Pastor William is more literal than most leaders we've had here. I feel our church can be a bit judgmental and narrow-minded anyway, but he's taken it to a new level. It honestly makes me feel uncomfortable at times, which is awful, because I look forward to Sunday mornings."

I snorted. "Your time is valuable. Why do you want to hang around with a bunch of people you don't agree with?"

She gave it some thought before she replied, "Not everyone at Patterson Street Church approaches the world like my mother and our pastor. Those two frustrate me because they're two of the loudest voices but preach some of the less compassionate tenets of our faith. Then the rest of the city believes everyone in the congregation is like Mom and William. It's not true." She looked at me. "Does that make sense?"

I could imagine how frustrating it would be having representatives who did not speak on your behalf, but their own. I nodded. "Yeah, it does. Have you thought of finding a different church?"

Her eyes widened, and she shook her head. "My mother would have kittens. Plus, I enjoy the ceremony of our traditional Sunday service. The ritual mentally resets and prepares me for the week."

I glanced back over my shoulder at the building. "What was William saying about an election?"

"Mother has a candidate, Joseph Stone, she's considering backing for Hopewell's next mayoral election," Emma said. "She'd asked Pastor William to review the candidate to help her decide."

My phone began to repeatedly buzz. "I'm sorry, let me check this." Then Emma's phone began to vibrate as well. I had texts from both Nate and Ben. I checked Ben's first.

*Where are you? Message me asap.*

Nate's text was nearly identical.

*Whereabouts are you right now? Give Trish or me a call.*

The sudden and similar nature of the messages, sent within moments of each other, gave me a feeling of uneasiness. I frowned at my phone. "Hey Em . . ."

Emma read a message on her phone. Her tone was urgent, and her words rushed. "Alex, I'm really sorry. I have to go."

I looked from her phone to her. "What's wrong?"

She fished for her car keys in her purse. "Something has happened at Another Chance. I need to be there right now."

"Do you want me to come along?" I'd finally gotten time alone with Emma to confront her about Mitch. If possible, I didn't want to let her out of my sight.

She shook her head. "No. I'm sorry. I'll call later." Emma gave a quick glance up and down the street before she rushed across it toward the parking lot, her phone already to her ear.

I messaged Ben back to let him know I'd been with Emma. As I crossed the street to walk to my car, my phone rang.

Nate's voice was uncharacteristically anxious. "Alex, where the hell are you? Are you okay?"

"I'm fine." Uneasiness morphed into dread and crept into my stomach. "Ben asked the same question. What's going on?"

"There are raids taking place across Hopewell." His tone sharpened and carried a snarl. "It's the map."

"What?" The hair at the nape of my neck rose. My inner wolf stirred from the sudden surge of anger that hit me. "Do you think it's Mitch?"

"Whoever it is, they're utilizing the Hopewell police department. Some officers showed up here at the club. Trish is dealing with them out front."

"How can I help? I'm downtown."

"We have everything handled here. Can you go to The Beacon and check in with them?"

"Yeah. Definitely."

"Thanks." Nate ended the call.

My phone buzzed yet again. Ben was at The Sound Refuge for a sound check and wanted me to meet him there. Was he aware of the raids? I quickly sent a reply so he wouldn't worry. *I'm okay. Need to stop by The Beacon first. Will see you afterward.*

I drew stares as I hurried and finally ran along the sidewalk. The Beacon was close enough; it'd be faster to get there on foot. Businesses along the way had police cars parked out front. I rounded the corner onto the street to the coffee house, and my anxiety spiked.

Flashing lights of the police cars could be seen from down the block. I slowed my run to a hurried walk. Three officers stood inside the entryway of the building. Another officer was posted at the front door.

The officer at the door folded his arms across his chest when I approached. "Sorry ma'am. No one is allowed inside the building at the moment."

"Why? Is something wrong?" I tried to look around him through the large windows. The police officers inside spoke to two employees behind the front counter. I recognized one of the baristas from when I visited with Ben.

"I'm going to ask you to step back, ma'am," the officer in front of me said. "You'll need to get your coffee elsewhere today."

"But my friend called me from inside. She's scared because she doesn't understand what's happening." A sudden commotion broke out at the counter, the sound of which reached us outside. The police officer turned toward the noise. I seized the opportunity to slip past him.

The smell of fear hit me as soon as I made it through the doorway. The officers' shouts were amplified within the small brick-walled room. The young barista I recognized had been pulled from behind the counter and handcuffed. He was read his rights while the other employee stood at the far back corner speaking on a phone. Another officer yelled at the second employee from across the counter.

I tried to move unnoticed through the crowded and chaotic entryway. One of the officers seized me by the arm and hauled me toward the stairs leading down into the seating area.

"M'am, we need you to stay out of the way. Wait downstairs with the others," he said.

I resisted the urge to wrench myself free from his grasp. "Why are you all here to arrest one kid? What did he do?"

"I said stay out of the way."

The handcuffed employee was steered toward the front door.

"Wait! You didn't answer me!" I said. "What has he done?"

The police officer turned toward me. "This is your last warning! If you don't back away, you'll be joining him. Is that understood?"

I glared at the officer, my chest rising and falling rapidly as the adrenaline and anger surged in my body. I wanted to stop them from taking the young man, but I couldn't help anyone from inside a police cruiser.

There was another disturbance outside at one of the police cruisers, and the two remaining officers dashed outside. I looked out the window, and my pulse lurched. Ben was recording the officers with his phone. He must have walked over after getting my message. One of the officers attempted to wrestle the phone away from him.

*No, no, no.* Why the hell did I tell him I'd be at The Beacon? He couldn't get arrested. I rushed to follow the officers outside. "Ben, stop! Give them the phone." He had the right to record the officers, but they seemed willing to argue that point.

Two other officers had already joined the fray. They worked together to hold Ben against the side of the cruiser. Were three police officers really needed for one skinny guy and his phone? The first officer wrenched Ben's phone away from him. One of the others steered him toward the backseat of a second cruiser.

I latched onto Ben's jacket sleeve to hold him back. "You have the phone. He wasn't doing anything wrong. Let him go!"

"He interfered with the arrest. Move out of the way." The officer pushed Ben forward. I felt my anger spike, and the creature inside me tried to claw her way to the surface. Ben looked back at me. He shook his head.

"They can't take you!" I said. Nothing good would come from being arrested while tethered. My fingers tightened on his sleeve. The familiar ache tingled in my hands. Golden eyes reflected back at me from his glasses.

Ben's eyes widened and he shook his head again. He mouthed at me, *Stop.*

I couldn't help him. My focus needed to be on suppressing the beast inside me or I'd wolf out in the middle of the day in front of the policemen. I wanted to scream in frustration. I let Ben's jacket slip past my fingers and watched helplessly, my hands clenched into fists. The police officers got into their cars. The barista was in the back seat of one cruiser, while Ben sat in the other. The police cars drove away from the coffee shop.

There was a rush of bodies as the patrons decided to exit the shop at once. A wisp of a woman entered, weaving past the departing customers. I followed in her wake. She spotted the young man behind the counter and hurried to him. They embraced, and she asked him, "What happened? Where is he?"

"They arrested him and took him to the police station." The stench of fear came off the young man in waves.

I spoke to the woman. "Trish Drake sent me. I tried to find out why the police were making the arrest and stop them, but they wouldn't tell me anything. I'm sorry."

"Hello." She looked at me as if she just noticed my presence. "I'm Heather. I own this business."

"I'm Alex," I said. "Do you know of any reason the police would arrest your employee?"

"No. He's my son, and he's done nothing wrong. I don't know why they would take him." Looking dazed, she reached for the edge of the countertop. "Please pass along my thanks to Patricia."

I nodded, stepped outside, and started toward the police station. I called Trish to tell her about the events at The Beacon. "Is Ben going to be okay?" I asked. "Or will he be in more trouble because he's tethered?"

"I'm not sure," she said. "Is Ben's apartment marked in any way on the map?"

"No." It was the first location I checked after mine the evening I'd gotten the map.

"I'm on my way to the police station to retrieve Nate," she said. "He didn't receive the police's drop-in visit well. I'll collect Ben, too."

A large weight lifted from my chest. "Trish, that'd be amazing. Should I meet you there?"

"It's your choice. If there are as many people there as I imagine, it may be a long wait."

"Are you able to do anything for all of them?" I wasn't sure how far Trish's reach went within the city's legal system. She obviously wielded influence if she'd been able to bail out Nate and me without any follow-up court date.

"We hope to. Reggie and I will be organizing an impromptu gathering for later tonight. Information and legal aid will be available for those whose friends and family were taken."

"Any sign of George and Leo?" I asked.

"None," she said. "I'll count that as a win for us."

"What can I do?" I'd failed to prevent the barista and Ben from being taken, but maybe I could be useful in some other way.

"Can you spend the evening at the club?" she asked. "I'm not sure how long I'll be away. Your apartment was already targeted. Since Nate will not be staying at the station, I fear it's only a matter of time before someone other than the police is sent to Hell's Bells for him. You and Nate know what George and Leo look like and what to expect from them."

"Yes, of course," I agreed.

"Thank you. Be careful." She ended the call.

I took a deep breath in an attempt to slow my racing thoughts. Was it a good idea to leave Ben in the hands of someone I'd met only about a week ago? Trish did bail me out without being asked, so I decided to trust she'd help Ben too.

Altering my course, I headed toward Another Chance instead. I wouldn't visit the station until I was due there for my appointment with Anne. In the meantime, I could check on Emma.

I walked to the shelter, the thin layer of snow squeaking beneath my boots. It was so frigid, the cold air made the inside of my nose ache. The sun's brightness was unrelenting, causing me to squint against the blinding light reflecting off the snow. The usual crowd of people stood outside Another Chance, huddled together with cigarettes and steaming Styrofoam cups.

Inside the building, mixed among the odors of damp clothing and bulk-prepared food, was another sharp scent. Fear. Across the dining room, the door of Emma's office was cracked open and the light was on. I could hear her voice. I quietly pushed open the door to find her talking on the phone. She rubbed at her temple, her brow furrowed as she frowned down at her desk.

Emma looked up and waved me in as she continued her phone conversation. "Yes, I understand what the business owner said. However, we spoke to your department multiple times about Barbara Greene's mental illness. We agreed on how to proceed if anyone on your force encounters her. There's a detailed outline."

I entered the office, pushed the door closed, and sat down opposite her. Emma's cheeks flushed. "Yes. Yes, I'll be here all day. You also have my cell number." She slammed the office phone down on its receiver. Her head rested in her hands, and her elbows on the desk. "It is *so hard* to have patience with them."

"What happened, Em?"

Emma raised her head to look at me. "One of the shops over near the park reported Barbara to the police for shoplifting again. When she forgets her medicine, she gets confused. She doesn't understand she's taking items she should pay for. The police came here and arrested her."

"Shit, I'm sorry," I said. "Was that your emergency?"

She nodded. "Yes. By the time I got here, the police car was pulling away with her in the backseat."

"I'm sorry, Em. That's frustrating."

"Then they wouldn't let me see her at the station, so I don't know if she understands what's happening. When there's a lot of sudden activity, it disorients her." Emma sat up. "They're supposed to call me back, but who knows if that'll happen. What about you? Is everything okay?"

I frowned. "Not really. Did you notice all the police cars on the way back here?"

She shook her head. "I had tunnel vision. I tried to get here as fast as I could."

"There were a lot. Wizards and wolves are being arrested."

Emma's eyes widened. "Are you serious? Why?"

"Apparently all sorts of random reasons were given by officers, but the arrests were made at the same time at different locations. I was at The Beacon when they took away an employee."

She sat back in her seat. "Barbara. She's a wizard." Emma's cheeks reddened again. She frowned. "Who would do something like this?"

"We're not sure yet. Trish and Reginald are trying to find everyone who was taken first. Then they're going to look into who was responsible." I hesitated. "Em, I need to talk to you about Mitch. I'm sorry to drop it on you with all the other bullshit going on, but I think he's involved in this."

I expected immediate anger and resistance. She'd told me multiple times what she thought about my opinions of Mitch. But instead, her brow creased. "Why would you say that?"

"Remember the night I followed him back to his condo? I told you I was protecting Mitch from those guys who attacked Ben?" I shook my head. "I was wrong. Now I know that I interrupted a meeting between the three. Shortie and the Ox are working for Mitch. They met him at Patterson Street Church after one of your meetings. He gave them a city map. Many of the marked map locations are where arrests were made today."

The color drained from Emma's complexion. It made her skin seem all the more like porcelain. She spoke quietly. "If that's true, why didn't you tell me sooner?"

I frowned, unsure I'd made the best choice in waiting. "Because I wasn't certain of all the details. I wanted to find those out first so Mitch couldn't discredit me. Then I had a difficult time getting you alone."

She nodded slowly. "He said you would make up stories like this about him. He told me you were trying to ruin the programs we're building here because of your jealousy."

Anger surged through me. "He's manipulating you, Em," I growled. "And trying to get rid of me."

She chose her words carefully. "He said the night we went to the show, he'd left his credit card at The Sound Refuge. When he left a second time, you were waiting outside and attacked him. We had a terrible fight over it because I didn't believe him, even though his shoulder was injured. You've never attacked anyone unless provoked." Emma swallowed and leaned forward. "Was Mitch the person who stabbed you?"

I frowned and nodded. "He called me an 'abomination' and said I wasn't 'worth saving.' Then he arranged to have me kidnapped by those two thugs he hired. They burned out my apartment last night."

She covered her open mouth with her hand. Her eyes widened and turned glassy.

"What is all this redemption bullshit he goes on about?" I asked. "Is it connected to what he's doing at The Mind Center? He has patient files on a lot of wizards and wolves. Is he trying to round us up for some weird experiment?

Emma blinked, and a tear slipped down her cheek. She remained speechless, staring at me.

"Mitch's family has so much pull, he has to be benefiting from or involved in the arrangement of today's raids. Do you know where he is right now?"

She sat back in her chair and slowly shook her head. "I don't know." Emma's gaze focused far beyond her office. She hadn't lowered her hand from her mouth. Her voice was quiet and frail. "I'm sorry. I need some time alone right now to think."

"Are you sure? I can stay and talk through this with you or even be here just to listen," I said.

She swallowed, and another tear slid over the curve of her cheek. "I'm sure."

"I'm sorry, Em." I was finally close to convincing her how awful Mitch was, so why didn't I feel any better? Instead of the triumphant vindication I'd expected, her reaction was creating more pain in my chest.

I walked around the desk and wrapped my arms around her. She leaned into my hug and placed her hand on my arm. "I'll be at Hell's Bells tonight," I said. "Please call me when you're ready to talk. I'll meet you anywhere you want."

Emma nodded, but avoided my gaze. I left Another Chance for the police station to see Anne and confirm the identities of George and Leo. My goal was to give Anne the information she needed without her learning how deeply involved I was with this mess, and how I'd kept that from her.

She was an excellent cop, and I was a terrible liar.

## 17

THE POLICE STATION was a chaotic bustle of activity. Searching the crowd, I couldn't see Trish anywhere. Anne met me in the lobby. She raised her brows at me in greeting and muttered, "Welcome to bedlam."

Following her through a maze of halls, I wondered how much the police were told about the synchronized raids they carried out. Did they question the orders they were given? "What's going on today? There are cruisers all over downtown."

Anne glanced back at me. "The majority of us don't know, hence the confusion up front. A select group was sent out about two hours ago. I wasn't even aware of it until they were bringing people in. Processing is a shit show right now."

We turned into a room packed full of desks. Anne led me to hers and sat down. She flipped open a folder and turned it to face me. "These are the two we picked up at the bridge. Are they the same two men who set a fire inside your apartment and tried to kidnap you?"

I looked down at the two mugshots and found familiar faces staring back up at me. I nodded. "Yes, that's them."

Anne read from another sheet in the file. "Meet George Marino and Leonard Whelan. It seems these two spend a lot of time together, including building their criminal records. They're both from out of state." She looked up from the page at me. "And the visit to your apartment wouldn't be their first offense for arson."

"So, repeat offenders. That doesn't surprise me," I said. "Are you able to arrest them now?"

Anne set the page aside on her desk. She leaned back in her chair and crossed one long leg over the other. She locked me in her patented analytical gaze. "I was wondering, Alex, was their attack on you the first time you met these two?"

My face flushed. *Dammit.* "No."

Anne frowned. It was more of a disappointed expression than an angry one. "I thought we agreed you would tell me things like this. Why didn't you say something sooner?"

That seemed to be the question of the day. I didn't have time or patience for this conversation right now. I wanted to find Trish and make sure Ben was okay. "I don't know. I'm sorry."

"I respect your choice to be a private person, but can you at least start meeting me halfway with something like this?" She motioned to the photos. "Who knows what else these two could be up to while they're here. From the looks of their records, they're the guys hired to shatter kneecaps. When they turn up, there are usually additional, more dangerous, people involved."

"I said I was sorry." What else did she want from me?

"Where have you seen them before?" she asked.

"They were talking to Mitch at Patterson Street Church one night. Mitch must've found out I saw them together, so he followed Ben and me after the show at The Sound Refuge. As you know, things escalated quickly after that." I was glad Mitch had sent George and Leo to my place instead of Ben's to look for me.

"You were lucky that night." Anne closed the cover of the folder. "To answer your question about your arsonists, yes. With you ID'ing them, we have enough now to arrest them. I'll be submitting an affidavit after we're done here."

"And Mitch? They're working for him."

She shook her head. "No. We'll be arresting George and Leo because of what happened at your apartment. We can't pick up Mitch just because he talked to them. It's not enough."

"So how do I prove he's involved?"

"You don't. You stay away from him," Anne said. "Have you talked to Emma yet about Mitch attacking you?"

I frowned. "Yes. I spoke to her about it before coming over to see you."

"It didn't go well?"

"She listened, but she was understandably upset."

Anne sat up and leaned toward me. "Are you ready to file a report against Mitch for the stabbing? We can do that right now."

I could tell she wanted me to do so. I shook my head. "Any progress with the Happy Chauvinists?"

Anne frowned. "All the facts and reasons to open up an investigation into the local chapter are there, but I'm getting pushback from my superiors. They're saying it's not worth the time, money, or PR mess it might create. They wouldn't even listen to Detective Grey. He thinks I'm on to something."

"Well, you have George and Leo to add to the mix now. Won't that help sell it?"

Anne shook her head. "I don't think those two have anything to do with the harassment and assaults by the Noble Sons."

I blinked. "I'm sorry, what?"

She tapped her fingertip on the folder holding George's and Leo's information. "I think these two are involved with our missing persons reports. They were trying to kidnap you."

Anne's words made me revisit what I thought I'd known about Mitch, George, and Leo. Emma said Mitch wasn't involved with the Noble Sons, but I assumed he lied to her. Could Mitch be targeting supernatural beings as well, but not with the same goal in mind? He'd babbled something about helping them.

"If we bring in George and Leo and charge them, I believe this sudden surge in missing persons cases is going to cease. And if we're careful, hopefully they'll tell us where to find the people they kidnapped." Anne tapped her finger again. "Alex, what else aren't you telling me?"

I shook my head. "We've got to find out more about Mitch. He isn't an innocent bystander in all of this."

"Let us bring in George and Leo and see what they tell us. Maybe they'll give up who they're taking orders from. Meanwhile, you can give some more thought to filing a report against Mitch."

"Okay. Are we done, then?" I moved to stand.

"Alex?"

Pausing, I looked at Anne. There it was again: the Anne Scan. "Yeah?" I settled back onto my chair.

"Ben was here earlier," she said. "He was with the woman and man who own that club."

"Was Ben released?" My pulse thudded in my ears. If they didn't keep him here, maybe he'd get off easy with the Committee as well.

Anne nodded. "They skipped the line and strolled right out of the station. It's like those two have a fast pass for this place." Her nails drummed on the folder. "I looked into Patricia Drake and Nathan Osterberg. They have lengthy criminal records. How did you meet them?"

"A community meeting." I swallowed. It was the truth, but it sounded fabricated even to me. Anne didn't know me as someone who'd run to attend any such meeting.

"Uh-huh." She leaned back in her chair. "Please be careful around the two of them. It was awful coming into work and learning you'd sat overnight in a cell. I couldn't do anything about it, and I'd hate for it to happen again."

She wanted to blame Trish and Nate for my arrest. I'd been the one who pushed Nate to help me. I dropped my gaze and nodded. "I'll be careful." Again, this was a conversation for another time.

Anne walked with me back toward the lobby area. We exchanged a quick hug before she opened the door into the loud and bustling room. The crowds hadn't thinned in the slightest. Voices bounced around the high-ceilinged room as bodies shuffled for positions at the desk windows.

I gave Anne a sympathetic look. "Good luck."

She smiled and shrugged. "Just another day."

I exited the building onto the sidewalk and took a deep breath of frigid air. Reginald would be interested in knowing George and Leo's full names. Even though Reginald might be upset with me, I also wanted to tell him about what happened to Ben. Since he was Ben's grandfather and a representative, he'd know if Ben had to worry about any disciplinary actions dealt by the Committee.

I reached for my phone and paused. Idling several parking spaces down the one-way street was a rusted, blue sedan. My nostrils flared as I walked toward the car, seeking any familiar scent. A police officer ushered a cuffed person into the back seat of the large vehicle. I recognized the smell of damp wool and the knit hat. It was Barbara.

"Hey!" I called out. The officer closed the car door and looked my way. Seeing me, he turned and walked briskly across the sidewalk back toward the building. I picked up my pace to intercept him, but he disappeared through an unmarked door in the wall of the police station. I turned back toward the sedan. George sat behind the steering wheel, wearing an expression first of surprise and then irritation. Leo was crammed into the passenger seat. In the back seat were two other people—a middle-aged man and Barbara.

Without thinking, I dashed across the sidewalk and lunged for the driver's side door handle. George cranked on the wheel and stomped on the gas pedal. The large car lurched into the one-way street, causing an approaching car behind it to slam on its brakes and blare its horn. The blue sedan accelerated. I raced down the slippery sidewalk parallel to it, dodging pedestrians. A red traffic light shone ahead at the intersection. I'd have another chance to get into the car. The beast within my body was already lurking right below my skin. The chase thrilled her. When I reached inside, her strength immediately warmed the muscles in my legs. A burst of speed allowed me to get ahead of the vehicle.

At the light, I swerved over through the pedestrian crosswalk to meet the car in the street. George scowled from behind the wheel as

Leo tapped on his partner's shoulder and pointed at me. Instead of stopping, the car engine revved as it accelerated. He planned to blow through the traffic light.

I tried to dodge back out of the way. My boot slipped on the slush in the crosswalk. I hopped up off the ground, and the front corner of the car struck me. I tucked my shoulder and rolled, not gracefully, along the edge of the car hood and fell to the street. More horns sounded as the sedan raced through the intersection. I sat up and yelled in frustration. My consolation prize was the license plate number of the retreating car.

Wincing, I stood. My shoulder and hip already began to throb. A few well-meaning pedestrians rushed into the street to see if I needed help. I shooed them away, repeatedly telling everyone I was okay. Thankfully I hadn't caused an accident. The traffic behind me started to back up, and cars at the intersection had stopped. It was time to leave before the congregation of gawkers grew any larger.

I limped from the scene as I dialed Anne's number. It rang through to voicemail. "It's Alex. I ran into George and Leo outside the station. They have a woman named Barbara Greene who was arrested from Another Chance today. An officer loaded her into the same sedan George and Leo had at my place. Em will be able to give you all the details on Barbara." I left the license plate number.

Still limping, I started toward Patterson Street Church to retrieve my car. I attempted a call to Trish on the way to alert her to the George and Leo sighting, but her phone rang through to voicemail. I tried Reginald next, hoping she was with him.

He answered the phone, the background a din of conversation. "Yes? Hello?"

"Hey Reginald, it's Alex. I have—"

"Hello?" he repeated.

"Hi. It's Alex."

"Miss Alex. One moment, please." The phone became muffled. When he spoke next, the noise in the background had faded. His tone was businesslike. "It is a touch chaotic here. Do you have any word from Ms. Drake?"

I frowned. She should be with him if she'd finished at the police station. "No, but I have the full names of the two men for you: George Marino and Leonard Whelan. My friend is a Hopewell police officer. She said George and Leo have existing criminal records in the Commoner's law system."

"Most helpful. Thank you."

"I need to ask you something about Ben." I paused, but he didn't reply. "Hello?"

"What's happened to Benjamin?" he asked.

"He was arrested at The Beacon coffeehouse. Some cops threw him in the back of the cruiser when he tried to film them." I heard muttering on Reginald's end of the line. "Is he going to be in trouble with the Committee?"

"Quite possibly." Reginald's tone had an edge to it. "Did he harm the officers?"

"What? No." I thought of the three men wrestling Ben against the car and taking his phone from him. "He didn't touch them."

"Thank goodness. His sentence may only be extended another year or two."

"What?" I was glad the archaic execution thing wasn't on the table, but it still seemed severe. "He didn't do anything wrong!"

"Miss Alex, I warned you something like this may happen if you didn't dissuade him. Benjamin has always struggled with self-control. As his . . . friend . . . I'd hoped you would remind him of the stakes."

His words caused me doubt. The type of relationship forming between Ben and me was unknown territory. Until meeting Trish and Nate, I didn't believe it was a possibility for me. I wasn't interested in being solely responsible for Ben's decisions though.

Reginald used my silence to change the subject. "Wasn't Ms. Drake intending to give Mr. Osterberg a ride home from the police station?"

"She should have been done with that by now. I was surprised she isn't with you." A slow dawning of dread unfurled in my stomach for the second time that day.

"Miss Alex, she and I had planned to visit William."

"I'm on my way there now." Ending the call, I risked the slippery pavement and lengthened my strides. Patterson Street Church's steeple emerged from the horizon line ahead of me.

THE ATMOSPHERE OF Patterson Street Church was starkly different from several hours earlier. Only a few people talked in the entryway. Some type of choral music was being practiced in the sanctuary. I hurried down the darkened halls, looking for the administrative offices.

The door to the office suite stood ajar, and I caught the combined scents of fear, blood, and another werewolf. I tried to enter, but the door wouldn't open all the way. I peeked around its edge instead. The church's security guard was lying facedown on the carpet. His boot stopped the door. With some wiggling and shimmying, I squeezed my body between the door and frame. I crouched beside the guard and was relieved to feel a pulse at his wrist. Trish's voice, a low growling tone, came from another office beyond the front desk.

Unlike the doorway I'd passed through, the door to the next office stood open. Trish's eyes burned a bright gold as she locked her gaze with mine. She stood beside a desk where William sat, his hair disheveled and his face sweaty and blotchy. A smear of blood dirtied his upper lip and the front of his white shirt. Items on the desk were in disarray, and one of the chairs in front of it was overturned.

"Trish, what're you doing?" I stepped into the office. She released a rumbling growl that immediately caused me to stop. The hair on the nape of my neck rose, and the beast inside me stirred.

"Leave," she said.

It took effort to keep my voice steady. "Reginald is waiting for you at the church." I glanced at William. His look of desperation, an unspoken plea to help him, irritated me.

"Tell him I'll be with him soon," Trish said.

"Come with me."

"Go!"

I flinched, and my pulse accelerated. "I'm not going to leave unless you're with me." If she decided to remove me, I wasn't confident I had any chance of resisting.

Her eyes narrowed and she bared her teeth. "Don't interfere."

I swallowed and gave a quick nod.

Pointing a finger at me, William shouted, "If you don't do something about this, I'll have you arrested as well!"

The speed of Trish's strike caught me by surprise. William's head was thrown back, and blood splattered across the desk.

"You don't get to speak to her," Trish snarled. She leaned over the desk and seized the stunned man's shirt collar with her clawed hand. Her ears had grown pointed, splitting the sleek curtain of her hair. She pulled him toward her, lifting him from his seat. "Beginning now, no one from your petty militia of self-righteous assholes is going to be talking to any of Reginald's or my people. You'll dissolve the group immediately. If you report Alex or me, no one on that Committee will be fast enough to stop me from tracking you down and killing you. Am I being clear?"

His eyes wide and watering, William nodded.

"Good." Trish smiled, exposing her pointed canines. "Now tell me about the map Mitch White had, and how he got it."

"What map?" William asked. Trish growled and twisted his collar. He squeezed his eyes shut. "I gave him a list from the Committee records!"

"Who organized the raids today?" I asked.

"It was Mitch. He needed a lot more of people. He used the confusion to hide that he took them." William whimpered. "Please, let me go."

Trish scanned the man's features before she released him. She straightened and glared down at William, but she spoke to me. "The White family has invested in the police department in the past. It's why it was so costly for me to have Nate and you released free of any breaking-and-entering charges."

"Anne mentioned resistance from her boss when she tried to take a closer look into the assaults and missing person reports," I said. But why go through all the trouble to bribe the police and coordinate an elaborate kidnapping scheme? "What does Mitch gain by abducting wolves and wizards?"

"He's naive and thinks they can be saved." William dabbed at his bloody nose with a handkerchief. "He's attempting to cure them at the therapy center he operates."

I looked at Trish. "The night he stabbed me, Mitch told me I couldn't be saved. He's also been messing around in Em's head to convince her using magic is wrong."

"That's all I know," William said. "I didn't tell him to kidnap people. There's nothing I can do."

Trish's eyes flashed, and she slammed her fist on the desk, startling William and me. A crack split across the surface of the wood. "Wrong!" she shouted at him. "Do not try to shirk all responsibility for his actions. You are his representative, his leader, just as you are with the Noble Sons. What did you expect scared men to do when you've villainized the people they fear? Your words have consequences. Always!"

William sat red-faced, silent, and shaking.

Trish trembled as well, but not from fear. Her voice dropped in volume and darkened. "Spineless bastards like you sicken me. You spew your nonsense, only interested in how it will elevate your wealth or social standing. You never consider how it will affect the people you're meant to serve." She leaned toward William, her claws raking the desk's surface. He shrunk back as if he could melt away into his chair. "But who gives a shit about them or who they might harm, right?" she said.

"Your followers have served their purpose." Her nostrils flared, and she ran her tongue over her sharp teeth.

The look in her eyes as she watched William made me uneasy. "Trish," I said, my voice soft, "he's been warned. Reginald needs your help."

She straightened, turned her back on William, and strode past me out of the office. I gave the cowering man a last glance before I followed her. Trish's features shifted, her ears disappearing back beneath her hair and her hands regaining their human shape. We stepped over the security guard and walked briskly down the hallway toward the entrance of the church.

"Do you think he's going to report you anyway?" I asked.

"No," she said. "He values his own welfare above anyone else's. My warning should buy us a reprieve from his minions while Reginald presents our evidence to the Committee." She pushed through the front doors and stopped outside, taking a deep breath.

"So William formed the Noble Sons, then inflamed the members' fears enough that they threatened and attacked our people," I said. "Seems like a conflict of interest with his Committee job, doesn't it?"

Trish released a shaking exhale as a burst of steam into the winter air. Her eyes were a warm brown hue again. "He should lose his seat for this."

"And then there's Mitch, who used the list of names William gave him to create a map to locate wolves and wizards in Hopewell. George and Leo were hired to abduct them," I said. "These raids to grab more people at once seem desperate. Mitch must know we're moving in on him." I certainly hadn't kept my intentions of shutting him down a secret from him.

"I don't want anyone else taken," she said. "Are you still able to help Nate watch over those at Hell's Bells tonight while I'm with Reginald?" she asked.

"Yes." There wasn't a shred of doubt or hesitation. I wanted to help protect the other wolves.

"Nate is close to securing the second Mind Center's location and entry information," Trish said. "Hopefully it will lead us to the missing wolves and wizards."

And I'd finally have answers as to what Mitch was doing to Emma, and how to stop it from ever happening again.

# 18

BEN AND I arrived together at Hell's Bells later that evening. At the door, I asked to speak to Nate. The burly doorman pointed across the lounge to where Nate was seated on one of the sofas. Emma was next to him. She looked down at her folded hands as she spoke. Nate sat forward in his seat, elbows resting on his knees, nodding occasionally.

Stares tracked Ben and me as we crossed the room together. Unlike our previous visit to the club, people were taking notice of him. The restlessness and tension in the air was palpable. And with that was the smell of fear. It was everywhere today. The combined scent of that and the other wolves triggered something in my own body, raising both my heart rate and the hairs on the nape of my neck.

Emma and Nate looked up when we reached them. Nate stood. "Thanks for coming over to help."

"I feel like I'm accepting a stick of dynamite," I said. "Besides the stress level being through the roof, how is everyone?"

His expression was grim. "They're strung pretty tight after today. Some of the younger ones had friends or family taken. There's a lot of anger, so be careful." He pointed at Ben but spoke to me, "And don't let him wander off alone here tonight. If someone jumps him, give them a rough shake by the scruff. They should back down after that."

"Thanks for the warning," I said.

Nate motioned to Emma. "She showed up asking for you. We've been talking about the second location for The Mind Center."

"What?" My pulse stuttered. I looked at Emma.

She nodded. "I want to help."

Nate continued, "We can go over there tomorrow to scout the place out. Right now, we watch over our people. I'll take downstairs if you're okay monitoring this area."

I nodded. "We'll keep an eye on the door."

Nate gave Ben a clap on the shoulder. "Sticking around? You've got a pair on you, wizard. I like it. Alex seems to enjoy having you nearby, so for her sake, try not to get eaten tonight."

Ben nodded and watched his feet.

Nate turned and bowed with a flourish toward Emma, wiggling his eyebrows and grinning. "Thank you, again."

Emma smiled. "You're welcome."

Nate turned and crossed the lounge. After a brief word with the doorman, he descended the stairs into the noise and dark below.

I took Nate's vacated seat next to Emma. "What convinced you?" I asked.

Ben sat down next to me as Emma spoke. "It's something I stumbled upon when I went to one of my appointments." She took a deep breath. "The second location for The Mind Center is in a warehouse district outside the city. After my first few appointments at the main clinic, I was asked to begin going to appointments there."

"Was Mitch the one treating you, Em?" I asked.

She bit at her bottom lip when it began to tremble. She nodded before inhaling a slow, purposeful breath and continuing. "I arrived at one of my appointments early. The second location was always less busy, so it was only the receptionist and me. I asked to use the bathroom. He directed me around the corner to the end of the lobby."

Her gaze unfocused as she recalled details of the memory. "My phone rang. It was Another Chance, so I stepped through a pair of doors into a hallway for some privacy. There were two more sets of doors there. After my call, my curiosity got the best of me, and I peeked through a glass panel in one of the doors. It was a type of hospital wing. There were nurses and a doctor. I thought I'd trespassed into an area not meant for clients, so I turned back."

"Did Mitch ever find out you went back there?" I asked.

Emma's eyes refocused on me. "I asked Mitch a few days later why they chose such a large space for the second location. He said they bought a larger building with hopes to expand as the business grew." She shook her head. "He didn't mention the area I'd seen. The whole experience was odd. I hadn't thought about it again until you spoke with me earlier."

"Have you talked to Anne today?"

Her jaw clenched, and she nodded. She took a deep, shaky breath. I didn't know if she was going to start crying or shouting. "She told me what happened outside the police station. I want to help Barbara make it back safely. If anything I know about The Mind Center can help Nate and you do that, I'll share it with you."

Emma's words loosened a vise from around my heart. I leaned forward and pulled her into a tight hug. The familiar fragrance of her perfume comforted me as she returned my hug and began to cry. I was thankful she did, so I could be the stoic one. A light touch landed at the small of my back, a silent gesture of support from Ben.

After Emma shared her recollection of The Mind Center's second building and where it was located, Ben and I walked her to the entrance of the club. She smiled as she looked from him to me, reaching out for my hands. "I don't need to know the details, but promise me you and Nate will be careful."

I grinned and squeezed her hands. "I promise. Celebratory night out when Barbara is home and the bad guys are behind bars?"

"Definitely." She gave Ben and me both a quick hug and left.

Ben and I returned to the sofas to post up as sentries for the rest of the night. I sat close to him, my thigh snuggly pressed against his, so the other wolves would know he was with me. Or that's what I told myself anyway. Really, any excuse would do.

Ben didn't notice and was already busy writing in the small notepad he carried. *Seems you've been busy.*

I told him everything, from Nate's and my confrontation with George and Leo to the files we found after breaking into Mitch's office at The Mind Center. The corners of Ben's mouth dipped downward. He became visibly agitated when I recounted being attacked and losing my apartment to the fire.

Ben scribbled on the notepad. *Endangering yourself to do the Committee's work? What're they doing to protect you?*

"Reginald set wards on my apartment."

*A lot of good that did,* he wrote.

"I met with Trish and Reginald yesterday morning. Apparently, after you and I ran into Aiden at the cathedral, he rattled the nerves of the Committee members. Our few allies decided not to help because they're scared of losing their seats."

Ben shook his head. *If you're caught breaking in or something else goes wrong, they'll tether you. Let Trish and Reginald handle it.*

I chewed at my thumbnail and looked up from the notepad at Ben. I wasn't sure what to do. He placed his hand flat over the center of his chest before moving it in a clockwise, circular motion. It was the sign for "please."

The original plan of finding out who George and Leo were, and what Mitch was doing to Emma, had escalated into something larger. What I'd untangled in my efforts to protect Emma affected a lot more people like us—those who are different, who wished to live their lives in peace like anyone else. I felt an odd sense of responsibility to expose the wrongs being inflicted upon them. Is this what Nate was talking about?

*You're a wolf. We take care of each other.*

I reached over and stilled Ben's hand. "I'll think about it."

His brow unknitted and he managed a small smile. He signed "thank you" and lifted my hand from his chest to kiss my fingertips. His touch was so gentle, something I'd rarely experienced in my rushed, one-off encounters with other men.

The creature inside me stretched within my chest, lured by the heat of his breath on my skin. I'm sure our hunger for Ben shone through my golden eyes. I didn't make any effort to hide it from him.

The remainder of the evening at Hell's Bells was uneventful. The atmospheric tension within the club dissipated throughout the night. I was grateful, the last week having been physically and emotionally taxing.

I gave Ben a ride back to his apartment after the club closed. If Ben was up for it, I had no intention of immediately returning to the cot in Trish and Nate's apartment. I sent them a brief text so they wouldn't worry.

By the time we pulled into the parking lot behind Rear Window, my inner wolf paced behind my ribcage. We were nearly delirious from Ben's scent in the confined quarters of the car. I put the car in park and held my breath, my hand resting on the key.

Smiling, Ben stole a glance at me and motioned toward the building. "Would you like—"

"Yes." I switched off the ignition.

We reached the first landing of the stairs before my hands were on him. My tongue was in his mouth, and I pressed as much of my body as possible along the length of his. If we didn't make it into the apartment, the creature reveling in his touch would take him where we stood. Alleyway, bathroom stall, stairwell, it made no difference to her.

I parted from him, and he was quick to follow me up to the door. My hands slipped into his back pockets to find the key. Face flushed, he fumbled with the lock. The door gave way behind my back. I seized a handful of his jacket and pulled him into the dark apartment. The door barely closed before I reached for the zipper of his jeans.

"Wait." His hand closed over mine.

"What? Why?"

He placed a delicate kiss at the corner of my mouth. "Slow down. There's no need to rush."

A throaty growl escaped me. I didn't want to slow down, and the beast within me didn't either. She wanted him, and I harnessed that confidence. Otherwise, it didn't work.

I quickly shed my jacket and boots. My jeans and shirt went next. I helped Ben pull his shirt off over his head and dropped it onto the floor atop the pile of my clothes.

He caught my hands, now tipped with claws. "Let's not—"

I kissed him to stop any more words from interrupting us. We stumbled to the center of the room. Strength fired through my muscles, and my inner wolf lunged. I twisted my body, Ben cursed as he lost his balance, and we tumbled to the floor.

I rolled atop him, pinning him beneath me.

His hands grasped the sides of my thighs. My body briefly tensed from the echoes of dark memories trapped deep within it.

Even with doubt surfacing in my clouded mind, the beast driving my actions refused to release Ben. My clawed hands ran over his chest, and I leaned forward to take a taste of his warm skin. He was delicious. I couldn't saturate my senses with him fast enough. A low and constant growl vibrated in my chest.

I wanted to devour him.

Ben propped himself up onto his elbows. My tongue passed over the skin near his collarbone. His neck. He inhaled sharply and his fingers tightened on my thighs. "Alex, wait."

Why was he still talking? I snarled and caught his bottom lip between my pointed teeth. He flinched and moved a hand from my leg to his mouth, frowning.

I froze, my pulse thundering in my ears. That bright copper taste from a time my body refused to forget was on my tongue again.

Ben pressed his fingertips to his lip. His brow furrowed, and his gaze twitched from his bloody fingers to me. Another scent, sharp and acidic, disrupted his own. Fear.

What the *hell* was I thinking? I pushed away. Her prey taken from her, the creature inside me rioted. Pain twisted my guts. My words were pinched. "I'm so sorry."

He sat up and reached for my hand. "Wait."

I shook my head and hurried over to my discarded clothes. For the first time since we came crashing into the apartment, the chill in the air caused me to shiver.

Still frowning, Ben stood. He turned on the lamp beside the sofa. "Can we please talk?"

"No." Wasn't the fact I'd messed everything up obvious? I pulled on and zipped up my jeans, a difficult task with the enlarged and grotesque state of my hands.

"Are you leaving?"

"Yes."

"Alex, please stop."

I halted, my balled-up shirt clasped tight to cover my chest. "What?" A growl edged my words. "What do you want?"

Ben blinked. "What do I . . ." He gave a short laugh. "I'd like us to discuss what the hell just happened." When I didn't reply, he sat down on the couch and held out his hand. "You can talk to me. What's going on?"

I blinked back tears. "This was a stupid idea." *Careless.*

His eyebrows raised. "Really? Because I thought it was very much a *great* idea. At first, anyway. But I asked you to slow down, repeatedly, and you ignored me."

I shook my head again. "I can't. If I slow down, it all goes to hell. It confuses her." Those toxic memories would be recalled in vivid detail. My inner wolf would interpret Ben as a threat. "She'll do more than give you a bloody lip." I pulled on my shirt and tossed him his. "I'm sorry. I wanted to be closer to you."

"But it felt like you weren't here."

A sharp ache thrummed in my chest. I swallowed to steady my voice. "This is what I have to give right now. It's the only way I know how to be with someone."

"Okay." Ben wiped his fingers clean on his jeans. "Then we can wait. I don't mind waiting. When you're ready, you can let me know." His friendly smile surfaced. "Can you stay over anyway?" He motioned to the mattress. "You can have the bed. I'll take the couch."

"What? You're not pissed?"

"Not like before. I have a better understanding now." He put on his shirt and stood. "It's up to you, but you're welcome to sleep here. Don't feel like you have to run away from this."

Part of me bristled at his assumption. "I'm not running away." I was absolutely trying to run. Ben stepped toward me, and my inner wolf attempted to leap forward to meet him. I held up my clawed hand and backstepped. "Give me a minute to cool down."

He stopped. "Sure. Whatever you need."

With my arms wrapped tight about myself, as if I weren't fully clothed, I waited outside the soft circle of lamplight. He got a pillow from the bed and grabbed some blankets. When Ben walked down the hall to the bathroom, I slunk to the mattress, undressed, and slipped beneath the sheet and quilt.

The fabric was strong with his scent. I closed my eyes, inhaling deeply and slowly exhaling. *It's okay. You're safe.* The agitated beast within me quieted. With knuckles aching and popping, my hands shifted back. I offered her a new possibility. *He's safe.*

Ben came back from the bathroom and settled onto the couch. The lamp was switched off. "Goodnight, Alex."

"Goodnight." My dreams were blissfully nightmare-free.


LATER THAT MORNING, I awoke feeling warm and content. The quilts on Ben's bed and his scent comfortably enveloped me. He was fast asleep on the sofa, his arms wrapped around his pillow. I got up and silently padded to the bathroom. On the way back, I stopped beside the couch.

His face was turned toward me and half obscured by the pillow and his hair. The bruising around his eye and cheekbone had healed to a dirty yellow hue. I crouched beside him and brushed the backs of my fingers along his bristled cheek and jawline.

My touch caused a small change in the rhythm of his breath. His eyelids fluttered open, and he smiled blearily. "Morning."

The way he smiled at me gave my stomach a funny flipping sort of feeling. My face warmed and I stood. "Good morning."

"Thanks for staying."

"It's preferable to a cot," I said.

He chuckled. "Have you tried the coffee? I can start some for us."

"No work today, then?"

There was a pause before he suddenly sat up. "What time is it?" He blinked away sleep as he pawed at the discarded clothing beside the couch. He grabbed his jeans and looked through the pockets until he found his phone. His eyes widened and he mouthed a curse. Looking at me, he managed a mixed expression of apology and panic. "I'm late. I need to go."

"Go. It's all right. I'll be down later." I took the seat he vacated on the couch and watched him frantically dress. There was an impressive juggling of a coffee maker, a toothbrush, and shoelaces before he rushed over to me. He handed over his key, hesitated, and kissed my cheek. I inhaled deeply to fill my lungs with him. Then he was out the door, a brief blast of cold air making its way inside. I pulled the still-warm blankets around me as the repetitive dripping sound of the coffee maker filled the empty apartment.

Without Ben's company, I grew restless. I gathered my clothes off the floor of the chilly apartment. After dressing, I took a seat at Ben's small table with a cup of coffee and my phone. I had missed calls from Emma and Nate, but no voice or text messages.

After calling Emma back and having to leave a message as usual, I called Nate.

He didn't bother with a greeting when he answered. "What are you doing right now?"

"Not much. Is everything okay over there?"

"Yeah, no uninvited guests. I'm getting ready to drive out to that off-site location." When I didn't reply he added, "For The Mind Center."

"Right. Sorry, I'm not quite awake yet." And barely had caffeine in me.

"Where are you? I can pick you up."

"I'm downtown at Rear Window."

"I'll see you in ten to fifteen." There was a click as he ended the call.

I chewed at my thumbnail, checking the time. I'd told Ben I would consider letting Trish and Reginald complete our investigation into The Mind Center. But it wouldn't hurt to drive out and simply get a look at the building and location. I put on my jacket and boots, grabbed a mug of coffee, and left the apartment. The change in temperature was drastic. An icy wind blew powdery snow around me as I carefully descended the stairs. I re-entered the building and walked into Rear Window.

Music greeted me in the record store, and I spotted Ben among the aisles. He referenced a clipboard as he filed some records away. I felt foolish but couldn't help smiling as I approached. "Hey there."

Ben looked up from his work, smiled, and signed, "Hello." He saw the cup of coffee, raised his eyebrows, and pointed at himself.

I nodded and handed the mug over to him. He signed his thanks. I glanced up at the front of the store. Another employee, someone I hadn't met before, stood behind the desk. Ben tapped on my arm. He pointed to a note he'd written. *Have a break in a few. Want to get food?*

"I would, but Nate is on his way here to pick me up. We're driving out to The Mind Center's second location." Ben's brows drew together. I placed my hand on his wrist before he could start writing. "We're only scouting it out. We'll be careful."

*Something the Committee should do instead? Pass them the lead?*

I shook my head. "It's something low risk I can do to help. If it gets too intense, we'll leave."

A bell jingled at the front of the shop. Nate was in the entryway. He made eye contact with me before browsing a display as he waited. I turned back to Ben. "I need to go. Dinner instead?"

His attention moved from Nate to me. He frowned.

"We'll be okay." I handed Ben the apartment key. "I look forward to hanging out with you more later."

Ben's smile was weak. He turned his attention back to the clipboard, and I walked to the front of the store.

Nate looked up. "Ready?"

The icy wind assailed us as soon as we were outside. We got into Nate's car, and my sense of smell was once again pummeled by the awful odor of cigarettes. I suppressed a gag. "Nate, you have to kick this smoking habit."

"Yeah, I know." He started the car and turned down the radio.

The bulky door protested with a groan as I pulled it shut and cracked the window. "How can you stand the smell?"

"Addictions aren't known for being sensible. At least it dampens the stink of that wizard you rolled in." He drove toward the highway. "Did you enjoy your late-night snack?"

"Don't be crude." I looked out the window, my cheeks hot. "And it's none of your business."

He glanced over at me. "Dammit. That doesn't sound like we'll be rid of him anytime soon." I shot him a mock glare, and he chuckled. "While you were out, Trish got home."

"How did things turn out at the church?"

"She and Reginald spoke with a lot of people," he said. "As we suspected, the raids were synchronized across Hopewell. Both businesses and residences were targeted."

I nodded. "As noted on the map. How's Trish holding up? She must be exhausted." And hopefully not tempted to revisit William.

"She made it home, but not to bed. When I left, she was on the phone trying to find more bail money for people who can't afford it."

"What about you?" I said. "How do you feel about all of this?"

He paused before replying, "I've never had patience with willful ignorance or the abuse of power. Too many people are hurting or dead because of it, including people I love and care for. I see Trish struggle every day trying to do what is right for everyone in what is considered the correct way." He gave me another glance. "I'm a *burn-it-all-down-and-start-over* kind of guy. There's a good reason Trish is in charge and I'm not. She has the patience and stamina for the long game. I respect her decisions. We do it her way."

"It's nice," I said. "What you two have." Their relationship had a level of intimacy I didn't think was available to me. I'd assumed, like my career, it'd been lost the moment my inner wolf awoke.

"You're goddamn right." Nate flashed his toothy grin.

He took the next highway exit, landing us in a giant industrial park south of the city center. Occasional roars overhead came from traffic in and out of the airport nearby. The industrial area itself was a maze. Twisting roads wound between clusters of large, nondescript warehouses.

He turned into a parking lot among a large group of cars. Nate referenced the map on his phone and pointed across the street to yet another plain warehouse. "That's the place." He reached across me and took a set of binoculars from the glove compartment.

I arched an eyebrow at him. "Professional creep?"

"I birdwatch." He lifted and adjusted the binoculars before scanning across the building. "The main entrance is at the front, right corner. I can see the logo on the door. There's also a side door near what looks like loading docks. We'll probably use that."

"Have you looked into the security yet?" I asked.

"It's pretty standard issue for warehouses in this area." He lowered the binoculars. "There'll be a camera at each of the entrances and alarms at the doors. Forcing our way in won't give us much time to search around such a large place before the police arrive."

"Maybe we disrupt the cameras?" It worked at the first location. We were caught because Mitch had awful timing.

"I don't have that connection for this place. The only wizard you have in your pockets can't cast magic, and I don't know any well enough to ask. Unfortunately, we're lacking the hacker other heist teams employ, so I'm not sure how we'd do that." He drummed his fingers on the steering wheel.

"Emma gave us a description of the layout, but I don't see her wanting to sneak in with us. What if we ask someone from that community group at The Village Pub to help?" I asked.

Nate smirked. "They write letters. They don't help break into warehouses under the cover of night. We're not going to find a magic user willing to be put on the Committee's radar if we get caught." He looked at me. "I already have a few calls in to people I know. We'll get in there."

Watching the warehouse across the street, I chewed at my thumbnail.

"Alex, I'm catching a whiff of hesitation. I don't like hesitation," Nate said. "Are you still in or not?"

My heart thudded in my ribcage. Mitch had somehow poisoned Emma's mind, nearly convincing her that her talent for healing was more of a curse to deny than a gift to embrace. There were others he'd taken who would be told the same. I couldn't let that happen.

Reginald would only be starting the process of submitting our evidence to the Committee. This was the quickest way I could see of helping Emma, finding Barbara, and shutting down Mitch. I lowered my hand and nodded. "Yeah, I'm in."

Nate grinned and handed me the binoculars. "I was hoping you'd say that."

I raised the binoculars to take a closer look at the building across the street. My stomach convulsed, and I broke into a cold sweat. Parked at The Mind Center's front entrance, covered in an undisturbed layer of the previous night's snowfall, was Emma's car.

# 19

I PACED IN front of the bar at Hell's Bells, my mind racing with all the awful things Emma could be facing at The Mind Center warehouse. The beast inside of me strained and struggled against my hold. Occasional snarling noises escaped my lips.

"Christ, Alex, sit down." Nate sat at the bar watching me. "We'll go tonight."

"She'd tried calling me!" I'd looked more closely at the missed call from Emma. The timestamp said it was made after she'd left Hell's Bells. In my excitement to get Ben back to his place, I'd completely missed it.

Nate shrugged. "There's nothing you can do about it right now."

"We can call the police," I said. "I'll call Anne and send her in there to get Emma."

Nate shook his head. "We talked about this twice already. Mitch isn't going to let that happen, and we'll be in there before your cop friend can get her warrant."

We'd argued the entire ride back from the warehouse, and now we were a good ten minutes into arguing at the club. I'd already begun recycling my material with him.

I stopped. "We'll report him to the Committee—"

"—and that dick William will tell Mitch," Nate said.

Repeated calls to Emma didn't lend any insight into why her car was at the warehouse. It seemed her phone was turned off. My mind was stuck in a panic loop.

"Listen," Nate said. "I don't like it, but I've put a rush on the keys. Let me take you back to Rear Window, and you can get something to eat with your wizard. I'll call when it's time for us to go."

I shook my head and continued to pace. "I can't do that." My stomach was tied into so many knots, there was no way I could eat.

He shrugged again. "Or stay here and wear a hole in our floor."

Growling, I stormed outside for some fresh air. An IT company van sat near the front doors of Hell's Bells. I examined the van, running my hand over the vinyl lettering on the side. Nate had the van replicated and even found us some shirts with the same company's logo embroidered on the breast pocket. The last items we were waiting for were the vendor keycards for the loading dock.

I checked the time and found only ten minutes had passed since the last time I'd looked. Maybe I should go see Ben. He didn't know about my decision to break into the warehouse, so I could tell him. How would he react? Would he try to stop me? Or would he insist on helping?

Reginald asked me to keep Ben out of any activities that would put him in the Committee crosshairs. I pulled my phone from my pocket and sent Ben a message.

*Change of plans. Helping with something at Hell's Bells. Will message you later.*

WHAT SEEMED LIKE an eternity later, Nate pulled the van up to the warehouse's side entrance near two large garage doors. The keycard gained us access without a problem.

We entered the building, and the scents of sawdust and fresh paint filled my nose. Hollow clicking noises preceded large industrial lights that flickered on far overhead. The cavernous room was nearly empty except for tall stacks of shipping crates closer to the loading dock doors. Our footfalls on the concrete floor sounded painfully loud as they echoed throughout the room. We walked toward a double doorway in the back corner.

When we stepped through the doorway, the dramatic change in space was disconcerting. Fluorescent lights flickered on in the ceiling to reveal a long and narrow hallway stretching ahead of us. It felt claustrophobic in comparison to the open area we'd left. There were no windows along the hall, only closed metal doors on either side. I looked at Nate, lowering my voice in the heavy silence of the place. "Any opinion as to where we should start?"

He shook his head, so I opened the door across the hall. The lights clicked on inside the room, and the stink of industrial disinfectant burned my nostrils. It was bigger than a physician's exam room but had a similar layout. A piece of equipment that looked like a cross between an exam table and a large dental chair was bolted to the floor. Lights were mounted on several metal arms secured to the ceiling. I backed away, goosebumps rising along my skin at the sight of restraints on the chair.

On the opposite wall, across from the door, was a long, darkened window. Nate opened the interior door to the area behind the glass. He gave a low whistle. I crossed the room to join him. "What is it?"

He walked further into a type of observation room. "What the hell are they doing out here?" Consoles of monitors and computers crowded the space. The monitors displayed the empty room on the other side of the glass. I looked back at the long window and could see out into the exam room.

"Are they experimenting on people?" Voicing the question aloud agitated my inner wolf. Her rising anger propelled me forward. "I'm going to check the next room." It was almost a carbon copy of the one I'd left. I exited into the hall and pulled the door shut. "Same thing."

Nate opened the door across from me. He looked back. "Same."

"Let's keep moving." We continued to the end of the hall and passed through another set of double doors. The hall split toward both right and left. We turned down the left hall and through yet another set of double doors. The hall was a more comfortable width and matched the hospital floor description Emma told us about. Each identical door along the hall had a narrow window and a chart posted on a clipboard outside.

Nate lifted one of the charts from its hook. He read the front, replaced it, moved to the next door, and read the next chart. "Come here and look at this."

I stopped when I heard movement from down the hallway. My breath caught and I looked at Nate. He was frozen in place, his nostrils flaring as he stared intently in the direction of the noise. My heartbeat drummed in my ears as we waited. The sounds of an opening door, receding footsteps, and then a clicking noise as the door closed traveled to us from down the hall. I slowly exhaled.

"Do you want to leave?" Nate said.

"No. Who knows if we'll get in here again." I looked at the clipboard as he handed it to me. "What did you want to show me?"

"This name looks familiar," he said. "Can you check it against that list from Mitch's office?"

I flipped back through the photos on my phone. Sure enough, the name was there. "Yeah, he's on the list. So are Mitch's supernatural patients eventually locked up here?"

Nate had already moved on to the next door. He read the patient's name to me. "Barbara Greene. That's who you're looking for, isn't it?"

My eyes widened. "Yes. She was arrested at Another Chance, and then taken from the police station by George and Leo." I returned the clipboard and joined Nate. He tried the door handle of Barbara's room. It was locked. I shielded the window from the light with my hand so I could get a glimpse inside the room. The room was too dark even for me.

"Alex, let's try these." Nate was beside me with a key ring.

I looked at the keys and back at him. "Where . . ."

He started testing keys in the lock. "There's some sort of reception area a few doors down. It's probably who's here with us. The computer is on with a card game on the screen."

"They left the keys out?" It wasn't the stellar security I imagined for a place like this.

"You're assuming everyone appointed to a security-sensitive position is competent." The doorknob turned. He flashed a grin and opened the door. A strong stench of fear and sweat wafted out. The hallway light angled into the dark room. Quiet murmuring came from within its depths.

Nate and I both waited, but no one stepped into the light. Nate's eye color shifted, and he cautiously stepped into the room.

The door down the hall from us opened again. "Nate!" My voice was hushed and urgent. "Someone's coming."

He looked back at me, his eyes reflecting the hall lights. A sudden rush of energy pulled past me into the dark. Nate had already dove toward the floor as I leapt back out of the doorway. A blast of force rocketed out of the room. It bent the metal doorframe it passed through and crashed into the wall across from the door. Chunks of drywall debris tumbled to the tile floor from the new crater.

A voice shouted from down the hall. "You! Step away from there!" A security guard had spotted me and ran toward us.

My heart racing, I looked into the room to see if Nate was okay. He scuttled backward along the floor to clear a path for a figure rushing into the light. Her eyes were wild, and her hair was a gray, snarled mess, but it was Barbara.

Seeing me in the doorway, she shrieked unintelligible words and waved me away. Another blast of force arched from her fingertips and curved toward me. I tried to sidestep again. My shield flared to life and deflected most of the attack that clipped me and spun my body to collide with the wall. I cried out as my shoulder put a deep divot into its surface, but at least I still had all my limbs.

Barbara ran from the room and hesitated, blinking in the bright lights of the hall. She was barefoot and in a hospital gown.

"Stop!" The guard halted his advance about ten feet away. He yelled at Barbara, "Back in the room, patient!"

Barbara's gaze moved slowly from me to the security guard. She leisurely raised an open palm toward him. The guard drew his gun and repeated, "I said, back in your room! Now!"

The surface of my skin began to tingle. "Get out of her way!"

Another blast of force was released. The gun popped, and Barbara's shoulder twitched. The guard's weapon was blown from his hand along with several fingers. He screamed as he cradled his mangled hand.

Barbara turned toward me and lowered bloodied fingers from the gunshot wound in her shoulder. She looked dazed. Seemingly seeing me for the first time, she asked in a slurred voice, "Alex? Is that you?"

I hurried to her side. "Yes, it's me."

She studied her wet fingers. "I think something is wrong."

Nate ran from her room. He scowled at the injured guard. "It's time to haul ass out of here. We don't want to be hanging around when he calls up his friends."

"I'm not going to leave without Emma." I put my hand on Barbara's shoulder and tried to meet her wandering gaze. "We're going to get you home." The stain of fresh blood was spreading through the fabric of the hospital gown.

"Do you think she's able to keep up with us?" Nate said.

The maimed guard stumbled behind the reception area. The beast inside me sensed the injured man, still a threat to us, and pushed a snarl past my lips. My legs flooded with warm strength. I sprinted toward him, leapt, and barely cleared the counter to tackle him. A good amount of the counter's contents and his chair came with us. At least he hadn't reached the phone. I grabbed the receiver of said phone beside me and smashed it on the tiled floor.

Nate rushed over, heaved the guard halfway to his feet, and knocked him unconscious with a single swift punch. He removed the small two-way radio at the guard's belt. It met the same fate as the desk phone. "You're going to have to make some hard choices if we're going to make it out of here, Alex."

I looked at the remains of the guard's hand and the pooling blood. "We have to do something about his hand."

"Do you want to find Emma or not?" Nate growled. "We have to go!"

"What if he loses too much blood?"

Nate growled and seized the man's sleeve at the shoulder. He tore the fabric with a jerk of his clawed hand. "If you absolutely need to, make a call when our asses are clear of this place." He tore the fabric lengthwise again, using the strips to wrap the injury and bind the security guard's wrists behind him.

I left Nate's side to hurry down the hall, quickly checking the names on the remaining clipboards. More people were being held in the rooms, but none were Emma. If we released them now, would they be as confused, and therefore as dangerous, as Barbara? It would make getting everyone out of here in time all the more difficult.

"We'll be back for you," I said more for myself than the patients that couldn't hear me anyway. I rushed to Barbara, urging her, "Let's go." She nodded absently as I guided her into an awkward hurried walk.

"Leave her," Nate said. "We'll come back."

"No!" I snarled. "We came here for Barbara and Emma."

"Where are we going, Alex?" Barbara smiled fondly at me.

I tried to keep my tone calm. "We're going to find Emma and get a cup of coffee together. We need to hurry though. She's waiting for us, and we don't want to be late."

We pushed through the double doors into the hall's intersection. I looked back at Nate. "Can you wait here with her? I'll be able to move faster. I'll find Em and bring her back here."

"You're going to go anyway, aren't you?" he asked.

I nodded.

Nate cursed and shook his head. "Go."

"Barbara," I took her wrinkled hand in mine. "My friend Nate is going to wait here with you while I go get Emma. I'll be right back."

She patted my hand. "Hurry before the coffee gets cold, dear."

I left the two of them in the hall and pushed through the second set of double doors. The odors of fresh paint and new carpeting lingered in the dark hallway. Inching down the hall, I scented the air until I found the vanilla fragrance I was seeking. The door to the room was locked.

I pressed my ear against the door, seeking any sign of movement or conversation inside. Nothing. I lowered my voice and spoke near the doorframe. "Em? Are you in there?"

There was rustling movement and hurried footsteps within the room. Emma spoke from the other side of the door. "Alex?" She started to sob. "He locked me in here."

"Shh, hold on. I'll get you out." I stepped back from the door to look it over. It had a wood finish with a handle more like a lever than a doorknob. A keyhole was situated at the lever's pivot point. "I'll be right back. I'm going to look for a key."

I crept a short distance to find a small lobby. The front desk was there, as well as a handful of waiting-room chairs. I started toward the desk but froze when headlights turned into the parking lot. Several cars drove toward the front door.

Time for Plan B.

I hurried back to the room where Emma was being kept. When I reached for my inner wolf's strength, she wrestled against me to get free. Sweat broke out on my forehead, and a surge of strength warmed my limbs. I wrenched on the door handle and pushed against the door. The lever broke off into my hand, but the door remained locked. I pitched it aside with a growl.

Car doors slammed outside.

"Stand back from the door," I shouted for Emma to hear. A few solid strikes with the heel of my boot finally broke the locking mechanism. The door swung open, triggering a shrieking alarm.

Disheveled and bleary-eyed, Emma rushed out. She launched straight into a hug. "I came here to talk to him and see for myself." Her sobbing voice was muffled by my jacket. "I didn't want it to be true."

My stomach dropped as Mitch and two other security guards entered through the front doors. "Em, we have to go. Now. Quickly." I pulled her along with me back down the hall. Mitch shouted from behind us. We burst through the double doors where Nate and Barbara waited.

"Barbara!" Emma released my hand and embraced the woman.

Nate cursed, seeing the security guards and Mitch. He held open one of the doors to the right of us. "Let's go!" We all passed through into the long hallway leading to the loading dock.

"Barbara is too slow. Can you carry her?" I asked Nate.

He looked cautiously at Barbara. "As long as she doesn't cleave me in two for doing it."

The door swung closed behind us. Emma grasped Barbara's hands and crouched to catch the woman's attention. "Barbara, you've been injured. We want to help you. Alex's friend Nate is going to carry you, okay?"

Barbara looked skeptically at Nate and considered the offer. "Don't get handsy with me, young man."

He crouched, and I helped her onto his back. The door behind us began to open. I turned and pushed back against it, slamming it closed to the sounds of startled surprise. Nate stood and adjusted Barbara's weight. He advanced more swiftly down the hall toward the loading dock. Emma ran beside them.

The force behind the door I held closed increased. The soles of my boots squeaked on the tile as I was pushed gradually backward. Unfortunately, I'd have to deal with the security guards and Mitch. They were too close now, so I wouldn't be able to outrun them.

Nate's voice called from the end of the hall. "Alex! Come on!"

"Keep going!" I spared a glance back. The door closed behind the three of them. Collecting all the frustration, fear, and anger roiling inside me, I surrendered more control to my inner wolf. Another wave of heat pulsed throughout my body. My hands shifted, cartilage popping and nails distorting, as she was allowed more freedom. I leapt back from the door.

The two men looked surprised as they suddenly gained access to the hallway. I seized the guard closest to me, pulling his arm upward while ducking my shoulder under his body. With little effort, I bent forward and hauled his weight up and over my body. His mass brought him crashing to the floor in front of me. I stepped on his chest and twisted sharply on the arm I held, popping the limb out of the joint. He screamed, and the beast inside me delighted at the sound.

I didn't hear the gunshot before the force of it hit my bicep. My ears ringing, I looked at the second guard. The gun he still had raised at me shook. His eyes were wide and his face pale. The scent of his fear stoked the anger churning inside of me. With an inhuman snarl, I seized his weapon and slammed it across the side of his head. He crumpled. Panting, I wrestled with the slippery hold I had of the beast raging behind my ribcage. The weapon slipped from my claw-tipped fingers and clattered to the floor.

Mitch was nowhere in sight. The coward. I stepped over the first fallen guard, breaking into a jog down the hall toward the loading dock. I didn't see Nate, Emma, or Barbara anywhere in the bigger room. Sprinting across the large space, I burst through the exit doors into the icy cold night. Mitch stood outside with three more guards, their guns drawn. They'd been waiting for me. The van was gone.

# 20

MITCH SMILED. "YOUR friends have left. It seems you'll be staying with us." He spoke to one of the guards. "Send someone after that van."

The man nodded and jogged back to the front entrance. Mitch motioned to the two remaining guards. "Take her inside." The guards cautiously approached me. A growl rumbled up from my throat. My inner wolf pulled my lips back to expose pointed teeth. The guards halted and gave each other an unsure glance.

Mitch sighed and ran a hand over his face. "Alex, it's been a disappointing evening. I don't have the patience right now for tantrums. The next time you act out, these men have permission to fire on you. Again."

I studied the two guards, weighing my options. They both carried firearms. I didn't know if Mitch was armed. I'd never dealt with guns before and wasn't sure how much damage my body could take. My arm already throbbed from the wound I'd taken from the guard inside. I lowered my gaze and raised my hands, allowing a guard to approach. The man secured my hands behind my back with some type of tie. He and the other guard escorted me back into the building.

The group of us followed the same route Nate and I had taken earlier. "You've forced me into a really difficult position tonight," Mitch said. "Not only is our location compromised, but the good work we're doing is also at risk."

I snorted. "Taking an old lady away from those who care about her, locking her up, and then brainwashing her is 'good work'?"

"Don't mistake yourself for a savior," Mitch said. "Did you consider the patient's well-being before selfishly kidnapping her from the safety of her hospital room? Her treatment is incomplete. Because of you, she's even more of a danger to herself and others than she was before."

"Her name is Barbara, jackass. And now that Em knows what an evil bastard you are, she can fix the messed-up thoughts you've planted in Barbara's mind."

We passed into the long narrow hallway off the loading dock. The injured guards at the end of the hall were already gone. The guards stopped me in front of one of the many doors, and Mitch moved past us to open it.

"I haven't given up on Emma," he said. "She's so close to being our first successful case." He stepped aside, and the guards escorted me into the room.

Unlike before, the long arms holding the lights were pulled down and positioned around the chair. A woman in a physician's coat passed into the back room with a clipboard. There was a humming noise in the room as if a lot of equipment or fans were being run. A wheeled cart with a metal tray sat beside the exam chair. Waiting in the tray was an assortment of what looked like medical instruments.

I broke into a cold sweat. "Let me go!" I struggled not only with my captors, but also with the creature pushing forward into my consciousness. This time she was winning. Growling erupted from deep within me. My ears and feet began to lengthen. My toes curled painfully within the confines of my boots.

Mitch slammed the door closed and shouted to the back room. The woman emerged and hurried to the cart beside the chair. She grabbed a syringe from the tray.

"No, no, no—" My next violent shove against the guards gained me a few paces. Fear turned into panic. The edges of my vision blurred as the doctor came at me. I heard a wild bout of snarling and vaguely comprehended it was escaping my own body. The needle was like a bee sting. My body rapidly became distant and lethargic. At some point the guards released their hold on me. I'm not sure I even made it a step closer to the door before everything went dark.

MY EYES OPENED, and I turned my head away from the blazing lights above. There was the same white noise of humming fans. I attempted to sit up, but my legs and arms were restrained. Everything snapped back into focus. I was reclined in the strange chair in the exam room. Instead of the button-up shirt and jeans I wore when Nate and I broke in, I had on a hospital gown like Barbara's. The gunshot wound in my arm was dressed. Mitch and the guards were nowhere to be seen. Movement in white drew my attention to the doctor. She stopped by the side of the chair and fed a syringe into the IV beside me.

"What're you doing?" I jerked my arm to pull against the strap across my wrist. It held.

She glanced at me from behind her glasses, her lips pressed into a grim line before walking away. Her voice was barely audible through the doorway of the small interior room behind the one-way window. "The patient is awake."

My limbs began to tingle and feel distant. The bright lights overhead pulsed. I turned my head again and partially lowered my eyelids. The door opened and Mitch entered. The doctor greeted him and passed him a clipboard. I couldn't hear what they were discussing. He nodded, sat down on a stool, and rolled up beside the chair I was bound to. I struggled to focus on him.

"How are you feeling, Alex?"

My tongue felt thick in my mouth. "You should let me go before someone comes looking for me."

He tilted his head. His smile was sympathetic. "No one is coming to look for you."

"If they don't come, the police will." Stringing words together to form sentences was a challenge. "We know you took people during the raid for weird mind experiments. We have proof of what you're doing."

He looked through the chart. "Is that all the poor woman is to you? Proof of your conspiracy theory?"

"You messed around in her head and confused her, like you were doing with Emma."

Mitch continued as if explaining a complex situation to a child. "Our patient has been retrieved and returned safely to her room. She's exhausted from all the confusion *you* caused her. Thankfully, she wasn't injured in the process."

"Your guard shot her!"

"No, you're mistaken," he said. "The guard was the person injured. You don't remember?"

His blatant lie fueled my anger. I pulled on the restraints again, but they held. I stopped, and dread crept into my consciousness. If they'd retrieved Barbara, where were Nate and Emma? "Where are my friends?"

"Your 'friend'? Which friend?" He flipped a sheet of paper on the clipboard. "Patricia Drake. Past charges include aggravated assault, conspiracy, extortion, criminal harassment, racketeering, and solicitation. Benjamin Sharpe. Past charges include assault, conspiracy, disturbing the peace, criminal harassment, forgery, minor in possession, and voluntary manslaughter. Nathan Osterberg. Past charges include aggravated assault, arson, burglary, disorderly conduct, drug possession, forgery, open container, theft, and vandalism." Mitch lowered the clipboard to look at me. "And now Mr. Osterberg is being held on charges of kidnapping."

His words made me feel sick. "You're making all of this up."

"Am I?" Mitch's tone was frustratingly smug. "Do you really feel you've chosen the right people to surround yourself with, Alex? Are they *good* people, or are you being used for their personal agendas? And to expose Emma to them." He raised his brows and shook his head. "I'm surprised she tolerated you as long as she did."

The creature inside of me rallied against whatever it was the doctor dumped into my veins. My eyes narrowed at Mitch, and I released a low growl. The sound barely left my throat before a jolt of sharp pain, originating from the restraints, coursed through my body. I gasped in surprise.

"Please refrain from giving in to your curse while we're having our discussion. This equipment is designed to remind you that embracing that monster is the wrong choice." Mitch smiled. "How much do you know about tethering?"

My response was a searing glare.

"Let me explain. Tethering to keep the peace doesn't work," he said.

"The one thing we agree on."

"Depending on who serves on the Committee, sentences are inconsistent and results are widely varied. Eventually the offender is back in the same situation as before. No reform is achieved. He lives day to day, saddled with these abnormalities, with no support. It's a barbaric practice that, for your kind, eventually leads to death." He raised a finger. "But why wait until a crime is committed? Instead, what if we offer preventative treatment?"

My mouth went dry and nausea twisted my stomach. Mitch truly believed he was *helping* supernatural beings by brainwashing them. He was forging ahead with the confidence his solution was the correct one. He was the good guy. It was more frightening than if his intentions were purely malicious.

Mitch's eyes lit up. "The mind is a malleable machine. With this type of therapy, we could curb and eventually eliminate the ability to cause harm. The option to entertain the primal urges your kind is cursed with would be removed altogether. If the choice wasn't available, your people couldn't make the wrong one, repeatedly, as they so often do."

His words were a hot knife twisted in my gut. "It's not a choice! Our gifts are in our blood. It's who we are!" I winced as another streak of pain was sent into my body from the restraints.

"Is it, though? It seems your first offense didn't occur until later in life." The paper on the clipboard rustled. "Let's take a closer look at when you decided it was acceptable to entertain these monstrous urges. To begin, you had the choice to prevent the situation from ever happening. Why didn't you invite a friend so you weren't running alone that day?"

All the air left my body. My pulse thundered in my ears. From far away, my voice asked, "How did you get that information?"

Mitch ignored me. "Why didn't you go in the afternoon when more people would have been in the area? Is it possible you sent the young man false signals? What exactly were you wearing?"

I felt as if my body had been plunged into a bath of icy water. The humming of the fans, the beeping equipment, and the intense lighting faded. Mitch's voice mingled with my mother's sobs in my ears.

*My mother gently helps me disrobe from the cold sweatpants stained with mud and blood. My grandmother's hands feel like warm leather on my trembling arms. The young woman in the mirror stares back at me. Her eyes glow gold. She's being burned alive from the inside out.*

"Finally, Alex, you could've called for help. Instead, you turned to violence. You attacked the man. He barely escaped alive. His promising athletic career was taken from him. He may still have lingering pain while jogging. Such out-of-control behavior and blatant disregard for the rules would warrant tethering. In my professional opinion, it's a classic example of a woman making a string of bad decisions."

Roaring filled my ears. The anger coiled down inside of me exploded from my hold. A white-hot rage flushed through me, burning off the lethargy in my limbs. The fog around the edges of my mind cleared. My full attention was directed at him, this man telling me who I should be. No matter how patient I was, how many times I worked within the rules, it would never stop. I could contort myself into every configuration possible, but it wouldn't be enough. He'd still feel threatened by my existence.

I gave him my rehearsed smile. The solution was obvious. I would have to kill him.

Snarling ferociously, I wrenched against the restraints. Another sharp jolt of pain elicited an animal-like yelp from me. The severity of the pain was rapidly overcome by the urge to tear this man apart. I ripped my clawed hand free. The act seemed difficult before. Now I'm unsure how the bindings held me back. Mitch leapt up, knocked the stool over, and shouted at the long window across the room. A light stinging sensation traveled up my other arm before my wrist's expanding width broke the strap holding it in place. The restraints on my ankles easily snapped.

"What are you waiting for?" Mitch yelled.

The doctor approached us, carrying not another needle but a tranquilizer rifle. The stink of fear permeated the room and further powered the raging beast inside me. The door burst open, and two guards rushed in from their posts in the hallway. Both pulled up short. Their eyes widened and the color drained from their faces. One of the guards screamed as I hoisted him aloft and launched him at the doctor. The man's body collided with her, and the rifle pinwheeled away from her grasp.

I seized the second man's forearm as he raised it to fire his gun. His bones snapped like twigs in my large hand, and again screams echoed off the walls of the room. The gun clattered onto the floor, and I shoved him back out of the room. I slammed the door and awkwardly flipped the lock before scanning the room for Mitch. My nostrils flared and I found his scent. It led me to the smaller room behind the long window.

The door to the interior room was locked. I lowered my shoulder and threw my body against it with a resounding thud. The metal door dented but held. I screamed in frustration, and the sound left my jaws as a roar. I slammed my bulk against the barrier again. It buckled and vibrated in its frame but still didn't open. I pried at the door's top edge where the bent metal strained at its hinges. My claws found purchase, and with the sound of screeching metal and snapping bolts, I tore the door loose.

Something stung me in the back of the leg. Snarling, I turned. The guard I'd thrown into the doctor stood behind me, trembling, with his gun pointed at me. Before he could fire again, I swung the door I held and struck his body. The force of the blow knocked him off his feet and halfway across the room. He landed in a heap on the tile floor and didn't move. I tossed the improvised weapon aside and noticed the main door stood open again. The doctor was gone. Sounds of shouting and gunfire echoed from down the hall.

I heard and smelled Mitch before he attempted to duck around me. My hand clamped down over his shoulder, and my claws sunk through muscle to his shoulder blade and collarbone. He shrieked, limbs flailing, as I drug him back to the exam chair. I lifted his body with ease and dropped him into the seat.

The span of my distorted, hair-covered hand easily encircled the width of his neck. He was so insignificant, reeking of urine and fear. I lowered my face toward his and peeled my lips back into a fanged smile. A long string of saliva slipped down from between my enlarged, serrated teeth to land on his chest.

"No," he sobbed. "Please."

I leaned my massive weight forward against my hand, and his pleading was choked into silence. There was a choice to make. I could watch the light slowly fade from his eyes, or I could take everything from him in an instant with one swipe of my claws. What would he think is the right choice? The good choice?

I tried to ask him but was only able to utter guttural huffing and growling noises. A second attempt yielded the same results. I drew back from the chair, disoriented. Mitch's hands flew to his throat. He gasped for air and coughed. My head struck one of the lighting fixtures suspended from the ceiling.

Something felt wrong. My knees were bent backward, and my balance was different. The remains of one of my boots was laced around the top of my ankle. My feet were huge, misshapen, and covered in gray hair. Each elongated toe ended in a sharp, talon-like nail that clicked on the tile.

I swung my gaze to the long, one-way window on the wall beside me. An enormous, canid-like monster with gray fur and rage-filled golden eyes stared back at me. I recoiled and screamed. The werewolf pulled back from the mirror, lifted her massive shaggy head, and released a blood-curdling howl.

Mitch scurried past me. My confusion vanished. I dropped to all fours and gave chase out of the room. As I attempted to turn into the hallway, I slid on the tile and collided with the opposite wall. Mitch gained a short lead before I recovered my footing with a scrabbling of nails. I leapt forward onto his back and brought him crashing to the ground.

The chaotic noises I'd heard earlier were amplified by the hallway and competed for my attention. The doors at both ends of the hall were open. I held the weakly struggling man in place as I scanned the area, and my nose scanned the air. Traces of other wolves came from the direction of the loading dock. Footfalls approached from the opposite end of the hall, and with them a more familiar scent.

"Alex!" Nate ran toward me.

The sudden sight of him sent a wave of uncertainty through me. Doubt chilled the rabid anger I'd been feeling seconds before. Why was I in the hall? Something inside my core struggled painfully against me, as if I were being torn in half. A noise between a whine and whimper left my body. I looked down at the bare nape of Mitch's neck, and the anger resurged. One quick snap of my jaws is all it would take.

Nate's voice reached me. "We have what we need! Leave him!"

More doubt and confusion. I backed away from Mitch. He remained on his stomach, groaning and half-conscious. The heels of my hands pressed to my temples, I wrestled to regain control of my mind and body. Another angry stab of pain flared within me like my insides were on fire. My scream of agony sounded more human than animal. Bile flooded my mouth, and I braced a hand against the wall for support. My joints shifted and slid sickeningly under my skin. Each leg felt broken and the bones realigned. The hair and talons on my feet had receded. Cries turned to sobs of relief. My legs were mine again. Then I vomited.

I wiped my mouth on my tattered hospital gown. "Holy. Hell."

Nate's eyes were wide. "What did he do to jack up your shifting so bad?"

Of course he'd think that. The other werewolves knew how to keep their shit together. They were in control of the creatures sharing a body with them. I leaned back against the wall and didn't answer, ashamed he'd found me in such a state.

"Or did you let her loose?" When I remained silent, Nate shook his head. "It doesn't matter right now. You're safe." He pushed his jacket at me. "Put this on so I can hug you without feeling funny inside."

Hands shaking, I put the jacket on. Nate helped me zip it up. Adrenaline still coursed heavily in my body, and all of my senses buzzed with information.

Nate grabbed me into a rib-bruising hug. I never imagined the smell of cigarette smoke and unwashed wolf being linked to a feeling of relief. He released me. "We came back as soon as we could."

"Mitch told me they captured all of you." I cinched the remains of my hospital gown around my waist with one of the split sleeves.

"No. Emma and Barbara are safe."

"Did you get everyone out of those hospital rooms?" I looked down the hall from where he approached.

"We found about a dozen. They're already being driven back to the club. Reginald and Trish are waiting for them." He glanced back over his shoulder as well. "Let's go. We wanted to be in and out before they called more guards in."

A weak groan drew our attention to the hallway floor. Mitch lay prone on the tile at my bare feet. The shoulder area of his suit jacket was a mess of ripped fabric and blood. It looked as if he'd been attacked by a bear. My stomach clenched. I wasn't sure what made me feel more sick: the sight of the grisly wound or the fact I'd almost taken his life.

"Alex." Nate's hand settled on my shoulder. "We need to go."

He turned to go, but I grabbed his hand. "Nate?"

"Yeah?" He stopped and looked back.

"Please don't tell anyone else about this. About how you found me."

The corners of his mouth dipped down.

A prickling sensation raced across the surface of my skin. Flashes of blue lighting flickered from the loading dock. Suddenly there was a resounding boom that echoed down the hall. Nate and I ran toward the loading dock.

# 21

CHAOS GREETED US upon entering the enormous room. I gagged from the combined smells of burned hair, gun powder, and blood. The amount of magic-wielding made the air crackle like electricity. More guards lay unconscious beyond the doorway.

My inner wolf responded to the feedback my senses fed her. I doubled over and clutched at my gut. "No. Please." She twisted within me, desperately seeking freedom. Panting and sweating, I stopped her from taking complete control. The pain in my body dulled, energizing strength charged my muscles, and my hands morphed into the claw-like form the other werewolves were already sporting.

George's short, stout figure was surrounded by a ring of low-burning flames. The burning barrier shifted as he moved but didn't scorch the paved floor. His focus was on two werewolves, whom I didn't recognize, cautiously circling him. George shouted a string of words, and the fire expanded outward in a pulse-like wave. The werewolves braced against the attack, and the flames split harmlessly around their figures.

Nate started toward the group, looking back at me. "I have these guys." He pointed across the room. "Get Ruth and tell her we're leaving."

Across the large expanse of floor, Leo was with another person I didn't recognize, presumably Ruth, near the stacks of shipping containers. He was in the process of smashing one of the wooden crates in his effort to get to the woman. The containers were jostled, causing the tall stack to momentarily sway. I sprinted across the room toward them.

The floor was littered with scraps of broken wood and large pieces of unassembled furniture and equipment. Leo heard my approach. His expression morphed from initial surprise into irritated anger. These guys never seemed happy to see me. It was enough of a distraction for Ruth to land a solid strike. Leo grunted in pain, and the young woman leapt spryly out of the way. He turned to swipe at her with huge taloned hands. I reached him and tore into the back of his legs with my claws.

Leo howled in agony. As he pivoted back toward me, parts of his body changed shape. I heard sounds like someone cracking and popping their knuckles, only it was throughout his entire body. His muscles slid beneath the surface of his skin like enormous eels. With a wet tearing noise, his skin split at the joints. His hands broadened, and his fingers elongated even further. Fur sprouted from Leo's face, neck, arms, and hands as his ears lengthened to points.

My stomach lurched as his jawbone cracked and extended to make room for large, jagged teeth. Eyes wide, I flinched away. My memory flashed back to the reflection in the one-way mirror. Leo leered down at me as he raised a massive, clawed hand above his shaggy head.

I was only spared thanks to Ruth. She ferociously attacked the hulking werewolf looming over me. He gave another roar and seized her upper arm. Leo jerked her small body toward him like a ragdoll. I cried out as the creature's immense jaws clamped down over the woman's clavicle with a moist crunch.

Her shriek of pain was abruptly silenced when the enormous werewolf snapped his head to and fro once. He let the limp body fall from his dripping maw before he turned blazing eyes onto me. I suddenly understood why Mitch had pissed his pants.

I ran.

Outmatching Leo with brute force wasn't an option, but he wasn't the most brilliant person I'd met. I dashed toward the stack of shipping crates. Leo dropped to all fours behind me in pursuit, the threat of which caused my inner wolf to thrash within the restraints of my control.

I leapt forward and upward, barely catching hold of the second crate's upper edge. The tower pitched unsteadily away from the impact of my body before rocking back into place again. I grunted with effort and heaved myself up onto the crate. Leo's claws hit the crate below me with the sound of an ax sinking into wood. The unsteady tower shook and teetered again.

I lowered my shoulder and braced it against the next large crate to move it. It barely budged. Terrified, I reached deeper for more strength, allowing the creature inside me more control. She uncurled further within my chest, pushing heat into my limbs. The wood groaned as I pushed the heavy crate toward the edge.

Leo spotted me from below and snarled. He ripped his claw free in a shower of splinters. The movement caused the crate to pitch violently toward him. I scrambled up over my crate and attempted to leap away as the entire tower of shipping crates crashed down onto Leo.

The edge of my crate snagged the hospital gown I wore, and I was pulled ten feet downward to land on top of shattered crates and strewn equipment. When the avalanche of containers and noise ceased, the air was aswirl with sawdust. I lay on my back panting, staring up at the metal grid of the warehouse's ceiling.

"Alex?" It was Nate.

I sat up, coughing and waving away the sawdust. "I'm okay." I stood unsteadily and looked around for any sign of Leo. I'd avoided being crushed. It seemed he had not. I picked my way through the mess, searching for Ruth and hoping she was still alive.

Nate ran up beside me and tossed broken boards and packing material aside as we searched. "Everyone is out except for—" We both felt the shift in the air around us before the large jet of blue flames struck us. The shield on my breastbone flared with burning pain but deflected the attack. The wood carcasses of the crates smoldered and caught fire. Nate snarled and refocused on George, who walked across the large expanse of the room toward us.

I continued looking for Ruth's body, my search growing more frantic by the moment. She was lying unconscious close to the edge of the debris. The injuries Leo had inflicted upon her almost caused me to puke a second time. Scooping her up into my arms, I hurried toward the exit. Nate carried on his dance around George to keep the man occupied.

I propped open the back door with my body. Another woman, wearing a knit cap and pacing outside in the parking lot, hurried to help me. She gingerly took Ruth from me. "How many more?"

"Nate and me." I answered. She nodded and carried the injured woman across the street where an idling car waited. I stepped back in the building and winced against the sudden high trilling noise of the fire alarm. Halfway between the exit and the mess of shipping crates, Nate and George still moved around each other. The wizard had his switchblade out, taking intermittent slashes at the werewolf.

Nate yelped and stumbled, retreating from the grinning wizard. George reached into his jacket and withdrew another blade. It was identical to the weapon Mitch had used against me. The switchblade George had been holding was sunk to the handle near Nate's collarbone.

The reek of burned flesh filled my nostrils as Nate drew closer to me. He snarled in anger and pain, gradually retreating from the wizard even as George cautiously followed.

"Nate, everyone is out." I got a better look at the blade lodged in his body. There was no way to simply pull it free. We wouldn't be able to deal with the blood loss.

He nodded, licking his lips as he watched George. Beads of sweat stood out on his forehead and upper lip. "You ready?" he asked me.

My gaze jerked between the wizard, the exit, and Nate. "Yeah."

"Go!"

We sprung into motion. I hit the door first, making it outside into the brisk air. An accelerating engine signaled the car's arrival from across the street. It slid to a stop on the icy surface. The woman who helped with Ruth was driving. The warehouse door clicked, and I looked behind me. Nate wasn't there. I rushed back toward the door and tried to yank it open. It was locked. "Nate!" I pounded on the barrier with my fist.

The door abruptly swung open again and almost cracked me in the face. Nate stumbled out. He was panting, smelled of blood, and wove like a drunk. The warehouse door closed behind him and didn't open again.

Nate collapsed into the front seat of the car. He uttered a steady stream of cuss words. I slammed his door shut and hopped into the back seat with Ruth. With the sound of spinning tires seeking traction, our car peeled out of the parking lot.

I turned in my seat to look back. There was no movement outside the building. As we drove through the winding streets of the complex, we heard approaching sirens. Our driver pulled over to the road's shoulder. Two city firetrucks and multiple police cars sped past us in the opposite direction.

Our driver pulled away again, and I reached for my phone. I didn't have it. I leaned forward in my seat, asking the woman behind the wheel, "Do you have a phone I can use?"

She handed it back to me, and I dialed Emma's number. The call rang a few times before being sent to voicemail. I looked at the time. It was after four in the morning. I sent a text instead. *Emma, this is Alex. Nate is hurt really bad. We need your help. We'll be at Hell's Bells in about ten minutes.*

I leaned forward again, reaching past the front seat to place my hand on Nate's shoulder. "Thank you for coming back for me."

He covered my hand with his own. It was wet with blood. I recognized the scent. It belonged to George.

SEVERAL PEOPLE WERE gathered outside Hell's Bells when we arrived. Our driver passed Ruth off to others who waited to assist us. I opened Nate's door to help him. The collar of his shirt was soaked with sweat.

"Alex?" Trish strode toward the car from the building. She enfolded me into a tight hug. "I'm so glad you're safely back with us." Her body tensed when she saw Nate. She released me with a strained smile. "I'll bring him inside. Please join the others and have your injuries tended to."

I stepped aside. "I tried to contact Emma. She helped heal my wound when Mitch attacked me with the silver dagger."

"She's here waiting for you. She hasn't left since they returned." Trish helped Nate from the car. Despite the obvious severity of Nate's injury, she remained stoic. He gave her a meek, almost apologetic smile, murmuring something for only her to hear. Trish shook her head, but her features softened. She lifted and carried him into the building.

The front lounge was being used as a type of triage center. Someone called my name again. Emma's small figure hurried across the lounge area toward me. She looked as if she'd been sleeping, her eyes bloodshot and her clothes wrinkled. "What did he do to you? Your leg!"

"I'm okay for now, Em," I said. "Nate is really hurting. Can you help?" She nodded. "Yes, of course."

We passed a handful of people clustered together near the bar and talking in hushed tones. Emma and I hurried down the hall to Nate and Trish's apartment. I knocked on the door and heard Trish invite us in. Emma and I entered to find Nate seated at their small kitchen table.

His unfocused gaze jerked upward at the sound of the door. He appeared ashen, and his chest rose and fell rapidly. He growled in a low tone of warning when Emma walked toward the table. His eyes burned a copper hue as he tracked her movement.

Trish joined us from the back hall, carrying a handful of towels. She set them beside a pair of leather gloves on the tabletop. Moving to Nate's side, she placed her hand lightly on his back. His growling receded at her touch. She motioned Emma to a chair beside Nate. "I'll remove the blade. What else can we do so you are able to concentrate?"

Emma sat down, eyeing the handle of the knife protruding from his shirt. The corners of her mouth turned down and she swallowed.

"Alex, I'm not sure I can cast the spell fast enough before he loses too much blood."

Trish's tone was stern. "We don't have time for hesitation. If you can't help, you need to leave."

"Em, you can do this. We're here to help you," I said. "Tell us what to do."

Emma nodded. Her voice wavered. "Okay. Alex, can you cover my hand and the wound with a towel when the knife is removed?"

"Yes." I grabbed one of the thick towels from the table.

Emma looked at Trish. "Can you please try to hold him in place while I work?"

Trish nodded as she put on the leather gloves. Nate began growling again, confused by the sudden activity around him. Trish wrapped her fingers around the handle of the blade, eliciting a loud snarl from Nate. She leaned forward to murmur near his ear. Her free hand rested on the front of his damp shirt. Again, her presence calmed him. Trish looked at Emma. The smaller woman trembled despite the determined look on her face. My heart thudded in my chest as I waited with the towel.

Emma gave Trish a curt nod. Everything that happened next was a blur of motion. Trish braced her palm on Nate's chest and jerked the blade free. She tossed the blade aside. The stench of burned flesh was suddenly heavy, making me queasy. Emma's small hand covered the gash. Blood leaked rapidly between her fingers.

I covered and pressed against her hand and the wound with the towel. The tingling sensation of Emma drawing on her magic danced along my skin. Trish restrained Nate from swiping at me with one of his taloned hands. He bared his teeth at us and let loose a fresh bout of snarls.

Emma didn't notice. She'd fallen into her trance of casting. Gradually, Nate quieted. He sagged in his chair. Trish remained beside him, whispering to him and periodically brushing his damp hair away from his forehead. Emma's eyelids rose and she looked at me. "The bleeding should be stopped."

I peeled back the towel. The underside was soaked in fresh blood. Emma lifted her hand. Through the slash in Nate's shirt and a smear of blood, there was a delicate scar. I breathed a sigh of awe and relief. "Em, you're amazing."

Emma stared at her shaking, blood-covered palm and fingers. She swallowed rapidly as her face turned from a sickly green to gray. Her eyes rolled back. I caught her before she fell from her chair.

I moved Emma to the sofa in the apartment while Trish relocated Nate to their bedroom. Not more than a minute passed before Emma regained consciousness. She gave a weak smile. "I'm sorry. I've never dealt with so much blood, not even when I mended your stab wound. That was . . . a lot."

I chuckled. "Yes, it was."

"Is he okay?"

"He seems to be. Trish carried him to bed. Thank you for helping him. It would have been hairy without you." I cringed. "No pun intended."

Emma giggled as she pushed herself to a seated position. "You're welcome." She looked at the jacket I was wearing. Blood had begun to appear through the sleeve where it covered my bandaged arm. "What happened to you? I was so worried."

"I was shot—a few times." Her eyes widened, and I laughed. It's not something I'd ever expected to say so casually. Exhaustion was gaining on me, making everything seem ridiculous. I eased out of Nate's jacket, exposing my bandaged upper arm and the shredded hospital gown.

"What are you wearing?" she asked.

Mitch's horror-stricken features flashed in my mind. Shame and self-consciousness descended on me. I wrapped my arms around my barely concealed chest. "I woke up in a hospital gown. It got torn up when we were escaping."

A gray t-shirt and sweatpants were dropped in my lap. I looked up to see Trish. "You can wear these for now," she said. "Someone out front can stitch you up."

"No." Emma placed a hand on my knee. "I can take care of her."

Trish paused, lifting her chin as she studied the petite woman seated beside me. She finally nodded. "Thank you for lending your gift. He's sleeping comfortably. Because you pulled the poison from his body, his recovery should be quick."

"I'm glad to hear that." Emma smiled. "You're welcome."

Trish spoke to me as I changed into the clean clothes. "Reginald is in the front lounge. Will you join us after you're finished?"

"Yeah, we shouldn't be long," I said, sitting down again.

Trish left and Emma unraveled the bandage on my arm, revealing a hastily stitched-together wound. She gently placed her palm over the injury on my arm, and her eyelids lowered. "The bullet was removed," she murmured. Her language transitioned into softly spoken, unrecognizable words. The sharpness of the pain in my arm dulled and was replaced by a blossoming warmth. When she lifted her hand, the wound had transitioned from an angry red gash to the pink of newly mended skin.

"Your leg too," Emma ordered. She slid aside to let me place my foot up on the sofa.

I winced, the pain in my leg far greater than in my arm.

The second gunshot wound took more effort on Emma's part to heal. Her brow furrowed, and a sickening tugging sensation came from within the muscle of my leg. Finally, her fingers closed around a small object at the surface of my skin. As the glowing beneath my skin receded, her eyes opened. "Are you going to report this to Anne?" She held out her hand to me, offering me the bullet.

I turned the bullet over in my hand. Maybe it could be evidence to pass on to the police. My knowledge of police work was limited to television and the scraps of information I'd picked up from Anne. "I want to talk it through with Trish first. Since it involves others who were taken, I'm not sure what I can share."

"Trish is intense," Emma said with raised eyebrows. "She's the club owner you met at the community meeting?"

"Yeah, Nate and her. Trish is amazing. I wish I had the self-control she has," I said. After what happened tonight, I'd have to make it a priority. I couldn't lose control like that again. I frowned, wondering about the extent of the injuries I'd given Mitch's security guards and even Mitch himself.

Emma smiled. "Maybe Trish can teach you."

"Maybe."

# 22

WE RETURNED TO the front lounge and found Trish had had breakfast delivered. The aroma of warm bagels, cream cheese, and coffee made my stomach rumble. Injuries had been tended to, and those who had accompanied Nate to the warehouse chatted over their meals. I poured myself a cup of coffee and filled a plate with food before joining Emma, Trish, and Reginald at the far end of the lounge.

"Trish, where's Ruth?" I said. "Is she okay?"

"Her injuries were too extensive for us to treat here," Trish said. "She's been taken to the hospital. Charles Arztin will care for her."

Emma smiled. "Dad is the best healer in the city."

"And knows the importance of discretion," Trish said.

"I hadn't met Ruth before," I said, "and she saved me from being cleaved open by Leo. It's how she got hurt."

"You're a wolf," Trish said. "We take care of each other."

The feeling of community was new to me, but I liked it. I wanted to be a part of it. Even though my apartment was lost, being with the wolves gave me a sense of home I hadn't felt since leaving my family in New York.

"It's good to see you safe, Miss Alex." Reginald appeared uncharacteristically bleary-eyed. He sipped at his coffee, using a folded show flier as a coaster. He'd lost the suit jacket, loosened his tie, and rolled up the sleeves of his dress shirt. A tattooed pentagram, identical to Ben's, was on his forearm.

A mix of panic and guilt hit me. "Shit!" Ben. I'd forgotten to check in with him.

Reginald arched an eyebrow.

"I mean, thank you." I set my coffee and food aside and reached for my phone. Of course, I still didn't have it. "Hey Em, I need to use your phone."

"Is everything okay?" She dug through her purse and handed over her glittery, pink phone.

"Yeah. I'll only be a minute." I walked away from the group to the bar for some privacy. The message I sent to Ben let him know I didn't have my phone, was safe at Hell's Bells, and was unsure when I'd be able to see him next. I would meet up with him as soon as I could.

His response was immediate. *Do what you need to do. I don't mind the wait.*

*Thank you.* It was ridiculous a simple message could make me feel giddy, but it did. I erased the message thread before returning to the small group and handing Emma her phone. "Did everyone make it back to you?" I asked Reginald. "Nate said he'd found more people locked away in the hospital wing at The Mind Center warehouse."

"Yes," he glanced at Emma. "I was telling Miss Arztin I plan to visit Ms. Greene tomorrow to speak to her. I'm concerned about what effects Mitch White's questionable treatment had on her frail mental state. I also plan to ask her to share her experience with me. Her testimony will be key to our argument when I present it to the Committee."

"He tried to scramble my thoughts, too," I said. "Let me know if you'd like me to speak to the Committee about it."

"Thank you for volunteering, Miss Alex."

"Nate said the tethered wizard and wolf were also there?" Trish asked.

"Yes," I said around a mouthful of bagel. "George, the wizard, is the one who got Nate."

"The men are from Chicago," Reginald said. "George Marino and Leonard Whelan were tethered three years ago for kidnapping and killing a prominent wizard. They escaped the Chicago Delegation's territory this past spring. I find it unsettling that the two were missing for so long and we were not notified."

My thoughts turned to our frantic escape and the smell of George's blood in the car. "We were so focused on getting out of there, I'm not sure what happened to them." I stole a glance at Trish. She was focused on Reginald.

"George Marino is currently in the ICU at the hospital. Mitch White has denied any knowledge of who the man is," Reginald said. "Leonard Whelan was not found. The Delegation said they will be sending someone this afternoon to collect them."

"Did the Delegation have any insight on the altered tethers?" Trish asked.

Reginald frowned. "No. Father Aiden visited George Marino in the hospital. Marino was unconscious, but Father Aiden did see the man's tether. There were no visible alterations to the sigils of the spell."

I blinked, swallowing my food. "That doesn't make sense! I was standing right in front of him and saw it."

Reginald held up a hand with a nod. "I did not mean to imply you were being untruthful, Miss Alex. I witnessed the alteration myself in your memory. I will be researching the matter further. It's disturbing that someone has the knowledge to weaken tethers and is willing to do so."

I dropped my gaze to my food and changed the subject. "How can we be sure Mitch isn't going to pull on his family's strings in the police department and have us all arrested?" I asked. "I can imagine the story he'd spin about us breaking into and trashing the warehouse."

Trish answered. "Detective Grey is the Committee's contact in the Commoners' police department. He's promised us protection from the White family's influence while we present our case."

Reginald added, watching Trish. "Father Aiden said William agreed to testify in the case to the Committee. William claims Mitch to be a lone extremist and will also be delivering a statement from his church denouncing the young man's actions."

Trish smirked. "William realizes he won't be able to sway the Committee against us. He's scrambling to protect his seat."

Reginald set his empty coffee mug aside and gathered his jacket. "Ms. Drake, I think it is safe to say we can all enjoy some hard-earned rest. Will you see me out?"

"Of course, Reggie." Trish smiled as she stood. The two walked together toward the front door.

Emma sniffled beside me. She was trying to hide her tears. I reached over and took her hand in my own. "How're you doing?"

She shook her head and gave a short laugh. "I feel like an idiot."

"You're not an idiot," I said.

"I don't think he lied to me when he said he wanted to help people. He was so convinced he was doing the right thing, he almost had me believing it." She wiped away a tear with the heel of her hand. "What's infuriating is he has the resources to do so much good."

Emma leaned into me. Despite the relief that she was safe, my heart ached for my friend. It hurt to see her hurt. I wrapped my arms around her as she cried.


AFTER EMMA LEFT mid-morning, I crashed on one of the sofas in the lounge. It was early evening before Trish woke me with a gentle shake of my shoulder. I stretched and groaned as my body protested, via multiple aches and pains, the last twenty-four hours I'd put it through.

Trish smiled. "Will you stay here tonight?"

"I'll be back later, but first I want to see Ben." I sat up and stifled a yawn. "How's Nate?"

"Fast asleep." Her smile waned. "We talked this morning when I went to bed. He told me about what happened when he went back for you."

My pulse stuttered. "Oh?"

"He's concerned about you."

Heat rushed to my cheeks, and I looked away. "He told you about that?" Trish and Nate were so in sync with their inner wolves, wielded shifting so effortlessly, I probably seemed like a complete hack to them. "Well, now I know he's shit at keeping secrets. I won't make that mistake again."

"We don't keep secrets from each other," she said. "If you'll let us, Nate and I want to help you. To teach you. No wolf should live in fear of who they are."

My chest tightened. "She almost killed someone."

"She protected you." Trish's voice was soft. "Despite what you may have been told, she's not your enemy."

The being nestled inside me, whom I'd struggled against, who I was ordered to keep hidden . . . could she be a part of myself I could learn to accept? I wouldn't have been able to help Emma and the other wolves without her strength and her protection. I swallowed and forced myself to look at Trish. "Can you teach me to control her?"

Trish's smile returned. "We can help you to know her."

I threw myself at Trish, and she closed her arms around me. Her laughter was rich and warm. A sense of comfort, the same I'd felt when Nate embraced me, surged through my body.

We parted and Trish asked, "Would you like a shower and some different clothes before you go?"

"I smell awful, don't I?"

She wrinkled her nose. "I didn't smell you until I stepped out of the apartment and into the hall."

I laughed and accepted the offer. Driving over to Rear Window, I reflected on how life had hurled one hell of a curveball at me. I'd caught it, only right between the eyes. I'd been oblivious to the harm being inflicted on those who, like me, lived at society's edges. Now I was unsure I'd ever be able to look away.

As soon as I hit the front door of Rear Window Records, my heart rate sped up. Robert Smith's voice drifted from the speakers overhead, serenading me with "Just Like Heaven." I scanned the rows of bins for Ben. He stood at the register but heard the front door.

Seeing me, he moved from behind the counter. I rushed him, and he pulled me into a tight hug. His breath tickled my ear as he whispered. "I'm so glad you're okay."

Sara emerged from the back room. "Hey, Alex."

Ben released me. I put some space between us and gave Sara a small wave. "Sorry. And hello."

Ben scribbled on the back of a flier. He pushed it across the counter toward his coworker.

She read it. "What about those displays in the back?" He signed a single word, causing her to shrug. "I don't care, then. Knock yourself out." She addressed both of us. "But not here."

Ben and I walked together from the record store. He reached for my hand, but hesitated. He looked to me, lifting his eyebrows.

I nodded and took ahold of his hand. "I'm going to need a lot of food, a drink, multiple albums, and a large chunk of your time to cover everything that's happened since we last saw each other." I remembered the recent deposit to my bank account and grinned. "Food and drinks are on me. Think that's possible?"

Smiling, he signed, "Yes."

# Bonus Preview

Thank you for reading *Fear the Wolf*.
For a bonus preview of the next book in the Alex Steward series,
simply scan the QR code or visit the author's website at
**stefaniegilmour.com**

# Acknowledgements

THERE IS NO way I could have published this book alone.

Thank you to my husband and first reader, Josh, for your emotional support and honest feedback on many drafts. The rollercoaster ride to publish Alex's story was rough at times, and you stood by me like the fantastic partner you are. I love you.

While writing this book, I read *Women Who Run with Wolves* by Clarissa Pinkola Estés. At the suggestion of Allison Davis Maxon, M.S, LMFT, I also read *The Body Keeps the Score: Brain, Mind, and Body in the Healing of Trauma* by Bessel van der Kolk, M.D. The work of these two authors, an important conversation with Allison about the effects of trauma, and the experiences shared with me by women throughout my life, helped to shape Alex's story. To all of you, I extend my deepest thanks.

Rebecca Cooper, Diane Telgen, and M.A. Hinkle, your expertise in publishing and writing made this book better. I appreciate your patience and care in mentoring an anxious writer with more than her share of questions. Thank you.

Shout-out to the beta-readers for *Fear the Wolf*! Logan Austin, Emily Bevilacqua, Kelly Bungee Rogers, Hailey Fournier, Jen Hefko, Hillary Robin, Olivia Smith, Allison Spooner, and James Tingley. I cannot say often enough how much I value your time and feedback.

Logan, my critique partner, your enthusiastic support of Alex (and Ben), gentle nudges to push the story further, and numerous co-write sessions kept me writing when I wanted to give up. Your friendship is a gift. Thank you.

And finally, to my family and friends who supported me in too many ways to list here, thank you. I'm so grateful to have you in my life and along for this ride.

# Stefanie Gilmour

STEFANIE IS A graphic designer who enjoys creepy and fantastical stories. Her short fiction has been published in *The Quiet Ones* literary magazine.

Plants, concerts, books, and writing are a few of her favorite things. She's a Midwest native and lives there with her patient husband and their tolerant cats.

stefaniegilmour.com
Facebook.com/AuthorStefanieGilmour
Instagram: @StefGilmour